THE VANCOUVER SPLIT

JOHN BIRMINGHAM

SIMON AND SCHUSTER • NEW YORK

FOR JIMMY GREENE
AND FOR DIANA BYE

THE VANCOUVER SPLIT

1

Wednesday and/or Thursday.   Here in the hospital routine is the thing. Show and Tell every morning. And breakfast, lunch and dinner are regular, of course. I haven't been here long enough to be positive, but I'll bet next Wednesday is roast beef and next Thursday is veal. No major objections—at least I'm not stuck eating the garbage they probably serve at Bellevue or another of those nonprivate New York hospitals—but this atmosphere doesn't leave me much trivia to talk about with my doctor. He gets annoyed when I sit there and say nothing, which is what I've done practically every time I've seen him. But what the hell am I supposed to talk about? My drawings? No, I hate it when right away they start trying to interpret those sketches; I surely don't want to do it myself. My fellow patients? Some *real* freaks. There's a lot to say about each of them, but I'm thinking more about myself and my own head these days. My family life? Early childhood traumas, perhaps? Actually, I don't have a vivid recollection of much of my life before the time a car hit me when I was fourteen. When I think of the life of Steve Gibbons, I mainly think of what happened over the last three years, between the ages

9

of fourteen and seventeen. Well, eighteen, practically. I'll be eighteen in less than two months. Happy birthday. So what does this doctor want to hear about? My hitchhiking adventures? I have told those stories to plenty of drivers as they gave me lifts as far as they went my way. So where would the doctor want me to begin? Even if I only tell about the times on the road after I hooked up with my friend, John, there are a lot of stories. And I can't enjoy telling all those stories to a psychiatrist. When I tell stories, I like to have an audience that will appreciate the adventures, not some shrink who will look down to analyze the stories from behind his academic desk. To tell the truth, I've always had a distaste for shrinks; whenever I talk with one, I end up feeling that I've just opened up part of my soul to a cop.

Friday. This is crazy; I obviously don't belong in here with these maniacs. By now the doctor and nurses see that, too. The only reason they signed me up so quickly in the first place was that I told them something about a bad acid trip. The mention of LSD was the password to get myself into this hospital last week. At that time, the hospital seemed like the only place left for me, the only place where I might survive. Maybe it was, but now I feel alien. Being an alien has its advantages, of course. This morning, at group therapy, I observed the proceedings like a newspaper reporter. The whole thing was so predictable that I didn't need to take notes. (What the hospital is all about: the security of predictability.) I waited for them to ask for my comments and then I gave it to them. I told them that they were all deceiving themselves, each in his own way. One girl in this place is a corny kind of crazy. Sometimes I guess that she must have read about a crazy person in a corny book or seen one on a corny television program and then decided that that was the way to be, to survive. So anyway, she runs around this place carrying a doll which she calls Doctor Kildare. She talks to that doll more than she talks to anybody else. This morning she refused to join us in group therapy because her doll wasn't with her. The nurse began politely explaining to her

10

that everybody had to attend group therapy. I was impatient to get the show going and over with. "Why don't you stop talking about that stupid doll like it's going to do something for you," I groaned. "It's nothing more than an old hunk of plastic which should have been junked years ago." That girl freaked out when I said that to her. She was screaming that Doctor Kildare was not a doll and that he was better than me any day and that kind of nonsense. Finally, she joined us at the meeting without her doll. Everybody talked about one another at the meeting. The only thing they said about me was that I had the face of an angel and the heart of a devil. None of them even laughed.

Still Friday.   The routine does its work on me fast. My role in this hospital, particularly in group therapy, is defined. It is the same role I played a couple of months ago when John and I were staying in a youth hostel for travelers under eighteen in Vancouver, Canada. We were the oldest guys in the hostel. We'd also been on the road the longest, me since shortly after I turned sixteen when I made it official that I was finished with school. If the kids in that hostel had questions, I had answers. I was invulnerable. And I am invulnerable in this hospital. That sounds like sanity to me. So why won't my doctor grant me a pass so I can meet my chick, Peggy, tomorrow? I know why. He wants me to be miserable. He told me so himself, said he wants to keep me from creating a Mental Hospital Utopia, with the securities of the hospital for when I'm feeling paranoid and the excitements of Manhattan for when I'm bored. Makes sense. Well, fuck him, all men strive for their Utopia! Does he think he's God, with the right to deny me paradise? Maybe I'll elope tomorrow, get drunk, spend the night with Peggy, and return Sunday.

Meanwhile, here I am, drawing sketches and writing rambling notes. I wrote John a letter and told him about this place. I also duplicated my better drawings on a Xerox machine they have here. I'm trying anything to keep my head cool. (Is that all you worry about, what's cool and what isn't?)

11

Saturday. Talked with Peggy in the morning. Ten minutes after I hung up the phone, my doctor told me I could have the pass for the evening. I should be overjoyed, but I'm scared. And I'd been thinking Peggy was an ideal chick for me to see. After all, I've known her for years, and she had nothing to do with the crazy things that led me to this place. She's simply a pretty girl I happen to be digging, as I did when I knew her in high school. So why is the idea of seeing her making me so paranoid? Am I afraid that I'm not in shape to play our usual ego games? Maybe it's only my mood today. I suppose I can avoid seeing her by sticking to my story that they wouldn't grant me a pass. This is ridiculous. I'll probably buy a gallon of wine and drink it on my way downtown to meet her. Then when I see her, I'll vomit at her feet and pass out. Great! At last I'm able to reach a realistic solution to a suicidal problem!

Saturday's end. Actually, it's two o'clock on Sunday morning. Daylight Saving Time has officially ended. I met Peggy at five thirty under the arch in Washington Square Park. Then we walked east to Seventh Street. I let myself into the apartment, and John was out. So Peggy and I bought a bottle of Vodka and some o.j. and we mixed screwdrivers. Then we went uptown to see *Performance,* a movie I'd already seen. I was so smashed I could barely stand. And in the lobby of the theater, we ran into one of my nurses and her boyfriend. I guess I didn't make a wonderful impression. But what do they expect from a nuthouse patient?

Sunday. Today I feel productive. I started and completed a two by three feet poster-sized painting. I'm never able to devote more than a day to one work of art, but I think this one came out well. It's of a guy standing with each foot on top of a hill. Shackles around his wrists bind him to both of the hills. The sky is black and planet earth looms over his left shoulder. He is looking off despairingly to his right. The hills and his body are enveloped in flames. The content of this painting is not typical of my art; most

12

of my paintings are filled with action and blood and guts. But I think this one turned out okay for a new subject.

The nurse who saw me at the movies stopped in my room this evening. She is very attractive, with shining brown hair down to her ass. I wonder how hard it is to make nurses in this place. I was wondering what they'd do if I got caught, and the nurse was admiring my painting. After all, I'm a nut, right? Nuts are expected to break the rules. Besides, my roommate was out. Then she turned to me and said, "By the way, Stevie, you don't have to worry about me ratting to your doctor about you getting stoned on pot yesterday. I thought it would ease your mind if I mentioned that." I laughed and said, "I hadn't been smoking anything but cigarettes; I was drunk out of my mind." Then she smiled knowingly and said in a stage whisper, "Oh, come now, Stevie, I know that after you try pot you don't go back to boozing." I smiled back and conceded that she was too slick for me. She was gone before I could get back into my fantasies.

Monday.   More artwork during the day. My mother visited me this evening. I appreciate her effort—I really do—but I wish she wouldn't bother. She is doing it out of obligation. We have nothing much to say to one another, so her visits are tense. What common ground do we have as a base for conversation? I haven't seen many movies lately, and our reading tastes differ. So I show her my artwork. She generally encourages me, though she says a lot of the stuff is gross. The only piece my mother did not comment on was my big painting. She was taken aback when she saw that one. I'm sure she reacted strongly to it, but she didn't say and I didn't ask.

Tuesday.   I told you I'm in a lot better shape than the rest of these people. My doctor is talking about what I'll be doing when I get out—sounding like he means quite soon.

Midweek.   Very busy. I am working on puppet heads for a psycho puppet show. I wangled another pass for the end of the week.

13

Friday.   I stopped downtown at the Seventh Street apartment, but John was out again. The subway ride put me uptight. I'd felt worse, but I considered heading straight back to the hospital to take it easy. No, that might have been a bad move. Since I couldn't guess how an early reappearance would affect my future chances at hospital passes, I decided to stay downtown. I sat on the mattress on the floor and listened to records. In the middle of "Old Man River" on Jeff Beck's *Truth* album, I switched the livingroom lamp to a red light bulb.

It was about nine or ten when I heard a loud banging on the apartment door. Had John forgotten his keys? "Stevie! Stevie, are you in there? John?" This was strange. It was my father's voice. He'd never been to the apartment before. I answered the door.

"Stevie, Jesus, I thought you weren't going to open up," he said.

"I had the music going pretty loud."

"I noticed. Are you okay?"

"Sure. Of course. What's happening?"

My father told me that my doctor had phoned him shortly after I left the hospital. Apparently, my doctor had just seen a couple of my most recent drawings, one or two of guys getting their heads chopped off, and the pictures convinced him that I was going to kill myself. My father and I relaxed and talked, and I turned him on to some music. Afterward, I telephoned my shrink and told him to stop being such an asshole. That made him angry. He said that I was being unfair, that he had only been concerned for my welfare. He was right, of course, but I had to assert myself so that my latest sketches would not count against me. Whether or not I decide to stay here, I want to maintain as much control as possible.

Sunday.   Back in the hospital. My shrink is losing patience with me. He wants me to talk with him. *Talk about anything! What happened while you were hitchhiking?* A lot of stuff. What do you want to hear about? *Why don't you tell me what you think was the point of what you were doing. Did you have goals?* Sure, I had

14

goals. My goal in life was to have a gassy time of it. *That doesn't tell me much.* Maybe not, but for me it says a lot. *Well, tell me about another kind of goal, like a particular place you wanted to go and see.* Ah, you're missing the point. Geographical goals were never the big thing. *Then what was the big thing? The amount of distance you could cover? What were you trying to prove?* All right, all right, I suppose there usually was a destination in mind when I traveled. When I left New York with John, for instance, we said we'd make it to San Francisco. But what I'm saying is that that was not the big thing. Man, before we thought a lot about hitting San Francisco, we zigzagged down to Florida, back up to Vermont, out to Colorado and south as far as New Mexico, back up to Wisconsin, and then out to Los Angeles and up the California coast. We didn't take the short route because getting to California was never the big thing. And as far as the idea of proving anything goes, just surviving the way you want to is proving plenty. All along, they tell you that you have to follow certain basic survival rules that they have already set down. Like they say you have to get that high school diploma, even if what you have to do to earn it is completely contrary to the way you want to run your life. That's horseshit. I'm not the same as everybody else; I have to discover my own survival rules. *So where do you find them? San Francisco?* What kind of crack is that? I told you San Francisco didn't mean that much as a goal. It was more like the goal in a game. The truth is that the most important things usually happened to me after I went beyond the original geographical goals. *So I am asking you what did happen? How does it happen? Do you ever find a place that you stop to accept, for better or for worse?* Man, I can't start telling you about every place I stopped.

2

I get excited and I get carried away. A cooler way to deal with my doctor might have been to keep giving him the kind of simple answers that would have left us clear of involvement. *Making it to San Francisco was my goal.* I don't know, though, would that have worked? Then he probably would have quizzed me about what happened over the next four or so months, between the time I accomplished that goal and the time I committed myself to his place of business. And his questions eventually would have brought him to Vancouver, where John and I went, where things got crazy. Four months. Should I have claimed partial amnesia?

But I don't forget.

It was the beginning of July when we did hit San Francisco. Being in a place where I already knew people, I felt secure. Right away, I brought John to Ellen's apartment near Market Street.

Ellen was an old lover of mine, from when I lived at her apartment during the previous fall. She was tied down by two kids. I had not been in touch with her since then; we had split up on bad terms, partly because she wanted me to father those kids. Ellen was in her early twenties and she took things too seriously. I made her laugh a lot of the time, though.

"She's bound to be home because of those kids," I told John before we climbed the stairs to her place on the second floor.

I banged on the door. When it opened, I grinned. Ellen looked up at me, beginning to smile herself. She had recognized me immediately; she did not seem surprised to see me.

"Okay, come on in," she said, pushing back the door and pointing our way into her livingroom with an open palm.

It was dusk, and the lights were off in the livingroom so that it looked pleasantly grainy, like a black and white photograph. I put down my knapsack and sleeping bag and sat on a mattress on the floor. John sat on his rolled sleeping bag.

Ellen sat next to me, but not too near me. She hugged her knees for a moment and tried to eye me suspiciously from the corner of her eye. She wasn't getting the effect she wanted with her gentle brown eyes, but I got the message. She wanted me to think I had to watch my step after my abrupt exit the last time.

"And where has the wind taken Stevie Gibbons since December?" she asked, turning to me with her wit.

"I've been around. I made it to New York for Christmas. Then John and I started hitching around. We've been partners for quite a while . . ."

"Partners in what?" she asked.

"In crime."

"Gigolo partners?"

"Ellen, I told you that story was strictly horseshit. How can you run around believing what you hear from a little girl with her fantasies about me? Sally was living in a dream world. You know that."

"I don't know what I believe after last fall."

I wasn't actually bothered that Ellen might think I was a gigolo. In a way, it was amusing that she still believed the story that Sally, an ex-girlfriend of mine, had told her. But I had to reassure Ellen if I wanted to get along with her while John and I stayed in San Francisco.

"I'm telling you what you can believe," I said firmly.

17

It was quiet a moment. Ellen let the subject drop, though it was still on her mind. She shifted herself so that her back rested against the wall. I was looking at her profile.

"Did you cut your hair, Ellen?"

"Oh, please don't even ask . . . Does it really look shorter?"

"Not shorter, just not longer."

"I'm afraid it's stopped where it is. Yours sure grew enough."

The room was growing darker, so Ellen walked across the room to light two candles near the window. The tenseness was still between us.

"Hey, John, what do you say we buy a bottle of wine and celebrate?" I suggested.

"Better than that, let's make sangria. We haven't done that in a while."

"Sangria! Beautiful!" It was what we needed.

"How do you make that?" Ellen asked.

"Tell me where there's a liquor store open and we'll show you," I said.

I was enthusiastic and Ellen seemed to be enjoying that. She said the liquor store across the street was open. Then John handed her a five-dollar bill.

"You'd better pick up the Burgundy since Steve and I are underage. We'll get the rest of it."

"Okay," Ellen said. "But could one of you stay here in case Lisa or Amoreena wakes up?"

John volunteered.

Ellen and I went downstairs and then split up. I ran to the grocery store to buy a quart of club soda, lemons, oranges and a grapefruit. When I arrived back at the apartment, I put them all in a mixing bowl.

"Ellen, you are about to experience the fabled Wine of Sweet Forgetfulness. This recipe was handed down to John and me by a mad physicist while we were tripping in the mountains of Aspen, Colorado."

"Really? You met him in Aspen?"

18

"We'd been traveling with him in his Volkswagen bus from Missouri to Aspen." I quartered the last orange and dropped the pieces into the Burgundy. "Man, there's nothing like hallucinating in a cool bowl of sangria. After one sip, I was begging this crazy scientist for his recipe. Then he said I could have it only if I promised to turn other people on to it wherever I went."

My brew was ready. I began by passing the bowl to Ellen. She sipped at first, to test it, and then she took a long drink. John, Ellen and I finished all three quarts and then sucked on the fruit.

"This is the best part," I said. "The fruit absorbs the alcohol so it really gets you smashed."

The phone rang. It was Ellen's sister, Kathy.

"Kathy, guess who just flew in my window? . . . No, somebody else. . . . Nope. . . . You'll never guess, Stevie Gibbons and his friend from New York. . . . Really. . . . Drunk? No, not really. I'm someplace else. The three of us just drank a bowl of ambrosia. . . ."

"No, it's sangria!" I yelled so that Kathy could hear me. "We drank the Wine of Sweet Forgetfulness. Sangria, not ambrosia."

"Kathy, this is like nothing else. This ambrosia is like . . ."

Watching Ellen talk, I was lying in the middle of the livingroom floor. She was looking good. She looked the same. Her straight red hair still touched her shoulders. She was still thin, but not slender enough to be a successful model, her latest aim. I think she wanted to model because she needed to prove to herself that she was good-looking. But she would never really make it. Her face was appealing, but it was not glamorous—the nose only slightly too prominent, the eyes lacking mystery.

John looked sleepy stretched out on the mattress. I felt impatient for Ellen to hang up the phone.

After a few more minutes of talking, Ellen put down the phone. She lay next to me on the floor and sighed. I am not sure what the sigh was about. The room was quiet. Then John said, "I've never seen an animal stare at me the way that that gray cat is staring right now." The cat was standing in the doorway to the

19

kitchen. Ellen rested her chin in her hands and said, "I know what you mean. She is the most compassionate cat I've ever known." Then I put my arm around Ellen's waist. "What about me?" I said. "Am I a compassionate cat?"

Early the next morning I heard kids tramping around the livingroom. I was alone in Ellen's room. I lit up a morning cigarette and wished there were a cup of coffee to prepare me for the world outside of her room. I waited about twenty minutes before stalking into the livingroom.

"How'd you sleep?" I said to John, and then cleared my throat.

"Great. This beats the side of the road."

I sat on the floor with my head against the windowsill, trying not to let the buzzing kids annoy me. Ellen was sponging off the kitchen table.

"Do you think Lisa remembers you, Stevie?" she asked.

"Hope not. She always had a thing against me."

"Oh, that, that was just a phase. I told you it was nothing personal. She wasn't digging anyone who shared her mother's room."

"Well, whatever it was, I hope she thinks I'm a new person."

Whether or not Lisa remembered me, she wasn't unfriendly. She was on the floor, pushing a plastic toy car around a rocking chair. Her bald-headed sister, Amoreena, was crawling, aimlessly it seemed, but she was smiling so it didn't matter. They were both wearing diapers, though Ellen said Lisa had been toilet-trained. Lisa's red hair, not as bright as her mother's, had grown longer and fuller since I'd last seen her. When she ran her car into the side of the rocking chair, she exclaimed, "Shit!" and then steered around it. She had grown some.

Now she was heading toward me. She pushed the car up to my feet without looking up at me. Then she stood up and held out the car, offering it to me.

"Stevie, you've got to admit that was nice," Ellen said from the kitchen.

"Sure, I admit it. Sure, it was very nice. Listen, John and I

20

thought we'd head over to City Lights for a while today. I'll try to find you some worthwhile reading matter." I'd noticed a book by the Maharishi Mahesh Yogi next to Ellen's bed; she was still into him.

"Okay, Stevie, but when you get back could you help me take Lisa and Amoreena to the park?"

"Sure, sure."

The sun rarely bakes San Francisco as hot as it did the day I took John to the North Beach section to show him the home of books by the Beat writers, the City Lights Bookshop.

"Man, I'm glad we're out of that apartment," I said to John on the trolley. "Ellen can make for a depressing atmosphere."

"Really? I was kind of enjoying our stay, appreciating the rest."

"Rest is one thing. I admit I enjoy the security of having a place to crash and a chick who digs me. But Ellen is into sitting in her apartment all day, chained to her kids and feeling sorry for herself."

"I don't know. I liked her on first impression. Maybe if we take her and the kids out, it'll bring her head up."

"Maybe. I mean I *like* her. She's *nice*. But she can really drag you down."

"Well, it's you who spends the most time with her. So where do you want to go? Farther north?"

"Yeah, I was thinking Vancouver. Now there's a far-out little town."

It didn't help us to keep cool when I forgot the exact location of the bookshop. I'd thought I knew where it was. With anyone but John I would have felt embarrassed, especially since I'd been talking as though I were an expert on Kerouac, Ginsberg, Burroughs and the entire Beat scene.

City Lights was hard to find because it didn't look special. In fact, my first visit to it was without initiation, and I'd assumed it was just another old bookshop. That was just before Kerouac died, and I was beginning to get into his writing. Having only read *On the Road* and *Dharma Bums,* I wanted to see what else he'd written. So I wandered into City Lights and asked a middle-aged man there if he stocked any books by Kerouac. The man politely showed me to the Kerouac section. As I was browsing, one of the guys who worked in the store tapped my shoulder. He was giggling in an annoying way so I asked what his problem was. "Do you know who you were talking to a minute ago?" he asked me. I answered that I had no idea. "That was Lawrence Ferlinghetti," he said.

John and I finally found the shop. This time I didn't need assistance. While browsing, I found a book I wanted called *The Yage Letters,* a collection of letters written by William Burroughs and Allen Ginsberg to each other. Each wrote his letters while traveling through South America. Burroughs went there before Ginsberg in search of yage, a drug that, according to some of the natives, will give its user telepathic powers.

I felt qualms about stealing from City Lights, but we were low on money. And shoplifting was easy at City Lights.

Kathy, Ellen's younger sister, had arrived. She said hi, but was not readily talkative. Kathy was bigger than Ellen, tall with large bones. Her hair was longer but not as red. When she spoke, you could tell that Kathy prided herself on her sharp ability to peg other people for what they are, where they're at. Yet she put on a dull, apathetic expression this afternoon. Whenever Kathy and I got together, we played verbal games, one of her favorite pastimes. She could be quite sarcastic, and sometimes the games were less than friendly.

"What book did you get?" Ellen asked.

"Yage Letters," I said, holding it up. "Letters by Burroughs and Ginsberg on the road. Maybe sometime after John and I go our separate ways we'll write a bunch of letters and put them together in a book."

"Yes. And you could title your half of the book *The Hot One,"* Kathy said. "Except then you'd be letting people in on the mysteries of your personality." She was in a mood.

"You're right. There is mystery, isn't there?" I said, grinning so that Kathy would think I was not going to let her put me up-tight.

"Hey, how much of the mystery are you leaving uncovered at this point?" John broke in. "Do they know your real name, or is that still part of the secret?"

I glared as though I wanted John to shut up.

He was smiling. John never did have a talent for putting people on. But Ellen was gullible. Especially with me, she believed crazy tales because she had a crazy image of me. To put on Ellen, talent was unnecessary. All you needed was imagination.

"Wait a minute, you mean your name isn't Stevie Gibbons?" Ellen said.

"Of course it is," I said. "Don't sweat about it. To you, I am Stevie Gibbons."

"But that's not your real name, the name your parents gave you?"

"Look, what's in a name?"

"But that's so weird. All this time I've known you I've thought of you as Stevie. Stevie Gibbons," Ellen said and then pondered it for a moment. "It's funny, but now it does sound like a made-up name."

"He's bullshitting you, Ellen," said Kathy, who wasn't sure her-self.

"Are you? Stevie, tell the truth."

"Remember the Connecticut people who knew you as Arlo?" John said. "And it started because one tripping freak thought you looked like Arlo Guthrie."

"Right. And I don't even vaguely look like Arlo, except for the curly hair."

"Of course. You are much better-looking. Blonder hair. Bluer eyes," Kathy said.

"I always kind of liked the name I used to use, Jim Steele," I said, ignoring Kathy.

23

"Yeah, I'd like to borrow that one sometime," John said.

"But I think your pen name—John—fits you better."

"Pen name? You're a writer?" Kathy asked John. "That's far out! So am I!"

"Writer? John's a published author. When we need money, all he has to do is give a speech at some college and they pay him."

"Steve, why don't you tell them your christened name?" John urged. "You've known them long enough."

"Sure, I know them, and that's exactly why I stick with the name Steve as far as they're concerned. I associate that name with Ellen and my other San Francisco friends. Stevie Gibbons expresses my West Coast identity," I said. And then turning to Ellen: "You see, John is one of the few people who can be sure of my name because he has known me longer than anybody."

"But I thought you two just met in New York," Ellen said.

"Far from it. In fact, I've known John since we were that high. Even before that, I first met John when we were infants. Matter of fact, John's mother and my mother met each other while they were having labor pains in a maternity ward. That's how they became friends."

"Is this the truth? Oh, you're bullshitting. You mean you both are nineteen-year-old Sagittarians?" Ellen said.

"Damn straight. We're astrological twins."

From the time I was sixteen, I'd made it habit to say I was nineteen, because sixteen and seventeen sounded awful.

"Wait a minute, John told me this morning that he was eighteen and a Virgo, so I know you're bullshitting now."

"Yeah, well he also told you his name was John, didn't he?"

I tried to keep the hoax going, but Ellen was not *that* gullible.

3

The story I was telling to Ellen, one my shrink later had to drag out of me, was not entirely fantasy—except, of course, for the part about us being born together.

Ellen hadn't heard the background on my friendship with John when I lived with her, however, because I hadn't even been thinking of John during the latter part of that fall. We hadn't really been in touch since junior high school, and we might not have gotten back in touch at all if I hadn't switched my plans and left California.

When I left Ellen, my plan was to hitchhike up and down the West Coast all winter. I started north, sleeping in my relic sleeping bag, usually near the ocean. When I came south again, I could still stay with friends in the cities—Ellen in San Francisco, my Uncle Mike near Los Angeles. Didn't need to know anybody in Vancouver because I found enough food and space in the hostels. It was all set. But at Christmas time, I felt that old urge to party with my first friends in New Jersey.

Going back was an irrational act. I had to hustle hard for plane fare. And even then I only had enough to fly from Denver, so I had to buy a navy pea coat and wool cap and hitch a thousand cold miles. Besides the hassles that went with crossing the country in winter, I would be unwelcomed by certain parties in New Jersey and I knew it. The cops in my hometown were still looking to put me in jail for a probation violation from when I was a drunken disorderly fifteen-year-old. My parents also were bearing a grudge, mainly my mother, so I was less than welcome at their house. But I had to hit New Jersey. If I didn't, I would have missed a couple of very stoned New Year's Eve parties.

Now I needed a place to stay on the East Coast, and I found one across the river from New Jersey, far from the cops in my hometown—at John's apartment. I had found out from a mutual friend that John was living on the Lower East Side of Manhattan, so I gave him a call.

My friendship with John was rooted in childhood, but since I had not talked with him in three years, I wondered how well I would relate to him now. I decided that the odds were in our favor. After all, John and I had been quote unquote best friends for years. When I was two and he was three we lived in the same Bronx lower-income housing project. And we became better friends later, after both our families moved to different parts of the New Jersey suburbs. We had a lot behind us. Also, I'd received a good impression of John when I saw him once in the summer of 1969, but we didn't talk that time because we were in a crowd at a wake for a dead friend and I didn't have much to say. I cannot say why I got a good impression at that wake. It may have been because John's hair hung past his shoulders and he looked hip, but I prefer to think it was something more than that, something less superficial. Anyway, the last time I'd spoken with John, we were both school kids, living at home with parents. Now I was on the road and John had his own apartment. And I'd heard that John was even getting a book published. Him, a published author. And me, of course, a road bum. Three years after and both of us had a title of distinction. Of course, my expectations about the whole thing

26

would have been less strange had John and I never met before.

It was an odd and dark hour when I arrived on the Lower East Side so I went straight to sleep on a mattress on the livingroom floor. I awoke early the next evening and John was already up.

Fully awake for the first time in days, it seemed, I checked out the apartment from bed. It was a long and narrow cave. I liked it right away. It was ideal for living on the Lower East Side—dark, secure and distinctly separate from the outdoors. Almost no natural light could find its way into the apartment, even in the afternoon. The livingroom windows faced Seventh Street, which becomes increasingly ugly and dirty east of Avenue A, so they were covered along with the rest of that wall by a heavy maroon cloth. Most of the apartment was painted off-white—the bricks that piled high to the cracked ceiling, the ceiling itself except for its fake beams, even the phony fireplace hole in the wall where John kept books. A light was on in the back room, a room that I knew from having stayed in other tub-in-kitchen Lower East Side apartments would not add greatly to the space of the apartment.

John walked barefoot into the kitchen to inspect the refrigerator. I watched new light creep along the floor and ceiling as the refrigerator door opened. I was thinking what to say. John was facing the light, but his blond hair hung so that I could not see his profile. He was wearing black Wranglers and a work shirt.

"Good morning," I said.

"More like good evening. How was the trip?"

"Okay. Lots of drinks on the plane."

"I figured."

"Christ, I nearly didn't make it. In Las Vegas, just before I got to Denver, they almost busted me in a casino for kicking a one-armed bandit. I was screaming and cursing at the machine and I had this fake ID in my wallet. I guess I was pretty smashed."

"Sounds typical."

"Right. At least they didn't bust me, though. Still, it was a drag losing that ID. You don't get over-twenty-one Canadian ID laid on you every day."

27

I wondered whether John meant it sounded typical of the cops or typical of me.

"Your sister told me about some phenomenal number of police hassles you've gone through recently."

"Which sister? When did you see one of my sisters?"

"Lorraine. I ran into her at the subway station near the bridge about a month ago."

"Far out! I just talked with her on the telephone for an hour last week, but I haven't seen her since the fall. How did she look?"

"Different. To me, anyway, she looked different. She was crashed out on acid at the time. Man, I hadn't seen her in . . . well, put it this way: The last time I saw her before that she was a pretty twelve-year-old wearing a pink jumper and man-tailored shirt."

I grinned, mainly to myself. Lorraine and I were probably the closest members of what at that time was not a tight family. I could picture how she looked.

"What was she wearing this time?"

"Black leather, ripped up jeans and boots. I didn't recognize her; she recognized me."

"Yeah, we've all been through some changes," I said, fumbling through the pocket of my pea coat, which lay next to the mattress; I came up with an unopened pack of Camels I'd bought at the airport.

After lighting up, I shook the flame off the head of the match and glanced around me for an ashtray. John passed me an empty Planters cashew can, and he suggested that we go sit in the back room to talk.

Adjusting my eyes to the bare lightbulb that hung from the ceiling in the back room took a while. The room was approximately eight by eight feet with an extra-long mattress on the floor to accommodate John's six three. A cheap component stereo system as well as John's record albums, mostly Rolling Stones, covered the top surface of a tall home-built loft. The loft stood above the foot of the mattress. The one window revealed a view of broken bottles in the alley. On the wall hung an oil painting of an enormous, raging, bursting sun over a turbulent ocean—like another window with a totally different view.

I recognized that painting. The artist was Patrick, a friend of John's and mine. He had died recently. That was the wake where John and I had seen each other.

"You plan to visit your family?" John asked.

"I'd like to see my sisters and brother all right, but my parents and I are not exactly on cordial terms. Last time I saw them, they were driving me to the airport to send me to stay with my uncle in California, and my mother made it clear enough that she didn't want to see me back for a while."

"Well, isn't it a while yet? How long have you been gone, since early September, isn't it?"

"You don't understand, man. It isn't just something I did to get her pissed off. It's a matter of years of living together that taught both my mother and me that we cannot live and get along under the same roof. We both know it. We knew it years ago. Man, when I was fifteen, my mother paid the rent on an apartment for me so that she would have me out of her house. It was a brilliant idea, me moving out."

John was sounding like a lot of people who cling to these sentimental notions about the bond between a mother and her child. I get this all the time when I'm hitchhiking. People who pick me up ask me what my mother thinks of me being on the road. My mother prefers to keep her distance from me, I tell them. They never believe it.

"You want to hear the kind of communication that went down between my parents and me when I lived at home? It was crazy. Here's a typical scene. This is two or three years ago, around the time that 'White Rabbit' by the Jefferson Airplane first came out. I remember because I was really getting into that forty-five of 'White Rabbit,' listening to it over and over while sitting in my bedroom, stoned on reds. Anyway, my father passes my room and sees me stoned, nodding, so he comes in and cracks my copy of 'White Rabbit' into about four pieces and then leaves. So I go out

29

and buy another copy and bring it home and start playing it over and over again. And when my father hears it, he breaks that copy. Man, this battle goes on for days until I buy the whole *Surrealistic Pillow* album and he gives up. We never talked about it the whole time."

"I guess that does sound pretty strange," John admitted. "I got into that song when it first came out, too, but my parents never broke it. Who knows, though, maybe that's partly because they never saw me listening to it stoned on reds. Actually, I've never done reds."

"No? You should try them. They're a sort of unusual down head. It's not something that's good to really get into, though." Then I shifted the conversation because I felt we had lots to talk about before we let ourselves be sucked into one of those endless discussions of dope. " 'White Rabbit,' man, that didn't come out so long after the time I got hit by that car. The time you visited me when I was in traction."

"Yeah, I remember. Connecting it with that song makes it seem like such a long time since the last time we talked . . ."

It had been that long. I was fourteen when that car hit me and fractured bones in my left leg and hip. John surprised me with a visit. After not seeing me for nearly two years, he walked into my corner of the hospital room wearing knee-high brown suede boots, chalk-striped pants and an epaulet jacket which concealed the balloon sleeves of his Tom Jones shirt. An English Mod. His hair covered the tops of his ears, too. At the time, I was sporting a body cast with a pin through my knee, but if I hadn't been stuck in bed, I sure as hell wouldn't have dressed anything like the way John did. For me, the junior high school trip meant being a hitter and I never lost a fight. I hung around with the Barbie Gang, a gang of kids who would have kicked John's ass had they caught him looking like that.

But we enjoyed a friendly visit despite differences. We joked about how the hospital food had made me as scrawny as John. I lay on my back scratching itchy spots under my cast with a knitting needle and relating anecdotes about trouble I'd gotten into in school. John mentioned something about having been kicked out for long hair.

Now I wondered how much John thought I had really changed since then. Not actually worried about it, I was curious about my image. Superficial changes in Lorraine were blatant, but in my case he didn't have as much to work with. For all I knew John thought I was a traveling greaser. My hair was still relatively short. And the last time John had seen me, at our friend's wake, I looked like the Boy Wonder with my boyish face beaming, naked and innocent, from under a crew cut. The cops had shaved my head. I wondered if John knew about that. I know it's supposed to be uncool to judge people by their outward appearance, but everyone does it, and I do it.

After all, I judged John quickly when I saw his picture in the local newspaper about a year before this, a few months before Patrick's wake. My father pointed out the article to me. It told about an underground newspaper that John was editing at his school. Interesting, yes, but I assumed that John would put out his underground paper for a while, then be accepted to a good college, and trim his hair in a few years so that he could land a nice, secure job. My father, however, being the intellectual college professor, dug the newspaper idea, but I never was able to relate to underground papers. They are supposed to bring a lot of people together, but for that kind of thing, I go to a concert. As far as reading goes, I prefer novels.

"We also saw each other at Patrick's wake, remember?" I said.

"I'm not going to forget that. You didn't look like you wanted to talk to anybody then."

"Yeah, it wasn't just Patrick being dead, I was disgusted by everyone's attitude about it. That was the first wake I was ever at and I didn't expect people to act like they were at a party."

"I don't know, I wasn't all that bothered by it," John said. "But I really thought it was in bad taste that they cut his hair for the casket."

"No, man, you're wrong about that one. Patrick cut it himself before he died. They just slicked it back behind his ears and gave him a shave. Patrick seemed to be into a thing of getting his head together around the time he died. I think he saw the haircut as a move toward sanity, in a way. He never said that, though; he just told me that he had decided it was time for a change. Did you know he was even enrolling in college for the fall?"

"Patrick? Going back to college?" John said.

"Yeah, they fixed it so he could go to Hunter."

"That's too much. Well, I guess you got a lot closer to him than I ever did. I heard you and he got busted together just before he died. My father showed me a mention of it in the paper. Said something about 'wreckless endangerment,' was that it? What the hell does that mean?"

4

The newspaper clipping is still in my wallet, a couple of paragraphs saying that Patrick and I were busted for wreckless endangerment. In the second degree.

On a summer afternoon, we had finished drinking most of a half gallon of Chianti, so we were pretty smashed when it happened. We began to stagger and laugh around Patrick's small, middle-class hometown in New York State. In fact, we were having a gassy time until we met some local punk greasers. They were a year or so younger on the average, but they were out to prove they had more balls.

"Faggot!" one of them shouted, leaning with coolie style against the candy store.

I gave them the finger.

"You see that, Jerry? The faggot flipped us the bird," the coolie said, turning toward his friends. Then turning back toward me: "What the fuck you think you're doing, faggot?"

I get belligerent when I am drunk and provoked. The old hitter in me comes out.

I repeated my gesture, explaining to the coolie that I was indi-

33

cating that he should go fuck himself, and followed up by tossing the remaining contents of my wine bottle in his face. Naturally, he was frenzied, lunging at me. There were eight of them, so I backed off and pulled a box-cutting razor out of my pocket. Patrick was somewhere behind me, probably too drunk to really know what was happening.

"Look out, man, he's got a blade!" several back-up boys shouted.

"Ah, look, the pussy needs a knife to fight me. What's the matter pussy, you need a blade to fight me?"

"I don't need a blade to take care of a shit like you."

I was so drunk, I let him talk me out of my knife. Then, to my surprise, his friends stood by as I proceeded to kick ass. They didn't interfere, in the interest of fair play, I suppose. But that didn't last long.

A local muscle-bound football player was strolling along the other side of the street, with his sports shirt over his shoulder. When he saw a hippie beating a regular guy, he stepped in. First, he seized my shoulders from behind so that I lost balance. Then he saw Patrick, drunken Patrick, stumbling toward him with the razor in his unsteady hand. Before Patrick could decide what he was doing, the jock whipped the razor out of his hand with his sports shirt. Most of what I recall from then on was being pinned to the ground while the coolie kicked me in the stomach.

"Take it easy, you're liable to kill him," one of the younger guys said in a worried tone. He wasn't worried enough to stop holding me down, though.

A funny thing was that while I was being kicked in the stomach, I kept looking up to see what was happening to Patrick. I don't even remember noticing the pain, but soon I was puking.

Cops were on the scene by then, but they waited to watch us get beaten for a while before they busted us. The last thing I remember was the cop yelling at Patrick for bleeding on the police car while they handcuffed us. After that, I passed out.

It was about eight o'clock when I came to, wondering what tramp's vomit I was lying in. I looked up and saw Patrick.

"Where are we?" I groaned.

"In jail. We got busted, you asshole."

Patrick was sitting with his bare feet on the cell's toilet so as to avoid my vomit. We both looked like slobs, smeared with blood and dirt. Patrick's hair was dirty and he had a week-old beard to off-set a long mustache. He was wearing an athletic tee-shirt with the word **DRAGONS** and a handsome home-drawn dragon on the back. My curly, blondish hair looked brown and electrified.

Soon Patrick's parents bailed him out. But I remained in jail for the next week. The cops let me talk with my mother on the phone, but she wouldn't listen to my side of the story. She kept saying, "This time you've really done it, Stevie, you've pulled a knife on someone." I don't know what the cops had told her, but at my arraignment they made it sound as if I had attempted premeditated murder. "Ah, what a bunch of horseshit!" I kept protesting. But my comments only prejudiced the judge against my case.

"I heard he looked bad, but I didn't guess he'd look this bad," one of the jailers said upon first seeing me. To which another replied: "You should have seen the one that got bailed out! He looked like Jesus Christ!"

Too much was going against me this time. For one thing, I found out that the coolie I was supposed to have endangered was the son of the editor of the local paper which was backing for re-election the judge who was hearing my case. Also, the cops found out soon enough that I was wanted by the cops in New Jersey.

The situation deteriorated. A jailer asked me to sign a document saying that I recognized the fact that the jail could not take responsibility for my possessions, or something like that. In my cooperative spirit, I read it and signed it along with a duplicate. Seconds later, one of the black trustees told me that the "duplicate" I'd signed was actually a document giving the cops legal permission to cut my hair. I'd signed my own death warrant. Instantly, I ran to the jailer, on his way out, snatched both papers and shredded them. He cursed with spit flying from his red face, but I only felt relief. From then on I wouldn't sign anything.

35

The next morning, the same jailer ordered me to follow him upstairs. I obeyed, though it worried me. Upstairs, a group of cops were waiting, equipped with scissors and barber shears. They grabbed me. I struggled, kicking at their balls with the heels of my boots and screaming that they'd have to cut off my head before they cut my hair. I guess they figured it wasn't worth the hassle because they let me go. They placed me in solitary confinement.

Solitary was not as bad as it might have been since it wasn't the usual solitary where you are left completely isolated with only a bucket for company. For me, solitary meant I was locked alone in the bullpen and the other prisoners were instructed not to talk with me. But a few of the black trustees talked with me anyway when they could get away with it. And occasionally they'd sneak a candy bar to me. To pass time, I scoured the floor for every flake of tobacco I could find and I did an incredible number of push-ups. I never seemed to wear myself out enough to sleep, though. I was too bored to sleep. A trustee gave me a stupid detective novel, so I read that a couple of times.

I kept wary the next time the jailer visited my cell. He ordered me to take off my boots, and I obeyed. Then he ordered me to follow him.

"Just a minute. If you think you're going to cut my hair, man, you'd better forget it because I'm not coming."

The jailer grinned. "Take it easy, son. It ain't worth the trouble to cut your hair. I just want you should have a shower. But if you want to stay looking like that . . ."

I was stinking. I felt desperate to get out of solitary for a while. I followed the cop.

This time, as soon as I walked in another room, the cops slapped cuffs on my wrists, my ankles, and then used a third pair of cuffs to connect one pair of cuffs to the other. They rendered me nearly helpless, but rushing adrenaline kept my body thrashing and screaming so that the entire county jail would know I didn't go down without a fight.

"Look, son, Frank here's a real good barber so you'll get a good haircut if you just take it easy. If you don't cooperate, we're going to shave your damn head. Now cut it out!"

I told them all to fuck themselves. Then one of them gripped his hand around my face to jerk my head back. I bit in. My teeth sunk into the fleshy part of his hand between the thumb and index finger. I tried to make my teeth touch.

That really started it. All the cops there began punching me until I was bruised and bleeding. Until the sheriff walked in.

"You fools! What in God's name do you think you're doing?" he said, giving me a spark of hope and a moment to take hold of my consciousness. "This boy has got to appear in court, so stop marking his face!"

So they continued beating me, but after that they left my face untouched. Until one of them clutched a handful of hair and buzzed up the left side of my head. I tried not to cry. Conceding defeat, I let them strip me of every hair on my head except for a little they left me to pinch on top. The razor machine was loud and powerful, but the hair fell slowly and quietly to the floor where it became useless waste, to be swept up by a broom.

Plotting revenge, I went on a silent hunger strike. My silent pouting must have looked to them as though I'd gone into a catatonic state because they actually seemed frightened. They acted more nervous, probably, than they would have if I'd opened up to let them know how I planned to slowly torture and terrorize each cop's family. But I kept all that locked inside me, so they thought I'd completely flipped out. They kept trying to be nice to me, telling me how good I looked, and coaxing me to eat. The only response I gave them for the next couple of days was to turn my face away from the mirror they wanted me to look into.

Anyway, they let me out of solitary for the remainder of my stay, improving my situation slightly. The only other good thing that happened was that I met a guy on my tier who was staying the night and had several grams of hashish sewn into the elastic of his underwear. We smoked it in a prison-fashioned aluminum foil pipe. Of course, the bad things that happened eclipsed the good. On top of everything else, one guy on my tier was threatening to fuck my ass. One morning, he came into my cell with some breakfast margarine and announced in front of the other prisoners that I had better start greasing my ass. I was scared shitless, but when the confrontation arrived, I managed to back the guy down, making it clear that I was ready with my fists. So it ended all right, but it didn't help my frayed nervous condition.

A friend of Patrick's family and mine found us a lawyer who was supposed to be the best in the county. The lawyer didn't make me feel much better when I saw him, though. He told me not to mention that the cops had cut my hair illegally because it would prejudice the judge against me. He told me he'd take my case if I wanted to sue the cops in a separate hearing.

When court date arrived, I was starving and falling to pieces. I was sitting on the left side of the courtroom when Patrick walked in with his parents and our friend who'd found the lawyer. Everyone was buzzing around Patrick, telling him not to worry, that all would turn out right. Meanwhile, I sat alone, wondering how Patrick would react when he saw me. For some reason, I was guessing that he might think my baldness funny, but I was wrong. When he saw me, he just looked sadly to the ground.

When Patrick died, I was temporarily staying at my parents' house in New Jersey with three of my four sisters and my younger brother. I was idling around the house most of the time. When I did go out, I had to avoid cops. I would duck under the dashboard whenever I rode in a car during the daytime.

One afternoon, I walked in the back door of the house while I was tripping on LSD. My mother was in the livingroom crying. "Stevie, Patrick is dead." I couldn't understand why she was crying. I thought that it was strange at this stage of the game, after all the conflicts we'd been through, for her to be so upset about me taking drugs. "Patrick is dead," she repeated. It didn't make sense. It took a few eternal moments to hit me. Patrick is dead. It hit me. I ran out of the house and caught a bus to a nearby hill, where I sat.

At the wake the next night I was sitting in the corner. People seemed somber at first, before it got to be like a party. Middle-aged friends of Patrick's parents took turns kneeling before the open casket to pray. I can't guess what was running through their heads. Young friends of Patrick also took turns, walking over to stand in front of the casket to check it out and then walking away. They looked serious. It must have occurred to each of them that it could have been any of us.

I sensed some kind of bad feelings toward me from Patrick's parents. At first, they seemed concerned about my unhappy quiet-ness, like a lot of other people there, like Patrick's old girlfriend who kept holding my hand and sobbing on my leather jacket, which I didn't dig. But when Patrick's parents chose guys to serve as pall-bearers, they didn't ask me. They even resorted to using John's father because John couldn't make the funeral the next day, but they didn't ask me.

The story everybody got which was supposed to be true was that Patrick had been running too much, overexerting himself, and then he smoked a pack of cigarettes after which he choked to death on his saliva—or something like that. Running. There is a symbol to be found there. Something about the way he did drugs, maybe? But perhaps the symbol doesn't fit. Patrick didn't do so much running around, not as much as I did, anyway. In fact, he never really broke away from his parents, except with his music. Patrick was a musician. He was flipped out. And he was trying to pull himself together that August. I could see him running in that way, getting himself into shape. But running as a symbol—I don't know. I am sure he killed himself.

While we were hitchhiking together, John must have heard the story of Patrick and me and how we got busted told to a dozen drivers. People who pick you up like to hear about your adven-tures. And I like telling the stories. It is ironic, though, that many of my stories that sound most exciting when I tell them were de-pressing when they happened.

39

One reason that I like to tell stories is that I am in the position to give the listener any image of Steve Gibbons that fits my mood. I can be a nature-loving commune freak or a bad-assed street fighter. The image I give can be affected by a number of things—like what book I read most recently. Matter of fact, I might not have been carrying that box-cutting razor had I not read a book called *Brighton Rock*, by Graham Greene. I got into that book. The main character is a lonely guy named Pinkie who carries vitriol and a razor.

I realize this is starting to sound self-deceptive. But believe me, I don't tell myself that the only reason I ever fought was that I was identifying with a character in some book. In fact, when I was in junior high school, I fought because I enjoyed it. I liked the contest. And I was good, so it was an ego trip. Before I was hit by that car, I even considered trying to box professionally one day. I sparred with a friend of mine who was near Golden Gloves, and he said I had talent, a natural left. I trained for a while and learned a few things, but I was never able to cut smoking down to less than a pack of cigarettes a day. And when my leg was smashed, any career plans were finished. It didn't bother me, though. I had never been that serious about it.

Even if my leg had never been injured, I would not have stayed with boxing. In a year or two, I decided it was a bad business. My attitude varied. Sometimes I would decide to fight only when necessary, and at other times the entire idea disgusted me. But I never became a pacifist; my temper would not afford me that. Besides, I don't like the way pacifism works. I could never let the fear of having the shit kicked out of me interfere with my freedom.

Occasionally, my later attitude toward fighting made me seem more vicious. I no longer viewed it as a contest with rules. If fighting was in order, then the point of it, as I saw it, is to hurt the other guy enough so that he doesn't hurt you. Rules are absurd. I remember one fight I wound up losing with a big greaser because I had referred to him as a "big douchebag" or something like that. He met me in the boys' lavatory and shoved me, saying,

"I hear you been calling me names, Gibbons." The next expected move would have been for me to shove him back and say, "That's right, you douchebag, you wanna make something of it?" But instead, I reached up, clamped my hands over the guy's ears and started bashing his head against the tile wall. Then I shoved him into one of the stalls and started pushing his head into the toilet. Surprisingly, I lost that fight because the greaser managed to kick my shin exactly at the spot where the bone had not finished healing. I landed on my back, writhing in pain. Then he jumped onto my stomach and it was ended.

Before we hit the road, John and I told nearly every one of our past adventure stories to one another at least once. John seemed entertained by my stories about violent episodes, but I wondered what he would have thought of me had he known me in junior high school. He might have hated my guts. But not surely, because people seem to admire qualities they don't have. For instance, Patrick often egged me on to do some insane things. But then, Patrick had a lot more psychopath in him than John did.

Anyway, I kept out of trouble while living at John's place. For a week in March, I held a job selling magazine subscriptions by telephone, the longest I'd remained with one job until that one. Countless times each day I began the same rap to disinterested secretaries: "Good afternoon, this is Mr. Day of the . . ." My boss, Miss Jones, told me to call myself Mr. Day and never to give out the company phone number. Our company was slightly crooked, I gathered. Naturally, I didn't care except that the job was tedious. I tried amusing myself by phoning John and other friends to bestow my deadpan Mr. Day rap. Still, the job was so boring that I couldn't resist taking off Wednesday. I called to tell my boss that I could not work because my sister had been involved in a car accident, but Miss Jones didn't seem to trust me. When I returned to work on Thursday, she eyed me suspiciously and asked, "What happened about that accident your sister was in?" I looked toward her solemnly, but without meeting her eyes, and replied, "She died." I said that funeral services were being arranged for the weekend, and so Miss Jones treated me tactfully after that. But I quit on Friday anyway because I didn't like her attitude.

Psychopath. I used that word too loosely. It was an exaggeration. The only person who actually used it to describe me was the high school disciplinarian, Tommasino. He once cited me as one of the two guys in my school he wouldn't touch. Actually, in some ways, it is a kind of neat reputation. I admit I am proud of it once in a while. But that is not the way I am.

After I'd been on the road for a while, I became notorious among some people for being a fuck-over, but I didn't always deserve that reputation either. Some people badmouthed me, saying that I only stayed in one place as long as there was a free meal and a place to crash. I suppose those people figured that that was my reason for staying at John's place before he and I hit the road. Those people pissed me off.

Reputations stick, though.

5

I came back to a reputation when I came back to Ellen's apartment in San Francisco, even though most of my old friends were gone. Sally had initiated the reputation thing. She was living at her sister's place, on the same block as Ellen, all part of a family, and Sally had told everybody about me while she was awaiting my arrival from Los Angeles. About how cool and fine I was. About what a rebel I was. Ellen later told me that she was sick of hearing about me before she met me. Of course, I didn't last long with Sally, and I wound up living with Ellen, and it all fit neatly with the image Sally had created of me.

That was last fall, a long time ago. Now I was on the road with John. Now Sally was back in New Jersey. Ellen told me where others went. I took only passing interest in most, and I avoided asking about Jainie, Sally's older sister, who was bearing a grudge against me. But I was curious about what had become of Matthew. Typically, he had been busted and deported back to Canada, to Vancouver.

I considered myself to be tighter friends with Matthew than with any of the other people I'd known in San Francisco. I wanted John to meet him and I dug the idea of seeing Matthew again, and so splitting for Vancouver seemed like a better idea than ever. But there was time to stick around for the Fourth of July.

"We can do the acid just before leaving for the fireworks. It'll be great! Come on, you can get somebody to watch the kids for one night, can't you?"

"I don't know. I mean I haven't tripped in . . ." Ellen's words faded out as she paused to figure how long it had been.

"So if it's been so long, then it's about time, don't you think?" I grinned. "What better way to celebrate the Fourth of July?"

John and Kathy weren't saying anything. I knew I'd have Ellen talked into it in a few minutes. She was wishy-washy; I could talk her into anything.

"I'm really not into tripping anymore, Stevie," Ellen said.

"But you'll dig it. You know you'll dig it," I persisted.

"I don't know . . ."

"What, just because the Maharishi says you shouldn't, you're not going to trip? Can't you see, Ellen? That guy just wants all attention focused on him so he can make his money."

I made my mistake when I brought up transcendental meditation. Suddenly, Ellen was vehement.

"Don't put it down! Just don't show your ignorance!"

"Why shouldn't I put that guy down? Everybody puts down the Maharishi because he's on a money power trip—touring with the Beach Boys, shit. Even John Lennon put him down and Lennon used to be into that meditation."

"That's John Lennon's paranoia—not mine."

I'd thought that a good LSD trip might lift Ellen out of her rut, but she now left me convinced that she was content in that rut.

"All right, then John and I'll trip. You know anyplace where we can cop a couple of hits of acid?"

"Maybe from Richard . . ." Ellen began.

"All Richard's got these days is THC," Kathy said.

"That's great. I've never done real THC," I said.

"But you've done fake THC?" Kathy asked sarcastically.

"Sort of. It's just that all the stuff that sells as THC on the East Coast is actually PCP, a trippy kind of animal tranquilizer. But maybe this Richard has the real thing—synthetic marijuana. We're a long way from the East Coast."

"Do I get to tell Stevie who is staying at Richard's place?" Kathy asked Ellen with a confidential smirk.

"Oh, right! Jainie is there, Stevie," Ellen said.

Jainie and I had had too much of one another when I was living with Sally. The place was Jainie's, paid for by her welfare check, and so I tried to get along with her. But the only times I got along with Jainie were when she was stoned on reds. Her grudge against me wouldn't have fazed me, except that she had always been a kind of scary figure in my mind. The ominous older sister. She was six feet two inches tall, and that added to her presence. Not that I thought for a moment she could beat me, I just didn't want to fight her. And a fight, from what I'd heard, was the only thing she wanted with me.

"What, is Jainie still down on me?" I asked, as though bewildered by the notion.

"She sure is," Kathy said. "Last I recall her mentioning your name it was to say how mad she was at herself for not punching you in the nose the last time she saw you."

"What's she so uptight about? Everybody at that apartment was a hassle for her head, not just me. Matter of fact, her biggest hassles were with Matthew."

"She is protecting Sally," Ellen said.

"Protecting her from what? I didn't do anything to that chick."

"Jainie doesn't look at it that way."

"Well, that's her problem. When can we cop from this guy Richard?"

Ellen offered to take John and me to Richard's anytime, so we left as soon as she had dressed the kids. Kathy came with us. I carried Amoreena in a papoose like a rucksack on my back. We looked like the makings of a commune as we trudged uphill. Quiet, sunny, but not oppressively hot, it felt like a Sunday.

A girl let us into Richard's house and told us to wait in the livingroom. We set the kids loose. Then John knelt down to thumb through records, and he finally put on *Let It Bleed*, the most recent Rolling Stones album at that time.

Ellen did introductions when Richard came in. She mentioned that we were fellow New Yorkers, and he asked me what I thought of how the Mets were doing. I had no idea of how they were doing.

I quickly got down to business. I told Richard we wanted four caps of THC. He said that the price was two dollars a cap, which meant that I now expected PCP, since two dollars was too inexpensive for genuine THC. I didn't say anything about it, though, because practically everything sold as THC was actually PCP. It wasn't really a burn. When people said THC, even outside of a dealing context, they usually meant PCP.

Richard said he needed our money in advance. We gave it to him, and he told us to wait. I knew that all he was going to do was walk a few houses away to his connection where he would buy about eight caps with our money. Then he'd give us four. It was irritating to think about, but that's business.

Richard was back with our dope before the second side of *Let It Bleed* was finished. John put the four caps into his pocket. I stood to leave.

"Isn't Jainie around today?" Ellen asked Richard.

"She just split yesterday. She flew up to Vancouver, said she was going to see her old man up there."

"She left? But she didn't even call me to let me know she was going."

"It was a sudden thing with her. She just got up and went."

"Do you know how long she's going to be up there?"

"She said she wasn't coming back."

On the way back to Ellen's place, John took a turn carrying Amoreena on his back. Lisa left Ellen's hand to walk several yards in front of us.

"So Matthew and Jainie are getting back together in Canada,"

46

Ellen said, sounding romantic about it. "You know, they haven't seen each other since Matthew was deported."

"It didn't occur to me that they'd get back together," I said. "I never was able to understand his thing with her."

"Oh, Stevie, you're just saying that because Jainie doesn't like you. She's a beautiful person. She is really pretty and she's nice . . ."

"I don't know. I wouldn't call her pretty."

"Oh, but she *is*. She has such pretty eyes."

"But she's so big."

"So what? . . . Lisa, come here! What is that in your hand?"

Lisa smiled and held high her handful of dog shit. We all laughed and Lisa laughed back. Then back at the apartment, Kathy, John and I settled in the livingroom while Ellen washed Lisa's hands to the sounds of protest. Finally, Ellen rejoined us.

"I was just thinking," I said. "I'd like to see Matthew again. John and I were talking about it the other day."

"John knows Matthew?" Ellen asked.

"No, but he's heard about him."

"You'd dig him," Ellen said to John. "Matthew is really like no one else."

"So I've heard," John said.

"That was such a crazy time," Kathy laughed. "When we were all together. Do you remember that bet he made with Stevie that time?"

Ellen and Kathy looked at each other and burst out laughing.

"Let me tell it," I said. "This bet was over whether or not Matthew could give himself a blow job. He tells me he can do it, no sweat, because he's double-jointed. And I say he can't. So I bet my leather jacket against this pair of pants he has. That gives him incredible odds, of course, but it's cool because I'm positive he can't do it. Then Matthew announces he's going to prove it to me, but that he wants to step into the back room to show me because he's embarrassed to perform in front of Ellen and Kathy. At this point, I know Matthew can't do it, because if he could, he'd be the first

47

to blow himself in front of everybody. Matthew wouldn't hesitate to do it on the street corner if he felt like it. Anyway, when we get into the other room, Matthew tells me he was just kidding around but that I should go along with the joke and give him my jacket for a few minutes. Then he and I go back into the livingroom. I'm saying, 'Holy shit, I never thought he could do *that*. Come on, Matthew, you proved your point, but you know how much that jacket means to me, so can I have it back?' And Matthew is keeping cool through the whole thing. Finally, he gave me my jacket back, saying he never really intended to take it, that the bet was unfair because I never could have known."

John was laughing at the story.

"Man, you think that's funny; the funniest part about it was that Ellen believed us. She really believed Matthew could give himself a blow job."

"Well . . . you guys put on such a convincing act," Ellen said defensively.

"Remember how uptight Stevie used to get because he always thought Matthew was going to try to make it with him?" Kathy said, launching her offensive again.

"All right . . . I was uptight in my youth."

Matthew had established quite a reputation. His sexual reputation went beyond that of a guy who balls a lot of chicks. He was always into something crazy. Also, he was bisexual, which doubled the possibilities, I suppose. Yet despite his sexual reputation, Ellen always insisted to me that she was never particularly interested in going to bed with Matthew. This surprised me; it seemed as though practically every chick I knew wanted to make it with Matthew. Another thing that surprised me was that Matthew never tried to make it with Ellen. He had things going with Kathy, Sally and of course Jainie, but not Ellen. The only time he ever made anything like an advance toward her was once when she was nursing Amoreena. He asked her to let him suck her breasts. She thought he was kidding, but he persisted, telling her that his mother had neglected him as a child, that this was vital to his psychological

48

well-being. So Ellen eventually let him suck. But they still never seemed to want to make it with one another.

We all missed the fireworks that night because John and I were so wrecked. It turned out to be PCP, as I'd suspected. My body felt heavy, but my limbs were buoyant. Moving sluggishly was easy. John and I were floating around Ellen's apartment together, but I didn't feel the closeness with him that I felt when we took other drugs together. Walking to the fireworks would have been like walking through water up to our necks. It didn't matter, though. The drug made me feel unenlightened.

The next day John and I packed our knapsacks, rolled our sleeping bags tightly and showered. Dressed, I went into the livingroom.

"Ready to check out, John?"

"Dooooo . . . dooo . . . dooooche*bag* . . . Stevie a dooooche*bag*!"

It was Lisa, straining and then beaming with pride as she completed her new word. She was being rewarded with Ellen's laughter. I felt paranoid for a moment. Ellen had taught Lisa a bit of New Jersey greaser jargon which had come from me.

"That's right, Lisa," she giggled.

Kathy was laughing, too. So was John. Then I joined them.

Ellen was kind to me just before John and I hit the road again, and I suppose we even had some crazy kind of understanding. She encouraged me to return to San Francisco after Vancouver. And she gave me five dollars' worth of food stamps as a going-away present. Then John and I kissed her and Kathy goodbye. "So long, douches," Kathy chuckled.

I was wondering how John's presence had affected the reputation I was leaving behind. Though Ellen and Kathy hadn't had time to get to know John well, he was definitely a calmer, more gentle presence. And at the same time, his presence was part of mine.

Of course, maybe nothing was changed; maybe Ellen had simply decided to accept me.

49

Anyway, it wasn't anything like the last time Ellen and I split up. After leaving on bad terms in November, I stopped at her place briefly in December on my way down from Vancouver. I needed five dollars so that I could eat on my way to Los Angeles. When I told Ellen that, she waved a five in front of my face and then snatched it away, saying, "Not until you tell me where your head is really at. I want to at least understand you, Stevie." With that, I turned around and left. I was having enough trouble trying to figure that one out for myself without going into it with her. I could panhandle the five dollars with less hassle.

6

So we hitched to Vancouver to drop in on Matthew.

But before we get there, I have to mention a friend of mine in California, one I did not visit this time around—my Uncle Mike. I was thinking of him while John and I were hitching out of the state, a hitch that took three days because of competition. Mike was responsible for getting me out to California in the first place, when I was sixteen. Before I flew off to live with him and his family, all my travels had been up and down the East Coast. I briefly thought about visiting Mike while John and I were in the Los Angeles area. But upon further consideration, it didn't seem like a good idea.

I lived at Mike's at the beginning of that fall, shortly after Patrick died. My parents were eager for me to leave their house because the hassles with the local police were forcing me to hang around all day. Then Mike invited me to stay at his place because he understood. He'd been in and out of trouble when he was my age, ran away from home after he was expelled from his Catholic high school for punching out a priest. That's why he could identify with me when he visited my parents in New Jersey just after the cops released me from jail. Mike learned that my parents were urging me to get out of their house. He also heard that I had recently been a long-haired hippie, but with my police-styled hair-cut, I guess Mike saw some of himself in me. "Steve," he said, "how'd you like to come out to California to live with me?"

It's funny, but when my uncle finally finished his visit with my parents, he was much more pissed off at them than I was. At the end of his brief visit, he had a clash with my father, because they'd gotten drunk together and about the only thing they had in common was their drinking habits. Both my parents were intellectual snobs, while Mike, my mother's brother, was a construction worker. Mike was intelligent, but he had had a different kind of education than my father had.

Anyway, Mike was holding a bottle of Johnny Walker Red in each fist when he first walked through the front door of my parents' house. And he had more stashed in the back of his Volkswagen bus. My father had just finished drinking a bottle of his cheaper whiskey before Mike arrived. And since my father is an alcoholic and my uncle drinks all the time, too, they decided to go to a bar when the bottles were empty. When I saw them leave, my father still had his cool, but my uncle was smashed. Then, at the bar, they nearly got into a fight.

"You think you know all just 'cause you wrote a book," Mike bellowed. "Well, I never wrote a book, but one damn thing's for sure that if I did it'd be twice as good as any fuckin' book you ever wrote. . . ."

My father put Mike down intellectually. Then Mike retorted: "If you wanna know the truth, I think Thomas Aquinas is a fag-got, anyway."

My father, an authority on Thomas Aquinas, at this point prac-tically challenged my uncle to a fight.

I heard the story from Mike and then again more objectively from my mother, who was also there. What I thought was funny about it was the way my uncle and my father switched roles. I can understand my uncle's point of view: even if you decide that intellectuality is pure horseshit, you still begin to feel inferior when somebody out-intellectualizes you. But I think my father was crazy for even considering taking on my uncle. Mike could have put him through the wall.

After that bar episode, Mike drove back to my parents' house and told me that we were taking off for California right away. As Mike's Volkswagen swerved at sixty miles per hour along the highway, he kept slamming his fist on the steering wheel and shouting, "I've never been so insulted in my entire life. Steve, I should have taken this fist and broken bones!" And I kept saying, "Yeah, you're right, but how 'bout letting me drive for a while?" Mike paid no attention and continued yelling his outrage. Fortunately it was late and so the roads were relatively empty.

Soon we stopped at a Howard Johnson's rest area. While a garage attendant filled our tank, Mike said, "Steve, if you're going to live with me, you'll need an allowance." He removed a ten and a five from his wallet and gave them to me. I asked him if he were sure he knew what he was doing, and he replied sure as he handed a ten to the garage attendant and told him to keep the change. We ate dinner at the restaurant, and when he'd finished his hamburger, which was in a few seconds, Mike called my mother from a phone booth. I knew he was talking to my mother because he was banging his fist against the glass of the booth and I could hear him yelling, "I've never been so insulted . . ." After he hung up the phone, we left. On our way out, Mike asked me, "Did you pay for our food?" I said no. "Good, we don't want to go around throwing our money away in these crappy joints."

The next day, after Mike had sobered up, I wound up going back to my parents' house, packing my clothes and then flying to California. Few of my plans worked out. I only attended school for two days before I decided again that it was horseshit, even in California, and the school officials told me they did not want me around school grounds because of my attitude. After that, I spent most evenings drinking with Mike. He would usually bring home a

53

bottle of whiskey for himself and a bottle of Chianti for me. I never seemed to notice his family much. His wife never bothered me because she was afraid of me for some reason. And Mike's fourteen-year-old son, Mike Junior, went to bed early or something.

Mike and I became good drinking partners, friends in a way. Even when my hair was growing noticeably longer, he would show me off to his pool hall friends. And I convinced him to grow his mustache and go a few extra weeks without a haircut. Still, Mike usually played the big brother role. "Steve," he would say to me when we were smashed. "Steve, I'm going to teach you how to break bones." One night, he decided to teach me how to break bones in the middle of his livingroom. I was pretty sure of myself; when I am drunk I think I can take on a bear. I thought I might even show Mike something, surprise him with my speed at least, catch him off-guard. I moved in. Wham! He nearly put me through the wall. I didn't give up, though. I moved in again. I moved in a couple of more times, and each time he knocked me on my ass. Finally, I managed to get a clear punch at his balls. That made him angry, but afterward he held more respect for me. He knew I was a streetfighting man.

After I'd been living at his house for a few weeks, Mike began talking about running away himself. His wife and kid were doing nothing for him but dragging his head down. He knew it and I knew it. But he would never leave. He was tied down to working his ass off for his split-level home and life.

Mike's main enjoyment was in spending the money he worked so hard to earn. He loved to flash it around and pretend he didn't take it seriously. When I first moved into his house, for instance, he told me he would buy me a motorcycle if I stayed in school. Then once when we were drunk, after I'd quit school, I reminded him about the motorcycle. "Hell, no, you can't have it. You didn't stay in school like you were supposed to," he said. But the next day he bought me a hundred-dollar ten-speed bicycle, *as a joke*. That was his kind of joke.

Soon I was on the road again, riding up and down the coast. I rode the bicycle to the Mexican border where I was turned back because my hair had already grown too long. Then I left the bike at my uncle's place and hitched north. I lived for a while in San Francisco with Sally and then I moved in with Ellen. Then I hitched some more, up to Vancouver and back. I finally wound up back at my uncle's place since things were bad in San Francisco and I had decided it was time to hit the East Coast again.

Today my uncle hates me for what happened then. I needed to return to the East, but it was too late in the winter to hitch. I called my mother and asked her for the money. When she refused me, I took the bike my uncle had given to me and sold it for fifty dollars. It was my bike, but my uncle was furious because he'd given it to his son while I was away. But my uncle never saw me or the bike again. Before he knew the bike was gone, I took twenty dollars from his house, hitched to Denver and from there I flew to New York.

I don't feel so badly about the act of ripping my uncle off; I just feel badly that he must have felt like a fool. When he discovered the bike and the money missing, he probably reasoned that the whole time I was staying at his place I was just taking him for a ride, taking him for his booze and his middle-class comforts. He undoubtedly thought that I saw him as a big simple greaser patsy. Sometimes when I talk about Mike, I can't resist making it sound like that's the way it was. I guess I feel funny or maybe ashamed to admit that I *liked* that big greaser. I did. And I wish he knew that even though I ripped him off.

Remembering that trip from Mike's place back to New York leaves me feeling awfully lonesome.

Now, on our way to Vancouver, it was different. I remember an old road bum once talking about that difference to John. His name was Abe. John and I had climbed the Grand Canyon with him and a bunch of other travelers, and we were all resting around a

55

campfire, singing, telling stories, sharing food and beer. Then Abe played a song we'd never heard before called "Me and Bobby Mc-Gee," a song he'd heard from Gordon Lightfoot, a Canadian singer. After that song was over, Abe cradled his guitar and commented to John that a musical instrument can mean a lot to a traveler. "This old guitar is invaluable to me," he said. Then John said, "I've gotten by pretty well without one so far." To which Abe laughed and said, "Sure, but you brought your friend."

John and I were traveling lucky. We didn't get busted in Washington, where police were notorious for jailing hitchhikers even on entrance ramps. And we were eventually able to sneak across the Canadian border after the customs official turned us back.

That was about a week and a half after we left Ellen's. The smug little official inside his blue blazer with the crest on the pocket had told us that they *might* let us across if we purchased round-trip bus tickets to Vancouver and if I got a note from my parents since I was under eighteen. A note from my parents was out of the question, so we decided to wait for nightfall when we would skulk across a nearby railroad bridge like convicts atop a prison wall. We waited in the middle of the border park: a well-designed composition of trimmed grass and shrubbery, dancing water sprinklers, sandblasted monuments above carefully arranged flower beds. Camouflage. Although members of the old people's organization that was holding a casual meeting in this park would scoot through customs hassle-free after their party, as far as John and I were concerned there might as well have stood a steel gray wall.

Not quite true. Sneaking across a steel gray wall would have been harder than hopping over the shrubbery, which is what we finally did. Toward late afternoon, I noticed two girls stepping out of a car on the north side of the bushes. I ran to them and spoke across the bushes about our predicament. They were stopping for a picnic, but they said they'd gladly give John and me a ride afterward. At about seven thirty, the girls returned to their car. Then John and I hopped over the bushes and into the backseat. They drove us to a point on the main highway several miles north of the border. We were in Vancouver before dark.

Our last ride let us off on Fourth Avenue, a double-lane thoroughfare where a lot of hip people nodded hello. "Nodders," Matthew used to call them. But enough with Matthew's cynicism, their friendliness was giving me a warm feeling about being back in Vancouver.

Everything seemed set, even though it wasn't. We'd made it, so not knowing Matthew's address didn't seem to matter. There were ways; I'd find out where he was living. I would call up Sally. She was bound to know.

John sat on the curb while I used a phone booth in front of a gas station. I was worried that my phony credit card number might not work in Canada, but the connection went through, and I soon heard a hello from one of Sally's brothers.

"Is Sally there?" I yelled, despite a relatively good connection.

Before I could get an answer, Sally's father was shouting for her brother to get back into bed. Then he grabbed the phone. "Who's calling at this time of night?"

"This is long distance. It's extremely important that I speak with Sally." I avoided saying my name because he knew me and hated me. When Sally got pissed off at her father, she used to tell him that I could beat him up.

"I don't give a damn. It's after eleven and Sally's asleep."

Click. He hung up. I dialed the number again, then gave the operator my credit card number and she put me through.

"Is Sally there?"

"Who in hell is this? I thought I told you . . ." her father began, and then interrupted himself by slamming down the receiver.

I gave it one more try, and this time luck was with me. Sally's father's bellowing had brought her to the phone.

"Sally, this is Stevie."

"Stevie? Where are you? Talk fast because my dad's going to kill me."

"I'm in Vancouver. I've got to have Matthew's address."

57

"I don't know where they're living now. Oh, have you heard about him and Jainie getting married?"

"Married? Are you joking?"

"I've got to get off now, Stevie, or my dad'll kill me. Call me back sometime during the day."

I was shocked.

"Did you get his address?" John asked as I stepped out of the booth.

"No. Guess what? Matthew and Jainie got married."

"Married? That doesn't sound like what I've heard of Matthew."

"No kidding. To tell the truth, I'm beginning to wonder just how well I do know that guy."

7

Matthew's address turned up only after John and I had settled in Vancouver, and after I'd nearly resigned myself to missing Matthew this time around.

Not that I hadn't been trying. The morning after our arrival, I began telephoning all the McLeods in the phone book. The fifth one listed was Matthew's mother. Speaking in a Scottish accent so loudly that I held the receiver a foot away from my ear, she said that Matthew was married and living at a new address. It was on Nineteenth.

So John and I hitched up Burrard to Nineteenth. Then we walked past cottagelike brick houses with adjoining garages and tidy lawns. As the house numbers grew closer to the one Matthew's mother had given me, the houses were bigger, many including two-car garages. Rotating lawn sprinklers dampened our sneakers. I was looking for a neighborhood eyesore with sturdy weeds in the front yard and peeling paint on the door. That would be Matthew's place. Another friend of mine was once arrested in the States for being a public eyesore. It was the only possibility that would make sense. But the neighborhood was uniformly trim, and Matthew did not live there.

To tell the truth, the realization that none of the house numbers corresponded with the one on my slip of paper comforted me. Looking for the place, John had been saying, "Do you really think Matthew lives in this area?" To which I responded: "I don't know, man. It's been a long time since I've seen him. He got married, so I guess he's been through some changes. But I don't know, this . . . this is a bit too heavy a change."

I more or less gave up then, but John and I set ourselves up to stay in Vancouver, anyway, because it was an easy place to live with little money. No jobs were available and everybody seemed to be on welfare. The conservative mayor was trying to change the situation, run the hippies out of town; but in the meantime there were two feed-ins in a schoolyard every day, and the town was loaded with free hostels.

We tried the Children's Aid Society on Broadway first because they referred you to the hostel that gave away meal tickets. We told workers there that we were both seventeen. Fortunately, John was a young-looking eighteen-year-old, and they didn't ask for ID. In our interviews, we both said we'd never stayed at their hostels before, which caused a minor confusion because they still had a ten-month-old Steven Gibbons file. It had slipped my mind that I'd given them my real name the last time I'd filed. Anyway, they gave us passes to the Catholic Charities Hostel after I explained that I had assumed they were talking about the last six months.

That hostel was on the downtown side of the city. Vancouver is divided by the Georgia Strait and then reconnected by a few bridges. The Children's Aid office, Fourth Avenue and Nineteenth are all on one side, the side where Kitslano Beach is located. To get to the hostel, on the downtown side, with its tall shining buildings, we crossed the Burrard Street Bridge.

Crossing that bridge reminded me of the World's Fair in New York. The sides of the bridge were decorated with banners which hung like colorful flags of the nations. But these designs didn't rep-

60

resent countries. Their colors swirled instead of following lines. I thought I saw Matthew on the bridge, but it was somebody else.

The Catholic Charities Hostel had an eight o'clock curfew, so we slept early. The atmosphere was like a YMCA. Twenty-five kids slept in the room with us, a lot of them French Canadians. I learned to take showers at night because they kicked us out early in the morning.

Two days later, at the eleven o'clock feed-in in a schoolyard near Kitslano Beach, John met a girl who knew where Matthew lived. I had been behind him on line, and he was sitting talking to her with a paper plate of food in his lap when I joined them on the lawn.

"You're from New York, too, eh?" the girl asked me.

"Right."

"That's so funny: I'm finding that I meet people from all over the place without ever leaving this town. Like I just met a married couple from New York, and now I meet you two from there . . ."

"Hold it. Who do you know from New York?" I blurted. "Did they just get married, just recently?"

She was talking about Matthew and Jainie, all right, though she had Matthew's origin wrong. She barely knew them. But at least she knew where they lived. And she seemed pleased to take us, the old friends, to see them after supper.

On the way, I explained briefly that Jainie would be unfriendly toward me for various personal reasons. I was really preparing myself.

This house was more like it, more like what I'd expected Matthew to rent. The house was small, shingled green and situated behind a large old house, only a few blocks from the feed-in. The entrance was on the side, where a couple of old mattresses were leaning against the house. We walked five steps up to the cluttered indoor porch. The refrigerator was on the porch, and the door next to it led into the kitchen.

Matthew, Jainie and another girl were all right there when the three of us paraded into the kitchen. Matthew and Jainie were both dressed in black tee-shirts and blue jean shorts which they'd cut off about a quarter inch below the crotch. With her back to us, Jainie was washing dishes. Matthew was sitting at the kitchen table near the door, working intently on brown strips of leather which he was weaving into a belt. Nobody acknowledged our entrance.

The girl we were with just stood there. I suppose she was waiting for the warm welcome for me, the old friend. I was uptight.

"Hey, man, could you spare a smoke?" I said to the top of Matthew's head after a minute.

He pulled an Export filter out of his pack on the table. As I put the cigarette into my mouth, Matthew knew he'd seen me before. He pointed at me, groping for words.

"Is yer name Stevie?"

What a way to put it. But I kept grinning and nodded.

"I didn't recognize ya cause yer hair's long and ya got a beard," he said, meaning the fuzz on my chin. "Far out. Look who it is, Jainie."

"Stevie Gibbons?" Jainie said, sounding almost gleeful.

I nodded nervously and kept smiling. For some reason, Jainie's wide, blue eyes seemed happy to see me.

"Ya look different," Matthew said. "Yer nose looks crookeder. What happened, ja get it broke in another fight?"

"No, nothing happened." Crazy Matthew, why couldn't he give a plain, simple, warm greeting?

"Well, whatcha doing up here?" Matthew asked.

"What do you mean what am I doing? I came to visit you!"

Matthew led me into the livingroom to show me his leather creations. He went into the closet, which was actually in the bedroom portion of the long room, and he pulled out a four-inch-wide, studded, brown leather belt. It looked camp. It was weighted down with jewels and big studs and smaller ones that formed peace symbol designs. When Matthew modeled it, it looked more like a girdle around his skinny hips.

"Far out, eh?" Matthew said.

"It sure is."

"Matthew's so funny; he shows that belt to everyone who comes in here," Jainie laughed from the kitchen.

"Matthew thinks he's a stud," the other girl said.

While Matthew ignored the digs from the kitchen, my attention was drawn there by that girl who was with Matthew and Jainie. Sitting with her back to the kitchen table, her knees jutted into view at the doorway between the kitchen and the livingroom. She was wearing a short, embroidered cotton nightshirt. She had it pulled tightly around her hips and was playing with the handful of excess nightshirt material that she had bunched in her lap. From where I stood, half of her was blocked from view by the edge of the doorway, but she had very pretty knees.

"That's Julie," Matthew grinned, catching me.

Then he sat down on a red arm chair with his feet to his ass and his knees pointing to his chin. His skinny body was folded like a roadmap. The illustrations covered his arms. Tattoos began at his wrists and continued to the sleeves of his tee-shirt. I looked for new ones, but they were all ones I'd already seen—a peacock, another kind of bird, the name Irene (of a girl he'd fallen in love with one drunken night but never saw again), among others.

"Listen, I'll see you soon," I said. "Right now John and I want to see what jobs they offer at Manpower."

"Ya gonna work?"

"We have practically no money left."

I cut the visit short because I didn't want to worry Jainie that John and I might try to move in. I wasn't planning an encore of the San Francisco performance.

John was talking with Jainie in the kitchen. The girl who had brought us here was gone.

Before we stepped outside, Julie asked us where we were headed. To the other side of the bridge, I told her. She asked us to wait a minute so she could walk with us part of the way. Then she went into the livingroom and put on a pair of blue jeans under her nightshirt. She was blond and cute, only about fifteen.

"Living with Matthew and Jainie is so cool . . . Matthew is so

63

cool," Julie was saying on our way down the avenue. "Like the other night, this dude I know, Bill, was telling us about a party he'd just split from. He was so uptight. He said he left the party because the boys were holding hands with boys and girls were holding hands with girls. Up 'til then, Matthew wasn't paying attention to Bill, but when he said that, Matthew started pulling his boots on. Then Matthew stood up and said, 'Where is it? There's nothing I like better than a *liberal* party.' "

Julie was dazzled by Matthew's charm, and she was not the first to be taken in. In San Francisco, Sally listened to and believed every word Matthew said. Once he told her that brushing teeth is bad because it removes too much of the organic green stuff that keeps teeth healthy. Matthew's teeth were corroded and crooked; and when he had a toothache, he would anesthetize himself with heroin and have the tooth pulled at the nearest free clinic. Yet Sally believed him, and I had to argue with her for a day before her sister, Jainie, told her to stop being stupid and brush her teeth.

Why these young girls believed Matthew is beyond me. He had experienced a lot in his twenty-three years, but he didn't look like a person to take seriously. His face had some handsome features—a strong jaw and a cleft chin—but his expressions made him look comical. He talked to you with his eyebrows arched, and he listened with his mouth hanging open.

Matthew was intelligent, but he had finished little formal schooling. At the age of eighteen, he was expelled from the eighth grade, and the only reason he had made it that far was that the police kept giving him the option to go back to school every time he was busted.

In some ways a general description of Matthew's appearance could fit John. They both stood over six feet and were both very skinny. Neither of them looked like gawks, though. They both had straight hair past their shoulders.

But they were two different kinds of skinny. Matthew's shoulders were broad and his bones larger than John's; they stuck sharply into his skin as though they might rip through in a few

64

places. John was a healthier kind of skinny. Also, Matthew and John had very different faces. John's was much younger, prettier. And John's teeth were white and even.

"So what do you think of them?" I asked John after Julie was gone.

"I really like Jainie. She's nothing like what I was expecting after . . ."

"Yeah, I haven't figured that out myself. So what did you think about Matthew?"

"He seems okay," John said positively. "I didn't get to talk with him much. . . . Actually, the one impression I got—you'll probably say this is bullshit—but isn't there something in his face that reminds you of Patrick?"

If it was there, I hadn't noticed it. But I was especially interested to hear any of John's reaction to Matthew because the two of them were so different from each other.

To my mind, they were opposites. Let me use this example: I could never picture John with tattoos. But tattoos were important to Matthew. In San Francisco, Matthew tried to convince all his friends to let him tattoo them with a pin and India ink. I almost let him put one on me once when I was drunk. Around that time, Matthew said he was planning to have a giant, full-color crucifixion scene tattooed onto his back as soon as he saved the money to pay for it. Matthew used to explain that the more painful a tattoo was, the more it proved you to be a man. This was another of his insane stories, like that one about brushing teeth. But sometimes I don't think he was entirely joking about this one.

Of the jobs posted in the crowded Manpower office, the only work that seemed to suit us was berry-picking. It paid seven cents per picked pound of blueberries. We were to meet the truck that takes workers out to the farm at seven A.M.

This was our first time on the road together with so little money. We'd left New York with a couple of hundred dollars from John's book money and a twenty-five-dollar check. Now we were down to that check and some change.

We would have still had a lot of money if we hadn't been busted in Madison, Wisconsin. It was just after the riots at the university in Madison, not long after the National Guard killed four students at Kent State, Ohio. John did a talk at the university, for which they paid him, but then the cops threw us in jail and fined us sixty dollars for hitchhiking.

I recall it now, but we didn't recall that sixty-dollar fine as we talked in the hostel that night; we weren't counting what we'd lost.

Kids were noisy, snapping towels at one another while we talked. Then John lent his shampoo to one of them. A mistake, he would get it back half empty.

"That work we're starting tomorrow, man," I said. "It's not going to pay too well, especially considering we'll be working a ten-hour day."

"True, but we don't need much in this town," John said.

"You're right," I said. "So there's no sense in us both getting up at six. Why don't you sleep in tomorrow."

John paused a moment. "Okay, I'll meet you at the late feed-in. Or at Matthew and Jainie's if you're late."

I earned six-fifty the next day, most of which we spent on dinner. After that I went back to being a bum because berry-picking wasn't worth it.

8

"It's just a feeling I have," John said. "We've come about as far as we're going to get from New York. I just have this feeling something's going to open up."

"You think a city trip might do it?" I asked.

With it drizzling outside, we had ducked into a Fourth Avenue coffee shop where we ran into Eric, a guy who was staying at Matthew's place that week. In a happy mood because he was going to head home to Calgary, Eric had given John and me each a tablet of LSD.

"I don't know," John said. "It's only a feeling."

"Okay, let's do it," I said, and put the tablet into my mouth.

"Your attitude toward tripping's changed, hasn't it?" John said.

"What, you mean since I was fifteen? Since the days of tripping every weekend? Man, that was crazy."

"No, I mean your attitude seems to have changed over the past couple of months."

"Who knows? Let's get out of here and enjoy it. You're starting to get me paranoid," I said, half-joking.

We walked to Kitslano Beach, where we could see mountains as well as the city.

True, I'd felt a strange uneasiness on my last few trips, but my attitude remained the same: Either you want to trip or you don't. I wasn't in a mood to sit down and analyze it.

"What do you say we start off with something light?" I suggested. "Like the Laurel and Hardy movie at the Magic Theater?"

John liked the idea. Then we decided to invite Matthew to come with us, so we went to his place.

We walked through the open kitchen door, and Jainie was on the couch reading a paperback. Matthew was looking for something in the closet.

"What are you guys up to?" Jainie asked, putting aside her book.

"Heading over to the Magic Theater to catch *Perils of Laurel and Hardy*—want to come?"

"Another night. Hey, are you getting off on acid or something?"

"Just starting to. What about you, Matthew? Want to come?"

Matthew had in his hand a Baggie of tablets which he'd fished out of the closet.

"Laurel and Hardy on acid—what a gas!" he said.

He ate one of the tablets and then put his denim jacket on over his black turtleneck sweater. "Bye, baby," he said to Jainie and kissed her.

"Bye, you guys have a good time," she said.

This was my first chance to talk with Matthew away from Jainie since John and I had arrived in Vancouver. I was glad for it. Not that I still disliked Jainie—I was beginning to enjoy her, in fact—but I never felt able to talk comfortably to Matthew with her around.

It had stopped drizzling but was still gray.

I asked Matthew what I'd wanted to ask when I first saw him—why did he marry Jainie? He said that she had to marry him to become a landed immigrant in Canada. Then he added that together they received a fat welfare check. I suspected other reasons, but Matthew said no more about it.

Walking along Fourth Avenue we met two young girls who knew Matthew. One of them cutely opened Matthew's jacket to poke at his ribs. She was wearing spidery eye makeup that looked spooky.

"Look at those bones, Betsy," she said. "Matthew is nothing but a skeleton."

Matthew grinned down at them.

"I can guess what you need, Matthew. You could use someone to fatten you up, eh?"

Matthew still grinned. Although I hadn't started tripping, I was getting visual effects. The girl's freckles looked like scales.

"Where are you going now, Matthew?" she asked.

"Movies."

"All right, we'll see you soon, eh?"

"Yeah, so long," Matthew said, and we went on toward the bridge. Then he turned to me: "What a drag, all the teenyboppers in this town wanna ball me."

"Come on, man, teenyboppers are fun," I said, not taking his remark too seriously.

"Yeah, sometimes they're fun," Matthew pondered. "But they're such a draggy ball."

"What are you talking, man; they're not draggy at all."

"Sure, they're okay fer once, but once one gets ya, she won't let go."

As he said that, Matthew demonstrated his point by lifting his left foot and shaking it as though a pesty little dog had its teeth clenched in the bottom of his blue jeans.

John and I laughed. And then I said, "You mean like Sally?"

Matthew didn't answer.

A Volkswagen bug took us across the Burrard Street Bridge. The driver let us off at the Georgia Street intersection, several blocks from the theater.

For those blocks, Matthew and I were walking abreast while John walked a few steps behind. Matthew's walk amused me. He was loose like a scarecrow, yet at the same time he managed to maintain a slickness about the way he carried himself, a self-assuredness.

"What about that chick who's staying at your place?" I asked.

"Julie? Would you call her a draggy teenybopper?"

"She ain't living with us no more."

"Why not?"

"She freaked out when me and Jainie tried to get her into bed. She said she'd ball me, but she ain't gonna sleep with another woman."

"I figured you had her there for a reason. She's a neat chick."

"She's young."

The theater was dingy and nearly empty. An old newsreel was already showing on the small screen. I sat with Matthew on my left and John on my right. The newsreel was about a bicycle race and the launching of a ship. They broke a good bottle of champagne.

I felt paranoid. LSD brought me to one extreme or another. Most of the times I tripped, I felt energy and emotions overflowing; it felt like the liquid inside me was about to spill out to connect me with the whole world. Other times on acid, however, I was hollow, empty, about to vanish. This time I was on my way to being invisible in my seat in the second row.

I decided to lose myself in the movie when it started. It helped. Laurel and Hardy were hilarious. The best scene was one in which Stan Laurel played the frustrated pea-chaser, chasing a pea with his spoon around his dish and onto the table and then around the room. Whenever I laughed, I nearly choked on my saliva.

Halfway through the movie, Matthew began to distract me. I could tell he was not tripping yet, and he was observing my trip.

People should never eat LSD at different times if they want to trip together. Otherwise, one person is on his way up when the other is on his way down. It's like playground swings; it is better to coordinate motions.

Matthew was in control. At the next funny part of the movie, he put his hand onto my leg. His knees were sticking in front of my seat. I was peaking; he knew I wanted him to stop. Then he had both of his hands on me, all over me. I was moving away so that I was practically sitting in John's seat. But John was so stoned that he didn't notice.

70

Before the movie was over, Matthew left me alone. The theater was large and hollow. The place seemed totally removed from the rest of Vancouver. But the movie ended before I forgot where I was.

Outside of the theatre, we stood around a coming attractions poster for a Marx Brothers movie. The sun had gone down.

"That oughta be a far-out flick, eh?" Matthew said.

"Sure," I said. "What do you say we buy a bottle of wine?"

"We've got a dollar bill left," John said. "Might as well spend it on something worthwhile."

"Far out. I'll throw in fifty cents," Matthew said. "I know just the wine."

The Government Liquor Store was several blocks away. Bums were panhandling outside it; I told them I'd give them the change from our bottle. Then Matthew bought Beau Sejour, a cheap purple wine. We backtracked a few blocks to drink sitting on the rear steps of the City Hall building. Matthew took long gulps; he was peaking on his LSD. When the bottle was empty, we all pissed into the bushes.

"Listen, John, we are out past the curfew already, so do you think it'll be cool if we stay at Beatty Street tonight?"

The Beatty Street Armory served as a hostel with no curfew. But before John could answer, Matthew commented, "Is that all ya worry about, what's cool and what isn't?"

I didn't mean the word *cool* in that way. Matthew's remark was so absurd that it shouldn't have put me uptight. But it did. I was uptight about the fact that Matthew was trying to put me uptight.

"Let's get another bottle of wine," Matthew said.

"Good idea," John said. "Are you going to buy it for us, Matthew?"

"I got fifty cents left. And Stevie's a good panhandler, ain'tcha, Stevie?"

"I'll panhandle the rest," I said. "But you guys have to stick with me while I do it."

John and Matthew had too much pride to panhandle. But I was

71

high on wine. And when I start panhandling, sometimes I even enjoy it. "Excuse me, sir, could you spare some change?" I said with conviction. And the money rolled in in quarters.

I remembered one lucky day I had been doing this on Wall Street in New York. When I asked one business man for change, he stopped and said that I looked like a healthy young man; why didn't I find a job? So I pulled out my wallet with my social security card and told him that I had been waiting all day for someone to ask me that question. "What position do you have in mind for me, sir? Junior executive, perhaps?" The business man chuckled and handed me a ten-dollar bill.

Luck wasn't quite that good in Vancouver, but we had enough for a quart of Beau Sejour in half an hour.

"Far out, let's get the wine," Matthew said.

"Hold it," I said. "Let's keep going a little longer and shoot for a half gallon." Then I turned to a couple and said, "Excuse me, could you spare a little change?" I got a dime.

"Ya ain't bad at this, Stevie. Didja ever consider it as a career?"

The next people to pass us on Georgia Street looked like prime targets, two straight-looking drunks about our age. One of them, a husky guy with glasses, was staggering blindly. His friend, wearing a cowboy hat, was high and giggling as he helped the football player along the sidewalk.

"Hey, man, do you think you could spare some change so my friends and I could buy a bottle of wine," I said, figuring he was a happy drunk who would be eager to put others into the same spirit.

The football player stood close to me so that he could focus on my face through his rimless glasses. "You want some wine, eh? What about pills? Would you want pills instead? Or H? How 'bout it? Didja ever crank the big H?" His breath was hot alcoholic fumes in my face as he did a clumsy pantomime of a person injecting himself in the arm with a hypodermic needle.

"No smack today, man, I'd just like a small contribution for our wine fund," I grinned, hoping to get what I wanted after watching the drunk's show.

"Well, *I've* cranked the big H," he said. "You can bet your life on that, boy. I've done it all, more than you done in your life. And I'm rough, too . . ."

"I'll bet you are," I said, humoring him.

"He may not be rough, but drunk he is," said the friend with the hat.

"Yeah, well listen, can you spare any change for wine? It would be sincerely appreciated."

"Boy, if you want money from me, you have to *crawl* for it. You want a dollar, boy? I'm gonna watch you *crawl* in front of me for it."

That remark pissed me off. The football player was on his drunken ego trip, and he was threatening mine. I stood my ground as he dug into his pocket for money.

"I don't mind crawling," I said, coolly.

"Yeah, boy, you better crawl for this dollar right now, 'cause if you don't . . ."

He waved a two-dollar bill in front of my face as his friend begged him to cool it. Then he tossed it at the gutter. I was ready. I bent down to pick it up. His hand pushed on my back, shoving me to the ground. I was ready. I spun around and stung him in the head. I punched him about eight times before he knew what was happening. His glasses fell off and shattered. But before I could hit him again, his friend pulled me down from behind by my hair so that my head was a few inches from the concrete. He had me. He told me to give him the two dollars. Where were Matthew and John? I loosened my fist. Then the guy with the hat took the two-dollar bill and released me. When I was up, I ran about twenty feet up the street to where Matthew and John were standing.

"Didja get the money?" Matthew said.

He knew I didn't have the money; he was putting me down for going through all that for nothing.

"How could I get the money with that guy on top of me?" I yelled.

"If ya had any sense, ya wouldn't have come on like a greaser in

73

the first place. Then ya wouldn't have had to hit the guy to get the money."

"I hit the guy because I thought I had *men* backing me up. Where were you guys when that drunk's friend had me on the ground?"

I knew Matthew's weak point, and he knew mine.

"As long as I've known ya, Stevie, ya ain't been able to come up to a guy without getting aggressive. Half the time I see ya, yer coming on like a greaser."

"Matthew, I'm *glad* I hit that fucker. Didn't you see the shit he was trying to pull on me? I'm *glad* I broke his glasses and I hope they cost him a lot of money. I would have that two bucks, too, if I had *men* to back me up."

"It ain't just hitting the guy that I'm talking about. It's that whole greaser come-on of yours. Ya can't even relate to a guy without showing yer aggressions. I told ya before what that means."

"Oh, don't start giving me your tired old horseshit again, Matthew," I groaned.

"I know it's cliché, but it's cliché 'cause it's true. There ain't no way ya can fight that. It's a definite sign of being gay."

Practically every homosexual I've met, particularly Matthew, is in the habit of calling half of your actions definite signs of repressed homosexuality. I think Matthew believed that the entire world is gay, but that he was part of that honest minority of people who admit it to themselves.

Instead of buying another bottle of wine, we decided to drink coffee at the White Lunch Cafeteria on Granville Street, a few blocks from the Magic Theater. The White Lunch was near a lot of movie theaters and dumpy hotels, on a block that reminded me of Forty-Second Street in New York.

The lighting in the cafeteria seemed to spotlight every blemish on every scabby face of the patrons. I tried to avoid looking into the mirrors that covered one wall to make the place look bigger. We put two coffees and a milk for John on one tray and then sat in the last booth in the back. I felt more secure with my back to the

74

wall. I folded my hands on the table and placed my chin at a comfortable spot on top of them. We were quiet.

In the booth in front of ours, three guys were laughing. One of them was obviously peaking on LSD. He was coughing and laughing, bleary-eyed, and repeating, "I got off on it." After a few minutes, he turned around to face us and said, "I don't know about you, but I got off on it." His apple cheeks were smeared with dirt. He looked stunned for a moment, with his hand on his oily head. Then he pointed at Matthew.

"The first thing I noticed about you was your tattoo."

He said it as a rhyme. Matthew grinned and left his right arm on top of the backrest so that the freak could hallucinate on his peacock.

The tripping freak was practically hysterical when he pointed at John and said, "And you, too, you are skinny, too." John grinned back.

Then the tripping eyes moved to my face, with my chin still on the back of my hands. "I can't tell you what's wrong with you," he said. "It's bad vibes all around. But it's cool. I got off on it."

That made me feel terrible. Was I giving off bad vibes? I lifted my head off the table and smiled to show him that he had misread my tired face. But he only repeated, "It's cool. I got off on it."

When we stood up to leave, I was annoyed at the freak for bringing me down, but I showed no more bad vibes. On our way out, he grabbed Matthew's arm and said, "You don't have to go yet. Don't you understand? I got off on it! You can too!" .

"Yeah, I can dig it," Matthew said.

John and I slept on the floor at Matthew and Jainie's that night. When we came in, Jainie was reading in bed with her knees up under the covers. "Did you boys have a good time?" she smiled. John just told her that the movie was a gas.

It seemed like time to hit the road again, as it often did after even a good acid trip.

We had to pick a direction. Ellen would welcome another visit

75

from us, it occurred to me, but I had been doing more than enough backtracking. Besides, John had a better idea. He showed me an ad in *Rolling Stone* magazine for a "Strawberry Fields" rock festival in Moncton, New Brunswick. It would mean a marathon hitch. We had only a week to cross the continent in time for the festival.

That was Friday, and we prepared to set out Saturday morning.

We needed cash. John asked Matthew, who had a bank account, to cash the twenty-five-dollar check he'd been saving in his wallet. It was a publisher's check; John had received it for writing an article in the spring. "Ya mean ya really write stuff and get paid for it like this?" Matthew asked. I had already told Matthew, but I guess he hadn't believed me. Matthew was eager to cash the check to freak out the bank teller who was used to Matthew's welfare checks. So John endorsed the check over to Matthew on the back. Matthew took it and inspected it.

"Ya got an inferiority complex," Matthew said. "Yer name here is smaller than them other words."

"Start worrying about it, John," I said. "Matthew here is a noted amateur psychoanalyst."

Matthew's comment was ridiculous. John had as big an ego as any of us. If I were to interpret his small signature, I'd suggest that it indicated the way he held himself back more than the rest of us.

"I can just see Stevie's signature; I bet it's 'bout fifty feet high," Matthew laughed.

Matthew knew I was leaving, but he didn't stop those digs. We left on pretty good terms with him and Jainie, though.

That evening, John and I went to a basement full of discarded clothes on Beatty Street. It was owned by the Catholic Charities. A kid at the hostel had recommended it for picking up free clothes. John found a gray woolen all-weather coat which would be useful in the Canadian Rockies. I discovered an old-fashioned blue dress jacket which fit me perfectly. And to top that off, I found a Stetson hat—a beautiful hat with a secure fit. The clothes added to the feeling of newness that went with the venture we began on Saturday.

The small, gray-haired man who showed us through the piles of discarded clothes asked me curiously, "Where are you young fellows going? All the young fellows seem to be on their way somewhere this summer. Is it some sort of secret meeting?"

I told him something about the festival.

9

We never made it to New Brunswick. We might have, but hitch-hiker competition on the highway across Canada was like that on the California coast. And meeting new people sidetracked us. At one point we talked away three daylight hours, drinking wine, eating cheese and exchanging road stories with a crew of seven freaks from Massachusetts who were picnicking next to their Rambler at the roadside. After that, John and I decided to regain lost time by hopping freights instead of hitching. But then I slammed a car door on my pinkie; and the purple nail looked as though it would fall off, perhaps with my finger as well, if I attempted a leap onto some strange train. The last straw came when, after sleeping our first freezing night near the Rocky Mountains, John phoned New Brunswick Information and found out that the Strawberry Fields Festival in Moncton had been called off. It made sense to turn back.

We amused our competition when, without warning, John and I crossed the narrow highway to point our thumbs in the opposite direction. Now we no longer had competition because everybody else was headed east. The sunlight was fragmented by the tops of the tall trees. Waiting was more relaxed on our private side of the road. We only had a couple of hundred miles to go.

"I'm sure Vancouver has a lot more to offer than just what we got out of it," John said, sitting on his sleeping bag.

"Always the optimist. Yeah, I agree with you, though."

"I'm glad we're going back. I think you were right about what you were saying back in Oregon; we should tune in on one place for a while."

Like John, I was getting enthusiastic about Vancouver, so I applied my most effective hitching techniques, smiling and looking anxious with my arm outstretched. The cars were rounding the bend just slowly enough so that I could look each driver in the eye as though I were making an individual appeal.

"If only a Rolls Royce would pick us up, one with a stereo tape deck and a bathtub and a refrigerator and two pretty chicks," I said. "I need to relax. Why don't you take a turn?"

John hitched with his arm held high. In midafternoon, a blue Econoline van with Florida plates and a canoe on top stopped for us. The side door opened, and a guy and a girl took my gear to toss it into the back. John opened the front door and sat in the seat to the right of the driver. Before I could shut the door behind me, the van was rolling again.

"Where y'all headed?" the guy asked me.

"Vancouver. We just came from there yesterday. We were going to cross Canada, but hitching is a bitch on this road."

"Well, Vancouver is our last stop, so we can take y'all all the way."

"You people drove all the way from Florida?"

"That's right. Gainesville. Where did y'all start out?"

"New York. Hey, I know Gainesville. Matter of fact, John and I were staying in a cabin by a lake in Ocala National Forest, right near Gainesville."

Then I stopped to introduce myself. The guy introduced himself as Lee, and the girl was Joanna. Lee told me the driver was named Frank.

They were traveling in a comfortable van. It was bigger than a Volkswagen bus. The back part, where I sat, was equipped with two beds and storage space underneath. In back of the two front seats, two large speakers pointed at the beds. The tape deck was in front. The walls of the van were decorated with posters and several amateurish cartoons.

Lee and Joanna seemed like easygoing hippies. They had healthy glows. Lee was thin, good-looking, and had shoulder-length brown hair and a mustache. Joanna's hair was of about the same length and color. Her face was round and her eyes looked oriental when she smiled, which was often. She was chunky. They both listened with apparent interest when I told stories.

"Of all the states we've hitched through, Florida was the state that gave us the most hassles," I said.

"Hassles with the cops or with the people?" Lee asked.

"A little of both. For police, the Miami area is the worst. They're out to bust your chops. One time last year, I got busted and thrown in Dade County Jail for four days for jaywalking."

"I know. I'm glad it's not like that around Gainesville," Joanna said. "The only trouble we get is with the narcs."

"I never had hassles in Gainesville itself," I said. "But I nearly got killed when I was staying at that cabin in Ocala Forest. I was living there alone because John had split for New York to take care of some business, and I was enjoying a relaxing vacation until this redneck showed up. This happened one afternoon: I'm walking down to the lake, minding my own business, when I hear this noise coming from the direction of the cabin. I figure it's cool, you know, because the old freak who owns the place has a lot of friends. But I figure I should check it out anyway. In the cabin, I see this straight-looking dude fussing through the shelves, so I start to worry about my dope stash. I ask the guy what he's doing. He was startled by my arrival on the scene, but then suddenly he looks pissed. 'I'm checking something out; I think I have all the information I need,' he tells me. He said it like he had the goods on me boy and now I was in for trouble, but I couldn't figure it out, so I act cool about it. Then the guy splits. But he comes back the same day, and I see him standing over my garbage pit with some woman. She was his wife. So anyway, I ask the guy what he's doing by my garbage pit, and he answers, 'I have all the proof I need. You stole my groceries, you lousy punk!' So I say, 'Hold it, man, what are you talking about? I never saw your groceries.' And he says, 'I have proof. I marked the cans. . . . I should have killed you as soon as I laid eyes on you!' That pissed me off, so I say, 'With *what*!' And suddenly he gets bright red in the face and says, 'With *what*? With *what*? With *this*! With my *toy*!' And he pulls this big pistol out of his pocket and shoves it in my face. Now I've seen these Westerns where the one guy pulls his gun on the other at close range and you wonder why the other guy doesn't just knock it out of his hand as soon as the guy with the gun looks a bit off guard. Well, I don't wonder about that anymore. Man, I was shitting in my pants. So I turn to the guy's wife and start begging her, 'Please ma'am, I didn't steal any groceries. Please tell your husband not to shoot me.' And she just muttered something about how these people get when they play around with that LSD. Her husband never shot me, but he said he'd be back with the cops."

"So what happened? Did he bring the cops?" Joanna asked.

"No. He did come back, though. It was about two hours later; I hear more sounds around the cabin, and I'm feeling a little paranoid because I just finished a joint. Then I hear the guy's voice. 'Steve? Are you in there, Steve?' I gave him my name when he was waving that gun in my face. But anyway, this time I'm not about to give the guy another chance to murder me. I pick up a broom and wait behind the door ready to beat the guy's brains out if I have to. Then I hear him calling my name again, and he sounds friendly for some reason. I can't figure it out, you know, so I say, 'What do you want?' And he steps into the cabin and sees me standing there next to my broom, and he says, 'I thought you could use some smokes since you're way out in these woods without a car.' And the guy

81

tosses a couple packs of Marlboros onto the table. I was still cautious, but soon I realized that the guy had found his groceries or something and that this was his way of apologizing."

Lee and Joanna seemed entertained by my story, so I told more. I was expecting them to respond with stories of their own, but they just listened.

Late afternoon, the van turned off the main highway and stopped. Frank turned around and said, "According to my map here, there ought to be a campsite about a mile down this side road. Should I check it out?" Lee and Joanna said it was a good idea, so we went to seek the site.

The campsite was overstocked with tourists, but it was beautiful. It was on a clear lake which reflected the tall trees and mountains and the blue sky.

We found room for our van and sleeping bags between an elderly couple with a camper and a family with a trailer. Then John and I helped Frank flip the canoe off the roof of the van. After setting it in the water, we paddled smoothly across the lake to the other side where there were no people. Lee, Joanna and I went first, and then Lee went back to pick up Frank and John. We all washed and then we enjoyed a swim for as long as we could tolerate the cold. After that, we dried on a flat rock in the sun. Cool breezes raised goose bumps all over my body. The lake was peaceful except for one buzzing motorboat.

"Do you believe that? Those guys are watching us through binoculars," John said, pointing at the motorboat. We all laughed.

"The poor bastard probably thinks we're all chicks," I said.

After more sunbathing, we put on our clothes and paddled back to the other side. This time, I paddled with Frank. I wanted a chance to talk with him because he looked like he was about thirty and I figured him to be a wise, experienced hippie. He was hairy and built like a bear. His hair was long, but the hairline was receding. And he wore a mustache that continued down his chin and was about three inches long on each side. We reached shore before I could talk with him much.

When we were all back at our campsite, I suggested that we celebrate our getting together with a party. John added that we could buy wine and cheese in the last town we'd passed. So Frank drove and John went with him. After they'd left, Lee mentioned to me that he didn't drink wine much.

The party was rousing. Before dark, we sat at a picnic table, eating and talking. John had picked out Brie, Muenster and caraway cheese. Later, we sat in the back of the van with a gallon of red wine. Lee and Joanna passed up the bottle on its second time around. I urged them to drink with us, but Joanna held her stomach and said, "I'll get sick if I drink too much of that stuff." Then I said, "Oh, you guys are strictly potheads, huh?" Frank was indulging in long drinks.

"Steve, why don't y'all tell Frank some of those adventures y'all were telling us," Lee said.

"Like which story?"

"I don't know. Think of one y'all haven't told."

"Tell them where you picked up those jeans," John said.

"Oh yeah, these jeans came from Carson City Penitentiary," I said. "A four-time convicted murderer gave them to me."

"Are y'all making this up?" Joanna laughed.

"No, this is no shit," I said. I wasn't making it up. "John and I met this guy because he was the deputy sheriff in a small southern Colorado town where we got busted. It started: we're walking through the center of this town, minding our own business, when all of a sudden this cop in a cop car sees us and yells at us to walk on the other side of the road, facing traffic. So we promptly cross the road and continue walking toward the other side of town. But then John says, 'Wait a minute, we weren't even hitchhiking. He can't tell us what side of the street to walk on!' And I agree, so we cross the street again. Then a couple of minutes later, the same cop pulls up behind us and busts us. 'What for?' I ask him, and he tells me, 'For walking on the wrong side of the road.' "

"They had a law against *that*?" Joanna said.

"They did. But even if they didn't, it wouldn't have mattered.

Man, one thing I learned a long time ago is that if a cop wants to bust you, he can do it, no matter how clean you think you are. Anyway, we wound up spending four days in jail waiting for the judge. During that time, they told us we could work or sit in that empty jail cell, so we worked. One day we were shoveling rocks in a graveyard, and another day we mowed the deputy sheriff's lawn. That's how we met the deputy sheriff. Huck Sterling was his name. When he first came to our cell to take us to work, we figured he was the town old-timer who had nothing better to do than take prisoners to mow people's lawns. He had white hair and a red face, and he was quiet until I started talking with him. I asked him how long he'd lived in town, and he said three years. So I asked him where he lived before that, and he said Carson City Penitentiary. Then I asked him what for, and he couldn't suppress a little grin when he said, 'Murder.' "

"Didn't that scare you?" Joanna asked.

"Nah, he was past his murdering days. He just liked to talk about it. And it worked out well for me and John because we spent most of that day listening to his stories and telling some of our own before we had to mow his lawn. Man, this guy really got off on freaking people out with his stories and his reputation. He told us about how half of the town was scared shitless of him. Like one time he was in the local barbershop and the barber nervously asked him, 'Mr. Sterling, sir, just how many men did you kill?' And old Huck just counted for a minute on his fingers and said, 'Not countin' Mexicans and Indians?—Five.' Huck told me and John that he was bullshitting there to freak the guy out, that actually he had only killed four guys, and one of those times was an accident. He said the first time he killed someone was in a card game where he won a taxi from the cab driver he was playing with. The guys he was playing with accused him of cheating so he had to kill them with his service revolver. I think he said that was in the nineteen twenties. Anyway, he went to jail, and he got let out years later. Then he was put back into prison after a bank holdup. He was the shotgun man, and he was playing with a hair-trigger. It went off accidentally and blew the bank teller's head off."

"Oh, Jesus, wait a minute, how do you know this man wasn't bullshitting you?" Joanna asked.

"Well, I'm sure he was exaggerating, but I also know the basic story was true because he had two articles written up on him in a detective magazine and he showed us a bunch of other articles and photographs from when he was in prison. He had spent the second most time in prison of any man alive. He even showed us rough red rings around his ankles that came from wearing leg irons for all those years."

"But wasn't he down on hippies?"

"Yeah, but he liked me and John for a couple of reasons. For one thing, John told him that he was a writer and that he was interested in these stories and that he knew a publisher in New York who would pay a couple of thousand dollars in advance for the rights to Huck's story. Old Huck played it cool, like it didn't really make a difference to him whether or not John wrote up his story. But after John's rap, Huck put in the good word for us at the jail, so they treated us better. And Huck got along with me because I was always trying to match his stories with ones of my own. I told him jail stories that made him feel like there was a kind of bond between us."

"Y'all have stories to compete with this guy Huck's? This I've got to hear," Frank said.

"No, man, nothing big time like his stories. I just talked about a couple of months I spent in a children's jail in New Jersey. Huck was telling us about crazy psychopaths in prisons, so I told him about this little skinny kid we called Asthma when I was staying at the children's shelter."

"What did you call the kid? *Asthma*?" Frank asked.

"Right. He had asthma. He was skinny and weak, but nobody fucked around with him because we all knew he was crazy. He'd been in the shelter for longer than any of us, for shooting at a cop when he was fourteen. Even the guards were careful before they fucked around with Asthma. He was also the wealthiest kid in the

85

shelter. Wealth was measured in matches and he had books of them. While most kids were splitting their matches into cross sections before lighting a butt, Asthma was burning them a book at a time for fun. Anyway, the story I told to Huck Sterling was about a time Asthma kicked ass on one of the guards. Huck loved to hear about the guards getting beat up. I told Huck about the social scene at the shelter. Asthma and I sat at one particular lunch table where the in-crowd, all the oldest kids and the kids who'd been there longest, would sit. This one day, Asthma is making a lot of commotion so a big black guard tells him to sit at another table. Asthma tells him to fuck off, so the guard picks up Asthma's kicking body and sits him at the other table, humiliating him in front of everybody. Asthma knows he can't do anything about it there, so he waits. The next week, everybody has forgotten the incident, and we are playing softball in the yard. Asthma takes his turn at bat. As soon as he puts his hands on that bat, he starts chasing the guard around the yard, swinging like the guard's head is a softball. I saw him hit that guard pretty hard at least once."

"But Huck was there to guard y'all, right? So why did he like hearing about a kid beating a guard?" Frank asked.

"It's not the idea that Asthma was beating a guard," John said. "It was the idea that he was beating up a bully. Huck had a peculiar sense of morality behind all his stories, y'know. He liked us best after Steve talked about beating up a bully at the shelter. I don't think Huck saw much difference between guards and prisoners. They were all people to him, y'know, with bullies on both sides and weaklings on both sides. I think another reason that he liked us in a way was that we didn't complain to him about being busted and having to mow his lawn. He told us that the reason why so many men become fucked up in prison is that they whine so much about all the cards being stacked against them. What old Huck respected was a man who tried to better himself and never complained when the going got rough. You want to know who that old guy's hero was? Huck really admired Elvis Presley—the self-made man who didn't squawk when he got drafted."

Frank was engrossed in the stories. I am rarely one to refuse an audience, so I continued telling them until John, Frank and I were drunk and ready to sleep. I told Frank about the time I got busted with Patrick, about that time they shaved my head. He seemed impressed by the fact that my hair would have been that much longer if they hadn't cut it. Then John told a couple of stories about times we had on the road, mostly about the crazy people we met.

"You want to meet some unusual people," I said to Frank as we were rolling out our sleeping bags, "let me and John introduce you to Matthew and Jainie, this couple we know in Vancouver."

I say pointless things like that when I'm drunk.

10

The next morning, Frank was trying on my hat. He composed a serious expression which broke into a grin in the mirror on the door of the van.

I climbed out of my sleeping bag.

"I really dig this hat," Frank said. "But I think it fits y'all better than me. I'm going to look for a hat that fits me when we get to Vancouver."

"Do that," I said, taking the hat and putting it on my head.

"I guess I have a lot of ego still. I like to see myself in boots and a hat."

"Where are Lee and Joanna?"

"They went up to the outhouses. John's still sleeping."

I went to John's sleeping bag next to the picnic table. Only four fingers and some hair peeked out of the top of the lumpy bag. "Time to hit the road, Jack," I said, kicking the foot of the bag. The lumps rearranged, kicking up dust, and then John stuck his head out.

It was during those last miles to Vancouver that the idea of tripping came up. Lee and Joanna were talking about past trips when it began to sound like a good idea to me. Lee and Joanna, however, were not so sure.

I directed Frank straight to Matthew's place when we reached Vancouver. I went inside alone first, so as not to crowd Matthew and Jainie suddenly with new friends.

Matthew acted happy to see me; he didn't ask what had happened to my New Brunswick plans. I brought him out to the van right away. Wearing a pink tie-dyed tee-shirt, royal blue velvet pants and that enormous belt he showed me when I first showed up at his place, he climbed into the back of the van.

"Do y'all know of anyplace away from the city where we can go to relax tomorrow, because we've been traveling . . ." Joanna began.

"I got just the place," Matthew interrupted. "Wreck Beach—it's private and the cops don't hassle about bathing suits."

"Great! We can stay at Kitslano tonight," I said. "Then can you cop some acid for us before we go there in the morning?"

Naturally Matthew could do it. But Lee and Joanna were still hesitant about committing themselves to a trip. John and Frank were with me on the matter. Finally, we all decided to let the morning's weather decide for us.

Frank, John and I went to sleep shortly after dark by a log on Kitslano Beach. Lee and Joanna slept in the van.

The next morning was brilliantly sunny. I woke up with John sitting on the log next to my head.

"You awake, Steve?" he said.

"Yeah, give me a minute."

"I just want to warn you, there's an uptight scene between Frank and Lee and Joanna by the van."

"What kind of uptight scene?" I asked, sitting up and shaking sand out of my hair.

"They want to sell the van and split up."

"It's that uptight? What is this, they have an argument and right away they want to split up?"

"It's no sudden thing, man," John said. "I've been watching it coming since they picked us up. Haven't you noticed the way Frank practically never talks to them? It's like this: They came up here to find land and start a commune, but they were hating each other's guts after a week on the road."

"How did you find all this stuff out?"

"Talking with Frank. That first day, while we were going to get the wine, Frank was giving me his rap about how communes are where it's at, y'know. So I told him I thought that communes are a good idea if you really know what you are into, but that it's better to keep loose and be on the road when you're not so sure about those things. I didn't think I was being *too* convincing, but it set Frank to thinking."

"Christ, hadn't he thought about those things? He's been through enough already, hasn't he?"

"Steve, Frank only looks old. He's actually the same age as Lee and Joanna—twenty-one. He and Lee are college buddies, and they dropped out of school together."

"Man, I've got to wake up."

Frank had firmly decided to split from Lee and Joanna, so naturally they didn't want to trip together.

"I'm gonna cop on Fourth, at the Last Chance," Matthew told us at his house. "Wanna come with me, Stevie?"

"Is it cool if I go like this?" I asked. I was wearing no shirt or shoes.

"Sure," Matthew said. "They even let hippies in there."

The Last Chance turned out to be a dimly lit hippie hangout. People played chess and acted cool. Matthew found his connection and bought three tablets.

"Aren't you going to trip with us?" I asked on our way back.

"Nah, I'm too neurotic."

Back at Matthew's, Frank, John and I ate the LSD. Then Lee drove all of us to the beach, with Matthew dictating directions. We bought a gallon of Beaujolais on the way. Lee and Joanna left us at the top of a cliff and agreed to pick us up there at eight.

Then we carried wine, a blanket and a bag of Jainie's sandwiches as we followed Matthew down the many uneven wooden steps to the beach.

Getting to the place Matthew was talking about took ten minutes. The steps followed a steep path through woods. The beach wasn't visible until the bottom, and then we marched over rock piles to the section where people swam nude.

We dumped our things behind a log near the edge of the wooded cliff. Then we peeled off our clothes and tiptoed to the water. With my bare feet, getting past the sharp pebbles and shells at the shoreline was harder than adjusting to the cold water. At the edge of the water, I ran until it was deep enough to dive. A splash!— and then it was nothing for an instant but cold numbness. I pushed my head back into the air and shuddered. Matthew and John dove into the water behind me. Jainie was saying, "You fuckin' guys, man," and trying to duck the cold drops that flew as the bodies slapped the water. The last one in the water was Frank. The rest of us swam around, alternating backstrokes and crawls, and coaxing Frank to come in. "Come on, Frank, it's beautiful once you get used to it!" He was standing in water up to his knees, afraid to get his balls wet. It was comical. Our coaxing sounded as though we were encouraging a baby to take its first step. And there was Frank, the hairy bear, splashing his legs and shuddering. He finally walked in.

I was getting off on the acid while standing in the water. At first, I wondered about where I was. This wasn't an ocean because it had no breaking waves. But it seemed immense like an ocean. For an instant, it was imposingly immense, I thought. But that was a ridiculous paranoiac flash. I felt at peace with this water. There were waves but no breakers. The waves were hills of water that passed by me on their way to the edge. Each hill was a pulse. And I could not only see it, I could feel its extra force, like the pulse inside me. When it went by, it left behind a moment of calm, the pause. But the water was never really calm. It shimmered. The sun made it sparkle. It was liquid and shimmering, like the way my inside felt, not at all a bad feeling, more like a funny ticklish good feeling. And when I laughed the liquid feeling flowed out of my mouth, bringing tears and more laughter. The sensation reminded me a bit of the way you feel when you first realize that you are going to vomit. But this feeling was minus the nausea, without that bad part of the feeling. I just knew something was going to come up.

"Steve!" It was John. "Steve! Are you staying here or coming in?"

"What are you doing?"

"I'm going in."

I went with him. I suddenly realized that we were the only ones left in the water. Frank, Matthew and Jainie were walking toward our log. Other people were scattered along the beach, but the water was apparently too cold for them.

I felt refreshed. Matthew was trying to keep sand off the blanket as he spread it out. Frank was sitting on a towel, facing the water with his back to the log.

"Sit down and dry yerself in the sun," Matthew said. "Feels great!"

I did that. Then I asked Frank how he felt, and he grinned and said he felt fine. It looked like a good trip.

"Stevie and John, do either of you want sandwiches?" Jainie asked.

We declined.

Jainie sat on the blanket. Matthew was still tucking corners under the log.

"Oh Matthew, I wish I had a bathing suit. That man over there is staring at me. That's such a drag," Jainie said.

We all looked over. Some old guy with his clothes on was looming over us, about fifty feet away.

"If ya had a bathing suit, then you'd look as dumb as her," Matthew said, indicating a girl wearing a bikini, not far from the old guy.

"He'll leave in a minute," John said.

"We always get hassles with them voyeurs," Matthew said.

"Matthew, are you remembering that time . . ." Jainie began laughing. "Oh Matthew, that's so funny. You tell it."

The rest of us swiveled around on our log for Matthew's story.

"Me and Jainie are living in New York by Avenue B, right? We ain't got a lotta extra money, so we ain't got no curtains. We don't think it's necessary 'cause we live on the fifth floor anyhow. So this afternoon me and Jainie are balling on the bed when all of a sudden I can feel Jainie going stiff as a board, right? I mean she was like the fuckin' park bench. And she starts saying, 'M-M-M-Matthew . . . L-L-L-Look!' So I look over my shoulder and there's this guy standing up against the outside of the window. Ain't got no idea how he got there. It's like he flew. So I jump out of bed and go for this air rifle I got—looks like a shotgun, right? Now I'm standing there with a hard-on and a shotgun. That guy was so fuckin' scared. He took off down those fire escape steps . . ."

We were laughing. Matthew was the center of attention.

"I don't think it was the rifle that scared him, though," he added.

Then Matthew cushioned his head on Jainie's thigh, but he kept his lines coming. Except when we laughed, the rest of us were having a quiet trip.

I lay on a towel with my toes pointing toward the water and my head on our log. The sky was blank blue. Several birds soared across. They left trails like skywriters.

I glanced down at my body without moving my head. My chest was reddish tan with fine blond fleece. My legs were sick white. I stood up, shook sand out of my jeans and put them on. Then I screwed the cap off the wine bottle and took a long hit. I felt okay, but the wine seemed like a good way to cut the edge off of any twinges of paranoia that might arise. I was determined to enjoy this trip the way I used to always enjoy trips. I lit a cigarette.

"I'll be right back. I'm gonna bum a cigarette," Matthew told Jainie.

Frank and I both offered him one of ours.

"Nah, that's all right. Might as well get a free one."

93

When he returned, Matthew knelt next to John, who was sitting on the opposite end of the log from me.

"Check this out, all ya find these days are filter cigarettes," Matthew said, ripping off the filter and dropping it like a turd onto the sand. "Them guys who smoke through filters, they're scared to get at the heart of the cigarette. They ain't got no sense of their manhood."

"You know what I think of you today?" Jainie giggled. "Matthew, today I think you are a character."

Matthew continued as though there had been no interruption. "I used to go to this beach by San Francisco called Gay Beach. They called it that 'cause it was a nude beach and also 'cause a lot of faggots hung out there. I tell ya, ya couldn't bum a nonfilter cigarette there if yer life depended on it."

Things were happening, and I could hear everything Matthew was saying, yet the sun crossed the sky faster than I'd ever seen, like a cat crossing the road. I was drunk and chilly by the time the sun's rays were being broken by leaves.

People were putting layers of clothes back on when Matthew said, "Who wants to go dancing at the Manhattan tonight?"

"I'm up for it," John said enthusiastically, even though he didn't dance. "This cool breeze is making me want to let loose some energy."

"Right. I know what you mean," I said.

Only Frank looked unsettled. After a moment, he said, "Well, actually I'm feeling kind of spaced out. I don't know if I'd like getting in with a crowd of people."

"Don't sweat about that, Frank," Matthew said. "It'll be great. There'll be a lotta cool guys there. And then you'll walk in, all tripping and freaked out, and you'll show 'em where that's at. And then all the cool guys'll go home."

"Yeah, Frank, it'll be great," Jainie said.

Frank was grinning and ready to go. We gathered our things together and strolled down the beach toward the steps at the foot of the cliff. I carried my shirt and hat and jacket while walking between John and Frank. My jaws tensed, and my teeth ground together; a trace of speed must have been in the acid. I wished that the sun were still high because its warmth had been making me feel secure.

Keeping steady was difficult as we crossed the piles of rocks. On the other side, we passed through the bathing suit section.

Near the steps, Jainie's shorts fell into the water. "Shit, Matthew, look!" she said, hugging the blanket so that she wouldn't drop it, too. Matthew tossed the towels he was carrying onto the sand and fished the shorts out of the water. "Damn it, they're going to take so long to dry," Jainie complained. I didn't see why it mattered since Jainie was wearing long pants, but it bothered her. So Matthew, showing off his resourcefulness, gathered two handfuls of sticks and twigs from the woods, and he began to build a small, smoky fire. When a flame appeared, he flapped Jainie's shorts over it.

I dropped my hat and things behind a log, feeling impatient. The beach was becoming deserted. Then I noticed a girl wearing brown slacks and a brown sweater sitting next to her dog, gazing out to sea.

"Give me that wine. I'm going to get that chick," I said.

As I trotted up the beach toward her, I heard Matthew call behind me: "Yer barkin' up the wrong tree!"

I would use the dog to my advantage. I remembered a cold night outside a diner in Washington State when I saw a girl trying to catch her puppy. I caught it for her. And when I brought it back I said, "I sure envy that dog." She asked me why, and so I said, "Well, he's got a beautiful chick for a friend and a warm place to stay, while I'm out here alone in the cold." Ten minutes later, I was on my way home with that girl.

The Wreck Beach girl didn't notice me until I sat next to her and greeted her dog. It was a German shepherd. It growled at me viciously.

"Be careful, will you. My dog isn't feeling well," she said. "And he doesn't like strangers."

"It's okay. He'll be used to me in a second," I said. "Dogs can tell a lot about people, you know."

Then I told the girl about a dog that was given to me in Florida named Owsley that was half wolf and used to travel with me until he grew too big. I went on about how perceptive and smart my dog was. Then I introduced myself. She told me her name, but I can't remember it. She was friendlier after my dog rap. "Care for some wine?" I asked her. She said coldly that she didn't drink. I placed the bottle behind me and prayed it wasn't obvious that I was barely able to focus on her face. I could not interpret her expression, but her eyes were brown and pretty. I think she was wearing lipstick. "That's a nice-looking dog," I said. "How long have you had her?"

"Him," she corrected. Then suddenly the girl snapped at me, "What are these—friends of *yours*?"

Glancing around, I didn't see any of the rest of my crew. But then I looked up the beach in the water and saw Matthew, John, Frank and Jainie—in that order—with their legs wrapped around a log that they'd rolled out to sea. Together, they bobbed like a buoy, and every few seconds one of them fell off. They were laughing and yelling. At my distance, Matthew and John looked like pipe-cleaner figures wrapped around a cork cylinder.

"I never saw those people before in my life," I told the girl.

"Then why are they yelling at us?"

"Ahoy there!" Matthew shouted. "I'm Captain Pissgums and this is my perverted crew!" None of them were wearing clothes, except that Matthew had my hat on his head. It was too big for him.

"Don't pay attention to those maniacs. They're just trying to freeze themselves to death," I said to the girl. "Where do you live, anyway? Do you live near here? We can always split if those people are getting on your nerves."

"Listen, if those are your friends, you'd better tell them to go away because they will upset my dog."

"I told you. I never laid eyes on them before. Let's get out of here if they're bothering you."

Matthew waved a bony tattooed arm in the air. His voice sounded much nearer as he shouted, "Be cheerful my comrades! Don't let yer hearts fail! 'Cause yer bold harpooneer captain is striking the whale!"

The dog was growling.

"It looks like they're coming to bother us." I said. "Let's get out of here and not hassle with those freaks."

"Ahoy there, Stevie!" Matthew called, blowing the whole thing for me. "We've come for our wine!"

The dog barked viciously. The girl restrained it by its leash.

"My dog is very sick! Go away! You're upsetting my dog!"

"We are prepared to do battle for our wine!" John, Jainie and Frank were yelling and laughing.

I pushed the bottoms of my jeans up to my knees and waded into the water with the wine. "Here, take it and beat it!" When I turned around, one leg of my jeans fell into the water, and the girl was standing to leave.

"Where are you going?" I asked.

"Away from here. Your friends have made my dog sick enough."

I turned around again in time to see the crew on the log doing battle with a tiny rowboat. John, Frank and Jainie were walking in water up to their chests, aiming their log at the rowboat. The two guys in the boat were playing along, spinning in circles. Meanwhile, Matthew had gone to shore and was waving the wine bottle over his head and shouting, "So long, suckers!"

The water was black. The last embers of the sun were dying. It wasn't even worth telling the others how they had ruined things for me.

As I passed Matthew on my way to where I had left my jacket, I took my hat from him and put it on my head. I almost told him that I would have killed him if he'd dropped it in the water, but it wasn't worth it. I sat on a log. I was beginning to shiver. Acid paranoia was creeping up on me.

"What happened with the chick?" Frank asked me after drying himself.

"Nothing. She put me down," I said. Then I turned my eyes up

97

to Frank. "But I could have had her, man. I nearly had that chick. By a thin thread, I just about had her, but . . ."

Matthew was somewhere behind me saying, "Ah, he's just pissed off 'cause we blew his chance at that chickie." And Jainie said, "What? That uptight straight bitch he was talking to?"

Then John was with me. His eyes were dark and serious, contrasting with his blond hair. "Steve, you're not uptight because our show made that girl leave, are you?"

"Man, I could have had her. I almost had her . . ." I tried to explain.

"I don't give a shit about that, Steve. All I know is that we were having fun on that log—really having fun—and I don't think you should bring that down because you lost out on an uptight chick with a rabid dog."

John was annoyed. He rarely showed anger. And when he did, except when it was in a serious fight, the show of anger was so short-lived that I usually could not resist provoking it. "John's *pissed* . . . John's *pissed*," I would say over and over. I didn't joke like that this time, however, because I wanted to listen to him talk. "You getting upset about this, Steve, it's just a stoned melodrama," he was saying. Even if he weren't able to see the element of desperation in this situation, even though he was not as tuned in to my thinking and feeling as he usually was, I wanted to hear him talk because I knew that whatever he was saying would be coming from the heart. "You're blowing it up in your head. I can't even understand how you take this seriously." Was he trying to console me in this situation? Or was he actually unaware that something was tearing me apart? "Man, tomorrow you're going to think you were nuts for making such a big deal about this." I watched John's eyes. They must have been blurred. He was definitely stoned. In his daze, he didn't even notice that it was almost dark and that the tide was rising toward us. "All I know is that you should have been on that log with us." But that's the point: I wasn't on the log. I was trying to make that chick, and she put me down. "You're letting the ego trip become too important, that's all.

98

That trip is cool for a while, but when you let a thing like that girl putting you down get to you like this, then things are getting out of hand." The water was dark and sinister.

"Come on, you're shivering," John said. "We'd better get up these cliffs fast. The others are already at the top by now."

The woods were dark. We walked along the path. Then suddenly John shouted, "Let's go!" and we were running like locomotives. I felt powerful. I ran wildly, veering off the path and then finding it again. John was a few steps behind me, as though he were chasing me. I ran until I dropped. My heart was ready to explode my chest. Then I felt John's fists pounding on my back—like the roll of a kettle drum. I was up and running again, up uneven steps until I was certain I could run no farther. Then I felt John's fists again. It was insane, like a game. But I ran again.

I made it to the top.

11

This is ridiculous. I was very stoned and drunk; there's my excuse. But an excuse wouldn't do me any good. I needed a solution. What do you do when you've made an ass out of yourself? I could have let myself go, fallen completely apart so that none of this would mean anything to me. But it was too late for that because I had already climbed the cliff. A more practical solution—I decided to get more smashed, party all night until I dropped, and then I would wake in the morning unable to recall my name, no less my life story.

"Any more wine left in that bottle?" I called out as I approached the van.

"Is Stevie all right?" Jainie asked from inside the van.

" 'Course I'm all right," I said, poking my head in so she could see. "Let's get going if we're going dancing tonight!"

John and I climbed into the van, and Lee drove us to Fourth Avenue near Burrard, a few blocks from the Manhattan, which was on Broadway.

"What are you stopping here for, Lee? Aren't you coming with us?" I asked.

"Not tonight," Lee smiled.

"Stevie, we just decided we're too tired for dancing tonight," Jainie said.

"Come on, what are you, a bunch of party-asses? All right, all right, Frank and John and I will take over for the evening. What do you say, Frank, are you coming?"

"I wouldn't miss it."

"Okay, then let's go. Hey, would it be okay if I took that wine along?"

"We chipped the handle on our way up," Jainie said. "You'll cut yourself."

"Then just give me one more hit here." I took the bottle and chugged until it was empty, and I cut myself in the process. I couldn't feel it, but blood was coating my hands. Some of it might have been wine. Anyway, Joanna bandaged my thumb with gauze from a first aid kit. I told her she was a beautiful nurse. I kissed her a few times as though I were going off to war. Then the van took off and we were on our own.

"Shit, I must have dropped my smokes in the van," I said, feeling the pockets of my jacket. "How much money do we have left, John?"

"Barely enough for the Manhattan, unless you want to try sneaking in."

"Don't worry about that," Frank said. "I'll buy y'all a pack at this gas station."

I assured him that I could bum smokes in the Manhattan, but Frank insisted. He trotted across the street while John and I sat on the curb.

Resting with my ass on a curb and my feet in a gutter feels utterly secure when I'm very drunk. I felt pretty good. I was thinking about what good partners John and I were, about all the times we'd pulled through together.

"Man, you know what?" I said to John. "Together, we're unbeatable. You know that? We should have gotten together when we were thirteen. No, when we were eight!"

"We *were* together when we were eight," John laughed.

101

"No, I mean on the road. I mean doing what we're doing now."

Frank was crossing the street again. For a moment I'd forgotten him. I'd been assuming that we were going to sit on that curb for the rest of the night. I could have easily done it, too.

Frank handed me a fresh box of Players. I put one between my lips, and John told me to turn it around because I was trying to light the filter. "That's good you noticed that, man. Tonight, you and Frank stick by me and make sure I don't get lost." We headed for the Manhattan.

"Listen, we've only got two bucks," John said to Frank. "Did Matthew say anything about whether or not we'll have to pay anything once we're in?"

"Y'all just stop worrying!" Frank insisted. "Don't you understand? I have *money*."

"Sure, but we don't want to start taking your money. . . ."

I put my hand on John's shoulder. "John, it's cool. Frank's got money."

It made no difference. The Manhattan was closed.

"What night is it tonight?" I asked.

"Tuesday, isn't it?" John said. Frank nodded.

"Tuesday night and the fucking place isn't open. Didn't that fucking Matthew tell us it was open?"

"Guess he was wrong."

"Fucking Matthew, man, can't even get a simple thing straight in his head."

"I'll say one thing for that Matthew," Frank commented. "Y'all weren't joking when y'all told me he was unusual. He has got to be the most unusual character . . ."

"Ah, Matthew's just a bum," I said. "That's all he'll ever be. Come on, let's get out of here."

John wanted to go to Beatty Street and sleep, but Frank was still energetic and enthusiastic.

"I want to have *adventures*," Frank announced. The man is *hungry*. "Would y'all believe me if I said I've been all the way from Florida without anything happening to me? Now I'm not putting

Lee and Joanna down or anything, but all I've done with them is drive and talk about plans."

John began to explain to Frank that it doesn't work just to say let's have some adventures.

I was digging what Frank was saying, however, because he meant that John and I were the kind of people to go with if you wanted adventures. I liked that idea. It made me want to show Frank an exciting evening, not to let him down.

"We'll ask the next person who passes for a place to crash and see what happens," I said.

This Broadway was different from Broadway in New York. Most of the buildings were three stories high. And there were few cars and fewer pedestrians.

A couple of girls passed on the other side of the street. "Excuse me, do you know of a place where we could crash tonight?" I called to them. They stopped and said they were sorry but the place they were staying was overloaded. I smiled and tipped my hat. After that, several people passed who suggested the Beatty Street Armory. When I said it was full-up tonight, one of them said, "What about Cool-Aid?" I told him that I wasn't in the mood to be ripped off. Then Frank asked me what Cool-Aid was. I told him it was a degenerate dump where I'd stayed nine months ago. "Only way to keep any of your belongings in there is to sleep on them and pray you don't roll over in your sleep." A few minutes later, a straight businessman passed. He didn't even acknowledge my presence when I asked him if he could spare change or a place to stay.

"These fucking people, man, they won't even spare us a little space on their floor," I said.

"Well, I'm sure we wouldn't give them space on our floor if we were home in New York," John said.

"But that's different. That's New York—Paranoia City. This is Vancouver."

Another straight-ass passed and grunted when I asked him for a place to crash. "Well, fuck you then!" I said. He walked ahead without looking back.

103

"Steve, let's be cool about this and go sleep on the floor at Beatty Street," John said. "It's better than walking around all night."

"We'll just ask a few more people," I said, spotting another prospect.

Frank nodded enthusiastically. He was enjoying himself.

The next prospect was passing at an even clip. He was another of these guys who pretend they have no peripheral vision. And he didn't even bother to slow down when he said no to me. "Fuck you then," I said. "That's right, fuck yourself!" Then Frank's voice sounded defiantly after mine, "He said fuck you, mister. Fuck you!" The guy stopped and turned around to glare at me. "He said fuck you!" Frank shouted again, proclaiming our rebellion against the world. "That's right!" I shouted. "That's right, fuck you!" The guy was still standing there indignantly. He was challenging me.

Whipping my hat off in fury, I ran up to the guy and punched him in the face, with a right and then a left.

He stood there. Then I felt John tugging me back by both arms. He was saying, "I'm really sorry about this. He's drunk. You'll do best just to leave. I'm really sorry . . ." The guy was still standing there, incredulous. Then he took his time to remove a handkerchief from his pocket and dab the cuts on his face.

It was all still in my head, the entire day, gone too fast, all the emotional switches, the geographical switches, the idea switches, all there at the same time as it flashed by, like a mile of film yanked through a projector. . . .

Wait a minute, did I just . . . ?

"Come on, let's get out of here," John said.

"Let me go, John," I said. "I owe this man an apology. . . . I'm sorry about this, really, I'm sorry I hit you. I'm drunk and fucked up, man. I can't explain it. But I want you to know all long-hairs aren't like me. I don't want you to go around with a bad impression of all longhairs just because you had the misfortune to meet one exceptional fuck-up. I'm just drunk . . ." I was genuinely sorry.

104

"I don't think alcohol is your problem," the guy said, still shaken up.

"Well, I apologize, anyway. Do you accept my apology?"

"What is your name?"

For a split second, I felt an impulse to hit the guy again for not accepting my sincere apology.

Then Frank broke in, "Hold on, let me say something here. I want to explain something. I know Steve, here, hit y'all in the face —and he shouldn't have done that—but I think it would be good if y'all tried to understand why he did it. Remember that y'all don't know where he's been, what he's gone through. I see y'all are wearing bell-bottoms. Well, Steve was wearing bell-bottoms years ago when y'all probably made fun when a longhaired freak went by— am I right? People don't like freaks who express themselves by looking different. And Steve has had to fight that longer than most people I've met. And y'all know what else? They put him in jail for looking different. The cops put Steve in jail and shaved his head. . . ."

Now *I* was incredulous. Frank wasn't joking, nor trying to add insult to the injury my victim had suffered; rather, he was sincerely trying to help this guy to understand the hardships of being a hippie. Where do I begin to tell Frank he's wrong? I never wore bell-bottoms.

"Hold it, Frank, just hold it," I said. "I hit that guy because I'm fucked up. People can't go around hitting strangers for no reason and then telling them about the hardships of life. There's only one reason, man. I'm fucked up! I *deserved* to have my head shaved. I pulled a knife on somebody. . . ."

Now Frank withdrew, to think about what I was saying, I suppose. Then I apologized once more, telling my victim that I was the fuck-up, the black sheep, an exception.

"Will you apologize to me when you are sober?" he asked me.

I agreed to do it. He arranged for me to meet him at five P.M. the next day outside where he worked on Broadway. Now Frank was ardently looking forward to the next day when we would settle the mess. We repeated the address my victim had given us over and over so it would be embedded in our memories. Then we went inside the nearest apartment building to sit on the carpeted steps.

"John, were you there? Were you watching? Did I really hit that guy for no reason?"

"That's how it went."

"He didn't even say something to provoke me?"

"Nothing, unless you want to call stopping and looking at you provocation."

"Is that ever fucked," I muttered and rested my chin on my knee. Then another thing occurred to me: "Where's my hat? What did I do with my hat?"

"I'm not sure," Frank said. "Maybe y'all left it in the van?"

"No, I brought it with me. I was wearing it. . . . Maybe I left it where we were sitting on the curb—remember, John?"

"I know what you did with it," John said. "You took it off when you went to hit that guy. It's probably back there."

"Let's go. Oh, man, I can't lose that hat."

We walked up the street to the spot where I'd punched out that guy, and we scoured the area for a half-block radius. We double-checked.

"Forget it, Steve, that hat's gone," John said.

"Wait, let's think," Frank said, even less willing than me to abandon the search. "Where else could you have lost it?"

"Forget it, man. I lost that hat and I deserve it for hitting that guy," I said, exasperated. "Somebody else has it now, unless . . . unless I left it in the van! Are you sure I brought it with me, John?"

"You were wearing it."

The three of us slumped against the wall of the nearest building and slid down to sit on the sidewalk. I was tired. The way everything was happening—it was like road trip, like the way John and I had been traveling, five or six towns in a week when we were in the States. But we had decided to slow down. Slow down. Right, I could organize these things in my head tomorrow. Meanwhile . . .

"Let's go and find a place to crash," I said.

We tried Burrard Street. A girl there suggested Cool-Aid, but Frank explained to her that it was a rip-off scene. I was tempted in a moment of weakness to knock on Matthew's door, but no, I would never live that down. No, we'd find a place; we'd done it before.

Then I spotted a bare-footed freak standing beneath a street lamp. He couldn't have been far from home without shoes, I figured, and he wasn't. When I asked for a place to stay, he told us to follow him.

The way he walked looked funny. He wasn't bending his knees or elbows as he waddled down Fifth Avenue. He was brawny and with a paunch, and he was gripping the cuffs of his sleeves in each hand. I couldn't figure out what his expression was behind his scraggly reddish-blond hair and beard. He looked crazy, in a way. I asked him his name.

"Peter," he said, soft-spoken.

He was bringing us into a small and dark house. Then we had to be quiet as he led us through an obstacle course of sleeping bodies on the livingroom floor.

"Whose place is this? I mean who lives here all the time?" Frank whispered as we climbed the stairs to the attic.

"I don't know," Peter said.

"Well, how did y'all get here?"

"A man invited me."

None of this mattered to me, so I flopped onto the first mattress, which was on the floor next to the stairs. The mattress was lumpy, but I still don't understand why one of those bodies on the livingroom floor hadn't claimed it first. No matter, I shut my eyes.

Naturally, I couldn't sleep. It was either a trace of amphetamine or the LSD itself that was doing it to me; my eyelids weren't even heavy. I lay awake with my eyes open for the next hour or so. I could see nothing but darkness—and things I managed to find in the darkness. I kept uncomfortably conscious of my dilated pupils, wide open like an unhinged door with wind pouring through. Every time I thought of it, I squeezed my eyes shut. But they wouldn't stay shut.

Frank, Peter and John were at the other end of the attic. Frank and Peter were talking, Frank in a whisper, Peter in his normal voice which was softer than Frank's whisper.

"Where are y'all sleeping tonight?" Frank asked.

"I'm not. I'm tripping tonight."

"Far out. Y'all took acid? So did we. We've been tripping all day. I still feel it."

"Want to snort some more now?"

"No, no thanks, I've had enough."

Then there was a sniffing sound.

"What do y'all do?" Frank asked.

"Do?"

"Yeah, how do y'all spend your time, your life?"

"I cruise around."

"That's far out. I just came from Florida—Gainesville, if y'all know where that is. Now I'm digging being on the road." Then after a pause, Frank went on, "What were y'all before, I mean before this?"

"College student."

"So was I. I was a regular straight student before I freaked out and quit. Then I was doing leather work in my leather shop in Gainesville, before I came up here. Where did y'all start out?"

"Massachusetts."

"Did y'all leave there for any reason?"

"It was a small town. . . . I was dealing. . . . They busted my party. . . . They were busting me and my partner 'cause a fifteen-year-old chick was there. . . . I had to leave," Peter said, with long pauses between sentences.

"Wow, that's something. Can y'all go back home now? Or would they put y'all into jail?"

"Guess I can go back. Don't want to, though."

"What are y'all doing there?"

"Digging my fingernails. Look."

108

"That's long. Don't y'all ever cut them?"

"Not too much. They're useful."

"Oh, y'all like to scratch yourself?"

"That . . . and also they're good to snort acid with."

"Yeah, that's fun. We had an incredible trip today. But there was one big bummer. My friend over there, Steve, he lost his hat."

"Hat mean a lot to him?"

"Yeah, it was a beautiful hat."

"Well, what's *he* like? What kind of guy is he?"

Frank paused, thinking, I suppose. Then he said, "He's the kind of guy who wears a hat."

12

"I don't believe Stevie, boy. This boy's on a hair-trigger," Jainie said as Frank was describing the way I punched out that guy on Broadway.

"Steve is going to try and straighten it all out with him later," Frank said. "The man gave us an address where we're meeting him at five o'clock."

"Do you still intend to meet him?" John asked me.

"I don't know," I mumbled. "You think I should?"

"I believe Steve is a man of his word," Frank stated.

Frank's statement trapped me, but I didn't hold it against him because he hadn't meant it in a snotty way. In fact, it was a compliment. He never spoke with irony.

I would have skipped that appointment if Frank hadn't been there. I would have told myself I deserved a vacation from everything having to do with yesterday. John wouldn't have pestered me about it, though he would have kept the appointment were he in my situation. And Matthew, of course, wouldn't even have talked about it. But the appointment meant a lot to Frank. Not just that keeping it was the right thing to do; Frank was thrilled by the opportunity to effect meaningful communication.

So we waited out the afternoon in Matthew's smoky livingroom, smoky because Lee and Joanna had split the cost of a pound of grass with Matthew and they liked to test their merchandise. Lee was rolling joints as thick as cigarettes, two and three at a time. Yet he and Joanna were the only ones smoking, for the most part. Matthew took a few quick tokes to test the quality, but then he was more concerned with dividing his grass into even *lids*, the word in this case being a euphemism for the skimpy ounces Matthew sold on Fourth Avenue.

When we started to leave, at quarter to five, Matthew invited Frank, John and I to go dancing at the Parlour.

"How do I know it'll be open?" I said sarcastically.

"I'm sure 'bout it. This is a better place than the Manhattan. There's gonna be the best Vancouver group playing, the Jackals."

"I don't know, Matthew. I don't know if I'm in the mood really."

"Lots of chickies," Matthew grinned.

"Yeah, all right, maybe."

We left and took the van to Broadway. Then John stayed and listened to music in the van while Frank and I waited on a park bench. Five to five. We were on time. I had no idea of what the guy we were waiting for looked like, but Frank said he would recognize the guy. I hoped he was wrong.

At twenty after five, when John stepped out of the van, I no longer minded waiting because I was confident that the guy wasn't going to show up.

"Hasn't he shown up yet?" John asked.

"No," Frank said.

"Well, he's got a lot of nerve."

We gave it five more minutes and then rushed to the schoolyard to catch the feed-in. John was encouraging me to come to the Parlour and bring my head up that evening.

Matthew was dressed up when we got back to his place. He had on his crushed velvet pants and a matching blue shirt with gold sparkles, and he was tying the laces on his blue shoes.

"Look at this, man," I laughed. "Matthew, the fop!"

"Hey, those are nice pants, boy," Jainie protested. "I went to a lot of trouble to steal Matthew those pants."

Actually, I wasn't offended by Matthew's clothes so much as I was by the fact that they left me looking shabby by comparison, especially since I hadn't taken a shower since before yesterday's trip.

And I got more sweaty later at the Parlour, but not from dancing. To get in without paying the two dollars admission, John, Frank and I made a deal with the road manager of the band that was playing that night; we carried the band equipment upstairs to the dance floor. Those speakers were heavy; nobody was doing us a favor.

I was exhausted. I looked at the small dance floor, surrounded on three sides by long tables with chairs. The fourth side was reserved for the band. I wasn't going to dance with spectators on three sides. I looked over to the small bar. It didn't serve liquor. I was depressed.

So I sat next to a wall at the end of a table. Fortunately, the lights were low. I rested my chin on my hands. Matthew was charming a couple of girls on the other side of the room. John and Frank were buying Cokes. Then I noticed two girls stepping out of the ladies' room on my side of the room.

My chin slipped off the table. One of those girls was standing with one long leg bent forward, in a model's pose, as she lit a cigarette. Her hair was styled in a short shag. She was wearing tight, creased, unfaded denim flare-bottomed pants and a tight charcoal gray sweater over one of the slinkiest bodies I'd ever seen. Her body was slender, but not in a delicate way. The sweater was a pullover with a collar and three buttons that ran down from her neck, all opened. Her neck—I just noticed that—it was the one part that looked delicate, very pretty. Her eyes were big, round and darkened with enough mascara so that a blink of those eyes made me think for a moment she was waving at me. The makeup was

112

tastefully applied, though. She was careful about that, as she was about the way she carried herself. Although the Parlour was still relatively empty, she must have known somebody was observing her. But she hadn't really looked in my direction, I don't think. She paused, holding the cigarette lightly between her teeth. This chick was a fox. She switched her pose once, inhaling her cigarette so as to make you envy the smoke, and then she went with her friend to the other side of the room.

I felt more wasted than ever knowing I was in no shape to talk with this girl. My hair was dirty. The curls were matted. The left knee of my jeans was torn. And I probably had a few pimples; I hadn't checked. Any other night and that chick would be mine, I kept telling myself. And that depressed me more.

"I assume you saw her," John said, arriving on my side of the room with a Coke.

"The chick with the Mick Jagger haircut? I sure did."

My mind hadn't left her, but by the time the band started playing I had retreated to my original position with my chin on the table. It was some mediocre band, not the Jackals. I felt embarrassed for the drummer, with his heavy, thumping solos.

The slinky girl wound up on our side of the room again. She pointed at two empty seats and then sat next to John with her friend on her right. Soon John was talking to her. Then so was Frank. And so was Matthew. Matthew practically had to lean on Frank's lap to talk to her, but he was keeping his cool. It was ridiculous. My chin remained on the table.

Matthew asked the beautiful girl to dance, but wound up dancing with her friend, for one reason or another. I got a kick out of watching him dance, even though he wasn't great. Back at our table, he rolled a few joints and passed them around. I took a few tokes.

Then Frank took a turn dancing with the friend, and that was more embarrassing to me than the drum solo. The girl looked bored, and Frank seemed self-conscious, with his big ass shaking slightly and his hands moving back and forth in front of his belly.

113

He kept smiling, though. And I shouldn't criticize, of course, since I wasn't trying. But I had to look away.

Suddenly, an old bum burst onto the dance floor and gave me a number to watch. In his baggy pants, pulled tight at the top like a potato sack, this old guy was thrashing like an epileptic. The floor began to clear. People stopped dancing to stand and watch. And watch out—the grizzly-bearded hobo wasn't looking out for anybody, until he picked out a girl who was also dancing wildly. At first she tried to outdance him, shaking all over. She was a head taller than him, and her tits were rolling and bouncing like jelly through her translucent blouse. To compete with her, he squatted while he shook and made gestures with both hands that wanted to pull her to him. One minute she seemed to be enjoying herself, and the next she seemed intimidated by the old man's ribald gestures. Practically drooling, he was trying every suggestive move he could think of short of grabbing his balls. When the music finally stopped, the girl looked relieved. She went back to her boyfriend, and the hobo went to the opposite side of the room, where we were sitting.

"Yer doing great," Matthew told him. "Ya ain't quitting now are ya?"

"Oh, boys, she is really sumpin'. Boys, I gotta catch a breather," he said, coughing. He was missing several teeth.

"Well, take a good hit on this," Matthew said, putting a joint in front of the hobo's face.

After trying to catch his breath, the hobo put the joint in his mouth and took a toke with no hands. But as soon as he took the joint out of his mouth, the smoke spewed out.

"Have all yer want," Matthew said. "But ya gotta hold it down longer."

"I know, I know. Don't need to tell old Willy 'bout this," he insisted, inhaling another lungful and then blowing it out as if the idea were to smoke up the room.

When the band started another number, Old Willy started another conniption.

114

It wasn't so exciting the second time around, so I went over to Frank and told him I was going to crash at Beatty Street, that I'd see him later.

"Y'all won't see us again 'til the feed-in tomorrow. Tonight John and I are staying with the girls, here, Miki and Ann," Frank gloated. The girls were sitting next to Frank at this point, but he didn't even bother to introduce me. John was stepping out of the men's room.

I went outside to pick up my knapsack and sleeping bag from Frank's van. I didn't feel like going to Beatty Street, to sleep in that huge armory with those hundreds of kids, half of them not knowing when to shut up. At least the Catholic Charities Hostel had few enough kids so that I could yell at them to shut up. But it was too late for Catholic Charities, so I wandered around Vancouver until three in the morning. Then I went to Beatty Street.

Sure, I was excluded from the fun, but I was too tired at that point to let it bother me.

13

Frank was still gloating on the morning feed-in line.

"Miki and Ann said John and I are welcome to stay with them as long as we want to," he told me, with the air of a kid telling you he's having his birthday party this week and you're not invited.

"Think it would be cool with them if I crashed there, too?"

"I don't know, Steve. They might not like it if we invite other people."

I let the subject drop while I picked up my breakfast. One of the girls who worked at the feed-in smiled as she dumped a ladle of pasty porridge into my cardboard bowl. I felt better this morning, clean after a morning shower. Oatmeal was the part of breakfast I usually skipped, but today I was famished. Moving down the long fold-out table, I took a styrofoam cup of milk and two very hard-boiled eggs like hot stones. Then I sat a spoonful of brown sugar on top of my porridge, and the melting sugar seeped into the steaming cereal like dog shit on a snow pile.

John was sitting on the grass against the fence, already finished his breakfast, and I sat next to him. I asked him if he thought the

116

girls would mind if I stayed at their place.

"Why not? They may dress like jet-setters, but they don't seem to put themselves above running a crash pad."

"Well, Frank said it might put them uptight if any more people move in."

"Forget it, Steve. He just wants to keep you from forgetting that Miki and Ann picked *us* up, not you. He thinks you're hot shit."

It turned out that Frank and John were not fucking these chicks, though Miki and Ann had practically invited them to move in. I couldn't figure it out.

"Either they want yer cocks or they think ya got money," was what Matthew said about it when we visited his house after the feed-in.

Afterward, while Frank was meeting with Lee and Joanna to decide what they were going to do with the van, I spoke with John alone. We were sitting near a volleyball game in the park adjacent to Kitslano Beach.

"The one thing I don't understand, man, is why you guys aren't fucking these chicks," I said.

"Well, Frank isn't exactly passionate over Ann, and let me tell you, Steve, Miki doesn't come across to me as the most together girl."

"What? She has to pass a psychological before you ball her?"

"No, well, actually she put me down. She seems to dig me, but I guess not as much as I thought."

"Then she's a *little cock-tease*," I said, talking to myself more than John. The idea was sparking anger in me before I'd seen her in action. At the same time, I was thinking of myself as a guy who knew how to handle a cock-tease.

I was going to find out about this chick.

John introduced me to her apartment, in the Kitslano area, near the opposite end of the beach from the Burrard Street Bridge. We went in through the back way, by way of a gravel driveway that sliced through the middle of the block. Miki's apartment was on the ground floor. We stepped down into a small, concrete patio that

117

went with the apartment. Then John pulled open the glass sliding door and we were in the livingroom.

The apartment was designed like an elaborate motel room, the kind I expect to be furnished with a sofa with plastic slipcovers and a glass-surfaced coffee table and a portable television on a portable stand. But this place was naked. The walls were a flat white blank. The kitchenette was mostly stainless steel with a formica-topped table against the partition that separated it from the rest of the apartment. In the livingroom, a small television was alone plugged into the wall near the sliding door.

"A third girl lives here, but she's moving out," John said. "She has already taken most of the furniture. She and Miki don't get along."

The third roommate hadn't cleaned out the bedroom yet. There were two beds and a dresser. And the next room, the bathroom, was sparkling with the sterility of Howard Johnson's. Somebody lived here. The open mirror door on the medicine cabinet revealed a disarray of toothpaste, makeup, mascara, Noxema and deodorant.

"Just compare this apartment to ours in New York," John said. "I like ours better."

"So do I, but just think of the different personalities they reflect."

We went back into the livingroom and sat on the floor, with sunlight shining through the glass door. Miki and Ann were due to show up at about five. What would we do then? I talked with John about it. I wanted to take them to a place with an atmosphere more relaxing than this sterile apartment.

Wreck Beach. Of course.

When Miki and Ann showed up, just a few minutes after Frank pulled up with the van, I made it sound as if the Wreck Beach idea had spontaneously popped into my head.

"I've never been there," Miki said. "Is it nice?"

"Oh yeah, it's beautiful," I said.

"Is it like Kitslano?"

"It's much nicer than Kitslano."

"Oh good, because I like Kitslano a lot."

118

So we went straight out to the van. Ann sat in front with Frank while Miki talked in the back with John and me.

She was even sexier in daylight, but Miki also looked younger than she had at the Parlour. She had seemed dark and mysterious at the Parlour, the dim lighting and her makeup making it impossible to see the softness of her face. But now she looked about eighteen. She was smiling and animated, and it was sexy. She talked about Toronto, her hometown, and about her trip west from Toronto in her MG Midget, the car she'd just sold. She liked sports cars. "I phoned my mom in Toronto this afternoon to tell her I sold the Midget and about my new job with the phone company. She was glad I got the job, but she still kept asking me to come home. My mom misses me terribly whenever I don't see her for more than a few days."

"You're a telephone operator?" I asked.

She nodded.

"That's great. You can give me a new credit card number. I've been using the same number for months now."

Miki was speechless, tongue-tied like a kid whose teacher ordered her to hand over the private note she'd been passing to a classmate. She looked younger.

"Don't they give you access to credit card numbers?" I said.

"Sure, but . . ." she began. "I really shouldn't give them out."

"You mean you feel loyalty to the phone company?" I laughed.

"Yeah, kind of . . . as long as I'm working for them."

This made Miki even more intriguing to me. I'd never met a hip telephone operator who on principle refused to give out credit card numbers.

Taking Miki and Ann to Wreck Beach turned out to be a disaster. But how was I to know they wouldn't like a nude beach? They were too uptight to say anything about it. Frank, John and I were pulling off our pants while the girls sat on a blanket. Then Miki said casually, "We don't feel like swimming today." The worst part about it was that they kept looking in other directions while we were standing around them without our clothes.

119

I felt naked and unguarded. Although it had been years since I'd felt embarrassed taking my clothes off in front of other people, I still felt more comfortable when the other people were doing it with me, so that none of us felt at a disadvantage.

As we were leaving Wreck Beach after a quick swim, Miki said she liked Kitslano better.

That night, before we all slept in our clothes on the livingroom floor, we talked. But most of us were not saying much. Frank told a bit about some girlfriend he had when he was eight years old and about the hassles her mother gave him because he was always hugging and kissing with her. John asked Ann when the third roommate came in.

"Sometime later," Ann said, glancing in Miki's direction. Then she went on, "I hope she moves out of here tomorrow. She's such a bitch."

Ann had a droning voice which made her seem bored. Her looks fit her voice. Her eyes were a dull gray, and she had several beauty marks—moles—on her face. Her hair looked like ironed straw. Split ends stuck out all over her head, but the hair was evenly chopped off near the middle of her back. I doubt I would have noticed the split ends so much if it wasn't so obvious that Ann fought to keep her hair like silk. She should have let herself go. Actually, she wasn't ugly, just plain. But she was struggling to be television-actress beautiful. "I must get to sleep early tonight. If I don't have enough sleep, I get those unsightly gray circles under my eyes," she said. She already had them.

Miki, meanwhile, was wriggling on the floor near John. He should have pounced on her. I wanted to. Then she stood up to get a glass of water from the kitchen. On her way, she did some playful lion cub wrestling with Frank, and made cute remarks like, "So, I see you can lift all a hundred and fifteen pounds of me." Frank was a horny bear.

"Miki," I said. "You are a femme fatale."

Ah, but she was beautiful.

14

"Look at these stinkin' pigs on the floor here," the boyfriend said. He was standing arrogantly with his hands on his hips. He'd been drinking.

"Hey, buddy, find out who y'all are talking to before y'all go around calling people pigs," Frank retorted.

"I already found out. I can *smell* pigs."

The barrel-chested boyfriend was playing the junior high school game, with Miki and Ann's hefty third roommate next to him. She was the one who really wanted to antagonize us out of her apartment; but she wasn't going to succeed, not even with the help of her boyfriend, because we had the right to be there. Miki and Ann had invited us. And they would have been there in the livingroom drinking wine with us, except that they were out on their Friday night. . . . Where the hell were those chicks, anyway?

"Look fuck-off," Frank shouted. "Why don't y'all just leave if y'all are looking to start something."

"Hey *pig,* this is *her* place, not yours."

"That may be right, but the other girls who live here told us we are welcome to stay."

121

"Yeah, *dink*?"

"Dink! Oh, that's a good one. Steve, have y'all heard that one?"

"Hey, *fudd*!"

The roommate's boyfriend could have written a glossary, but I was determined not to involve myself. I was clutching the neck of my wine bottle, ready to bash the guy over the head if he tried something. But until he did, I was going to keep my mouth shut.

A few epithets later, the boyfriend followed his girl into the bedroom.

"That burns me, the way he walks in here and calls us pigs for no reason like that," Frank said. He was worked up. "It's a dumb thing to fight about, but I get so angry . . ."

Frank was not sure whether or not he had acted properly, so I said, "It's cool, Frank. We avoided that fight, so it's cool."

"I just don't know how I should handle myself when I get that angry. Some people in Gainesville used to put me down for it, because I get so pissed off sometimes the only thing I know to do is crush the thing that's pissing me off."

"It's cool, Frank. It's cool."

"But what do y'all do when a guy comes on like that, when he won't be reasonable?"

"I don't know," John said. "But I would hate to see what would have happened if that had come to a fight. That guy was built like an ox."

"Ah, y'all don't need to worry about that. I'm big, and Steve here's fast as shit," Frank said, exposing his pride.

"Well, it would have messed up the apartment, anyway," John said. "That girl must be more than just a little pissed off at Miki to put her boyfriend up to that nonsense."

Frank thought about it, and then he told us he was going to try to straighten out the situation for all concerned.

After a while, the boyfriend came out of the bedroom and crossed through the livingroom to leave through the sliding door.

"Hey, I apologize for sounding off at y'all before."

"Sure, forget about it," the boyfriend said in a low tone.

122

"If y'all want, maybe we could talk about it," Frank offered.

"Yeah, sure, some other time," he said. He'd just finished balling, so the argument no longer mattered.

But Frank didn't give up. He went into the bedroom to lend an understanding ear to Miki and Ann's roommate. He was in there for about fifteen minutes.

He said she seemed reasonable when he came back into the livingroom, though he still didn't completely understand her dispute with Miki.

"Her name is Bernadette. She says she doesn't have anything against us but she hates Miki. She says Miki's forcing her to move out of her own apartment. And she says she used to be good friends with Ann, but Miki turned Ann against her."

"She sounds like a real paranoid," I said.

"Well, she's really down on Miki. She even accuses her of stealing some of her jewelry."

"She's probably uptight because she's straight and Miki brings hippies in here," I said.

123

15

Miki and Ann were out until after I fell asleep Friday night, and then they slept late in the bedroom Saturday morning.

They were awake when Frank, John and I came back from the feed-in, and Ann met us in the driveway. She was hopped up about something.

"Come inside. Miki has something she's got to show you."

"What is it?" I asked, never a fan of guessing games.

"I'm not sure. Pills. You have to come and see."

We followed Ann, who seemed out of breath, through the living-room and into the bedroom where Miki was standing with a Baggie that contained tiny tablets.

"Where'd you get this?" I asked, taking the plastic bag to examine it.

"We found it under a bush, in a brown paper bag. What do you think it is? Do you think it's acid?"

I was estimating to myself the number of tablets in the Baggie. It looked like about a hundred.

"Is this all you found?" I asked Miki.

"We found seven of them all together," she said, opening the top drawer of her dresser to show us six more Baggies, all identical, each with a red stripe seal on top. "Ann and I were walking along the sidewalk when we noticed a bag under a bush . . ."

I poured the tabs onto the top of the dresser and began counting in groups of ten. There were exactly one hundred. Obviously, it was a dealer's stash.

"I'm just scared we'll get arrested if it is acid," Miki said. "What should we do with it?"

"John, why don't you take out one of those Baggies and see how many you count," I said. Then turning to Miki: "I guess you should find out what it is."

"But they might arrest us if we do that."

"Not necessarily. There's a freak bus that hangs around the feed-in as a general information center. They'll analyze your dope for you if you give them a sample. Another way you can do it is to check the chart they have posted in the Beatty Street Armory. It lists all the types of acid in town and tells you what kind of trip you're headed for."

"Exactly a hundred," John said.

"I can do it for you if you don't want to hassle with it," I offered.

"You'd do that for us?" Miki said.

"Sure, if you like."

"Oh, thanks a lot, Steve. . . . But what do we do if it *is* acid?"

"Well, that's up to you. It's risky, of course. And the guy who lost it will be looking for it, so you'll have to be discreet. You'd probably be best off fronting the pills to somebody to sell them for you."

"But we don't know anyone. . . . Do you think you guys would want to do it?"

"If you like. Look, why don't you give me this Baggie for now, and I'll check it out for you."

"Thanks, Steve," Miki said gratefully.

Then John, Frank and I left through the sliding door. I stuffed the Baggie into the pocket of my jeans. It was another sunny day.

125

In the driveway, I could no longer control my excitement. I was saying to John, "Do you believe this, man? Do you *realize* what we just struck? John, acid prices are *down* now, so that means we've only got about five hundred bucks worth of dope in that apartment. And that's if we deal it all in one shot! Shit, if we can ship it to New York, imagine what it'll be worth then!"

"Except who do you know in New York who trips?" John said.

"Good point. But still, it's worth plenty right here! And if we're worried about hassles from whoever lost it, we can always bring it to Calgary . . ."

Just then, a car grinding up the gravel right behind us startled me. The LSD in my pocket had me jittery. I jumped out of the way, ready to curse the car for not slowing down.

But then the car not only slowed down, it stopped. Two middle-aged men in plaid sports shirts leaped out of their respective sides of the car. What do these guys want? A hassle or something? A fight? They're crazy; there are three of us. . . . Then they flashed police identification, with a quick flap of the wallet.

"You! Empty your pockets on the hood of the car!" the smaller, flat-faced cop began with Frank.

Frank placed his wallet and roach clip on the front of the car. "What's this?" the cop asked, picking up the roach clip. Frank explained to him that it was an item he sold in his leather shop, which he ran in Florida. Quick thinking, Frank. Then the cop checked his wallet and rattled through the standard rigmarole questions about how long he'd been in Canada and what he was doing during his visit.

John's turn was next. From his pockets came some change, his wallet and the same roach clip. "What's this?" the cop said, repeating his question about the roach clip, to see if the stories checked, I suppose. "Those are tweezers," John said. "Tweezers?" the cop said. He was playing; he knew they weren't tweezers. But he didn't hassle John about it because he was anxious to get to me.

I dug my hands into my pockets and then put a jackknife and my roach clip on the car. Now there were triplet roach clips.

126

"What's this?" the cop sneered. "Those are tweezers," I said. The cop put a big, toothy grin on his wide, pushed-in face. "Well now, you boys seem to have a problem!" Then he turned to me and said, "Now are you *sure* that's everything you got in your pocket?" I paused. "Sure, I'm sure." And then, smiling, I pulled my pockets inside out. Empty. The cop hadn't expected that. His expression changed to a frown and he started scanning the ground around us. His partner went to the bushes that outlined the driveway and looked through them as though he'd lost his best golf ball.

Frank was whispering to John, "What did he do with it?" Incredible. Fortunately, John shushed him with a glare before either of the cops noticed that we had something to say to one another.

The tall partner returned from the bushes, frustrated, and said to John, "Do you use drugs?" These cops must have been partners for a long time because they talked with exactly the same bark. John replied that he rarely used drugs except for an occasional aspirin. Then the cop fired the same question at me: "What about you? Do you use drugs?" He was using the questions to stall.

"I use aspirin," I answered.

"That's all?"

"Well, if I get an unusually severe headache, I try Anacin." I was letting the cop know I was innocent enough to afford wisecracks.

"I believe you boys know what we're looking for."

"How could we know? You haven't told us yet."

"You're gonna stand there and tell me you haven't seen a plastic bag with white pills in it?" He was staring me in the eye at close range.

"Where was I supposed to have seen it?"

"A plastic bag with a red seal along the top?"

"Look, this is getting absurd. I don't know what you're talking about."

He kept staring me in the eye, waiting for me to crack. His smaller partner sat in the car, lighting a cigarette and jotting something down on a piece of paper.

127

"Excuse me, officer, but could you spare a smoke?" I asked from where I was standing, to break the tension.

"Consider yourself lucky I don't bust you for that," the cop muttered without looking up.

"For *what*?"

He looked up and glared at me. "You really want to get busted, don't you! There's a public ordinance against begging on the street."

"That's absurd! I was just trying to be friendly, making conversation so long as you officers are wasting your time and ours detaining us for no reason."

They made us stand there for a while after the last thing I said. They wanted at least to feel they'd had the last laugh, even though they didn't get the treat of busting us. Finally, they let us go. We walked casually in the direction of Matthew and Jainie's. I could hear the cop car backing up, but we did not look back.

"Steve, I don't know how, when or where, but I am impressed," John said, keeping his eyes fixed straight ahead. "When that cop told you to empty your pockets, I went beyond nervousness. I was just counting the years in prison."

I grinned nervously. I was still on edge, and I'm sure John was exaggerating when he said that he had passed that point. I felt the way I had after the first time the cops in New York State tried to shave my head, almost a year before this.

"Come on, open up, Steve," Frank said impatiently. "Will you tell us what y'all did?"

I reached into my pants and pulled out the Baggie for a second, long enough for them to see it, and then I slipped it into my pocket.

"I don't believe it! I thought you'd somehow miraculously tossed the acid over the bushes," John said. "Thank God they hassled me and Frank before you."

"I know," I said. "Just imagine how I felt after that, bullshitting that cop with a hundred tabs of acid under my balls. It's enough to make me want to start wearing underwear."

For the next block, I walked without talking, trying to shake the shakes. But though my nerves were frazzled, I felt proud for having saved the day.

Before going into Matthew's house, we reviewed the sequence of events and came to all the scary, obvious, yet seemingly far-fetched conclusions. How did those cops know exactly what they were looking for? Was the fact that they pounced on us right after we left Miki's apartment merely a coincidence? I figured that, if this acid was very hot, Matthew would have a connection through which I could unload the seven hundred tabs in one shot. I would wait for the right time to ask him about it. Meanwhile, we had to keep cool, play this thing right. . . .

Matthew was pacing around his livingroom, saying things to Jainie when we walked in. As soon as he saw me, he waved me into the room.

"I wantcha to test something out," he said, squatting next to a pound brick of grass in the middle of the floor. He rolled a quick joint. Then he passed it to John, saying, "Take a hit on that and tell me how ya like it."

John lit the joint with a match that I gave him, and he took a toke. He held it in. When he let it out, it was with a burst of laughter, with smoke exploding out his nose and mouth. "You guys are hovering around me like I'm a judge in your contest."

"Well, how is it?" Matthew said seriously. "Didja get stoned?"

"It's the kind of buzz you get from sniffing a campfire, not a grass high."

"I oughta kill them motherfuckers. What's it taste like? Alfalfa, right?"

John shrugged and passed the joint to me. It was not grass. I confirmed John's opinion.

"I got it figured out what they did," Matthew said. "They took a buncha alfalfa and wrapped it with a layer of grass to trick me into buying it. Selling me a brick of pet food, I oughta kill them . . ."

"Just bring it back and demand your money back," Jainie said.

"That's what I'm gonna do," Matthew said, zipping up his

129

boots. "You guys coming with me?"

John and I went with him, while Frank went to meet Joanna and Lee. We walked briskly down the street, with Matthew still cursing the dealers who'd burned him.

Matthew led us to the back door of a candy store, and he banged on the door. A short hippie answered it, recognized Matthew, and then we followed him down to the basement. It was cool and dark. The hippie turned around in the middle of the room, waiting for Matthew to state his business.

"Gimme my money back or get me a pound of real dope."

"What's the trouble?" the hippie said indifferently.

"I coulda bought this much fuckin' alfalfa fer less than a buck at the pet store," Matthew said, slamming the brick of grass and alfalfa mixture, or whatever, against the hippie's chest.

Matthew was a man in control. He was doing it and in just the correct way. The hippie felt the weight of the brick against his chest, but not so much that he could claim Matthew had done any more than return a bad brick. I wondered if my presence was having an effect on Matthew's performance.

The hippie knew his act as well. Without flinching, he handed the paper bag back to Matthew. Then he said, "Follow me," and went outside without talk of refunds. The stairs were narrow so that we had to march single file with the hippie taking the lead, taking his time, squeezing creaking sounds out of the stairs with his boots. He was taking us to discuss the matter with his partner, who lived in a large house on the same block. None of us attempted to start conversation along the way. No hellos, no names, no introductions; even when the acne-faced partner answered his front door, it was impersonal business. We passed through his livingroom, which was arranged like a garage sale, with dusty lamps and chairs and things. Behind that mess, the kitchen was less cluttered. A bare table stood in the center of the kitchen. Over that table, Matthew dropped his brick—to show its worth—as if it were a stack of yesterday's papers. Our attention focused on it, plopped on the table, the brick in question, like a defective Silvertone television, with Matthew saying to the Sears salesman: Brother, I don't even give a shit if RCA did make the parts; that TV don't turn on!

Still, the dealers never spoke of refunds. That's not the question, Brother. I mean, it makes no sense to talk money-back-guarantees when you have a solid brick of fine dope in front of you. I mean, nobody ever told anybody it was Michoácan.

The acne-faced partner skipped upstairs for a moment to return with another brick which was wrapped in green plastic. Bracing it on the table next to Matthew's brick, he stabbed through the plastic with a kitchen knife and then ripped open the package.

"Look at it. Healthy green leaves. Check those stalks. Both of these bricks came from the same lot. Identical. Perfectly good dope."

Matthew studied twigs from both bricks. So did John and I, but we did not comment. They did resemble thin marijuana sticks. Then Matthew threw down the twigs, saying, "I don't give a fuck fer yer brick. All I know is, my brick is a lotta pet food with maybe a few good twigs mixed in."

"What's the matter with you? Just look! This is all good dope, man," the small hippie said, grabbing fistfuls of grass from both bricks.

The idea was to convince Matthew that he and his friends were such stoned freaks that they only *thought* they weren't getting off on this grass. Quite often, it is not the fault of the drug but of the user's state of mind that he does not get high. These dealers were telling us, in so many words, that we were too spaced out and crazy to dig the *subtlety* of this fine dope.

Being that I am no great connoisseur of marijuana, this ploy was beginning to work on me. Of course, I would never let them know that.

"Check this leaf," Matthew said, sticking to his guns. "That's an alfalfa plant. I checked it out in the pet store this morning. Same stuff they keep in the hamster cage."

There was an uncomfortably long pause. All of us stood staring at the piles of shredded plants, victims of our battle. Then the

131

acne-faced partner said to Matthew, "Okay, we'll take you to our man and you can talk it over with him." Matthew collected his greens and stuffed them into his crumpled brown bag. We began filing out of the house.

But then the short hippie said to me and John, "Not you two." Apparently their man didn't like crowds. I looked to Matthew. He nodded that it was cool for John and me to leave, that he could handle this himself. Was he trying to prove something to me? At first, I was going to insist that we keep the sides even, but then I figured Matthew knew what he was doing. So we walked quietly out the front door. When the five of us reached the first corner, John and I turned to go to Miki's.

Miki's apartment looked more vacant than ever. Miki and Ann were out, working for the phone company. And the third room-mate, Bernadette, had moved her bed out as her final insult, leaving a solitary twin-sized bed in the bedroom.

I checked the top drawer of Miki's dresser. The acid was missing. Immediately, I began pulling out drawers and slamming them shut. I finally found the six Baggies under Miki's rainbow of underpants in the bottom drawer.

"That's odd that she went to the trouble of hiding the acid and then only moved it to the bottom drawer," John said.

"That might indicate that she's not a crafty narc, but just a police informer."

John laughed. "I was sure she was a narc. I had it all figured out. At first I even figured that the reason this place isn't furnished is because they are using it temporarily to set up a few quick busts. But just think how paranoid we sound, Steve."

"True, but you should never rule something out as a possibility just because somebody might accuse you of being a paranoid for thinking it," I said. "But I've figured it out, man. Miki is innocent. I must have been being careless about the dope because we're in Vancouver. I keep forgetting that cops are cops, in the United States and outside of it. I probably put that Baggie into my pocket after we stepped outside, and the cops must have seen it before it was in my pocket."

132

"Ah, this is insane," John laughed. "I think I'm going to spend the rest of this afternoon in the library."

So John went to the library while I went back to Matthew's to see what kind of acid deal I could arrange with him. John said he'd see me at the five-thirty feed-in.

Before going into Matthew's house, I stashed the seven Baggies in a hole under a rock under a bush in the driveway behind Matthew's house. Nobody knew where it was but me.

16

"Ain't no such thing as somebody who don't look like a narc," Matthew said. "That's how they getcha. They get a chick to getcha 'cause nobody thinks a chick's gonna turn out to be a narc."

He was amusing himself, trying to start me wondering about Miki again; I'd told him about our close call with the cops near Miki's apartment.

Meanwhile, I was trying to get Matthew serious to find out if he could unload the seven hundred tabs of acid for me. He finally said he'd do it, but I would have felt more secure had he sounded more serious and definite when he said it.

Ordinarily, Matthew wouldn't joke about dealing, but this afternoon he was still edgy from his confrontation with the dealers who'd sold him that brick of bad dope—alfalfa, he claimed. He'd gotten his money back, though.

"Hey, ya know what I heard one of them guys, one of them dealers, say after I stepped outside? I was just splitting and I could hear one of 'em say to the other: 'Shit, the fifth brick we got back.' "

134

Though nervous, Matthew was as proud for having asserted himself to those dealers as I was after asserting myself to those cops earlier that day.

"I tell ya, I knew that stuff was alfalfa," Matthew chuckled. "Them guys knew it, too."

Soon we heard Frank coming through the kitchen doorway. Frank seemed big and noisy when he walked in on a group, but he livened things up in his own way sometimes with his big grin and his ideas.

"I have some presents for y'all, Matthew," he called out.

Matthew went into the kitchen, and then Jainie and I followed. Frank was dumping an armload of tools onto the kitchen table.

"I don't guess I'll be starting myself another leather shop, so y'all can have my tools."

Matthew thanked Frank and began checking out the tools. He played with a leather punch, a gadget that resembled a paper punch, except that the leather punch was bigger and had a wheel of different-sized studs for selecting hole sizes.

Frank swelled, enjoying his Santa Claus role. He pulled at the left end of his mustache, the longest hairs of which actually grew out of his chin, and it stretched down his neck.

"Well, I phoned Florida for the rest of my savings so I can buy the van from Lee and Joanna. My folks are wiring the money today."

"What are Lee and Joanna going to do?" I asked.

"They found a place in Stanley Park to sleep, for now. Then they're hitching back east."

I liked the idea of having the van around.

Suddenly, three furious guys burst into the kitchen. They lined up, three abreast. Everything stopped.

"McLeod! You rip-off! Who the hell do you think you are, ripping *us* off!"

The guy in the middle was doing the barking. He was flanked by two other longhaired guys who, by their arrogance, looked as if they ought to be cradling submachine guns.

135

Matthew began blurting out words. But it was coming out in stutters. His face was turning red. Then he steadied himself enough to yell at them.

"Nobody comes in my house like that! Nobody!"

His face was burning brighter. I didn't understand: I'd never seen him like this. Then he scooped up a leather tool from the table. A small, hook-shaped knife. He waved it in threat.

"Get outa here motherfuckers! I'll kill ya! I'll cut yer fuckin' eyes out! I'll rip yer fuckin' nuts out!"

His arm was trembling. He was practically bawling.

"Get the fuck out! I'll tear yer balls out!"

"Be cool, Matthew," Jainie said firmly. "If you can't keep cool I want you out of here right now."

"Nobody comes in my house . . ."

These guys didn't scare me. I hadn't even realized who they were right away. But I was both startled and scared by Matthew's reaction to them.

I collected myself. Then I stepped in front of Matthew, whose knife was now lowered.

"Hold it, you guys have some cooling to do, too," I said. "You come busting in here without explaining what you're after; that's not going to get any of us anywhere. Now why don't you explain your problem so we can discuss it like reasonable people?"

If there weren't three of them, I would have stood uncomfortably close as I addressed the main guy so as to intimidate him. Circumstances as they were, however, I tried to appeal to him as a reasonable gentleman.

"McLeod copped a pound from us," he said, lowering his voice. "Then he brought it back saying it was bad dope. We gave him his money back and then he had the balls to give us back our brick a quarter pound short."

"Well, we have to figure out what the mistake is," I said, "because I was with Matthew the whole time when he unsealed that brick and when he tested it out and when he returned it and during all the time in between, and I only saw him take three joints out of

136

that brick the whole time."

"Listen, we weighed that brick this afternoon and it was a quarter pound under. Are you saying our scale is bad, too?"

"Look, man, we're not getting anyplace standing here arguing. Why don't you show us the pound? We'll weigh it together and then talk about it."

I was being reasonable and they knew it. So Frank, Matthew and I went out with these dealers. Actually, the move was no boon for us, and there were disadvantages to moving onto their turf. But at least it gave us time to think.

They took us to a dimly lit one-room warehouse that must have been even older than Matthew's house. It was empty except for packages and junk stacked against the wall. And a long wooden table and some chairs stood in the center of the room. It was set up like an oversized kids' clubhouse.

It was three of us and three of them and a scale. I felt at ease with those odds. After all, Frank was big enough to take on two of these guys.

Then another guy walked in. He had a big beard and a big belly, but he didn't look like much. I figured I could take him. I began thinking it would be better if John were with us. Not that John was a fighter, but it's better to keep numbers even.

Then another guy walked in. And he had a friend. It began to look like a convention.

Well, boys, looks like we'll have to talk our way out of this one. . . .

They set up the scale on the table and brought out the brick. As the main man delicately pushed the sliding weight toward the one-pound mark, there was the kind of hush that precedes the opening of an envelope that contains the name of the prizewinner.

And the winner is . . . It was two ounces underweight.

Matthew most likely got the brick two ounces underweight, but to say that would be to ask for a fight. So I continued being reasonable.

"Look, you guys don't even seem to have your story straight. I thought you said the brick was a quarter pound under."

The main man was ready to concede me that much. "I guess we made a mistake about that. But two ounces is still a rip-off."

"I got no reason to rip you guys off 'cause that ain't even grass," Matthew broke in. "I told ya before, I wouldn't take it fer free. I ain't got no hamster, and all ya got there is alfalfa, the same stuff I seen in the pet store this morning."

There was a long pause. I wasn't sure what was coming next, but I was glad Matthew had made a comeback.

The main guy finally said, "Listen, you three go wait outside while we talk this over."

We went outside to wait. Frank was the only one of us who talked. He asked questions that demanded a fortune-teller. What do we think they're going to decide to do? He wasn't scared, though. This was pure adventure for him. Matthew, however, was still visibly nervous. I told myself that the reason was that Matthew was the only one of us who knew these people and what they might do to him.

Before long, a guy opened the door and motioned for us to come in. The main dealer was standing at the table. "Okay, it's cool," he told us. But then he told Matthew to buy some alfalfa at the pet store and bring it to him the next day. To make the comparison, he said. Matthew agreed to do it, and then we left.

Walking back toward Matthew's house, Matthew asked me a few questions about alfalfa. He was not even sure if they sold it in pet stores.

I did chores in a hurry before meeting John at the feed-in. First, I arranged to meet Matthew later so we could transact the big acid deal. Matthew knew somebody who might buy all the acid that evening. Then I went to my secret hole under the bushes and found all seven Baggies intact.

At the feed-in, I told John what had happened.

"Man, I never felt so sorry for Matthew," I said. "I know he'll

138

have completely forgotten about it by tomorrow, but I feel horrible thinking about how he broke down like that. And then the way I had to step in for him. You know the way he and I always have this competition thing going between us. Man, I wish we could just drop that whole competition game. If it weren't for that, I wouldn't have felt so bad that he freaked out like that."

"Those guys sound like a bunch of longhaired gangsters," John said.

"That's exactly what they are, man."

It was almost our turn to have slabs of ham forked onto our plates. The feed-in lines grew longer every day. I was bored with having to wait on lines for meals. Of course, I would not have to wait much longer. Money for seven hundred tabs of acid would be in my pocket within days, hopefully hours. Maybe we would be taking Miki out that night, drinking and partying straight through to Sunday. I only ate half of my meal and then hurried John as if we had a train to catch.

Jainie was the only one home when we got there.

"Where's Matthew?" I asked.

"He went to meet his connection. He said to tell you guys to give me the acid so I can bring it to him. Okay?" Jainie was standing and ready to go.

Naturally, parting with the acid left an unsettled feeling in my stomach, like letting somebody try out your brand new motorcycle. But I gave Jainie the seven Baggies without hesitation.

"Okay, you guys wait here and I'll be back."

John and I sat on the livingroom couch. I thumbed through a few moronic confession magazines that Matthew's mother had generously dropped off for Jainie to read, not that Jainie had any use for them. Then I picked at several loose threads on the armrest.

"What kind of deal are we going to give Miki?" John asked.

I let go of the threads.

"I don't know. You really think she expects anything out of this? I mean, she seemed overjoyed when we took the dope off her hands."

139

I was not saying anything definite because I had not yet resolved the obvious conflict. I had suppressed my thoughts about it, hoping to make the deal smoothly and then maybe share the rewards with Miki by way of taking her out and buying her dinners and drinks. Now I was stalling to see if John had strong feelings on the subject.

I assumed he would say Miki deserved a cut. He might be right. And then, he might not. In any event, his idea would probably be more definite than mine. My principles were solid with regard to the way I let people treat me—nobody fucks over Steve Gibbons— but when it came to the way I treated other people, my principles were fuzzy. From lack of exercise, I admit. Often I simply acted toward people in the way they expected me to act. I cared about people, but I've met a lot of people who expected me to take advantage of them.

John had principles on which he was fuzzy, too. They were particularly the ones on which I was strongest. John was inclined to let people take advantage of him; I told him that a lot. He was in the habit of lending out his money, for example, even to people who were likely never going to pay him back. I would laugh at it. "What? What?" I would laugh. "You mean you gave Joe Blow another five when you know you're not going to get back that ten you lent him last month? You're nuts, man, you're really nuts!"

John wasn't jumping at the chance to donate our money to Miki, however, despite my assumption. He was unsure, saying, "I'm still not satisfied with your explanation of why those cops jumped up behind us this morning. There's something about that and something about Miki . . ."

"She's a foxy chick, that's all." I was reminding myself of that, too, because I wanted to remember not to start tossing my money in the air like confetti the next time she flashed me a cute smile.

In the middle of our conversation, Jainie rushed into the room and plopped into a chair opposite us.

"What's happening?" I asked her.

"I just couldn't go through with this whole trip without letting

140

you guys know what's happening," she said, out of breath. "I had to come back to let you know so you won't keep your hopes up there."

"What trip? What's happening? Can't Matthew pull off the deal?"

"I have to tell you, Stevie, that acid is very hot. Matthew found it out about an hour ago from Murphy, his connection. That acid was ripped off."

"So what's your point? We have to bring it someplace else to unload?"

"No, no, that acid was ripped off from Murphy's partner, Brian. There was only one way we could do it: we had to give it back."

"What do you mean? We could bring it to Calgary, or to New York, even," I said excitedly.

"No, we already did it. It was the only way, Stevie. They've got a tight dealing scene here in Kitslano, and we can't let it get fucked over by rip-offs. Matthew and I figured you wouldn't dig the idea, but I had to come back here right away to tell you where it's at. I wouldn't feel right letting you guys sit here thinking you're rich, y'know?"

I acted out-of-character and didn't explode at Jainie, for several reasons. For one, the notion that I was going to be several hundred dollars richer had all along seemed more like a dream than reality; the closest I'd ever come to having that much money at one time was when I was saving for a pedigree dog with money I earned from a newspaper route I ran in junior high school. Another reason was that Jainie was Jainie, and I still didn't feel entirely comfortable with her. But my main reason was that she probably expected me to blow up, and I wanted to show her that she hadn't pegged my character so accurately.

"Man, you don't think I have any kind of scruples at all, do you," I said.

I genuinely felt insulted that she and Matthew had not given me and John the opportunity to return the acid ourselves.

"It's not that, Stevie. I think you have scruples, but this was the

141

only way I could see to do it. Don't you understand? In your shoes, I probably would have taken off with the acid, but that's because you don't have to live here. You've got to understand that the scene here in Kitslano is really tight, and Matthew and I are part of it. We live here."

The Mafia is really tight, too, I thought.

"That really shows a lack of respect for Stevie and me that you didn't try to talk to us about it," John said.

Jainie furrowed her brow. She looked discomfited.

"Oh, Stevie, I know you think none of us trust you, but we do. It's just that, well, we had to do it our way because we live here and you don't, that's all. It's the difference between being on the road and being settled down. How else can I say it?"

We paused. It was done. I let the argument drop.

"Anyhow, now Matthew has made good friends of Murphy and Brian, and they say they'll front him all the dope he can deal," Jainie said.

My reaction to this was anger at Matthew. I believed that Jainie believed in what she was saying, but I was willing to bet that Matthew simply saw the whole affair as another hustle, one in which he was coming out on top. He'd made good contacts with big dealers who were now willing to give him dope one day and let him pay for it the next, after he'd sold it at the usual profit. And all this was happening because Matthew returned the acid that *we* had given to him.

Then Jainie continued, "And I'm sure, if you guys want, Matthew will tell Murphy and Brian that you were the ones to come up with the acid in the first place. If he puts in the word for you, they'll probably front acid to you guys, too."

My head began to cool. At least we might get something out of this.

"I guess Matthew feels better now," I said. "It's good for him that he has some dealers on his side."

"You mean as opposed to those assholes who came in here this afternoon?"

"Yeah, right. I felt awful about that. I never saw Matthew so freaked."

"Oh, he gets like that under certain circumstances, but it's because he doesn't want to hurt anyone. It's like a defense, you understand. Matthew cares so much about other people. When someone invades his territory like that, he knows he has to freak out because he might hurt them otherwise. You know?"

I did not reply. In a way, I thought it was nice that Jainie was covering for Matthew, but I also thought her explanation was far-fetched. I thought about what an amazing job of rationalizing two friends are able to do for each other. I am a skillful rationalizer on my own, but when I get together with a friend—John, for example, —we can outrationalize most people, if we want to. Between the pair of us, one is bound to produce a rationalization that vaguely fits into somebody's concept of reality. Then all the other has to do is to affirm it and maybe reinforce the explanation a bit. It's like bending the cardboard cutout in your hand so it will fit into the wrong part of the jigsaw puzzle.

Of course, rationalization is something I believe in avoiding. I'm against self-deception. John and I could have done it if we'd had the chance to take all the acid money without giving Miki a cut. We could have. But we wouldn't have fooled ourselves. And under those circumstances, I would have done more to maintain my self-respect if I simply ripped her off without rationalizing about it.

Later that evening, we caught Miki and Ann at their place just before they went out for a Saturday night in Gastown, a section of the city with a lot of bars. Miki looked finer every time I saw her. This evening she looked older, the way she looked the first time I saw her. She was dressed in a violet crepe shirt and her unfaded denim bell-bottoms, which I noticed were taken in on the inside seam so that they would fit snugly around her slender legs. In her high-heeled gray suede boots, she was taller, five eight or so. I had still never seen her without eye makeup.

I told Miki about our tangle with the undercover cops, and she

143

seemed genuinely alarmed. Then I told her that we had discovered
the dealer to whom the acid belonged and had returned it. Miki
paused, glanced in Ann's direction and said, "Oh." Then she said
to Ann that they ought to get going.

17

Sunday seemed serious. Even with the dope deals done, even joking around with Matthew and Jainie, there was that undercurrent. They were going to cop heroin that evening, and I wanted some. I was waiting for the right time to ask them. We talked as usual in the meantime.

"Those fuckers, boy, those guys who busted in here yesterday . . ." Jainie said, clenching her fist. "Now they're badmouthing Matthew all over Fourth Street, telling everyone not to buy Matthew's grass."

"Tell what ya said to that chick," Matthew chuckled. "Stevie'll dig this."

"No, I don't want to tell it," Jainie said, looking like she was going to blush. She was big and strong-looking, but with her blue eyes and very red lips Jainie had some little-girl expressions that reminded me of her sister, Sally.

"This chick, a friend of them dealers, she came up to Jainie today, right?" Matthew said. "So this chick says to Jainie: 'Ya better tell yer old man to be cool about his deals or my boys are

145

gonna have to get heavy with him.' So then Jainie says to her . . .
Go ahead, Jainie, you say it."

"I didn't like this chick's attitude," Jainie said. "So I just said to
her: 'You better tell your boys to lay off my old man or I might
have to get heavy with *you.*' "

I laughed and congratulated Jainie on her style.

Later, I caught her alone in the kitchen for a moment, and I
asked if she would cop heroin for me, too. She was only buying for
herself and Matthew, she stated. That was more of her condescend-
ing attitude toward me. She was saying that they knew how to handle it, but that I did not.

I felt I knew heroin as well as Jainie did.

The life of a drug-user is a series of times of masking and un-
masking himself, I used to say to John. LSD left you naked.
Heroin was the ultimate mask.

At one time, of course, I was nervous about trying heroin. They
had brainwashed me into believing that one or two shots would
addict me. But when I finally did break away from the old ideas,
it was as if I'd cut the string on a catapult. I went all the way, willing to try any drug once. Since my hometown was upper-middle-
class, a wide variety was available. A supply to meet the demand,
you understand.

We exercised our imagination. One summer a friend of mine
copped a tank of nitric oxide, the sweet gas some dentists give
you when they fill your teeth. We hooked it up to where the
oxygen tank belonged in his parents' fallout shelter. Then four of
us went inside and sealed the shelter shut. We turned on the gas.
We took the whole thing more lightly then than I was taking it
today.

I finally got the heroin. I caught Matthew alone at his house
early that evening. He'd already bought it, and he had some extra.
Frank was with me at the time, so I invited him to try some. He
was eager: he'd never done it before.

Heroin sold in Vancouver in capsules for fifteen dollars each.
Although we only had part of one of those capsules, it looked like

146

plenty to stone three of us after I sprinkled the powder onto a sheet of paper on Miki's kitchen table. Since I was the only one of us who'd even tried it before, it wouldn't take much.

I divided the powder into three tiny mounds, but then John told me he didn't want any. Although I didn't mind getting high with Frank, I wanted to get high with John, so I urged him to reconsider. It didn't surprise me, however, when John turned me down.

I went ahead and rolled a matchbook cover into a cylinder through which to snort the dope. Meanwhile, I told Frank we would snort only two thirds of what we had. I spoke like an expert, the way I spoke about a lot of things in Frank's presence. I let Frank snort first.

John slid into his sleeping bag on the livingroom floor and relaxed with his hands clasped behind his head.

After a snort through each nostril, I settled on the floor near John, with my back against the wall. Wanting to feel as secure as possible, I got up again to turn off the kitchenette light so that the room was lit only indirectly by the bathroom light. Then I sat against the wall again and untied my brown leather jacket, which was attached to my rolled sleeping bag. I spread the leather like an afghan over my legs and smoothed it with my palms. That always made me feel secure. Given to me by a friend in Connecticut, this leather had traveled with me almost since I first hit the road.

Canada was beginning to make me feel paranoid in the way that the United States always did, I was thinking. First it was the cops and then it was those megalomaniac dealers. I slid my hand into the sleeve of my jacket to feel the hidden leather stash pockets. Stash pockets—what a sign of paranoia! But at least I hadn't felt the need to use them since we left the States. Of course, that was partly because we hadn't much dope or money to hide in them.

Those pockets contained a history of their own. I had them sewn in by a shoe repairman on the Lower East Side in New York before John and I left. Naturally, it did not seem odd to the repairman that I wanted secret pockets; he assumed that I was trying to avoid losing my money when the junkies in our neighbor-

147

hood mugged me. Since then, the pockets passed many stringent tests. In Florida, when John and I were busted for hitchhiking in North Miami Beach, the cops searched carefully through our packs, opened our toothpaste tubes, ordered us to remove our sneakers, made us stand with our feet apart against a storefront window, and then they felt around our crotches before handcuffing us, a spectacle for the vacationing elderly couples. Yet those cops never found the hash and psilocybin that were neatly tucked away in my stash pockets.

The craziest part of this was where I'd found the idea for the pockets. I was watching a repeat of *The Man from UNCLE* on television. Napoleon Solo, the hero, was transporting secret documents through enemy THRUSH territory. He had stash pockets located as mine were placed, on the bottoms of the insides of his sleeves, so that the documents were in the part of his sleeve that was closest to the ground when he stretched his arms out perpendicular to his body. The reasoning behind this was that they only feel the tops of your arms in a quick frisk.

I felt the dope coming on.

Frank, who had been sitting across the room from me, went into the kitchenette and switched on the light. I asked him what he was doing.

"I'm going to snort some more. I want to get good and high," he said.

I told him I didn't think he needed any more, but he insisted on taking another snort. Then he turned the light off and sat down again.

The leather on my lap was smooth and supple. I loved that leather. I once gave the jacket to John to keep—I'd thought that I'd had it long enough and that it was time to pass it on to a real friend—but I asked John to give it back to me within a week. John was often amused by the way I babied the jacket, and he said I was too sentimental about *things*. He was not one to be upset by something like the loss of a hat.

I was noticing ripped seams and a few rough spots. I decided I

148

would pay to have the jacket reconditioned when John and I made it back to New York.

"Y'all won't believe what my parents said when I called to tell them to send me the rest of my savings," Frank said.

I just realized that he was wanting to talk.

"They asked me if I was ready to straighten out and come home. Can y'all believe that?"

I said that it certainly was an unperceptive thing to say. Frank didn't look well to me.

"You feeling all right, man?"

"I'm just feeling a little sick to my stomach is all."

"Well, take it easy. You'll feel better soon. Sometimes you feel a bit queasy the first time you do smack."

I hadn't anticipated this. Since I didn't get sick the first time I did heroin, I had forgotten that many people do. It's the poison. Frank would get over it, but it was bound to worry me in the meantime.

Frank was closing his eyes.

"Oh, Frank, there's one thing you've got to remember, Frank. That's to stay awake. Keep your eyes open, okay? You'll feel better soon." Christ, I hoped he wasn't about to start ODing on me.

Then Frank jumped up and ran into the bathroom. He was in there retching for about five minutes. Well, it was better than ODing, I thought.

I went into the kitchenette and switched on the light. Frank was nuts. He had snorted almost all of the rest of the heroin. What was he trying to prove? That he could keep up with me and even do me one better when it came to doing dope? John was asleep and the girls were out on the town. I would have gladly traded duties with any of them.

When Frank came back from his five minutes of staring into the toilet bowl, he said he felt okay. He looked more nauseated than ever. But Frank had a way of smiling most of the time. Even as he was deciding whether or not to charge back to the toilet, the corners of his mouth were turned up.

149

He made his decision. Charge! From then on, it was back and forth until we went to sleep around one o'clock.

I was wishing Frank were not so intent on following my lead. It had seemed good for his head at first. John and I turned him on to being uncool, drinking and gallivanting around. But now he seemed determined to go all the way with me. And farther, wherever possible. Even when it meant retching.

18

It was time to find a positive step for all of us to take. I thought about it the next afternoon as I panhandled next to the Coming Attractions window of the Magic Theater, and I saw possibilities, positive possibilities. Miki was a possibility, still waiting to be ventured into. What was I, becoming an introvert? Of course, Frank's van widened the range of options. And there was still that opening to deal acid on the streets. What did I have to complain about? This city was saturated with raw materials, so to speak. It was only a matter of pulling things together to make things happen.

That's when it came to me: We would take Miki and Ann to the Jethro Tull concert at the Vancouver Agrodome. All we needed was money. . . .

"Excuse me, sir, could you spare some change?"

John was keeping me company as I collected the dimes and quarters. I was competing with a congregation of Hare Krishna people up the block.

"We're doing okay," I said to John. "Keep going with luck like this and we may not need to delve into that last twenty to get the tickets."

Then I spotted some hippies climbing out of a California Volkswagen bus. They headed our way.

"Stake a fellow American to a meal?"

Between the three of them, they came up with thirty cents for me.

"Hey, how long do you think we're going to be sticking with Frank?" John asked.

"I don't know," I said. "What, is he really starting to get on your nerves?"

"Sometimes. But it's not that so much; I just think it would be better if he didn't see himself as partners with us."

"Well, I've got to admit, man, that van has gotten to be a security for me."

"Sure, I don't mind having the van around myself, but I'd like it better if he knew that we don't really have anything to give him . . . unless you want to call making his decisions for him giving him something."

"Hold it, let me hit this guy," I said. And then, after coming back empty-handed, "What the hell, Frank's digging it, right? Let's just think about getting to that concert for now. It'll be great, man. We'll get Matthew and Jainie and everybody into the van, maybe bring a couple bottles of wine, then make it on over to the Agrodome."

The next guy heading our way was on crutches because his right leg was amputated above the knee. He was grinning broadly at me and John. I could count the black spaces between his teeth. His hair was dirty and greasy, but neatly combed; the path of his comb was marked by rigid grooves. The hair was dark, but he looked old and sick. He was a hobo—I expected no money from him—but I began a friendly conversation with him by asking him if he could spare change.

"Times are hard, buddy," he said, still smiling.

"Sure are," I said. "But never let it get you down."

"No, sir. Not on a day as pretty as today, anyhow," he said. "You fellas come from here or where?"

"New York."

"Oh, a long ways from home. Up here to keep outa that draft, are ya?"

"Not this time. No, we're just passing through."

Many Canadians seemed to think all young American males were in Canada to beat the draft.

"You ain't been through the service yet, have ya? You look kinda young."

"They haven't called us yet, but we don't sweat about it. John's got number two hundred in that lottery they just started, and I've got a bum leg," I said, referring to my left leg which was broken in the car accident. Of course, I was too young to register for the draft, but I figured that my leg would keep me out when that time came.

"So they don't wantcha 'cause of your leg. Well, I'm with you there," the hobo said, looking down and chuckling at his stump. It was covered by his right trouser leg which was safety-pinned up so that it wouldn't flap around in the wind like a flag. "They blowed this one off in the war for me."

He mentioned a particular war, but I don't recall which one it was. It was one of them. He was an American.

A businessman was walking along Granville toward us. "Excuse me just a second, man, I think I see a good prospect," I said to the hobo. But I returned without any more money.

"Like I say, times are hard," the hobo said, and laughed through his nose. The hair was growing out of his nose like damp stalks. Their roots might have been the capillaries in his blood-shot eyes. "Well, buddies, I'd like to help you out, but I ain't got no kinda money to speak of. But I can always offer you a drink, if that suits you."

"Friend, I'd love to join you in a drink," I said.

He reached into his back pocket with a forearm the size of Popeye the Sailor's and brought out a flask-shaped bottle with the words *Bay Rum* printed on its label.

"Man, you're crazy! You shouldn't be drinking that stuff!" I

153

said. "Don't you know what that stuff does to you, to your liver?"

"It's okay, buddy. My system is used to it," he said, before taking a quick swig and gasping. "Sure you don't want some?"

I tried to dissuade the hobo from drinking it himself, but he knew all about bay rum. It made no difference to him that it was an after-shave lotion; all that mattered was the alcohol content. Thinking about it bothered me after he left because I'd read a few newspaper articles about bums who were found dead in the gutter with bottles of bay rum in their pockets.

•

I told Matthew and Jainie about the hobo with his bay rum when John and I stopped by their house before the five-thirty feed-in.

"Them guys all drink it," Matthew said. "It only costs 'em a buck a bottle. If ya ever need a meal and all ya got is a dollar, one of them guys will tradeja a pair of his meal tickets fer one of them bottles."

"You wouldn't do that, would you?" I asked, though I knew Matthew was only saying it to shock us. "Man, I've got a lot more scruples than somebody who'd pull something like that."

Matthew didn't comment. Then I hit him and Jainie with our idea about organizing a party to go to the Jethro Tull concert. They liked the idea. Matthew said he might cop some MDA.

MDA. The ideal concert drug has to be MDA. I was not positive of what it was, except that I knew its effects since I'd done it before. Somebody once told me MDA was originally discovered by a scientist who was trying to perfect a synthetic mescaline. But its effect is different from that of mescaline. It is not psychedelic. It comes on more like a combination of speed and cocaine. Sometimes it charges you with speedy energy, while other times you don't mind sitting quietly. One positive effect: it makes you dig people. And it makes you very horny. Sometimes it is cut with cocaine.

At the feed-in, we met Frank and told him of our project. He was thrilled by the idea. And by the idea of taking MDA. He had never done it before.

154

Miki and Ann were also enthused when we invited them to the concert, but not quite so when I mentioned MDA.

"I've given up chemicals," Miki said quickly.

"But have you tried MDA?" I asked. "It's not a psychedelic, y'know. No need to worry about freaking out or anything. It's mild. You'll dig it."

"Not a psychedelic, eh?" Miki said. "Well . . . I'll wait to see how I feel when we go."

Ann looked lost. Later, when I had a chance to speak to her alone for a moment in the bedroom, she confessed that she had never tried anything stronger than grass or liquor. "It's unbelievable, Steve, but I used to be so straight until Miki moved in here. She's so hip. She's great. She has turned me on to so many things. Good vibes."

Good vibes. Well, whatever that meant, Ann seemed to be open to the new.

Friday came. The concert was to start at eight P.M. Frank drove me, John, Miki and Ann to pick up Matthew and Jainie at seven thirty. They were waiting for us outside. They climbed in the back, while I was sitting in the front seat next to Frank so that I could prime myself for the concert by listening to Frank's Jethro Tull tape through the headphones. I took off the headphones when Matthew started distributing capsules of MDA. Miki, John and Ann ate one each. Then Frank took one and Matthew ate one. That left one for me and an extra since Jainie wasn't taking any.

"Hey, Matthew, would it be cool if I took the extra? I've already done one; I'd like to see how I get off on two."

Matthew put the extra in my hand.

"Listen, I'll split it with you if you like," I offered.

"It's cool. Take it yerself."

I twisted the clear capsules to loosen the halves. Then I found a Marvel comic book on the floor of the van and set it onto my lap. The capsules were tightly packed; I had to tap the first one like a

ketchup bottle before the white powder fell onto the comic book.
"What are you doing, Steve?" Ann called from the back.

"Snorting's the only way to do it," I said. "It hits you faster and harder."

I snorted the MDA off the comic book, pinching my left nostril closed and sweeping in air like a vacuum cleaner until the powder was gone. The stinging chemical taste dripped onto the back of my mouth. My sinuses were dripping and burning, so I sniffed a few times. I shuddered.

Frank was driving while I snorted the second hit of MDA. A few specks spilled when we hit a bump in the driveway, but I got almost all of it, this time with my right nostril pinched. It burned, but at least now there was symmetry of feeling. The numbness spread to the back of my head.

I turned my head around. Matthew was sitting with his arm resting on the back of Frank's seat. His face held no expression; I was unable to guess what he was thinking, if anything. Miki and Ann, behind Matthew, were in their own little world. And John was miles away in the rear of the van, laughing and talking with Jainie. I couldn't even reckon what *he* was thinking. So I faced front and put my mind on the cars in front of us.

The MDA was hitting me too hard. Everything blurred as though my eyes were a movie camera that was trying to scan a 180-degree radius in three seconds. I focused on a stationary object, the tape deck. It was still not clear. I kept thinking: What frame of mind is this drug forcing me into? But I couldn't answer any questions because they attacked me too fast. And that was just it: There was no frame of mind. The frame had been lifted or broken. Or it simply did not exist, never did.

I was losing energy the way the top half of an hourglass loses sand. My face must have been white like putty.

"Steve, how are y'all feeling?" Frank asked, obviously sensing something wrong.

"No," I said.

It had taken me long seconds to answer him.

156

"Do y'all feel up to going to the concert?"

I ran what Frank was saying through my mind. The sounds of his words were not in Frank's usual tone. He must have been worried. *Panicked,* even. But I did not feel that; I was distant from whatever Frank was feeling. He was talking about the concert. *The* concert. I'd forgotten. It had slipped my mind that we had a destination. I felt like I was in a car with a group of strangers who had picked me up hitchhiking. It was as though these people would stop when they reached their planned destination, but I would stand with my thumb out again and keep going, around and around.

Around and around the van, people were buzzing. "We have to turn back. Stevie's freaking out." The words were repeating, sounding more distant each time until I could no longer hear them. I felt the same.

A hand clasped firmly on my shoulder. It was John's.

"How you doing, man?" he started. And then he began talking faster. And faster. His talking kept accelerating faster.

"Isn't that great? I've been sitting back there talking with Jainie and digging the Stones' tape, and I don't believe how good this is. It's like being with someone you like, even if you're alone, but of course you're not alone, man, you've got all your friends around you, and they're all going with you, wherever you go. Hey, isn't it a gas riding around in this van? I'm enjoying it, just sitting back there, and then Matthew mentioned to me that you didn't feel so good, so I wanted to come up here to talk to you. But Jainie said I should stay back there because she thought I might get depressed by talking with you if you don't feel too well, but isn't that ridiculous? I mean, I just wanted to come up here to talk to you, to see how you *really* feel because if there's one person I'm really tight with, man, if there's one person I can say I know, it's you, right?"

I nodded and then John went on talking faster while he squeezed my shoulder tightly.

"Well, Matthew told me that you were feeling bad, but I figured that you probably don't actually feel *bad,* you probably feel uptight and maybe not too sure of yourself because you're not sure of *how* you feel. It's like any new experience y'know. You can only think of it in the light of your other experiences. It's like that time we took PCP down in San Francisco, remember? We thought it was going to be THC, but then it turned out to be PCP, y'know, so I got more stoned and in a different way from what I'd expected. So at first, I let it scare me because I was thinking what a horrible drug it was because it weighted you down like that. But I should have let myself dig the experience as long as I was going through it. And I finally did let myself dig it. All I needed to do was to decide that I wanted to pull my energy together, so I did it. I simply breathed deeply. *Really* deeply. I took in the air so that I could feel it. And it wasn't even hard to do when I decided to do it. Which is funny since that was a draining drug no matter how you looked at it; it sucked the stuff right out of you. But this, man, this MDA really gives you the energy you need if you let it, if you *feel* it. If you just take it slow because you've got plenty of time and breathe *in,* feel that air. Just breathe like this and feel how good it feels."

John breathed in air so loudly that it sounded like a wind whistling through trees. Meanwhile, I was nodding at what he was saying. I didn't think John would bullshit me.

Then I tried it. And it worked! John had put his finger on it, somehow. The air that I drew into my lungs served as the ballast I badly needed. And before we reached the Agrodome, I was surging with energy. I felt ready to fly on the music.

Still, John did not quit talking to me. He went on, repeating many of the things he had already said, until he was sure I felt secure. Then we all piled out of the van and onto the macadam of the Agrodome parking lot. Everybody else was acting as if nothing had happened.

In the parking lot, it began to seem surreal. Along with hundreds of other people, we left our auto and paraded beneath looming streetlamps toward the stadiumlike building. I felt like part of a flock.

And the inside of the Agrodome was our home, where we all got together. It reminded me of a smaller version of New York's Madison Square Garden, which hardly means it was small. There were two or three levels, all filled with seats, above the arena. The arena, where we went, was partially covered with seats, but a generous area in front of the stage was left open for dancing. It was immensely crowded.

John was still talking. And I was still getting off on it. His rap veered off onto tangents, but he was mainly saying how great it was that neither of us could possibly flip out so long as we stuck together because we cared about each other. He was obviously proud of having talked me off a freak-out. Love is all you need, right?

"We keep going because we share," he said, coming up with ideas off the top of his head. "It's like—if I have a hundred dollars and you have a dollar, then we both have a hundred and one dollars. You see, there's where a lot of people foul up when they think they have us figured out. What they don't see is that it works both ways. If you have a hundred and I have a buck, it's still the same. If you panhandle a few bucks and I have a few bucks from some article, it's all ours. . . ."

"Man, I'm glad to hear you say that."

I really was. It had bothered me at times that John was always the one to pay the rent in New York and he invariably had the most money in his pocket. So I had hoped that my panhandling and berry-picking meant something to him. Sometimes there's nothing better than a stoned conversation between friends.

"Hey, I think we lost Miki and Ann," John said, scanning the area in back of us.

We had been in our own little world.

"We'll catch them later," I said.

"Right, but I hope they make out okay on MDA."

"Don't worry, let's just catch up to Matthew and Jainie."

Before the show began, a group of people on the stage passed cans around the audience to collect money for a bail fund for some-

159

body who had been busted. "Don't think this money is going to *them*," the longhaired announcer began, referring to cops in general. "It's for *you!* As soon as we get this money back after the trial, it goes back into the bail fund to be used for any of our brothers and sisters who get busted." John and I tossed some change into the can when it passed our way.

Then the show started. Fleetwood Mac was on first. And they were fine. The lead guitarist was singing a rock and roll medley with his guitar swung low—and the joint was rocking.

"Isn't it fine to be tall!" Jainie said to John, as she, he and Matthew were able to see over most of the other heads. Then she added, "I just wish we had room to dance."

The concert went quickly. John and I wandered happily around, trying not to step on the bodies of the freaks who were totally zonked out on the floor. We ran into Frank, who was euphorically stoned out of his mind. He was dancing with a very young-looking girl and they both seemed elated. Fleetwood Mac did their set plus one encore.

There was a break.

The next figure at the front of the stage was a mad magician. He appeared there suddenly with a silver wand in his hand. He streaked silver through the air. Then he placed an end of the wand to his lips. He was balanced on one foot with his right foot resting on his left knee. He blew a melody before singing:

"Nothing is easy, though time gets you worried, my friend it's okay . . ."

It was Ian Anderson, lead singer and flutist for Jethro Tull, dressed in heavy boots and an old checked coat with long tails dangling as he whirled around to conduct his band with the flute. He moved quickly from song to song, flinging back his hair and bearded head and staring at the audience with piercing eyes as he blew the notes in short bursts that built up and up and up until he sneezed into his flute.

"I've got no money coming in, but I can't be sad/That was the best cup of coffee I ever had . . ."

Man, I'm glad you said that.

160

19

I was drunk.

"Miki, I love ya. I love ya, but I'm pissed," I was yelling from inside Frank's van.

Frank, John and I had been waiting with our bottle of Beau Sejour. Miki and Ann hadn't come to the van after the concert, so we had parked the van by their apartment to wait for them.

"Miki, do you hear me? I've been worrying about you! Doesn't that mean anything? How was I to know you hadn't freaked out on MDA or something?"

Miki poked her head through the door of the van and flashed me one of her cutest guilty smiles.

"Come on in here, Miki."

"No, you said you're pissed," she said and withdrew her head from the van.

"I'm only pissed 'cause I love ya!" I yelled.

Bitch, she wasn't afraid to join me because I was pissed; she and Ann had brought a string of new boyfriends home with them. I could hear them. That's how I knew it when she was finally home.

"Isn't she beautiful, man," I said to John.

"Anything you say, Steve," John replied in a monotone. He was more sober than me, and it seemed that he was generally fed-up with Miki and her antics.

"She's so beautiful," I said. "I'll tell ya, what I wouldn't give to ball her right now."

"But what do y'all do when your chick is sixteen and lives with her folks?" Frank asked. "I met the greatest chick tonight, but damn, she's so young."

What the hell was I supposed to suggest? Kidnap her, for Chrissake. . . .

"Ah, Miki, if you only knew what you are doing to me. . . ."

I woke up in the van the next morning. Assuming it was too late for the feed-in, I went through the glass sliding door into the apartment where new knapsacks and sleeping bags were strewn all over the livingroom floor. The girls were already out. I heard voices in the bedroom, so I went in.

"Morning, Steve," John said as I looked at the neatly bearded guy on the bed. "Oh, this is Brian. You remember Brian, the man whose acid we found."

"Oh yeah! Right!" I said, figuring foggily that he was here to front us acid or something.

"He's asking questions about Miki," John said.

"Oh yeah? What kind of questions?" I asked.

"She stole my stash," Brian began. "I am inquiring to see if she has been doing this to other people."

"What do you mean? How could she get at your stash?" I asked.

"She and her friend were the last ones in my apartment, aside from close friends, before I discovered it was missing. I made the mistake of allowing them to go into my kitchen alone. Part of my stash was in the refrigerator. The girls came out with food."

"Wow . . . Holy shit . . ." I was saying, mostly to myself. Then I added, "No, I don't think she's been ripping any other people off."

"Do you think we should run her out of town?"

That gangster remark came from a fourth guy in the room, a friend of Brian's.

"No, that doesn't seem to be necessary," Brian stated evenly.

Brian's friend, I later learned, was an ex-boyfriend of Miki's. It was turning out that a lot of people were letting themselves get hung-up about that chick.

Frank, meanwhile, wasn't feeling hung-up at all. The morning had told him all was well and that MDA was the kick. He had already walked to Matthew's place to find out about a possible MDA connection when John and I met him in the driveway next to his van.

"Matthew gave me this address where I can cop an ounce of MDA for three hundred dollars," Frank said. "That's three hundred caps. Y'all want to come with me?"

"Three hundred dollars! Man, won't that break you?" I said.

"Well, it won't leave me much, but I'll make it all back dealing."

"Let's go."

The three of us drove to the address of Matthew's connection. The block on which we copped, I later learned, was known as "Chemical Row." The Row consisted of three or four old houses which served as centers for quantity dealing of all kinds of drugs; at that time MDA was the favorite.

Frank made his deal through a gray-faced girl who insisted that he give her a few hits worth of the powder for her role in the transaction. She was a middleman, undoubtedly a temporary crasher at the house. She was wearing a madras plaid shirt with sleeves rolled below her elbows, but high enough to reveal gray stripes that ran down the veins of her left arm, stripes that matched the color of the circles around her eyes.

With that deal done, we drove to Burrard Street and then across the bridge to a drugstore on Granville Street. Frank pulled the van over but kept the motor running. I ran into the drugstore with Frank's money and bought three boxes of clear gelatin capsules, a hundred in each box, and three pairs of disposable surgical rubber gloves. I noticed that you didn't need a prescription to buy syringes in Vancouver.

Although the cashier in the drugstore had seemed nonchalant, we were nervous as we drove back to Miki's. When we got there, we shut ourselves into the bedroom and began capping MDA.

Capping required more patience than it takes to thread a needle because the capsules were slippery. And I'm not certain whether the fault was with those gloves or me, but the rubber hindered the process. After capping about ten hits, I removed the gloves to free my sweaty hands. Between the three of us, we capped 278 generous hits from that ounce—not a bad count. Frank and I were enjoying it because we were getting high from the powder we were snorting out of our fingernails.

"This is so far out!" Frank exclaimed. "I'll tell y'all what I'm gonna do. I'll front a hundred caps to y'all now and all y'all have to pay me back is a hundred after it's sold."

"Great! Great!" I said. "With a drug like this, I'll have your money for you in no time at all."

Money! It was finally coming through. And dealing MDA would bring me more profit than dealing LSD. Street prices for MDA were about three dollars a hit. I could sell it for two-fifty and please a lot of people as well as myself.

This deserved a celebration. We decided to go to the Parlour that night. But not wearing our tired old pauper's duds, we would dress in clothes that would suit our spirit.

Frank drove us to a newly opened clothes shop that we had seen advertised in the *Georgia Straight,* Vancouver's underground paper. "Jelly Beans for Jeans." They stocked piles of pants in a spectrum of colors and textures. After leafing through several stacks, accustoming myself to the ten ninety-nine minimum price tag, I found a pair of royal purple denim bell-bottoms which I tried on. The salesman was gay, and I had a hard time keeping him from joining me in the dressing booth. He kept on peering over the Old-West-barroom type swinging doors of the booth and asking me if I were managing all right. I guess he didn't believe I was capable of put-

164

ting on a pair of pants. While I was modeling the pants in the mirror outside of the booth, he pulled off the tags before I'd even made my decision about the purchase.

Before I was able to make my decision, I went back into the dressing booth to examine my Carson City Penitentiary jeans with the patch on the knee. It was about time for a new pair of pants, I thought. Hell, those jeans were so old that they had buttons instead of a zipper at the fly. I thought about maybe buying a pair of black Wranglers, like the pair John had given me back in New York, the ones I had left behind in that Colorado jail cell. But I decided on the purple. It would be good for my head to run around looking like a jet-setter, the way Miki did. And why shouldn't I add a bright color to my life?

For once, I was meek about asking John for the money, since it was going to leave us with about eight bucks. But when I asked, he laughed—he could see how much those pants meant to me— and he said that we were nearly broke anyway, so why not.

"Thanks a lot, man, really," I said. "I'm starting dealing tomorrow, so I'll earn us this much and more, you'll see."

Frank, meanwhile, had picked out two pairs of pants in his size, one of them of startling white material and the other the same as my pair.

"Which one of these do y'all think I should buy?" he asked us.

"Take the white," I said immediately. "We don't want to go running around looking like the Bobbsey Twins."

Frank returned the purple pair to its stack, and then he changed from his blue denim bells into the tight whites. He wore them out of the store.

"I wish my ass was smaller so I'd look better in these pants," he said as we boarded the van.

"Yeah, right," I said, realizing right away that it was the wrong thing to say.

"Well at least I have a big chest," Frank blurted, rushing to his own defense.

I let it drop. It didn't matter. I was satisfied with the way I

165

looked. Being big like Frank had its advantages, of course, but in the long run I preferred to live with my own size.

We drove to Matthew's. Before going in I said to John, "You don't really like these pants, do you." It wasn't a question. I could sense it.

"Ah, they don't bother me," John said.

He did not like the pants.

We went into the house, and it was model time again.

"Turn around, Stevie," Jainie said. "They're really nice, boy. I love to see people get into colors."

"Them pants make ya look real faggy," Matthew said offhandedly.

Fuck you, Matthew.

I would have stayed longer to tell Matthew and Jainie about my MDA dealing prospect, but to tell the truth I felt self-conscious about my new pants. The way people were acting at first reminded me of the way they acted after I had my head shaved. It was only five o'clock, but I urged Frank and John to come with me so we would get to the feed-in before that line grew too long.

We went to the Parlour that night. It was a bore. We stuck it out for a few hours. Frank was having fun dancing with some girl, but there wasn't anybody who looked especially tempting to John and me. So we left. We let Frank stay to have a good time, and we hitched to Matthew's.

Lights were out in Matthew's house, so I called for him beneath his bedroom window. I tried to call loudly enough so that he'd hear me if he were awake, but softly so that I wouldn't wake him. The window swung open—it had hinges at the top—and Jainie stuck her head out.

"Oh, sorry, did I wake you?" I asked.

"No, that's all right. I was just lying here, thinking, you know."

"Where's Matthew?"

"He's out. He'll be back later."

"We just came from the Parlour. It was a drag."

"So where are you guys crashing tonight? Still at that chick Miki's?"

"Yeah, right. Holy shit! I didn't even tell you this afternoon. We found out how Miki got that acid, the seven hundred tabs, you know? She stole it. We talked with Brian, that dealer, this morning, and he's positive Miki's a little rip-off."

"You fuckin' guys, man," Jainie laughed. We were always coming to her and Matthew with our stories.

Then she said, "Come inside. I'd like to talk with you."

So John and I went in through the kitchen. The light was on in the livingroom when we got there, about forty watts behind a yellow shade. Jainie was sitting on the sofa, wearing black denim pants and a shiny purple shirt. I sat on the other end of the sofa. John made himself comfortable on the floor.

For one reason or another, we got to talking about our wishes, our desires. John was saying that he would like to get out of the city for a while, and we all agreed.

"Sometime we should all get together, but under different conditions," he said.

"I'll tell you what I could dig, boy," Jainie said. "Just getting out somewhere and going off and being *alone*, just me and Matthew. Shit, do you realize we've been married a month now and there's always been someone *around*. Running this house is a trip and I'm into it, right. But it can get to be a hassle when you really want to go off and be alone."

"Are we starting to get on your nerves coming around all the time?" I asked.

"No, that's not it. I really dig you guys coming around with all your crazy trips. It's just that Matthew and I could really dig getting out, way off someplace, and getting into something else for a change. Something easy, you understand. I know it's hard for you guys to see, in a way, because you guys are on the road, really out there, wherever you want to be. But it's different when you're committed to a house and a community like this. It's good. But it's just

167

different, you understand. There are these things that you have to make work."

"It's different, but both ways wear you down in their own way," John said.

"Right. Right. Don't I know it."

"I think we know it too, y'know," John said. "After all, it's not as though it's been like this all our lives. We did come from someplace. We do have that apartment back in New York."

"Yeah, I believe you," Jainie laughed. "You told me about that before. I guess I'm just talking mostly about my own needs, the kind of trips I've been running through."

"I suppose it's a lot like what you went through in San Francisco," I said, bringing up the subject I hadn't dared to mention before now.

Jainie laughed. "You mean I'm into my same old Jainie trip? Being a stable mother image for anyone who needs it? And letting that hurt my own head? No, it's not that bad. I've gotten a lot together since San Francisco."

"To tell the truth, I was wondering why you weren't pissed at me when I first showed up here," I said, but from my reading of Jainie's face, she didn't know what I meant. "When I saw Ellen and Kathy in California before we came up here, they were warning me that you were really pissed at me. It kind of surprised me when you acted friendly."

"Shit, man, I didn't even know you were talking about *that*. I was thinking about my last few months in San Francisco. What you're talking about is so long ago. I even forgot what it was that I was so angry about. . . ."

We went on to talk about the last October and November in San Francisco, about the people we knew, about Ellen, about Kathy, about Ellen's husband and the kids. Then I brought up Sally, Jainie's sister. I was easing us onto the subject of why Jainie had been pissed.

"I just got a letter from Sally," Jainie said.

168

"I suppose you were mostly pissed because you thought I fucked her over."

"I know. I know. Oh, boy, was I angry! That was for a while there. But that was a long time ago."

That it was part of the distant past wasn't enough to make me drop the subject. I wanted to set one thing straight. "Everybody blames me for that, but I didn't simply fuck her over. Things went badly between us, but it was both our doing. It was a bad time."

"You're telling me it was a bad time, boy. Who do you think was supporting all you guys? But, Stevie, can't you understand why I was so angry? Sally was my sister just out from New Jersey, her first time away from the parents, you know, and I wanted it to go so well for her. I wanted for her to be happy, but she was lost out there. Before you came to stay with us, all she used to talk about was how fine everything's gonna be when Stevie gets here. Everything's gonna be just *fine,* you know? Stevie, she really loved you. Well, maybe it was only puppy love, whatever that is, but she was feeling it. She believed that you could make everything better."

"I suppose I didn't do that, did I?" I said sadly.

"No-o-o-o-o-o," Janie said. But then she saw it was depressing me so she said, "But that was so long ago. And you know what I just said in a letter to Sally? I wrote and told her that Stevie Gibbons is here and he's really nice now."

That gave my head a lift.

"And shit, I was going through my own problems at that time," Jainie went on. "All you had to worry about was: Did Matthew get to break Sally's virginity before you did? I had other hassles. That whole scene between me, Matthew and Sally before you came . . . oh, God! . . . I'm remembering this one time when I heard those two talking behind my back. Sally was saying that she had never realized what a bitch I was, and Matthew was going along with it because he wanted to ball her. They weren't even lowering their voices. So I ran into the room where they were talking

169

and I started *screaming,* 'You two should listen to yourselves! You're supposed to be my sister! And you're supposed to be my *lover!'* I was crying; I felt like I was . . ."

Jainie was getting herself upset. She was very emotional; I thought she was going to start crying right there.

"Did I mention to you I'm starting dealing MDA tomorrow?" I said, to change the subject.

"Really? That's good," Jainie said, paying little attention. "It was so long since I thought of any of that scene of last fall. I'd practically forgotten about it. I haven't really thought about many of the things that happened before this spring in . . . Stevie, you don't know, but I cut myself. Then I had to come up here to Vancouver right away because Matthew is the one person who knows me well enough. I went into the bathroom where I was and found a razor blade. I know it was a stupid thing to do. I wouldn't have done it at all if I wasn't so drunk. I was so drunk, boy. But I cut myself really good. Then I just stood there watching it. . . ."

She was talking about a suicide attempt as though it were simply another episode, one of the sad ones. It scared me. But I pretended I wasn't shocked. I had never noticed those scars on her wrists.

During the next half hour, we managed to find lighter subjects for discussion. We returned to our talk about getting out of the city. Jainie was saying that she and Matthew would like to get out to Vancouver Island . . .

Then we heard a couple of voices outside. One of them was Matthew's.

"Is she in?"

"Guess so. Hope she ain't been waiting up fer us," Matthew said. He sounded smashed.

"Will she be mad?"

The kitchen door opened with a slow creak. Then Matthew must have seen Jainie slouched with her legs extended off the sofa because he marched straight into the livingroom.

"Evening, baby," he said, bending over to kiss Jainie.

"Matthew, you're drunk," Jainie giggled.

"I know it. Is it okay if Tim stays here tonight?"

Matthew was kneeling on the floor between Jainie's knees and hugging her around the waist.

"It's okay with me."

"Didja hear that?" he said to Tim, who was standing in the center of the room. "It's okay, ya can stay here."

Tim was quiet. He looked up at the ceiling for a moment so that his styled, layer-cut blond hair fell back in thick billows against his shoulders. I must confess I was impressed. Tim was the prettiest, perhaps even one of the most strikingly beautiful guys I'd ever seen. He was not very tall, five eight maybe, and he was quite thin. His face was what was unusual. The features all went together perfectly, the thin straight nose, the somewhat high cheekbones and his gray eyes. It was obvious that he had worked hard to make his hair look like that: falling in rich, ruly waves, without a single broken strand. With that hair, he reminded me of a proud Afghan that doubtless had a good master somewhere to take meticulous care of him. But this beauty didn't impress me so much as did the fact that Tim was with Matthew. Actually, I was impressed that Matthew had a boyfriend like this.

Matthew caught my notice of Tim. He sprang off of Jainie's legs as if they were parallel bars and turned around to switch on the radio. Then he spoke with Tim as though they were the only ones in the room. The act was for my benefit.

"Didn'tcha get off on that cute blond boy I was dancing with tonight? I never seen him at the club before."

Tim said nothing; he was not cooperating. He seemed self-conscious, maybe because he felt that he and Matthew had abruptly barged in on our conversation, like a couple of drunken bums who want to talk to you while you feel like being alone on a park bench.

Matthew crossed the room and bounced onto the bed in the bedroom. He straightened his velvet pants. I wasn't in the mood for the show.

"We tried to cop some MDA, but there ain't no dealers hanging

171

around Fourth Street tonight."

"I have MDA if you want some," I offered.

Matthew jumped up like a pogo stick. "Far *out!*"

I removed three of the capsules from the box of a hundred in my pocket. Matthew urged us to join him and Tim, but that wasn't our mood. He and Tim snorted half a cap each and then ate one. For the next few minutes, they were both pacing the livingroom floor, shuddering and sniffing.

When the sniffing was over, Tim said, "You people looked really peaceful when we walked in. I really hope we didn't break something up."

"No, that's all right. We were having a nice talk," Jainie said. "I think we'll go for a walk now to finish it."

She made eye contact with me and with John and then we all stood to leave. Matthew and Tim told us to come back soon.

Walking along Third Street, quietly at first, we strolled through the shadow of the trees and then the light of the streetlamps at each corner. It was like passing through a series of tunnels.

"That's so fine when we just talk like that," Jainie finally said. "We should all get together to do that more often."

John and I agreed.

Then Jainie said, "I'm a little uptight about going back home now. You heard what they were saying before they came in. Maybe they don't want me there."

I was thinking the same, but I didn't comment.

We were hidden in the shadow of a tree, halfway between corners, when I spotted Miki and Ann crossing Burrard Street. I saw them before either of them saw us. But when they did recognize us, Miki darted to her right, down Burrard Street. Jainie, John and I hastened our pace to meet Ann.

"What's the matter with Miki?" I asked when we were near enough to her so that I didn't have to yell.

"She's so messed up," Ann said, discomposed. "She found out that you all know she robbed Brian's drugs. She's scared that you're

172

going to be mad and say something about it."

I glanced down Burrard Street to see Miki waiting halfway down the block. She knew I could see her; she looked like a cornered fugitive. Then she began walking back in our direction.

"I didn't want her to take it. I was scared. We were at Brian's apartment and we were looking for food in his refrigerator when Miki found all that acid behind the cole slaw. And she took it! I was so scared, I had to say we'd found it."

Miki was approaching. She smiled and said, "Hi there! I was just looking for my dog. Have you seen her? I thought she might have run down this block."

"I didn't even know you own a dog," I said.

"Didn't I tell you? She came out here with me in my Midget. Just me and my dog. That dog loves me more than anything. Too bad I had to leave her with a friend. I wish they'd let us keep a dog in our apartment building. Otherwise she might not be lost now."

"What kind of dog is it?" I asked.

"The biggest, most beautiful Saint Bernard you ever saw. You like dogs, too, eh? Well, I'm going to go down this block again to look some more. Nice seeing you. Bye bye."

Miki looked very young when she lied like that.

"I'll help you look," John said and followed her down the block.

I watched Miki skip away. I admired her and wondered about her.

"I don't believe it, she's so crazy," Ann said, after they were out of sight. Ann was obviously thrilled by the idea of having such a nutty friend, but she spoke as though she were concerned for Miki's health.

"What I can't believe is that a chick like that works for the phone company," I said, right away realizing that Ann might be offended by my slur on phone company employees. But she wasn't. She didn't catch on to things like that.

"You can't trust anything she says, Steve. It's all lies. She never worked with me at the phone company. She keeps saying these

173

things, and I don't want to say they're not true while she's standing right there. You understand, don't you, Steve?"

"Is she really from Toronto?" I asked.

"Yes, but she never owned a car. She flew out here. And that dog of hers—God, she's always talking about her dog—she bought it here in Vancouver, before she moved into my apartment. But it is not lost."

"Holy shit, man, why does she say all those things? What's the matter with the true story?"

"I don't know. She just does it. Her real name isn't even Miki. She made that up, too."

How ironic, I thought, that this was a chick who had every other guy in Vancouver desperate to get into her pants, and she hadn't even given them her real name.

Jainie was no longer involved with the conversation, so she announced she was going home. Then I walked Ann back to the apartment.

"What's her name if it isn't Miki?" I asked on the way.

"She hasn't told anyone, practically. It's Kay Ferguson."

Kay Ferguson! No, that doesn't fit at all.

When we arrived at the apartment, Miki and John were still out. Guys' sleeping bodies, about six of them, were scattered on the livingroom floor. These were the new boyfriends. Somebody had dragged the mattress off the bed and into the livingroom, and Frank was sleeping on it. The bedroom was empty.

In the bedroom with the door shut, Ann began complaining about her troubles, having to pay rent, working that awful job, having to sleep on that bed of springs without a mattress, all alone and coming home to an apartment loaded with strangers who take advantage of her generosity . . .

"And look, I burned my hand," she practically sobbed.

She was right. She had burned her hand on the stove or someplace. I hadn't noticed the gauze around it.

"Oh, Steve, I can't even take my shirt off it hurts so much," she said, with her usual dull pout.

174

So I helped her take her clothes off, and then she climbed into bed. I said good night and switched off the light on my way out. One or two drinks in me and the night would have taken a different turn. But no, I wasn't exactly wild about Ann.

I slept in the back of Frank's van that night. I was thinking about Miki—beautiful, lost Miki—and I decided that what she needed was a real friend.

20

It began to seem like a circus, with Miki and Ann bringing on new acts every other night, as soon as they tired of the old ones. But the old ones stayed. The apartment was rapidly becoming an exclusive crash pad, reserved exclusively for boyfriends of the tenants. Good vibes, as Ann might have put it.

Bad vibes, as I would put it. Competition left everybody tense. Hostilities mounted highest between my crew and the group of four road bums that Miki had brought home with her on the night of the Jethro Tull concert. The day after their arrival, that group asserted itself by stocking the refrigerator with groceries and then making a point of forbidding everybody but Miki and Ann to touch the food. What dirty tactics, they had taken over the refrigerator! Well, I wanted to avoid a hassle, so I spent most of my time from then on outside of the apartment, dealing MDA on Fourth Street and in Gastown.

But one evening, a supershow night at the circus, I did hang around the apartment while John and Frank were out. I was past letting Miki's antics bother me at that point, so I kept cool when she and Ann introduced me to Pierre and Paul, the latest finds. The French Canadians were cordial as we talked, while Miki and Ann went out again for a bit. Since the girls stayed out for a couple of hours, the conversation went deep. It was getting philosophical, so I said little, letting them expound their theories. Pierre, a muscular guy with a shag haircut, was spouting his existential attitude toward life. A regular Jean-Paul Sartre, he was. To illustrate his ideas with an immediate example, he pointed out that his big lucky break of the evening—getting picked up by two attractive young ladies, being handed the opportunity to spend the night with them—in reality was utterly worthless and meaningless to the world, to his life, to him and Paul, to the way they would feel next week. . . . Then Miki and Ann came in from the night, like a dream, through the sliding glass door—with three new boyfriends.

By the look on Pierre's face, it seemed his one-night-fuck was meaningless until he realized he wasn't going to get it. He and his partner moved on in the morning.

My fantasy that week was to get Miki out of the city. Quiet walks on the beach, gentle waves, sunsets—I wanted to turn that chick on to a little romance.

It didn't seem so unrealistic. Especially since Matthew and Jainie and Frank were all talking about taking the van out to Vancouver Island for a kind of retreat.

Why not? That's how I put it to her, and that was Miki's general reaction when I invited her to come with us to Vancouver Island. That was in the middle of the week, and she seemed to think it was a nice idea. But toward the end of the week, as the time to actually leave came closer, she wasn't so positive.

Meanwhile, I was dealing. MDA . . . MDA . . .

I enjoyed it in the beginning, playing the role of the Candy Man. My customers often came back to tell me how they liked the MDA, since many of them had never tried it before, and all reports were good. One girl came back, elated, fifteen minutes after I sold her a cap. I was dealing in the Travelers at the time, a Gastown hangout

177

where people drank beer around round tables and listened to music from the record machine. And this girl was stoned already. "You're beautiful!" she was saying. "You're one of the most beautiful boys I've ever seen in my whole life!" She wanted to kiss me, but she was with her boyfriend. "Give me three more," she said, slipping me a ten. I gave her the caps. But when I tried to give her the two-fifty change, she said, "No, you keep it—you're beautiful!" Her boyfriend was glaring at me. He took the two-fifty. He was not high.

I liked the work in the beginning. I was always as stoned as my customers.

I quickly learned the ways to do the most business in Vancouver. Fourth Avenue turned out not to be the best place. I started out there, often with Frank and the van nearby, advertising my product as people passed along the sidewalk. "MDA . . . MDA . . ." But I wasn't making much money that way because few hip people trusted that, the lowest form of street dealing. I soon learned that Gastown, on the other side of the bridge, was the place to make a mint. I sold fifteen caps in one afternoon of hanging around the main hangouts, Travelers and the Gastown Inn. All I had to do was sell one hit and satisfy one customer. The word spread. Then I sat back at my table, sipping beer and waiting for new customers to come to me. The places were big and noisy so I wasn't conspicuous.

I think it was Thursday that Miki began changing her mind about wanting to come with us to Vancouver Island.

"This city's a nice place, eh?" she said to me before going to the Manhattan with Ann that evening. Then: "I don't know if I can come with you, Steve. I'd have to take a whole week off from work, and they might not let me."

"Be serious, Kay."

She pretended she hadn't heard me call her by her real name, but she was as bad at hiding her paranoia as she was at lying.

I wasn't trying to get her paranoid. I had tried to say it in a light manner. It was no big deal that I knew her name. I wanted her to see that.

She left with Ann a few minutes later.

I was getting depressed because I wasn't making any money. For every cap I sold, I ate one myself and had a beer.

I was getting depressed because I was weary of hustles.

And I was getting depressed because I felt apart from John. I was always out dealing with Frank. I'd be crashed out on the MDA by the time I saw John.

"Don't you think you've been overdoing the MDA," he said to me on Saturday morning, before I went out. "I don't think I've seen you straight in a week."

"Oh Jesus, man, what are you supposed to be, my mother?"

John's face flushed and he said something like if I had any brains I'd watch myself. I hated that. Why couldn't he have waited until I was straight if he felt he had to say that? Now we were both uptight. John was in the front seat of Frank's van, shutting himself off by listening to Stones tapes on the headphones. It was like a fight we had in that Colorado jail cell after four days of having nothing to do but work for the man and then crawl back into the cage. I felt horrible, and I felt caged into it.

Naturally, we didn't stay angry at each other for long. But I still didn't have much fun dealing that day. I ate another cap of MDA.

Sunday morning, I blew my chance to get Miki out to Vancouver Island. I had been up all night and was desperate for a place to crash. Frank and John had claimed the van shortly after midnight, so that was out. And it was too late to go to the Beatty Street Armory. As I sat by the kitchenette table, thinking, people on the livingroom floor were starting to wake up. But the floor didn't appeal to me. I got up and paced around what space I could find. Then Ann, who was used to getting up early for work, came out of the bedroom to go to the bathroom. I asked her if I could sleep on her bed. She said yeah. I said thanks, really, thanks a lot,

179

and I waited for a turn at the bathroom. In my mind, that bed of springs was a velvet-covered water bed with goose down pillows. After washing my face and brushing my teeth, I went into the bedroom—only to be dumbfounded by the sight of Miki dozing on the bed. Her body was stretched out diagonally so that I couldn't even find room for myself. I started burning with anger. "Miki, Ann told me I could sleep in her bed," I said firmly. Opening her eyes, Miki whined, "No, I had to sleep on that floor all night!" I stood at the foot of the bed, exasperated. Miki thought she could get away with anything because she was beautiful. I took off my clothes. "What are you doing?" she said, looking at me. I pulled up the covers and sat in bed next to her. "What are you doing? Get off this bed! I'm sleeping here!" Then she turned over with her back to me to say that the argument was finished. But I stayed sitting next to her. "Get off!" Miki yelled one last time without looking at me. And then I shoved her onto the floor. That was one chick I never thought I'd be kicking out in the morning. She whimpered crocodile tears and left the room in a huff. I slept until midafternoon.

That night, for the first time, the sliding glass door was locked shut when we arrived at the apartment.

"That bitch! Well, if it's war she wants, it's war she'll get," I said to Frank and John.

I tapped on the glass harder and harder until it shook. I knew she could hear it, but nobody answered my knocking. I knocked steadily for about fifteen minutes, figuring I would keep that bitch and those bastards awake even if it left me without a place to crash.

After the sound of tapping had begun to get on my own nerves, I knocked on Ann's bedroom window. She woke up and let me into the livingroom where everybody was still pretending to be asleep. I slept on the floor.

The next morning, Miki didn't have the guts to admit she had locked me out. She didn't even act pissed about Sunday morning. She wasn't going to come with us to the Island, though.

I knew the trip to Vancouver Island could not be like my fantasies about it, but I felt a need to go, with or without Miki.

180

We gave dealing another try on Fourth Avenue, and Frank and I met a couple of girls and invited them to Vancouver Island. It happened just like that. We talked to them for half an hour in front of the Last Chance, telling them about our plans, and then we suggested they join us. Fortunately, they were impulsive chicks.

Their names were Wendy and Darlene. Right away it was plain that I went with Wendy and Frank went with Darlene.

On that matter, I didn't envy Frank. Darlene was nice, but she was big and embarrassingly boisterous. She was an ex-biker chick with big, sagging tits. You might have expected to find a tattoo somewhere in between them. She was wearing knee-high suede boots over skin-tight jeans. The first feature of her face you noticed were her full, expressive lips. She flaunted her horniness like a new pair of boots. Frank dug it.

Wendy, on the other hand, projected a subdued personality at first. She looked like a sweet young thing. Her skin was creamy white and delicate with a cluster of freckles spattered across the bridge of her nose. Her hair was blond and in the process of growing out of its page-boy length. Like Darlene, Wendy wore faded jeans, but unlike Darlene's jeans, Wendy's were clean so that they looked like a reflection of the sky or maybe of Wendy's eyes.

I was speeding when I met her; I had just traded three hits of MDA for a dime of methedrine. For that reason, Wendy's pretty face looked gorgeous.

After talking with her, however, my impression of Wendy changed. She came on quiet at the start, but once she began to talk she didn't shut up. Although I was the one who was speeding, she wound up doing nearly all the talking before I invited her to the Island. She came from Toronto. She told me about herself and all the dudes back in Toronto—Peter, Marvin, Larry, Sam, et al. She talked about how she was once a seconal freak and how she knew every junkie and speed freak in Toronto, but how those dudes made for a bad scene. A seventeen-year-old woman of the world, she was so convincing, she was *too* convincing. But since I was speeding and she had a pretty face, nothing she was saying both-

181

ered me. In fact, I decided I dug her. "I feel sorry for dudes," she said at one point. "They have to bend way out of their way to get a chick. Chicks don't have to do that. Like if I stand in the Last Chance for five minutes, I have more dudes than I can handle." I could see that Wendy was not unusually perceptive or aware—okay, so she wasn't the most together chick—but I was digging her. After all, she doesn't have to pass a psychological, does she?

We arranged to meet Wendy and Darlene in front of the Last Chance at eleven the next morning, Tuesday morning. Now Frank and I both felt optimistic. I figured Wendy might even lift my mind off Miki.

Leaving the crowd at Miki's, we stayed in the Beatty Street Armory that night, the night before we left.

John and I were talking with the kid on the bottom half of bunk sixty-seven, the bunk next to mine. He was fifteen, and this was his first time away from his home in Winnipeg. He was a funny kid. His hair was stringy and greasy and parted too close to his left ear. It swept across his forehead and rested on the frame of his glasses when he pushed it back with his hand. Other times it fell behind his glasses. I figured that he preferred not to see a lot of the time. Anyway, John had to get his toothbrush from his knapsack, so we took the kid outside to show him the van. He was impressed.

"Wow, you've got this set up real neat," he said. "Wow, beds and music—everything! Wow, neat cartoons and posters, too."

"It's okay," I said. "I liked the last one better, though, didn't you, John?"

"Right, the last one was one of the best."

"Whuddya mean last one?" the kid asked.

"The last van, the last van we had."

"Ya mean you had another van that was better than this?"

"Sure, man, it's boring when you trip around in the same old van all the time."

"Wow . . . wow . . ."

182

"And I dig the part where we turn other people on to vans, don't you, John?"

"Right, man, the joy of giving," John said, trying to make it seem that he was laughing out of joy or something.

"Wait, ya mean you give people buses like this and they don't have to pay you?" the kid said, catching on quickly.

I had nothing better to do, so I gave the kid a rap about a club that John and I belonged to that was set up by an eccentric millionnaire who had nothing better to do than give away vans to travelers. Few people actually belonged to the club, but once you were in, your membership was secure.

"The only rule they enforce is that you have to give away your latest van to somebody who will genuinely appreciate it after you're tired of it. Then the president of the club will send through a form so that you get your next van."

The kid kept shaking his head and saying wow. Then he eyed me through his oversized horn-rimmed glasses and said, "No shit, you really give away buses like this?"

"No shit," I said. "Most people don't believe me."

He thought about it for a minute and then said, "Ya think I could get into this club?"

"Well, there's an awfully long waiting list, you understand."

"Then d'ya think you could give me one of these vans? I'd really appreciate it."

"Actually, we're not tired of this one yet," I drawled. "But when we do get bored with it, I'll remember you, man."

21

The van wound up being packed with a larger crew than any of us had expected before we set out for Vancouver Island at noontime Tuesday. Although I had decided it was foolish to count on Wendy and Darlene making it, they were standing next to sleeping bags and knapsacks in front of the Last Chance at eleven sharp. From there, we went to pick up Matthew and Jainie. Since Jainie had not finished preparing salads and sandwiches, we had time to kill. I went to the bathroom to discreetly snort the rest of my methedrine. Then I helped everybody pack the van. Frank and I set a plywood board between the two beds in the back and covered it with a long cushion so that the entire back of the van was like a king-sized bed. With most of our gear stored under that bed, seven of us drove away to pick up the eighth and last member of our crew, Matthew's friend, Tim.

At the start of the trip, everybody was rather quiet, listening to my tape selections. In the front seat next to Frank, I thumbed through the tape collection in search of speedy music, and I played a Led Zepplin tape.

The ferry was an hour or two away. I took off my headphones once in a while to assist Frank with the directions. I was speeding; the intricacies of maps fascinated me.

At the dock for the ferries, we had to wait on a long line of cars. The line was so long that the ferry was filled before it was our turn to drive on board. Well, at least we were second in line for the next ferry. I took off the headphones when the tape ended, and I sensed the impatience of other members of the crew.

The impatience was of the type that brings people to invent car games, either word games or guessing games. I was more in the mood to listen to loud Led Zepplin.

But Frank thought of a game and needed the tape deck to play it. He dug through a storage box in the back of the van and found a microphone to attach to the tape deck. Then he found a blank tape. He plugged the mike into the tape machine and put on the blank tape. He switched the machine on to record.

"Good afternoon, ladies and gents, this is Friendly Frank's Freak Van and today we have a very special show to bring to y'all, an . . . unusual show. We're here today to bring y'all a special Freak Van interview with Steve Gibbons who I'm sure y'all have heard of. Steve . . . what have y'all got to say for yourself today?"

Frank was speaking into the mike in a mock radio announcer voice. I felt embarrassed by his clumsy effort to fool around. On the other hand, I admired any attempt to invent a way to have fun, so I played along with his game.

"Uuuuuuughaiiiiiiioooooooach!" I sounded into the mike.

"That there's a smart idea, Mr. Gibbons," Frank said. "Now we're looking over the rest of the Freak Van to see if we see other celebrities. And here's one now. We now have with us Matthew McLeod!"

"Hey, Frank, why doncha go out and interview some of the straight people in them other cars," Matthew said.

"Far out. I'll be right back, folks," Frank said into the mike.

Everybody in the van was hysterical. Frank, meanwhile, kept a straight face as he unscrewed the tape machine from its platform under the dash.

"Ya can tell 'em you're from KVAN radio news and ya wanna know what they think about the news that the last ferry just sunk and killed all the passengers," Matthew added.

Frank tucked the tape machine under his arm and stepped out of the van.

"Frank is so open to suggestion," Matthew laughed.

I jumped out of my side of the van and ran around to hold the tape machine. I stood back with the machine as Frank approached the car to the left of our van. He stretched the cord so that the mike was as near to that car as it would go.

"Good afternoon, y'all in there, this is KVAN radio and our listeners would like to know what y'all have to say about waiting for this ferry."

The driver rolled up his window and honked as Frank finished his statement.

Then we tried the car to the right of the van. We passed the tape machine through the front of the van to get it as near as possible to the car. Frank repeated his question, this time to a woman who was at the wheel of a large station wagon full of kids.

"I didn't hear you," she said.

Frank repeated his question. This time she heard him and she laughed. She gave us no answer, but she was friendly.

The cord attached to the tape machine was too short to reach the cars in front and in back of us, so we hopped back into our van to play what we had recorded.

"Didja hear that story they had on the radio last month?" Matthew asked me as Frank screwed the tape machine back onto its platform. "That one about the guy who was running around terrorizing the suburbs. He kept breaking into these middle-class straight people's houses, but he didn't rob anything from 'em. Instead he'd take a shit under a pillow in the bedroom. Can ya imagine that?"

"Are you shitting me, man?" I said.

186

"I dunno 'bout you, but I supported the guy."

Just then, Frank switched the tape machine to play.

"oooooooach!"

The sound blasted at top volume. Then Frank switched the machine to rewind again, and then back to play.

". . . unusual show. We're here today to bring y'all a special . . ."

"I don't sound like that, do I?" Frank said, slightly dismayed.

"Frank, nobody ever thinks he sounds like the sound of his voice on a tape recorder," I said.

But then some of my voice came on after my obscene noise, and I thought that maybe this *was* a faulty tape player. I winced.

"I see you don't dig the way your voice sounds either, Stevie," Jainie laughed from the back of the van. "It's so funny to watch people's faces when they hear a tape of their own voice, boy. Everyone thinks their voice sounds fucked up just because it sounds different from what they're used to hearing."

Then Matthew's voice came on the tape.

"I think Matthew talks fucked up whether he's on or off the tape," I said.

I can't explain what made me say that; it simply came to mind and I said it. Then I wished I hadn't. Matthew looked hurt and he made no quick comeback.

"What a fucked-up thing to say," Jainie said. "You've been acting like a shit all day, for the last few days as a matter of fact. I wonder if I like you at all anymore, Stevie."

I deserved it, but I was left feeling downcast. Also, I was unable to figure out what other shitty things I'd been doing. But I didn't want to ask Jainie about it, so I was left wondering. An uneasy silence filled the van for a few minutes until Matthew broke it.

"If I could get one thing 'bout myself changed, I'd add four inches to my height but stay at this same weight," Matthew said. "I think I'm gonna get new heels fer these boots."

We laughed. Matthew was not one to act hurt and sulky.

Between the price of the ticket for the van and the price of all

187

the individual passenger tickets, the ferry ride cost more than twenty dollars. After paying that, Frank drove us into the lowest level of the ferry. It resembled a greasy New York City parking lot. That level was hot and gloomy, so we immediately climbed three flights of stairs to the top level of the ferry.

I felt liberated at the top. My hair was blown back by the cold wind. Wendy, who along with Darlene and Tim had spoken little on our way to the boat, stood next to me against the railing. "Wow, it sure is windy," she said. It sure was, Wendy. The wind seemed to have scattered our crew into pairs that blew to different places on the deck. At that point, it was me and Wendy, Frank and Darlene, John and Jainie, Matthew and Tim. Few other passengers were on the deck with us because it was cold. Most of the passengers remained inside the enclosed part of the ferry where dark wooden benches, a lunch counter, and book and magazine stands made possible a comfortable trip.

By the time the boat launched itself to begin the journey, most of our crew were inside and exploring the ferry. Wendy and I bumped into Matthew and Tim at the lunch counter inside the enclosed section of the top level. They were buying vanilla milkshakes. Matthew and Tim took their drinks to a booth next to the window, and we joined them.

"Wanna taste?" Matthew offered, pointing at me with the plastic straw that stood in his milkshake.

"No, man, no thanks."

The idea of drinking something that thick and rich repelled me. But I did think of something I wanted. I got up and walked to the lunch counter for a moment to buy a pack of gum. I started chewing two sticks. When I returned to the booth, Wendy was sipping Matthew's shake. She licked her lips with a coated tongue.

"Where didja stash yer MDA? Ya ain't carrying it around in yer pocket, are ya?" Matthew asked.

"Don't sweat about it," I said. "We won't get busted. Frank and I hid our stashes behind the paneling in the van."

"It'll be a real gas to do that on the beach, eh?"

188

"Sure will," I said. "I think the city was getting my head down in a bad way."

"Have ya ever shot MDA?" Matthew asked me.

"No, have you?"

"Yep, I did it the first time last month. It's a whole other trip. When ya first start to rush, ya think everything's melting and yer gonna die fer sure. But then ya start digging the rush. I ain't never had a rush like it."

"Anything like speed?" I asked.

"Oh no, not at all," Tim said.

"I got a fit downstairs if ya wanna try it when we get on the beach," Matthew said.

"Great!" I said. "Hey, you think it would be cool if I did it now?"

"Sure, if ya wanna do it."

"Could you hit me?"

"Sure."

We went downstairs to the van after they finished their milk-shakes. Tim left us at the second level to look at the magazine rack.

"I'd probably miss if I hit myself," I told Matthew when we were in the van.

Actually, I had never hit myself before. And I wouldn't have known the best way to do it because I had always averted my eyes during the few times people had injected me with dope in the past. Not that I needed to mention anything about it, Matthew was eager to hit me up.

Lighting was poor inside the van since the parking lot level of the ferry lacked windows. Matthew took a few minutes looking for the needed equipment: the fit, a cord, a spoon and a water bottle.

"Maybe I should hit you," Wendy said. "I'm an expert hit. I never miss."

"Matthew knows what he's doing," I said.

I sat in the driver's seat after taking a cap of MDA out of my stash. Matthew sat in the other front seat and used the plastic cap that covered the needle to stir the MDA in half a spoonful of

189

water. The syringe was the disposable plastic kind. The few other times people had hit me up, they had used eyedroppers—home-fashioned syringes made with a point and a glass eyedropper. Anyway, the end result would be the same.

Matthew touched the point of the syringe to the solution in the spoon and gently pulled up on the flagger, the plastic plunger. When all of the solution had been sucked into the body of the syringe, he turned it point-end-up and gently snapped his middle finger against the syringe to tap air bubbles to the top. Then he pushed on the flagger so that the air went out through the point and a tiny bit of solution squirted out behind it.

Meanwhile, I was bending my arm and snapping it out straight as though I were doing curls with an imaginary dumbbell. When I saw the veins beginning to protrude, I choked the arm just above the elbow with the white cord so that the veins bulged like blocked-up hoses. Wendy was making me feel self-conscious by the way she was watching the ritual so intently.

It must have been getting on Matthew's nerves, too, but he didn't show it. Wendy watched over my shoulder as Matthew held my arm steady in his left hand and prodded the most prominent vein with the needle. I felt the slight prick as it broke through the skin. The needle was short and shining new. I could see its outline buried inside my vein. Then he pulled very gently back on the flagger. A bubble began to appear inside the plastic wall of the syringe.

"Ah, you missed!" Wendy exclaimed. "You should've let me do it for you in the first place, Steve. I told you I never miss."

Wendy's outburst made Matthew jittery as he slid the needle back out of my arm. Then he sat back in his seat and rubbed his forehead with the back of his hand.

"Give me that fit. Let me do it," Wendy said.

I was annoyed at her for making Matthew uneasy, but I let her hit me because I was weary of the suspense. Matthew and she traded places. Matthew did not seem anxious for me to give him a second try.

Wendy went through the same procedure as Matthew did, even did it at the same pace, and she maintained the air of a professional. She watched the point like a metalworker watching his drill press. When she pulled back on the flagger when the needle was again inside my vein, a bit of blood trickled into the fit. It had registered. The blood mixed with the smoky MDA solution to form a red cloud. Wendy slowly pushed the flagger down until all but a drop of blood had disappeared into my arm.

The rush hit me. It was like a four-hour MDA high that had been compressed into a few minutes. All the power, all the distortion, like an orgasm, it jolted my mind and body.

It tapered off . . .

"I told you I never miss," Wendy said as she cleaned up after us. "I've hit half the junkies in Toronto and you can ask any of them. I never miss."

Nobody congratulated her; she was obviously able to do that for herself.

Once I was able to walk easily again, we went back upstairs to air ourselves out on the deck. We met Jainie, John and Tim on a bench outside.

"Hi, baby," Matthew said.

"Don't even tell me what you guys have been doing because I don't want to hear about it, okay?" Jainie said.

It was understood.

"We've been trying to figure something out up here," John said. "We're trying to figure out if those sea gulls are flying as fast as this boat is cruising, or if they are just taking a ride in the boat's atmosphere. And then if the boat does have an atmosphere, Jainie wants to know how far out it reaches."

I looked at the gulls.

"I know the answer, but I forgot the scientific explanation for it," John said.

I had assumed we would reach our destination before dark. I suppose the word "island" had made me think of a place about the size of Manhattan Island. But night had fallen by the time the ferry dropped us off on the eastern coast of Vancouver Island, and we still had to drive two or three hours to get where we were going, Long Beach.

We packed ourselves into the van, in a different order this time, and the van party continued. We were crammed into the back like a package of hot dogs, with John against the back end and Wendy next to him and me next and then Jainie and Matthew and Tim. Frank was driving with Darlene next to him.

Half an hour of driving passed and Frank suggested we open one of the gallon bottles of wine he had brought with us. It was exactly what I needed. The spit in my mouth had bunched together into foamy pellets; I wanted to spit, but I wasn't quite vulgar enough to sit with seven other people and blow sticky gobs into a jar. Anyway, the wine washed it down. I passed the jug to Wendy, and she passed it to John. For the next twenty miles, the wine circulated around the back of the van. Finally, after all the others said they were sufficiently smashed, I stationed the bottle in my lap.

Inside the van was dark. Occasionally, another car would sneak behind us with its bright lights, like a guard shining his flashlight into the cell to check on a sleeping prisoner. All the cars seemed to attack with their high beams. I suppose they figured that they could leave their high beams gleaming since the traffic on the single-lane highway was light at that time of night. The bastards. Those cars were making me feel like I was being forcibly transported to someplace I wouldn't like, a jail or a concentration camp, not a sunny beach. It was enough to make me feel like taking over the wheel of the van to run some of them off the road.

I tried to dull the edge of the MDA/methedrine crash by drinking more wine, but my teeth continued grinding like mismatched gears. My jaw muscles ached, particularly when I opened my mouth. I wouldn't stick my tongue out for fear I might bite it off. I pressed my tongue against the backs of my teeth; the tongue felt like a prisoner. Maybe we should stop, I thought. Maybe I could get some sleep if I were inside my sleeping bag at the side of the road instead of being cramped inside the van. When I die, I hope they at least build a coffin that is long enough for my legs. I sat up so that the small of my back was pressed against the paneled wall of the van. My head had to bend forward to do it, but at least my legs were stretched. Now if I could only do the same thing with my jaws . . .

Matthew and Jainie, on my right, were half asleep already, or else in a drunken stupor. Their eyes were shut part of the time, anyway. Their heads were rested on the cushion and their four legs were folded and tangled among each other. It looked uncomfortable to me, but at least they were on their way to sleep.

I closed my eyes. Then I became too conscious of them, and I felt vulnerable. There they were, bulging out of the middle of my face, inside their elastic sockets: two big crushable spheres. Open the eyelids again! Think about the jaws! I'd rather let the tightness of my jaws vex me. Not the eyes.

John and Wendy were smiling and smashed on my left. I couldn't hear what they were talking about behind the droning of the van. Anyway, I wasn't interested. It was undoubtedly some horseshit. John was putting the make on her. He was drunk and probably saying anything that came to his head so that he wouldn't have to sleep alone that night. Those beaches get deathly cold. Crashed out on speed, a person can get to feeling awfully alone.

Which was my reason for going to the trouble of inviting Wendy. I was bringing her for me. From the start, it was plain: Wendy went with me and Darlene went with Frank. Frank was now in the driver's seat, keeping the sound droning, with Darlene next to him. But I was in the back, suffering both the discomfort of being jammed into a crowd and the sadness of being alone.

Sadness, horseshit, I was pissed. John looked cozy lying on the cushion with Wendy snuggled next to him. There he was, next to me, blatantly putting me down, kissing my chick, stealing from me for the night. He wasn't *that* drunk. He knew what he was doing. And I wasn't that stupid. I knew what he was saying. It wasn't so much the fact that he took my chick; I was angry about his mo-

193

tives behind it. He was doing it to show *me* where it was at. This was the ultimate putdown. How blindly stoned did he think I was? John was supposed to be my best friend, my partner, and now he was telling me this? *Fuck you, Steve Gibbons, you think you're so hot; well, I can take from you any chick you think that you've got.*

That was it. I had hit it. I *was* alone. Painful as it is to face the truth, it must be faced. No partner, no true friend would do this to me. I was angry, but I wouldn't hit him. No point in hitting him just because I had realized a truth in my life. I would restrain myself. I would simply tell him.

I tapped John's shoulder and whispered harshly into his ear: "We're splitting up, you filthy prick."

I could sense John's shock right away. He sat up and looked at me, but I wouldn't give him the satisfaction of meeting his eyes.

The next thing I knew, John was crawling over the row of bodies between him and the front of the van. He said something to Frank. Wendy was staring at me, but I wouldn't look at her either. I was as furious as ever, but I was also confused by whatever trick John was pulling. People were opening their eyes as John crawled over their bodies again. When he was back at my end of the van, he sat there quietly for a minute. Was he waiting for me to say something? I had already said it. Then John moved his head closer to me so I could hear him speaking in a low voice.

"I told Frank to pull over at the next town," he said.

"What's the point?" I said, still refusing to look him in the eye, and angry that he was pulling a trick like this.

"If we're splitting up, we're doing it now."

"Not yet. We'll talk about it later. Now I'm so pissed . . ."

"I'm not waiting. If we're splitting up, we're splitting up. I'm not taking suspense."

I was still angry, but the idea that John was leaving scared me. I didn't want him to go yet. We would talk about it later. I was too confused to discuss it now. I wasn't sure; maybe John wasn't deliberately putting me down. I wasn't positive enough of anything to talk. If I talked in this condition, anybody might bullshit me into

194

believing them. But, of course, John wouldn't bullshit me like that. Even if he did put me down, I knew him well enough to know he wouldn't try to con me like that. Maybe I should ask him. Maybe he was unaware of what he was doing to my head. I wasn't sure, so I could not let him leave yet. Maybe it was a dream, all happening inside my own head. If I judged it wrongly—if I was the fool—how could I explain it to him? Maybe we should talk now whether I liked it or not, I thought.

I looked at John. Tears were running down his face. He began the crawl to the front of the van again. What was happening hit me. I grabbed his shoulder.

"Wait, man, don't go yet. We'll talk about it."

"What are you doing? Just what the fuck do you think you're doing?" John was crying.

I pulled John back and hugged him so he wouldn't go. I talked as fast as I did the time I apologized to the guy I punched out for no reason in Vancouver. But this time I was talking to my friend.

"Forget what I said, man. I'm fucked up. You don't know what I was thinking. I worked this whole thing up in my head that you were putting me down."

"Just what the fuck do you think you're doing?" John repeated.

"We can't split up now. We're just getting started. We're friends. We shouldn't let a slut like this get in the way of our friendship. We started it together, we're going to finish it together, you and me, man, right?"

John was upset and not saying anything, so I went on talking for about five minutes, trying to get him to say he would stay.

"We'll stick together, man. I was just being stupid, getting jealous about that chick 'cause I dig her. You don't know her, man, I talked with her yesterday and she's fucked up, but I don't know why, but I dig her. But you can have her, man, she's yours. You won her. You're the better man. I want you to have her. Take her tonight, dig her."

"What makes me the better man because I'm with her?" John muttered.

195

"You're right, neither of us is the better man," I answered quickly, ready to agree with anything. "We're just great together. We're a team. John and Steve. We're going to keep on going, man, we're not going to let this slut split us up."

"You're really blowing my mind, Steve," Wendy said. "I don't know what's happening but if you think I'm coming on to John to split you two up . . ."

I hadn't thought anybody was listening to me, but Wendy was there so I had to deal with her.

"Right. Right. I understand. You dig John. He's yours. Everything's cool. We're all going to the beach together."

John now must have been as confused as I had been. But what counted was that he was staying with me—with us—and the van party was continuing.

When Frank stopped the van at the exit for the next town, I shouted to him to move on because John was coming to the beach with us.

At that point, Jainie said, "Good." Other than that, nobody said anything about it. Frank must have been more baffled than any of us.

Anyway, one thing made sense: I needed to take a piss or burst. So I asked Frank to pull the van to the side of the road for that reason. He said he also needed to piss, but that we should wait until we were well away from the town.

Frank parked the van at the roadside just in time. He, John and I climbed out. He and John went to the edge of the woods along the roadside while I stood in back of the van, waiting for the piss. The night air felt refreshing, especially since I was not wearing a shirt. My kidneys ached, and the urine took a long time to come out. I looked up at the millions of stars. Then I looked down at my bare feet on the pavement. I was standing at the edge of the empty highway.

A car was headed toward me, coming closer as I pissed. The headlights grew bigger and brighter. Then high beams flashed into my eyes like the flashgun of a camera. The bastards, I lifted my cock to aim my urine at them. The car was slowing. The headlights were spotlights. I was blinded. The car must have been near enough for me to hit it, but I was out of ammunition. I buttoned my fly.

It was a cop car.

Two cops stepped out of opposite sides of the car. They were both six feet tall. They walked toward me from two directions, cornering me against the van. As soon as I recognized that they were cops, I clasped my hands over my head.

"What are you doing?" one said belligerently.

"I'm taking a piss, sir."

"Can't you walk to the side of the road like your friends?"

"It was an emergency, sir."

Frank and John came back from the woods and flanked me on both sides. I felt more secure.

"Who's the driver here?" the first cop asked.

"I am, officer," Frank said.

"Show me your license and registration."

Frank took his wallet out of his pocket, and the cop shined his flashlight on the license and registration.

"How long have you been in this country?"

"Almost a month," Frank answered just as I said, "Two days—if you count today."

"We'll get to you," the cop told me. Then he asked Frank, "What do you do in Florida?"

Frank told him about his leather shop.

Then the first cop turned to John and me and told us to show him our ID. We went into the van, told everybody there not to worry, and then came back with our wallets.

"What do you do in New York?" the cop asked John.

John told him that he was a writer.

"What about you?" the cop addressed me.

"I'm a bum."

"No need to tell me that. I can see."

"We're just going to the beach for a short vacation," Frank said. "We're trying to obey the law."

"Don't you know it's illegal to drink and drive?"

197

"Yes, officer, but I haven't been drinking. Steve, here, is the only one who's had a little too much to drink."

"A little too much, eh?" the second cop said sarcastically. "Hey, what are you doing, anyhow?"

"Doing, sir?"

"Yeah, why the hands on the head?"

"I thought it would help your job, sir. You don't need to worry about me trying anything, sir."

"I think he's trying to air out his BO," the second cop said.

"Yes, sir, this does help me control my BO problem, sir."

"Well, it don't help us any," the second cop snickered. "Hey, what's he stoned on, anyway?"

"Steve? He just had a little too much to drink is all," Frank said.

"Don't give me that."

"It's MGA, sir. Too much MGA," I said.

"What?"

"MGA—mud, garbage and . . . acorns. A pleasant high, sir."

"All right, we're taking him in."

Jainie walked up next to me. "What's happening?" she asked.

"Steve's getting busted," John said.

"What for?" Jainie said indignantly.

"Don't give us trouble or we'll take in the whole carload of you," the first cop said, grabbing my elbow.

"Well, at least let me get his jacket. He looks so cold," Jainie said and ran into the van.

"We'll call about bail tomorrow, Steve. You'll hear from us," John said.

The cops were leading me to their car when Jainie came back with my jacket. Jainie stopped them and helped me put my leather on. Then she hugged me and kissed me and said, "Don't worry, Stevie, we'll get you out. We love you."

That made the cop angry. They pulled me by the arm and said to everybody else, "All of you, get into your truck before we take you all in."

With the rest of my crew inside the van, the second cop shoved me into the back of the cop car. Then he tried to put handcuffs onto my wrists. The metal claws of the cuffs pinched me and I squirmed. So he slugged me in the mouth. I tasted the blood. I began thrashing and tried to punch the cop back. He was now holding tightly onto my wrists. I kicked him in the knee, and he hit me again. Then I saw Jainie over the cop's shoulder, pulling him back by the material of his uniform. He whipped around. All seven members of my crew were standing around him like a posse that had come to get him. He put his hand to his gun handle.

"All right, all of you get back! Go back to your truck. I'm not going to hurt him. I'm trying to put the cuffs on him."

All eyes were fixed on the handle of that gun as they backed off and went back into the van. Then the cop slapped the cuffs on my wrists and slammed the door shut. He sat in the front seat next to his partner who was driving. They drove the cop car away before Frank drove his van away.

Along the dark highway, the second cop punched me from the front seat a few times until he thought I was unconscious.

But I wasn't unconscious.

When they least expected it, I seized the driver's shoulders and yanked back. The car began to veer off the highway, but the cop was an amazingly skillful driver. He maintained control of the car while his partner punched me one last time—hard—in the face.

Then I was out.

22

I woke up Wednesday morning to find my body on the cell floor, feeling like a sack of sand that had been dumped there. I recalled trying to piss on the cop car and fighting with the cops. And then I remembered the worst of it: that horrible paranoiac nightmare I'd had about John putting me down. I had told John we were splitting up. But my memory would go no further than that. I tried, but I couldn't remember whether or not I had straightened it out with John. I remembered wanting to straighten it out, but had I succeeded? Or would I never hear from him again?

Let me out of this hole!

I was locked in Port Alberni. My fellow prisoners were mostly Indians. They got worse treatment than I did, most of them bruised and scabby when I saw them.

Matter of fact, the cops were hospitable to me after I was inside their jail. They put food in front of me, and they didn't threaten to hit me.

The cops did threaten me in one way, though. They warned me that I should plead guilty to a misdemeanor of resisting arrest or else they would clout me with half a dozen more charges. This didn't add to my worries. Pleading guilty to misdemeanors had always made sense to me. I knew what to expect. They would deport me to the United States.

No lawyer, no shoes; but my luck in court two days later ran better than I'd expected. I gave the judge an impromptu story about me being a misfortunate New York University student who had come to Canada for his vacation and had gotten himself a bit too drunk for his own good. I told him that my schooling was important to me and that I was scheduled to resume classes in a couple of weeks, on the fourth of September. I threw myself at the mercy of the court. Splat. I passed out at the end of my testimony. That part was no act; I had been unable to sleep or eat in jail. Anyway, his honor figured that I would be the United States' problem within two weeks if he simply released me, so he let me go.

I zipped my jacket over my bare chest and rushed back to Vancouver. The first two lifts were short. Then I caught a ride on the back of a small Yamaha that took me the rest of the way to the ferry. I worked for that ride. The motorcyclist couldn't stop for me. He circled around and around like a merry-go-round next to me, riding as slowly as possible and yelling to me that the bike would stall and maybe not start again if he stopped. If I wanted the ride badly enough, I would have to leap onto the rear of the bike as he passed me, he was telling me. I was getting dizzy from watching his Japanese bike buzz in and out like a lawnmower. The next time it passed me, I lunged in but chickened out before I could jump onto the bike. The biker shouted that he'd try to pass more slowly the next time. It still seemed like he was zipping by at sixty, but I vaulted onto the rear of the bike the next time, feeling like Roy Rogers leaping onto Trigger from the rear because he's got no time to hassle with stirrups. The Yamaha rocked back and forth. My left foot scraped along the pavement.

Near the ferry station, I took a dozen paper towels from a gas station. I spent the next hour sitting bent over on the curb, soaking the blood out of my left foot with paper towels. I was trying to

201

scheme a way to get onto that ferry. But in the end, I didn't need to sneak. A man saw me sitting there, obviously feeling sorry for myself; he gave me money for a ticket, after listening to my tale of woe.

By the time I reached Vancouver, I had told my story to five or ten people, and I was bored with it. Stories, hell, I just wanted some food in my stomach.

My first stop was at Miki's. Nobody was home, so I invaded the refrigerator. Hamburger meat! About a pound and a half of it was waiting for me like a loyal friend. I squashed two mounds onto a skillet. Impatiently, I let it sizzle for a few minutes. I ate it blood rare. It tasted funny, but I hadn't eaten in a long time which might account for that.

Next, I went to Matthew and Jainie's to see if anybody was staying there. The door was wide open. They were home.

"Stevie!" Jainie whooped as I stumbled into the livingroom. "Shit, man, we've been so worried about you. How did you get back here? Everyone else is still back on the Island. John's trying to bail you out. . . ."

John was trying to bail me out. Then everything was cool.

"It's a long story, but I'm out."

"Oh, boy, look at your foot. Your poor foot, let me get something to put on that."

"It's okay. It's mostly healed."

"Well, you should at least wash the scab. I bet you could dig a bath."

"Yeah, later. Right now I want to catch some breath."

"Oh, Stevie, if it makes you feel any better, you didn't miss anything. It was so awful. The first night wasn't so bad. It was funny. We ran out of gas right after those cops busted you, so we all slept inside the van. And Matthew kept us up half the night making noises and telling scary stories. The rest of the trip was shit. You know what we wanted, Stevie; we just wanted people to leave us alone. Well, everybody kept coming to us with their stupid questions. Especially those stupid chicks, those chicks you guys brought along. They were unbelievable, boy. That chick, Wendy: she was totally freaked out because Tim was walking around without his pants. And that fat one, Darlene: she was too much. Every time Matthew and Tim walked down the beach for a while, that chick would say, 'Where are you boys going all by yourself?' I couldn't figure out if they were both really as stupid as they seemed. I never saw such dumb chicks."

Matthew chuckled, "That chick had the hots fer Tim so bad. She almost pinned him on the sand that night."

"That night!" Jainie laughed hysterically. "That was so funny. All those guys had their sleeping bags opened up so that they were sleeping together. But they all had the hots for someone else. Frank was there wrestling around trying to make Darlene while she was trying to make Tim. And Tim was totally unaware of the whole trip. He was lying there next to Darlene and talking to her like nothing was happening. I swear I don't think he even caught on that everybody was practically attacking each other."

"Who was Tim trying to make?" I asked.

Matthew and Jainie caught each other's glances for a moment. Then they burst out laughing.

"John?" I asked.

Then they laughed some more.

Jainie was right; I needed a bath. I went through the kitchen to the bathroom. After taking off my clothes and filling the tub, I sat in the hot water for about fifteen minutes without moving. I was beginning to feel sick to my stomach. I washed my hair with some of the shampoo that was on the corner of the tub. Then I took a piece of broken mirror and Matthew's razor from a shelf above the foot of the tub and I shaved the fuzz off my chin and upper lip. I also trimmed my sideburns so that they stopped about half an inch below my earlobes. Some people told me my face looked angelic. It didn't look angelic to me, though, except maybe around the eyes. I could feel where my nose was crooked from being broken in a few fights. I rubbed with my hand from my nose down to my chin and I felt a couple of pimples around my mouth. I studied them in the broken glass. Then I put it down. Pimples, even just one or two, depressed me. They clashed violently with my personality.

The tub water resembled sewage when I was done. Looking at it made me feel I had accomplished a lot. Then I went back into the livingroom.

Jainie took my pants, my only pair until I could reconnect with Frank's van, and she sewed a couple of rips in them. Now the pants were sturdy, and I felt less like I was falling apart.

By that time, however, I felt violently ill. A sharp pain was stabbing at the inside of my abdomen. I thought that the cops might have poisoned me, but then I remembered that I hadn't eaten any of their food that morning.

Finally, I vomited. I flushed the toilet right away. Then I felt better.

Frank showed up. That evening, while I was in the middle of planning to go back to the Island, he walked through the door with Darlene and Wendy behind him.

"Y'all got out of jail!" Frank exclaimed, after being taken aback upon first seeing me. "What a mix-up. John's out on the Island trying to bail y'all out."

"I guess he can cool it because I'm here."

"Did y'all get our messages? John left messages with the cops the morning after they took y'all in."

"No, man, those fuckers didn't tell me anything."

"Wow, I'm really glad to see y'all are out, Steve. How'd y'all manage it?"

I told an abbreviated version of my story while Frank and the girls sat on the floor to listen.

Then Frank described the Island scene, making it sound wonderful and the opposite of what Jainie had told me earlier. He told Matthew and Jainie that they should have stayed one more night because all the people who were living on the beach got together that night for an enormous celebration. About fifty people, he said, lived in the log huts on that beach. And Frank had brought every-

204

body together, with the help of a friend.

"It was far out. We turned the whole beach on with MDA. Then all the people sat around a hugh campfire and talked and dug on each other. It was beautiful," Frank beamed.

I looked at Wendy and she seemed somewhat indifferent, but Darlene was enthusiastically describing some of the people, particularly a family of kids. It sounded like a commune scene.

"Why'd you leave if you dug it so much?" I asked Frank.

"Well, Darlene here had to come back for some appointment today, and, well, I figured I'd drive back . . . But I'm going right back there tomorrow and y'all are welcome to come."

Frank loved the Island scene, but he was unable at that point in his life to sit still in one place even if he loved it. Anyway, I was happy to get a ride with him.

We talked a while longer at Matthew and Jainie's and tried to convince them to return to the Island with us. But they had had it with that Island.

Then we drove to Miki's. This time, she and Ann were home. Not only that, but they wanted to come with us to the Island the next day. Ann didn't mention what she would do about her job, and I didn't ask.

"Far out," Frank said. "We'll make it another party."

Yeah, I thought, smiling at Miki, who smiled back.

"I want to come, too," Wendy blurted.

"But, Wendy, I thought you said . . ." Darlene began.

"No, I want to go back with them. I'll meet you at your parents' in a week or so."

Darlene glared at Wendy as if to ask what the hell she was doing. But Wendy let the glare bounce off.

"By the way," Miki said. "None of you guys knows what happened to the hamburger meat that was in the refrigerator, eh?"

I looked guilty. "I'm really sorry about that, Miki, but I was starving when I got back here. I hadn't eaten in days."

"You *ate* that meat?"

"Yeah, what's the matter?"

205

"Steve, I got that meat for my dog. The butcher gave it to me free because it was bad."

I managed to keep from vomiting again before going to sleep.

The next morning, we set out once more. I'd better watch out for myself, I thought, or this could get monotonous. But this ride was nothing like the last one. This time, all my attention was focused on Miki. I talked with her on the way to the ferry and on the ferry. Ann sat in the front with Frank on the way and didn't talk much on the boat. But Wendy pried her way into my conversation with Miki at every opportunity.

"I wonder if those gulls have a home on the Island, or one near the city, or if they just keep going all the time," I said to Miki.

"They probably hang around the ferry most of the time," Wendy commented before Miki could speak.

I kept looking at Miki. Then I looked out to the horizon.

"I sure am looking forward to seeing John again, aren't you?" I said to Miki.

"Yes . . ." Miki said.

"I am, too. He loved that beach the last time I saw him just before we left . . ." Wendy said, beginning her lengthy description of John's state of mind.

Then we listened to the water slap the side of the ferry.

"You're really looking fine today, Miki," I said.

Wendy said nothing.

Hostilities were cooking by the time we were driving across the Island. I was sitting in the front seat next to Frank. After a while, Miki climbed over the metal cover on the engine to sit between us. The hot metal was starting to brand Miki's ass, so she wriggled onto the seat next to me.

"Am I bothering you, taking up half your seat, Steve?"

No, ma'am, not at all. I smiled.

"Stop the van, Frank! Stop the van!" Wendy shrieked from the back.

206

Frank pulled over to the side of the highway. Were we about to hit a dog? Or had Wendy misplaced her knapsack on the ferry? The back door opened and Wendy jumped out.

"Where are you going?" I called.

"Anyplace. No one wants me here, so I'm leaving. That's what you want. You don't care what happens to me. You act like I'm nothing."

I hopped out of the van onto the grassy shoulder of the road in time to grab Wendy's elbow. We played tug-of-war. I had to suppress laughter at the mawkish melodrama, but at the same time I didn't want to leave her stranded. A girl crazy enough to initiate a game like this might play it to the end. I yanked her into the van by her arm. Her body snapped back like a whip. But then I was gentle.

"Stay with us, Wendy. Of course we care what happens to you."

She sat on the cushion in the back of the van, rubbing her shoulder and pouting like a brat. Miki said she was sorry if she had put Wendy uptight. She hadn't realized . . . Then I put my arm around Wendy and she calmed down. The scene was still amusing me, and I was even thinking that Wendy was sweet in a crazy way.

I sat in the back with Miki and Wendy for the rest of the ride, thus violating a basic rule of hitchhikers' auto etiquette: Never give your driver a chauffeur complex by leaving him alone in the front of the vehicle. But I was keeping the peace by sitting with Wendy.

We reached our destination a couple of hours after nightfall. Frank turned the van onto a dirt road which we drove on at about twenty miles per hour for half a mile or so. The road became bumpy. We slowed down. The road was winding up and down a series of small but steep hills. "We need a land rover for this, Frank; are you sure we shouldn't park here and walk?" I yelled from the back. Frank said it wasn't much farther. Branches were sweeping both sides of the van. We were passing through a dark funnel.

Finally, we parked. Frank and Miki and Ann gathered their gear. "Aren't y'all coming down?" Frank asked me. I told him I was tired and would prefer to check it out in the morning. They left the van to me and Wendy.

I punched a tape into the tape deck, Rolling Stones' *Let It Bleed*. Then I checked my MDA stash. It was all there, along with the syringe.

"Hey, what do you say we do some MDA?" I said to Wendy.

She shook her head. "Not me. Do some yourself if you like."

"I like. Will you hit me?"

That brought a rise out of Wendy. It was as if I'd suggested we go dancing or on a picnic. She took the fit from my stash and prepared it for the injection. As she busied herself, she talked nonstop about how much everybody loved to get hit by her because she was so skillful. I watched the MDA solution gradually disappear from the spoon. She was a good hit, I admit. She held the syringe in front of my eyes as she tapped out the bubbles. She looked like a scientist studying a test tube. The hard steel was pointed up toward the light on the ceiling of the van. It gleamed like a silver dagger. Then she lowered the syringe and looked at me. I was ready. She put it in. Even that fine point looked thick as it punctured the rubber tube of my vein. I was straining as I pulled the cord tighter around my arm. Wendy pushed the cloudy solution into me. But then she pulled back out so that the solution returned to the syringe. The solution was redder. She slowly pushed it back in. Then she let it slide back out and into the syringe again. She was booting the shot. In, out, in, out . . . I've met junkies who insist booting is a pointless perversity. But what a picnic. Watching that in, out, in, out—watching the color of the solution glow redder with each rise—I was starting to get my rush. It was coming. Wendy emptied all but a drop from the fit and then she pulled it out.

I was still rushing while Wendy talked. She cleaned up after us. I lay back.

Wendy took a long time cleaning, fussing with this and that. It was making me impatient. Finally, I pulled her onto the cushion with me and kissed her. I started to lift her pink pullover. But she was lying rigidly, and it was like trying to take a pullover off a

208

mannequin. I felt more impatient and slightly frustrated. I sat up and quickly pulled off my own clothes. Then I kissed Wendy again and began pulling off her shirt again.

"What are you doing?"

"What do you mean what am I doing? I'm taking your clothes off."

"But it's cold in here."

"So we'll go under sleeping bags."

"It'll still be cold. I want to leave my clothes on."

"You'll be warm. Don't worry about that."

I was too stoned to understand the kind of game she was playing. Anyway, I pulled the shirt off the mannequin body. Then she sat up. Her shoulders were hunched and she wouldn't look at me.

"Stop, Steve, I'm scared."

"What's to be scared of?"

She started crying.

"I'm scared. I'm a virgin. You'll hurt me."

I was incredulous. I paused.

"Look, I won't hurt you."

"Yes you will. You know you will."

Another pause. Now it was left up to me. Either I do it or I don't. My body was greedy and surging with MDA. Wendy cried louder as I pulled off her jeans. Then she scurried to the back corner of the van and put up her knees to hide her face.

"Stop, Steve, I'm scared."

There was nothing I could do but try to be gentle. I was bored with chasing her around the van. I pulled her back onto the middle of the cushion.

A past conversation with Matthew. "I can't understand whatcha dig 'bout busting virgins," he said. "Man, you can't deny that it's one of the ultimate ego trips," I said. "Yer a sadist if I ever seen one." "I am not, Matthew. You can understand it, how much a chick digs you for it." "Bullshit. Ya ask any chick who's into sex what she thinks of her first ball. They all say it was the worst." "That's if they don't have an orgasm. But there's no greater ego

209

trip than knowing you gave a chick her first orgasm." "And knowing it won't be her last," Matthew laughed.

That night I practically had to rape Wendy. It was a drag.

The next morning, she wouldn't let me go anywhere without her.

23

Living on Vancouver Island was a fantasy. And it seemed to be a happy one for most of the community of travelers who had set their gear down on that beach.

The beach outlined Wreck Bay. It was U-shaped and curved subtly for about a mile. At any point on the U, you could see an island that looked nearby, but was actually many miles from all points on shore. At the bottom of the U, where the community centered itself, the beach was backed by wooded cliffs, on top of which the people parked their vehicles. But you could not see the cars or our van from the sand. The beach was in a wild state. At the foot of the thickly greened cliffs, hundreds of logs cluttered the sand. They must have drifted there during the winter from a northern logging camp. The tide had left them scattered in disorderly heaps, forming obstacle courses between the cliffs and the shore. Many logs leaned on other logs to form shaky seesaws. The arrangement was often deceptive. You might step onto a log that looked secure and find yourself wobbling, or worse, the log might spin on its fulcrum to flip you onto the sand.

Anyway, these logs were essential to the life-style of the beach community. In the midst of chaotic wood piles, people had constructed about thirty log huts of varying sizes and designs. Log tables and benches added classy touches to some of the huts. The logs were also burned and cooked over and sat around at night. They also formed bridges across the fresh spring water stream that flowed from the cliffs into the salty bay.

Wendy hit me up with a couple of caps of MDA early in the morning. Then she led me like a blind man down the steep path to the foot of the cliff, gripping my arm and talking to me as I watched everything but my step. Without looking at myself, I could feel sunshine bursting through the leaves to paint bright patterns all over my body.

I took the lead on the beach, absently pulling Wendy along as I looked for John. People smiled cheerfully as they passed and I smiled back. The community seemed like an entire city, which I had to search to find my friend.

We came across Tim first. He looked different, sitting on a log stirring a pot of beans over a fire. The only change I could pinpoint was that his beard was growing in. But the change went beyond that. I supposed it was mostly that I had associated Tim with the city and here he was apparently very much a part of this beach community.

I stood so that my body cast a shadow over his head. He looked up.

"Is this your place?" I asked.

He recognized me. Then he nodded. I could tell he also recognized from my shaking that I was stoned.

"Do you know where John is?" I asked.

"He's visiting with the family in the place in back of here," Tim said, indicating the direction with his hand.

Wendy and I climbed across a pile of logs to get to the hut on

212

the other side of Tim's. This hut was elaborate, with a plastic-covered roof and a camp area which was neatly surrounded by logs, like a corral. On one of those logs, a man was sitting with thin legs crossed as he whittled a hand-sized slab of wood. I spoke to the top of his brown cap on which was embroidered a simple, yellow flower design.

"Excuse me, do you know where John is?"

He looked up for a moment before responding. He had a gray walrus mustache and a weathered face.

"John, you mean the tall fellow, John?"

I nodded vigorously.

"He left here only a minute ago to fill a water jug. Said he'd be right back. Your name Steve by any chance?" He spoke calmly.

"That's me," I said, sitting with Wendy on the log across from him.

"We've heard quite a lot about you. You were put in jail on your way out here, is that right?"

"Yeah, right," I nodded, happy to discover I had achieved a degree of fame.

"You've known John a long time, is that right?" he asked me, still carving.

"Man, I've known John all my life."

"I remember. He said that to me. Well, you two must have stories to tell."

"We sure do," I said, shaking my knees up and down and feeling impatient.

The man rubbed his slab of wood with a piece of sandpaper and then inspected it. Then he handed it across to me.

"Well, there you have a spreading utensil of sorts."

I weighed the wood in my hand and rubbed its smooth surface with my thumb. The wood was hard and dark and it felt like ivory. I was amazed that a man who barely knew me would give me such a handsome present.

"You just made this and you're giving it to me?" I said.

The man was taken aback for a moment, during which I realized

213

that he had intended only to show the utensil to me, not give it to me. Then he said, "Well, if you'll find a use for it, it's yours."

I was embarrassed as I gave it back to him, but I appreciated his offer.

"I think I'm going to try to find John now," I said. "What's your name, for when I see you again?"

"I'm Graham. Do you know where the spring water begins?"

"No, is it far?"

"Not far, just follow the stream up the hill and you'll find a pipe sticking out of the cliff."

Wendy and I walked along logs next to the stream. At one of the log bridges, people were bathing in the spring water. I almost fell in at a few points. Then I spotted John coming down the cliff, a sight for stoned eyes. He saw me.

"Steve!" he called as he trotted up to us. "Miki told me you got here last night. I was wondering when you'd be coming down."

I grinned and sat on the log, shaking my knees up and down. John sat on the log across from me with his legs dangling. His expression changed to a more sober one.

"You look zonked."

"I am zonked, man. I'm so stoned . . ."

My words faded and there was quiet. I knew something was wrong because it was an uneasy silence. John looked different, as had Tim. He was wearing his usual clothes, jeans and a work shirt, but with his bare feet and a jug of water resting on the log next to him, he almost looked like a farm boy.

"Doesn't John look like he fits here," Wendy finally said.

"Yeah, you do, man." I nodded.

"It's a nice place," John said.

More silence. This was the first time I could remember feeling that John and I had nothing to say to one another. I was uptight. We sat for a few more minutes, with me quickly getting depressed. Finally, John said he was going to take the water to Graham's hut.

We followed him. He set down the jug next to one of the log benches and sat down. After a while of hovering around with noth-

214

ing to say, I went with Wendy back up to the van. I felt scared in a peculiar way. Wendy hit me up with a couple more caps of MDA.

That afternoon, I met Graham's family. Between him and his wife, Kathleen, they had four kids, three of them Graham's and one Kathleen's. Graham's kids were Geoffrey, twelve; Daisy, seven; and Tommy, six. They were nice kids, though Daisy was a bit of a showoff, running around rolling her own cigarettes and smoking them. But the one with whom I was most impressed was Kathleen's twelve-year-old son, Michael. He seemed extraordinarily loose for his age. He looked like any healthy twelve-year-old except that his thick brown hair fell to the middle of his back. He was wearing an Indian headband. He looked like a boy, but naturally most boys and girls of that age can pass for either sex if their parents don't force them into crew cuts or pink ruffles. So Wendy kept whispering to me, "Is that a boy or a girl?" I wanted to step on her face because she was giggly and whispering loudly enough for Michael to hear her. But it didn't faze Michael. He was much cooler than Wendy. He was cooler than me, for that matter.

Graham passed out bowls of hot millet to his family and to anybody else who wanted some. John and Tim each took a bowl, and Miki took a taste out of Tim's bowl. I wasn't hungry. I was thinking about what it would have been like if I had been raised in a family like this one. I liked my own family and didn't really know this one, but these kids plainly lived under less restrictions, less impositions than I had to live with at their ages. I wanted to talk with Michael.

After the meal, most of us meandered toward the shoreline. Wendy skipped into the water and frolicked like a dog. I could tell from the cold wet sand beneath my bare feet that the water was too cold for swimming. John and Tim sat against a log. I stood staring at Miki, who was gazing at Wendy and out to sea.

Miki was a girl out of her element. She was wearing high-heeled suede boots while everybody else was barefooted. She looked

215

down to the sand beneath her feet. Then she dug her heels into the damp sand. She etched big letters into it before the tide washed the letters away. MIKI. Swish, and it was gone. Again, she dug her heel into the sand, this time more deeply. MIKI. The new letters were fancier. And it took two of the gentle waves this time to erase the word completely.

I was still watching Miki as I sat on the sand next to Michael with my back to a log.

"Did she come out here with you?" Michael asked.

I took a few seconds to figure out that he was referring to Miki. Then I smiled and nodded. I kept looking at Miki.

"I'd sure like to ball her."

I looked at Michael and almost laughed, but then I just said, "Yeah, I know your feeling, man."

"Where are you from?" he asked.

"New York, originally. What about you?"

"I'm from Alabama, I guess, but I've lived in a lot of places."

"That's great. Is that what your family does, move from place to place?"

"Sometimes. Right now we have a kind of commune on the other side of this island."

"Hey, I wonder what that island out there in the bay is called. It looks mysterious, doesn't it? Do you think anybody lives on it?"

"That's an ancient Indian burial ground. No people are allowed on it 'cause they'll bother the spirits."

"Far out," I said, thinking that this kid knew a lot. Then I asked him a question that often annoyed me when people asked it of me. "How does your family support itself? What do you do for money?"

"We don't need much," he began with my usual answer. "Graham had a house in Alabama and we sold that . . ."

"So you're making it for a while on that?"

"Partly. We do some farming, too. Oh, and Graham had some credit cards," Michael laughed. "Some good ones, too. He had one from Penney's."

"You mean fake credit cards?" I said, impressed.

216

"Yes. They were lots of fun, until we were caught."

"How'd they catch you?"

"Oh, we got carried away with ourselves," Michael laughed harder. "We went into Penney's in the first place because it was Geoffrey's birthday. Graham told him he could have anything he wanted, so Geoffrey found this nice watch. So I said, 'Gee, that's a nice watch,' so Graham bought me one, too. Then we kept going. We bought presents for all of us all afternoon. Then the Penney's guy checked out our card."

I laughed along with Michael. Then we both gazed out to sea for a while.

"Did anybody get thrown in jail?" I asked finally.

"No, we got away with it."

That was what counted; how they got away with it didn't matter.

"Why do you shake so much all the time?" Michael asked me.

"I'm kind of stoned."

"What did you do to get like that?"

"MDA."

"I did MDA the first night when Frank brought it down for everyone, and I didn't get like that. I thought it was a love drug."

"How much did you do?" I asked him.

"Half a cap."

"Well, man, that makes all the difference. I've already done about four caps today. And I used a fit; I hit it."

"You mean you shot it with a needle?"

"Right."

"I never did that. Do you do it a lot?"

"I don't know. I guess I've been doing it quite a bit lately."

"Could you show me where you keep your needle, or fit, or whatever you call it?"

"What for?"

"Well, if you show me where it is, I'll break it for ya."

Since I knew I couldn't subsist on sunshine vitamin D and MDA for the rest of my life, I decided to eat before getting high again

217

that evening. I waited a few hours until late afternoon and then asked John if he knew of anyplace where I could find something to eat. John said he had a few cans of beans and soup. But then Miki said Ann had eaten a home-cooked lunch at Frank's hut and there might be food there for all of us. Miki took us there, leading us across the stream and heading north up the beach. On the way, she walked ahead with Wendy. They were laughing a lot, but I wasn't listening to the jokes.

Frank shared a hut with a new friend of his named Nick. When we walked up, Nick was scouring a frying pan with a handful of sand. He was muscular and tanned, wearing only a pair of denim cut-off shorts with a hunting knife at his hip. The hut was as elaborate as Graham's and even more orderly. It also included a camp area that was surrounded by logs. But unlike Graham's open setup, these logs were completely connected in a rectangle that connected to the hut so that visitors had to climb over it to get into Frank and Nick's space. Nick was obviously the neatness fanatic. He was cleaning pots and pans and utensils before eating what he had cooked in them.

"Where's Frank?" John asked.

"In there," Nick said, indicating the hut. I disliked him right away. He wore a yellow handlebar mustache and he had the most unfriendly blue eyes I'd ever seen.

Frank crawled out of the hut with a stack of plates in his hands; he and Nick were preparing to eat next to their fire.

"Hi, Frank, is it cool if we eat here with you?" I asked.

Frank frowned. I was taken aback. After all we'd been through, was he now going to begrudge me a meal? Was everybody turning against me?

"All right, come on in," he said.

I was tempted to tell him to fuck himself if that was his attitude, but I was hungry as a wolf. We all climbed over the log barrier and crawled inside the hut to wait for our supper.

The hut was cool and shady inside. The sand inside was cool, and it seemed different. This hut had plenty of room for the five of us: me, Wendy, Miki, John and Tim. In fact, it was more spacious and had a slightly higher ceiling than Frank's van.

Like a hostile waiter, Nick passed forks and plates of his spicy rice and vegetable mixture to us. He left and we ate quietly. I finished first.

"Man, this is delicious," John yelled out to Nick.

I agreed, but I kept my opinion to myself.

After Miki finished her meal, she whispered something to Wendy. They giggled. They were becoming buddies, and it was causing them to act like little kids around each other, playing games and keeping silly secrets.

"Did you ever notice that Tim never says anything?" Miki giggled.

"That's true. He's very quiet," Wendy agreed.

They tittered. I wasn't catching on to their game, but I didn't worry myself about it. Then I noticed Miki was smirking at John.

John crawled out of the hut and went to sit against a log on the opposite side of the enclosure. "That really was an excellent meal," he said again to Nick.

But he hadn't escaped Miki's smirk. She and Wendy lay down on their stomachs and grinned at him through the entrance of the hut. With their elbows in the sand, they had their heads propped up in their hands like a couple of kids watching television. It seemed silly, so I laughed.

Tim went outside next. He sat next to John and talked with him. The girls giggled and whispered something between each other again. Then they crawled out of the hut and went over to John and Tim. I followed.

Miki and Wendy crouched in front of John and Tim like two kids trying to tease their babysitters.

"Did you ever notice that wherever John goes Tim follows?" Miki said.

"Yes, that's true; you never see one without the other," Wendy agreed.

It was a comment many people had made about John and me.

219

And it made me feel jealous to hear it said about John and some-body else. Of course, Wendy was only saying it to put John up-tight; she was implying that he and Tim were fags. John looked more angry than uptight. In the past, people had suggested to me that John and I were fags. But I never let it put me uptight. I knew they only said it because they wanted to drive a wedge between us. They feared the instant conspiracy that our tight friendship formed. If I did get uptight about what people said, I was put uptight by the idea that somebody was trying to put me uptight. But now I was sad. What had happened to that close friendship?

The sun set us into a pink evening. Even the sand was pink. Cold pink.

"I'm getting my sneakers from the van," I said to Wendy. "This sand's getting too cold."

It was an invitation. She came with me up the cliff to the van. She wasn't a genius, but she knew what I wanted. Inside the van, she hit me up with a couple more caps of MDA. While I was still rushing, I stepped out of the van to cherish the chalky pastel sky before it turned black.

"Didn't you say you wanted your runners?" Wendy reminded me.

Sneakers, right. I rummaged through my knapsack to find them, a pair of torn blue deck shoes. After the day of walking bare-footed, wearing those sneakers made me feel that I could hop on nails. I ran down the path to the bottom of the cliff with Wendy, shouting behind me that I was going to kill myself. I did stumble and slide a few times, but I came up with nothing more serious than bruises.

The sun was down soon after that.

We walked to the shoreline so that we would have to cross a minimum of logs in the dark. Of course, the moon and galaxy of stars kept the beach from total darkness, and campfires were like torches along the beach. The greatest fire, one at the south edge of the community, was lighting the sky with flames that leaped at

220

least five feet above the tops of the burning logs. The logs were standing ten feet above the sand. The fire was designed like a frame of a teepee, and it had been ignited by a smaller fire inside. The fire had been built to attract people.

The fire drew me and Wendy to its heat. We joined about fifty other people who were talking and singing in a circle around it. Somebody passed me a joint. I took a deep toke, but it didn't alter my high. I later found out that the joints were filled with a tea that grew wild along the cliffs. It didn't get you high, but the people were having fun passing the joints around. It was part of the community spirit, which I can't say I felt a part of.

I was an observer, not a true link in the circle around the fire. I couldn't even get the guitar player to play one of my songs. He didn't know any blues. All he knew were Donovan tunes—"Catch the Wind" and "Colours"—not offensive but also not my requests. I thought maybe he'd know "Ramblin' Boy," but even his Donovan repertoire was limited.

After ten of the people softly sang "Josie," one guy who had been listening smiled and said, "It's gonna be all right . . . It's gonna be all right . . ." Most of the people seemed to understand, but one girl asked him what he meant. He kept smiling and replied, "We just sit here doing something simple like this and we know . . . It's gonna be all right . . ." Naturally, it was nice to see this guy happy, but I was thinking that he must have been living on this horseshoe strip of land for so long he'd forgotten about who and what were on the outside. I don't know, maybe he should never leave.

Wendy and I left and went up to sleep in the van again that night.

"How do you like staying on this beach?" Wendy asked me before hitting me up with some MDA.

"I don't know. What do you think?"

"Miki says she likes the city better because there's more to do. I think she's right."

I really didn't know. I was confused about the island scene and

221

about all of the sudden changes my friends seemed to be going through. It seemed that every time I got off and rushed on MDA, everybody was different in some way by the time I stopped rushing. Maybe all the changes were happening while I was oblivious to them, during my rushes. Anyway, at least the rushes were a constant in my life. I could count on them. I couldn't wait for Wendy to hit me up, to get to the MDA rush and the MDA fuck, to get back to my reality.

24

The next morning, before a lingering fog lifted, Frank changed his name. Now he was Daniel.

I didn't find this out until early afternoon when I went to ask Frank if I could borrow the keys to his van. I had trouble finding him. He wasn't near his hut, so I asked a few of his neighbors if they knew where I could find him. Most of them didn't know, but a Mexican girl who lived two huts away told me he was on top of the cliff. I thanked her and climbed the steep path which led me through a tunnel of bushes and trees. The tunnel opened up to the sky at the top.

And there was Frank, working with three other guys on his A-frame. The frame for the floor, made of four narrow logs with the bark still on them, had already been assembled. Frank was the only one of the workers who was standing. He was peeking into a How-To-Build-An-A-Frame book and then looking up to survey the area. With his hair tied back, he looked like the foreman of a work crew.

"Afternoon, Frank," I said.

223

He nodded to me and then looked back into his book.

"Looks like you're off to a good start with this thing. What happened, did you decide you wanted to live in something more classy than that hut down on the sand?"

"Those logs down there are going to be washed away this winter," Frank said. "The tide will come halfway up this cliff."

"So you decided you want to stay here this winter. . . . Well, that's far out; it's good that you dig it that much. Hey listen, Frank, would it be cool if I borrowed the keys to the van for a while so I can drive people to the store?"

Frank frowned and he said, "Y'all look too stoned for driving."

He was begrudging me his van keys, but it didn't irritate me. I was already accustomed to his new attitude toward me.

"It'll be cool; I'll ask John to drive," I said.

Frank paused and then handed me his keys.

"Thanks a lot, man," I said. "I'll get these back to you right after we get back."

Then one of the workers asked, "Have you decided what you're gonna do 'bout your floor, Daniel?"

And Frank answered, "I think I'll go ahead with the idea I told y'all about, fill this part in with concrete."

Wait a minute, maybe I was in the wrong place.

"Wait a minute, why did he call you Daniel?" I asked.

"That's my name. From here on y'all call me Daniel."

I shrugged. "Okay."

Then Nick popped up through the tunnel of trees. That guy projected an attitude that made you want to punch him out. He walked past me and up to Frank. He talked with Frank about the A-frame for a minute. Then he put his arms around him.

"Daniel, you and I are two of the few true friends in this world. We'd really do anything for each other. That's a rare thing."

"It sure is," Frank agreed.

I'd never seen a show quite like this before.

"If you ever need anything, all you have to do is ask," Nick said, still hugging Frank.

"I don't need anything at the moment, Nick."

"Daniel, can I have your watch?"

"Of course, Nick."

Frank pulled off his wristwatch and gave it to Nick. I was gaping at the transaction. Was this show put on just to shock me? I guess not.

"Well, I'll be back later with these keys, Frank," I said.

"Daniel."

"I mean Daniel."

I went back down to the beach and across the stream to the area of Graham's hut where I'd left Wendy and Miki earlier. On my way, I contemplated the Daniel bit. I couldn't figure it out, except that I assumed the name change was connected with Frank's new comradeship with that guy Nick.

I met John near Graham's hut. He said he'd drive us to the store in half an hour. Then I strolled along the shoreline with Wendy and had one of my rare serious conversations with her. She filled me in on a few of the changes Frank had gone through while I was in jail.

On Frank's second night on Wreck Bay (my third night in Port Alberni), he ate two hits of MDA and became enthralled by the simple nonmaterialistic life-style of the people on the beach. While everybody was sitting around the great campfire, Frank went to his van and came back with about eighty hits of MDA for the party. He began selling them at three for five dollars, then at a dollar fifty each, then in ten for ten sales and for free to people without money; money wasn't as important as it was to turn on the community. During the course of his fire sale, Frank traded hits of MDA for hits of mescaline and LSD. Of course, he wasn't a psychedelic dealer, so he ate the mescaline and acid. Then he evened it all out with two more hits of MDA. If our man Frank was going to turn the whole beach into MDA heads, he was going to maintain his own status as the biggest MDA head on the beach. He got zonked. He was one with the spirit of that community, watching groups of ten people rocking with their arms around each other in

225

"love circles." He was watching them singing and loving and all this because of a touch of magic that Frank had brought to these people. Just looking at this and feeling it and understanding it, Frank must have been on some kind of threshold. Cosmic consciousness, maybe? He was headed up and up toward the stars. There was no doubt, after all, he could *feel* it. He might have made it up there, too, but something stopped him. Some flaw in his consciousness, some impurity, perhaps a remnant of the brainwashing from his childhood that even the acid couldn't dissolve, some bit of conditioning that had branded his mind and would not vanish when he ordered it to go away; it stayed there to haunt him when he realized: "Holy fuck, I've just thrown away my savings!" Anyway, Nick was nearby and saw what was happening. He saw how stoned Frank was, so he appointed himself Frank's financial manager. He took Frank's money and took over the selling of the MDA. Now it was three dollars a hit. Any protest and Nick accused you of trying to rip off his main man, Frank, the new guru of Vancouver Island. Naturally, Frank and Nick became partners.

Wendy apparently disliked Nick as much as I did, which gave us something in common beyond our mutual fascination with needles. Her details did not explain Frank's switch in attitude toward me, but at least this new evidence left me confident that Frank was the crazy one and not me.

Wendy and I went up to the van to wait for John. While we waited, she hit me with two caps. By the time I had finished rushing, John was in the front seat of the van. Kathleen's son, Michael, sat in the front seat next to John. Miki and Tim boarded the back with me and Wendy.

The trip turned out to be an upset for John. The girls, Miki in particular, were shrieking as we drove slowly up and down the narrow path along the cliff. Miki kept screaming, "We're gonna fall over! We're gonna fall over!" and Wendy followed her lead. They were like kids on a roller coaster. John should have stopped and ordered them out of the van, but he was too proud of his driving. I told them to shut up, that John was doing fine, but the girls kept squealing. John's nerves were shot by the time we reached the store. He went into the store with us, bought an apple which was as red as his face, and went back to the van to regain his composure. I went back to the van while everybody else was still milling around the store. John was silent. "Are you okay?" I asked. He nodded. Then the others boarded the van with bags of canned foods and honey and bread. John still looked unnerved, but he turned the ignition key right away.

"Maybe we should rest here for a while," Michael said.

"No, I'm okay," John murmured.

"Wait a second, I forgot something," Michael blurted as he hopped out of the van.

Michael was inside the store for the next five minutes. Then he sauntered out chewing on a licorice stick. He sat again in the seat next to John.

"I think I'm ready to go now," he said.

We drove back to the cliff above Wreck Bay, this time without noise from Miki or Wendy. John parked the van in its original spot. Then he punched a tape of Dylan's third album into the tape player. The song began playing in the middle with, "One too many mornings and a thousand miles behind . . ." I opened the van door to let in the breeze and sunshine, and then John and Michael joined us in the back for a bread and honey feast.

It was the most delicious food I'd tasted in weeks. The honey made the bread feel scabrous like honeycomb on my tongue. "We're all going to come down with the runs," I warned as I took a bite out of my third slice.

Beginning the fourth slice, I spotted Frank climbing the cliff with Nick behind him. They marched up to the van.

"Y'all have the keys for me?" Frank asked.

I said yeah, sure, and John gave the keys to him.

"All right, y'all have to get out of the van now," Frank announced.

"What for?" Wendy asked.

"Because this van is for traveling, not for hanging around in."

227

"But Frank, there's no place else where we can listen to music," Wendy protested.

"That's too bad, but y'all have to get out."

Slowly and quietly, we all gathered our gear and filed out of the van. While we were doing it, Frank noticed his old extra sleeping bag on the floor of the van.

"I'm not going to need this sleeping bag. Does anyone want it?" he asked.

"I'll take it," Nick said just as everybody else started to open their mouths.

There was a hush while everybody but Frank glared at Nick. Then Tim, the most reserved of our crew, was the first one to comment:

"Those who step on people on their way up should bear in mind that they will meet the people again—on their way *down*."

Tim spoke softly and didn't bother to look at Nick, but Nick caught the message.

It looked like we were going to sleep on the beach that night. I carried my knapsack and sleeping bag as I headed toward the sand. Wendy was behind me and John and Tim were in front of me.

"Y'know, regardless of what that guy Nick is up to, I'm glad in a way that Frank kicked us out of his van," John said.

Tim looked at John in a way that said, you're nuts.

"Well, at least he's stopped letting *everybody* shit on him," John said.

25

John's birthday was coming up.

"He'll be nineteen years old in a few weeks," I told Miki and Wendy. "I've been friends with John for most of those years, but I've never celebrated a birthday with him. Nineteen years, man, that deserves a celebration, wouldn't you say?"

That's how I initiated the idea for the surprise party. A corny idea? Well, you have to picture it. There'd be the most outrageous campfire Wreck Bay had ever seen—a flaming skyscraper. And plenty of wine, you understand, enough gallon jugs so that we could douse out the fire if we had to. By the time those jugs were dry, people would be singing and dancing and whooping around the blaze like a tribe of stoned Indians. This would be a birthday party. I don't mean sitting around trying to embarrass John and singing "For He's a Jolly Good Douchebag"; we'd go way beyond that kind of stuff. We'd bring everybody together to have the ultimate gas; and without an overload of words everybody would know that this bash was happening in honor of my friend, John.

Miki and Wendy turned out to be regular little party planners.

To them, it was an exciting new scheme. And they couldn't wait to get back to the city, even if only for a quick stopover to pick up wine and food. We decided to have the party in a week. In the meantime, Miki and Wendy would ride to Vancouver with Frank, who was planning another of his runs that afternoon. They would return within a few days with the makings of the party and maybe even convince Matthew and Jainie to come along with them. With plans set, I gave Miki and Wendy nine capsules of MDA and the last of my change in case that would make a difference. Miki assured me she could sell the MDA.

Naturally, it had occurred to me that the party would also be a way for me to move closer to the island community. I still felt like an outsider, though I sensed a bond of sorts between myself and Graham's family. I don't know how they felt about that.

I sat with Wendy on a log between the beach and Graham's hut while she and Miki were waiting for Frank to finish loading his van. Ann passed by us and said that Frank and Nick were nearly ready. Ann, I'd forgotten about her. She seemed cheery. She must have made new friends during her first day on the beach. I hadn't seen her with Miki at all.

Later, Frank and Nick passed not far from us with armloads of food. They took the food to a simple hut near Graham's. A girl wearing overalls lived there, and they placed the food at the entrance to her hut. I could see everybody smiling. I saw Michael and his brother, Geoffrey, also outside that hut. Michael talked with that guy Nick. Then I saw Nick give him a red box. Michael turned around and headed in our direction.

"Hey, Steve, do you like raisins?" he asked when he reached us.

"Sure, I love them," I said.

"Well, put your hands together," he said, and he poured a hill of raisins into my cupped hands. "I got this box from Nick. He said I should take them, but he told me I shouldn't give anything to you. He said I shouldn't trust you. So I said, 'I want those raisins, but I'm gonna give some to Steve if you give 'em to me!' "

"Thanks a lot, man, really," I said.

Michael laughed, "I think I pissed him off pretty bad, but he gave me the raisins."

Then Michael poured a pile into Wendy's hands. I probably would have gone over and punched out that guy Nick if Michael hadn't already put him down for me. The raisins were delicious.

"Come on, let's go eat with Graham and my mom," Michael said.

We followed Michael and sat on the log bench with Kathleen and Graham. Michael's sister, Daisy, popped out of the hut to take her share of raisins. But she pocketed them instead of eating them.

"What do you plan to do with them?" Graham asked.

"Save 'em," Daisy said.

"She's gonna sell them to some sucker on the beach so's she can buy candy," Michael said.

I laughed because Michael was right. I'd seen Daisy exploiting her own cuteness to sell seashells and home-rolled cigarettes on the beach for nickels and dimes. I only heard one of her customers dicker over her price, and she dove down to a penny without hesitation.

Frank and Nick stopped by Graham's hut.

"We're 'bout ready. Meet me and Daniel by the bus in fifteen or twenty minutes," Nick said to Wendy. "Ann and Miki already know."

Wendy nodded.

"I'll see y'all again in a few days," Frank said, directing his words mainly to Graham.

"Okay, take things easy, Daniel," Graham said.

Frank and Nick turned around and headed up the cliff.

Then Graham turned to me and asked, "Do you know what's the secret behind Frank wanting everyone to call him Daniel?"

I almost answered that Frank was my servant and Daniel is Nick's, but I realized that that wouldn't be a cool thing to say. So I only said I hadn't figured it out yet.

"It's got me guessing," Graham said. "It's not so important to me what I call him, of course, but I can't understand why someone would want to change his own name."

I told Graham I'd let him know if I figured it out, and then Wendy and I took a short walk before she went to Frank's van. Since she was leaving for a few days, I asked her to get me off one last time. We stopped by the hut where we'd stayed with Miki and Tim and John the night before, where I'd stashed my knapsack. I took my fit and three capsules of MDA out of my knapsack. Wendy hit me up in our hut. I was still rushing when Wendy had to leave, so I said goodbye to her on the sand.

That afternoon, I felt a sore at the corner of my mouth. My face was beginning to break out. I took a bath and washed my hair in the spring water stream next to a log bridge. That water might have been ice if it weren't running.

The bath left me with an appetite, and I ate a good meal for a change that night. Some people who lived in a hut near Frank's had caught salmon, which they cooked in aluminum foil in the fire. Tim, John and I feasted with our neighbors.

Then the three of us slept in our hut, the one where I'd bumped into Tim on my first day on Wreck Bay. We didn't talk much.

The next morning was gray. I could see it through the spaces between the logs of our roof, through the foggy plastic that topped those logs. It was dreary gray like an old tennis ball, solid gray like a black and white photo of a blue sky. A number of people moved out of their huts that day, decided it was time to hit the road again. Hardly everybody, but enough went so that the beach seemed more lonely. When I stepped out of our hut to walk around that morning, most of the people who were not leaving were still inside their shelters, undoubtedly huddled inside their sleeping bags. The few people outside were warming their hands over campfires.

I took a quiet walk along the beach. The only way I could tell the shoreline was curved was by watching the changing position of the island in the middle of the bay. As I walked one way, it shifted along the horizon in the other direction. I watched it through steamy breath; it was like a floating island, somebody's raft. Then I turned around to look back at the cluster of huts on the sand. I had been walking for longer than I'd noticed. The huts were in the distance, far away enough so that I didn't notice the few people around their campfires. It was all very lonely, like an empty boardwalk or an abandoned amusement park.

I walked slowly back toward our hut. John and Tim were outside starting a smoky fire. I sat on a log and watched them. It was silent. I was letting myself slip into it, the silence, the sadness. I had to stop myself. Maybe a loud noise would change it.

"You guys feel like doing MDA with me?" I asked.

Tim turned around. "I'd like to," he said. Then he looked to John.

John switched his glances back and forth between the two of us. Then he said he'd like it, too.

I ducked into the hut and brought out my knapsack. I took out a handful of capsules. I ate one. John ate one. Tim snorted one.

"I'm going to hit a couple more," I said.

John's expression was blank as he looked at me. I wanted him to help me.

"Can you tie me off?" I asked.

John paused for a long moment. Then he said yes.

I prepared the shot, mixed the solution, drew it into the syringe. As I tapped the air bubbles to the top, I caught Tim staring, and it made me forget what I was doing for a second. Then he told me I shouldn't mind him, that he was always fascinated by the ritual. I went ahead. Tim mentioned something about how much he used to love to shoot speed and something about some months he spent in the hospital with hardly any marrow left in his bones. I was engrossed in my work. I hung my belt over my arm above the elbow. Then John pulled down on the loose ends of the belt with both of his hands. He was straining as the veins bulged. It made me nervous. I found a fat vein and slowly eased the point inside. It registered. The process took me longer than it should have, but I hit myself without a miss. Just before I started to rush, I caught a glimpse of John's blank white face staring at me.

233

The rush was timeless, a flash of nothing, another rush. It left me naked. There I was again, feeling stoned yet not altogether different from the way I'd felt an hour earlier. I was frightened.

Raindrops were falling into my hair. I looked up to the sky and then shielded my eyes with my arm. It suddenly began raining hard. I stuffed things into my knapsack. John and Tim were crawling into the hut. I followed.

John opened his sleeping bag. I was getting in his way as he spread it open with the nylon side to the sand. With it spread out, I sat on the zippered edge of the carpet. Tim split another cap of MDA with John, snorting it. Thousands of drops were tapping frantically on the plastic above us. We sat quietly for a long time, until the rain calmed down.

I was sitting with my knees up and my chin resting on my knees. I was hugging my folded legs with my right arm. With my left arm I skimmed my index finger across the surface of the sand. The fluid sand flowed over the top of the finger like a tiny breaking wave. I felt John looking at me.

"It's been a strange couple of days," he said.

I nodded, knocking my chin against my knee and forcing a smile.

"Strange . . . after all this time . . . to suddenly take a break . . ." John went on.

I was finding it difficult to force the smile.

"Friends for all that time . . . and then we suddenly stop like that for a few days . . ." John said, forcing his voice to sound louder and clearer.

I pressed my mouth against my knees.

"Funny, it seems like it's been much longer than a few days. . . . Might as well laugh about it, I guess. . . . Why not, right?" he said.

I hugged my legs tighter with both arms. We were quiet for a while.

"Might as well laugh because we're friends again now. . . . And we wouldn't want to sit around here crying in public," John said, letting out a halfhearted laugh that sounded more like a muffled sneeze.

I joined him in that laugh.

"I guess we have a lot of talking to catch up on," he said.

I nodded and mouthed the word, Yeah . . . No sound came out the first time, so I tried it again. "Yeah . . ."

John looked over to Tim. "Is it cool with you if we leave here for now?" he asked softly.

Tim nodded.

John and I crawled out of the hut. The light rain refreshed me. Standing up felt good. I didn't feel that we needed to say any more, but John wanted to talk. So we talked. We walked along the spring water stream and followed it to its source. Then we wandered through the woody area along the foot of the cliff.

"I was really scared for you, Steve. But then I guess something happened when you got here. When Miki first came down and told me you were out of jail and right there at the top of the hill, I was all happy, but then it seemed different when I saw you the next day, when you were all wrecked from your morning shot; I guess I suddenly felt I'd had enough of worrying about it. I mean I was still worried, but I didn't want to be, you know? I wanted to stick to only being annoyed. It pissed me off that you were abusing the drug that did a lot to bring the people on this beach together. It was like, all the other people but you had realized that the drug wasn't the important thing, and I couldn't understand how you could be that blind."

"Man, I felt so scared that first morning when I first came down," I said.

"Yeah, well, I was scared, too. I haven't been able to figure out what I'm supposed to do. Like just now, it seemed crazy to pull that belt around your arm. But I had asked Tim about it, and he persuaded me not to discourage you. He gave me his rap about when he was doing speed, and all he wanted to hear was a friend tell him not to do it. Then he said he'd run out and shoot up all the speed he could cop. I don't know . . . I was thinking that you

235

were really getting yourself strung out, but then Tim told me you were just digging on the needle."

I didn't want to talk about it. Shooting MDA already seemed like a detail of the past, irrelevant. I no longer felt the need for it. John and I were friends; we could surely find more pertinent subjects to talk about.

We sat on a slope near the foot of the cliff and we faced the bay. We must have talked for an hour there. Everything was coming out in words, and all our ideas made the most basic and simple kind of sense to us.

We looked at our fears. They seemed absurd. And the solution seemed simple and easy: Don't be afraid, friend.

I said that the first fear I'd felt on Wreck Bay was that John had become closer friends with Tim than he was with me.

Then John talked about his friendship with Tim in a way that made it sound surreal. He had never become such close friends with anybody as quickly as he did with Tim. That was fine, but the friendship had happened so fast that John hadn't had time to relate it in his own head to the rest of the Vancouver scene and to the rest of his friends. For a couple of days, John was friends on the beach with Tim and without any of his other Vancouver friends around. And then suddenly the Vancouver friends were around. Things changed fast.

"And were you watching those games Miki was playing with our heads?" John said. "I don't think you were there a lot of the time, but I wished she had stayed home. She kept trying to put me uptight by making her remarks hinting that Tim and I were doing a thing. Man, the day after she got here, Tim told me he wished I'd never known that he is gay. Miki was doing her job, man. That whole gay thing never made a difference until Miki showed up."

Miki had chosen as her point of attack one of the basic fears, a fear that stems straight out of the junior high school trip. Hell, not that trip again! How old was I? I was seventeen, not twelve. Yet clearly that absurd old trip was still junked somewhere in my consciousness, in John's consciousness. And somewhere along the

236

line of that old trip, somewhere at the beginning or in the middle or at the end of the push-me-fuck-you-yeah-sez-who junior high brand of conflict, there invariably came out the word: faggot. The word was a trigger, a marionette string that made people do strange things when it was pulled.

"But that's bullshit. I'm wrong to pin the whole blame on Miki for getting Tim uptight," John went on. "It might have been me. I don't know. Tim said he could sense me getting uptight. But he only said it after Miki and Wendy and you guys arrived. I don't know. I didn't think I was getting so uptight. I think a lot of it was Tim's paranoia. Like the other day, Kathleen asked us how long we'd known each other, and I told her three or four days. Man, that really blew her mind. She raved on about how much we seemed like old friends and how she pictured us together all the time. And I really dug that she said that. Really. I took it as a compliment. But Tim later asked me if Kathleen's remark had put me uptight, y'know?"

John probably had taken it as a compliment. But I also figured he had been uptight in some ways, as Tim had said. Paranoids are some of the more perceptive people, I think.

"What do you really think of Miki?" John asked me.

Miki. True, she had problems. Don't we all. To tell the truth, her problems were rarely the first things that came to my mind when I thought of her. I thought about her breasts before I gave thought to the complexities of her life. And lately, a fantasy about Miki had been recurring in my mind. I pictured John and me on heavy motorcycles cruising back home with Miki. I pictured myself roaring through my hometown on a chopped Harley, so fast that the cops couldn't catch me. And I pictured Miki clinging onto me tightly as I skidded to stops in front of the houses of my old friends. I would never have to stop at one place for too long; my engine would be rumbling and spitting like a monster as Miki grabbed onto me and we took off again. Okay, it's a crazy ego fantasy, one of me playing my role, living an image. But I could dig that. I was a realist. If I dug something I accepted that I dug it.

237

I admit I dug Miki mainly for her looks. Which brings up the question John was really asking, I suppose. Would I have dug Miki if she looked like Ann? Probably not. But that's because then she wouldn't be Miki. If that says something about the way I looked at chicks, I could accept it. I scorned idealism.

I scorned idealism—except when I was high and talking with a friend.

"I think Miki needs a friend," I said.

"I guess," John said.

We must have both been feeling idealistic. By the time we were exhausted from talk, we had decided we would always be open with each other and that we would not play competition games with each other. I was referring to my own paranoid scene in Frank's van when Wendy had taken John over me.

John laughed. "Steve, that was crazy. I was drunk and not thinking in any way of trying to put you down. And the only reason Wendy came on to me in the first place was because of the way you looked, I'm sure."

"What was wrong with the way I looked?" I asked, feeling a twinge of paranoia.

"It's hard to describe. But when you are doing that much MDA like that, something seems to leave your face. I don't mean something like a nose or an eye, just some of the character is missing. It leaves you with a different face."

This had not occurred to me.

"Will you do me a favor, man, and let me know if I ever get that look again," I said.

"Sure, Steve," John laughed. "We stick together and neither of us has to worry about falling apart."

I nodded vigorously. Love is all you need, right?

I was feeling pretty good and wanting everybody to be happy as we walked along the sand toward our hut. But that added to the sudden feeling of sadness I felt when I saw Tim walking along the shoreline alone.

"Should you go over and talk with Tim?" I asked.

238

"I'm still into talking with you."

John was not being perceptive. It surprised me.

"He looks kind of down," I said.

"I don't think so," John said. "He said it was cool. He's okay."

I knew that Tim wasn't okay. I saw his face before he ducked into our hut. I realized then that he loved John.

"I really think you should go and rap with Tim," I said again.

John agreed this time. He went to our hut and ducked inside.

26

I went to sleep early in the evening and woke up before most other people the next morning. While I ordinarily used the woods, this morning I brought my knapsack with me all the way up the beach and across the stream and past Frank's empty hut to one of the two outhouses on that end of the beach. I went inside the outhouse and sat on the wooden seat. The stink was overpowering, so I held my breath for as long as possible while I hit myself up with a couple of caps of MDA. Then I forgot about the stench. After my rush, I squirted a few drops of blood onto the wall below some unoriginal graffiti. Then I angrily stabbed the wall with the point of my fit. Before stepping outside, I dropped the syringe into the hole with the rest of the shit.

Tim hitchhiked back to Vancouver that day. I didn't talk with him much. While I had been asleep inside the hut the night before, Tim and John had been talking late into the night next to the fire. The only thing John told me Tim had said was that he hadn't realized that John and I were really friends. Tim had assumed that we just hung around together and told people we were friends. I don't entirely understand why it made a difference to him, but it did. So he left.

Over the next few days, the beach grew progressively quieter. A few new people moved into the abandoned huts, but more were moving out to hit the road again. And when Graham's family packed their gear to return to their land on the other side of Vancouver Island, I knew that the Wreck Bay community was dissolving before I could become a part of it as John had been a part of it. It was over, so I didn't let it bother me. I told Michael I would probably drop in on his place one of these days.

John and I moved into Graham's hut. We took long afternoon walks around the horseshoe strip of beach. And we lived for a few days on carrots and honey and several loaves of whole wheat bread which a Volkswagen van of freaks had been handing out one day. Except for diarrhea, our days were peaceful. I felt that I had at last found a place where I could cop a little serenity.

27

Those bitches, they never showed up. I kept waiting, telling myself something must have hung them up for a few days, trying to
believe they'd surely arrive with the wine any minute. Meanwhile,
my anger expanded. John could not understand it because I didn't
tell him about the party plan. "What are you getting yourself so
pissed at them about?" he said. "They're crazy, and you are, too,
if you're relying on them to get here." But this was not a simple
matter of reliability. After all that enthusiasm Miki and Wendy
had expressed for the idea of surprising John with a party, their
failure to show up now was a direct insult, an affront to both John
and me. I waited several extra days, though, to give them their
fair chance.

Another thing that kept me waiting at Wreck Bay was that a
huge ugly sore, an MDA reaction, had developed at the right corner of my mouth. And after a few days, the sore festered. I could
barely smile or open my mouth. It looked like the right third of my
lips had fallen off. And my face was breaking out in other places,

too. I'd never seen myself look so ugly. How could I think of facing Miki while I was looking like a leper? Although I wanted to beat that chick up, I wanted to be looking good while I did it.

Just before I resigned myself to looking like a monster for the rest of my life, a girl on the beach rescued my face from total consumption by turning me on to some Vitamin E. I applied it to the sore.

I could smile again when John and I left Wreck Bay the next day to hitch to Vancouver.

We stayed at the Beatty Street Armory that night. I felt stronger being back on our turf.

Miki's apartment was locked and empty when we went to it the next day. The curtain was drawn so that it covered most of the glass sliding door, but I was able to peek through a thin uncovered crack at the edge of the door. No show here, there were not even any props, not so much as a sleeping bag on the floor. Had Miki and Wendy skipped town with the loot?

We walked to Matthew and Jainie's place to see if they knew anything about it. And we were lucky; we caught them just before they stepped out their door. They were on their way to meet Lee and Joanna and go with them to sell belts and leather goods at a local fair.

"Where have you guys been?" Jainie asked. "Out there on that island all this time?"

"Yeah," I said. "Now we're trying to hunt down Miki and Wendy. Those chicks owe us some explanations, among other things."

Jainie rolled her eyes. "Shit, man, I think I've heard Miki's name enough to last me a long time. She's moved into that building right over there." Jainie pointed to a yellow tacky modern apartment building not far down the other side of the driveway in back of Matthew and Jainie's place. "I'll show you which apartment she lives in if you want, but after that I don't want to hear about her."

"What did she do to get you so down on her?"

243

"Forget it, Stevie, that chick's unbelievable. You know that brown tweed jacket I have, the really nice one? You've seen it. Well, I lost it a few days ago. And I was really down about losing it, too. Then I ran into that chick Wendy the next day. The first day after I lost the jacket and this chick Wendy is wearing it. I nearly fell over, boy. I said: 'What the fuck are you doing wearing my jacket?' And that chick Wendy said: 'What do you mean *your* jacket? Miki gave me this jacket as a present this morning.' I argued and I finally got it back, but I think I've had enough of Miki for a while."

"Miki really *is* nuts," I said. "Sounds like she's desperately trying to get caught."

"That ain't it," Matthew said. "She just don't give a shit 'cause she knows she can talk her way outa anything with them tits of hers."

Jainie insisted that they had to get going, so John and I walked with Matthew and Jainie along the gravel driveway as far as the modern yellow building.

"That's it," Jainie said, pointing to a corner apartment on the ground floor. "That one there. I wish you guys luck."

"Thanks," I said. "Hey, how long will you be away?"

"For one night. We'll see you guys tomorrow."

"If ya see Miki," Matthew said. "Tell her to keep away from our house."

John and I walked through a red wooden gate to check out Miki's apartment. We crossed a strip of lawn and stepped down onto a small concrete patio. The sliding door to the apartment was locked. I knocked on the glass.

"This is insane," John said. "They go to the trouble of moving and then wind up in an identical apartment in the same section of town."

"This one's even uglier than the last one," I said. "Piss yellow, man, who picks out that color? There must have been a sale."

Nobody answered my knocking. We went back out the gate and around the block to the front of the building. I buzzed the intercom button to their apartment. It was in Ann's name naturally. No answer. I leaned on it. Then one of the tenants came through the locked front door, and we slipped inside the building before the door shut. Miki's apartment was easy to find. A note was stuck in the letter slot on the door to the apartment:

Steve and John, Miki and I have gone to Calgary for two days or so. We'll be back by Thursday. Luv, Wendy.

An antiquated note. Today was Sunday.

"Those bitches, man, taking a Calgary vacation . . ." I said. The idea that they were doing it with money from the MDA I'd given them was making me feel like a total asshole. Just who did they think they were dealing with here?

"You think they'll be coming back at all?" John said.

"They won't if they know what's good for them," I said. "But yeah, they're coming back. Why else would they leave the note?"

We waited it out. We ate supper at the five-thirty feed-in. And then I did some panhandling near the library on Burrard Street. We brought a couple of dollars worth of food back across the bridge to Miki's place. They were still out. So we ate by Matthew's house. This second meal was tasty—tuna fish and Muenster cheese and orange juice—but it needed some spice. We checked inside the refrigerator on Matthew's porch. There wasn't much, but . . . potato salad! Jainie had left a pot of her delicious potato salad, probably only to be spoiled. John and I added that to make it a perfect meal.

The evening was pleasant, but it looked like another night at the Beatty Street hostel. I was sick of noisy Beatty Street. John and I started talking about possibly heading back to New York. I was as weary of hitchhiking as I was of living in an armory, so I told John about a way we could get free plane tickets through the Children's Aid Society. The idea that we had an apartment waiting on the lower East Side for us made New York appealing.

But we also had an apartment in Vancouver! A light switched on in Miki's place. The bitch, she was home. John and I ran around to the front of the building and buzzed. They buzzed back

245

to let us in the front door of the building without checking who we were through the intercom. I pounded on the front door to their apartment. There was talking inside, and then Miki opened the door.

She looked more beautiful than ever.

"Hi! We were just talking about you guys, wondering when you'd get here," Miki smiled. "Come on in."

I stared at her for a moment, her thin white hand holding the door. She waited with her lips parted, running her tongue over the glossy surface of her upper lip. I could think of nothing to say. We went inside, John walking ahead of us into the kitchen. I watched the delicate bones of Miki's shoulder blades through the sheer violet material of her blouse. It was the fine, glossy kind of material that clings like paint to the skin to highlight every shape with its color; that slick, sliding, almost fluid material that would slip like mercury onto the floor if you set it hanging off the edge of the table. I hoped Miki didn't notice me staring at the soft outline of her nipples when she turned around.

"Nice place, eh?" she said.

Place? Oh, right, the apartment.

"Yeah, sure," I said. It looked the same as her other place, except that this one was cleaner and its kitchen more definitely separated from the livingroom by the partition.

Miki took us into the livingroom to see Wendy with a couple of strangers sitting on a mattress on the floor. Wendy looked up and said hi.

"Steve and John, this is Huey and that's Jesse."

Everybody nodded. The situation was uneasy at first. But it wasn't that I felt threatened; these guys were dirty with unkempt scraggly beards, not Miki's types.

They turned out to be nice guys, though. Huey became particularly talkative once he got started. He was from Paterson, New Jersey, a fact that shoved Miki and Wendy into the background for a while.

"Paterson, New Jersey!" I exclaimed. "That's not far from

where my parents live. Hell, I forget the last time I met anybody from Paterson, New Jersey."

"It's far out, brother," Huey said. "It was Ginsberg's hometown."

"I never thought of it that way . . ."

"I'm goofing. It's a bummer. You'll never find me back there again."

"What were you into in Paterson?" John asked.

"Teaching Phys. Ed. at the high school."

"No shit!" I said. "Man, I never had a gym teacher who looked like you."

I tried to picture Huey with a whistle hanging around his neck and wearing a gray sweat suit. . . . All right, everybody! Jumping-jacks! One, two, one, two, one, two . . . No, it didn't fit at all, not with his scraggly goatee and shoulder-length brown hair, and especially not with his placid smile.

"They never saw a gym teacher like me either. But I quit before they had a chance to fire me," Huey said. "Brother, if you're from Jersey, you've got to meet my partner Davy when he gets here. The man's from Fort Lee; he's been through all that, like you and me."

"More people are coming here?" I said, dispirited. I'd hoped that the ratio of other people to Miki would stick at this level.

"Any time now," Huey said. "We're all partying tonight. My friends are out copping crystal. Could you dig some crystal tonight?"

I told Huey that I could definitely dig some. The prospect of getting off on crystal methedrine perked me up again.

"How are you digging Canada?" Huey asked.

"I'm digging it."

"Right, brother. Isn't it far out? This place is my dream. . . ."

The sliding glass door opened, and three guys walked into the livingroom. The guy in front, the one with short dirty blond hair and thick glasses, was grinning like an inexperienced shoplifter.

"You got it!" Huey exclaimed.

247

Then he and Jesse stood up and looked to John and me before following the other three guys into the bathroom. I got up and followed them. Inside the bathroom Huey organized everybody so that all six of us would fit. I was sitting next to Jesse on the edge of the pink bathtub.

"Where's your friend? Where's John?" Huey asked.

"He's not into speed," I said.

Huey felt he should have a fatherly talk with John about that, but he was eager to get down to the business at hand first. The guy with the thick glasses unfolded his small aluminum foil package as if there might be nitroglycerin inside. The magnifying effect of his glasses was making his eyes appear to bulge. I thought the way he was acting toward the speed—as if it were the last cup of water in a desert—was kind of disgusting, but I didn't say anything about it. Then he brought out the surprise party favors—two plastic syringes. Each of us took a turn hitting himself. I hit Jesse because he didn't know how to do it himself. Then I hit myself and came out of the bathroom rushing, not quite so intensely as with MDA, but rushing just the same.

John was at the kitchen table with Miki and Wendy. Huey was also there, already talking to John. Miki was beautiful. John was laughing about something. It was an inviting scene. So I sat on the floor against the wall next to John's chair and listened to Huey's rap:

"I can truly dig where you're at now, brother, because I was in just that same place myself last year. I was just at that stage where I was afraid to let myself really flip out because I was scared that a flip-out had to mean a freak-out. That's where it's at for you now, but you'll get to where you don't feel that way. I can dig you; you'll cool your way into it. Take it slow, the way you're doing. I dig that. I can dig why you don't feel up to speeding with us yet. You dig that you're young and you've got time. You just cool your way in there until you connect with where you know a flip-out is really at."

"Man, I can't understand what you're saying. I don't know

what you mean by flip-out and freak-out," John said.

Huey put his palms up in a gesture that meant: Stop the traffic because Huey understands. "I know. I know. IknowIknow-Iknow. You're really far out, you know that? *Really* far out. I can dig what you're saying, that it's the *words*. The *words* just can't make it, right?"

"What words?" John said.

"Exactly . . . Exactly . . . What words? The words are nothing, right? I dig what you're saying, brother. But you can *feel* the meaning, right? You can *feel* that I've placed your head for where it's at. That's why we have this beautiful connection."

Huey was apparently having nearly as much difficulty adjusting his glassy bloodshot eyes to focus on John's face as he was having with his effort to figure out where John's head was at. I was amused and enjoying Huey's crazy high.

"And this one here, brother, this one here . . ." Huey said, squeezing my forearm. "Just look at him! Isn't he far out?"

"You'd never know I was from Jersey," I said, joking.

Huey went hysterical. "Oh brother, you're so far out!"

"I thought you told me you came from New York, Steve," Miki said.

"Yeah, well, John and I have a place waiting for us in New York. That's where we actually live."

"You're not going back, are you?" Huey said.

"Matter of fact, we were just talking about it this evening. We've been on the road a long time and I was thinking it would be nice to settle down to a little security. Winter's coming up soon—"

"Oh no!" Huey exclaimed, shaking his head. "You can't do that. You made it all the way up here. What do you want to go back down for?"

"It's a kind of a far-out place if you get to know it," I said. "New York is such a concentration of everything."

"A concentration bummer, brother."

Huey was still shaking his head when his friend with the thick glasses tapped his shoulder. He asked Huey if he could dig another

249

rush, and then Huey and I got up and went into the bathroom. The arrangement was the same as before. This time Huey offered to hit Jesse.

"I can't do no more, Huey," Jesse told him. "I got to see my probation officer tomorrow so I got to catch some sleep tonight."

"Send a friend to tell the cop you're sick," Huey suggested.

"Send a friend to take your place," I suggested. "To cops, all hippies look alike."

Huey paused to stare at me for a moment. Then he went hysterical again. "To cops, all us hippies . . . *Right, brother, right!* You got it! Oh brother, you're so far out. You really dig what kind of space we're all into!"

Personally, I found Huey's reaction a lot funnier than my quip. Anyway, we got down to getting high, and Jesse let Huey hit him up. Each person squirted a fine spray of his blood into the sink when he was finished. Then Huey and I returned to our positions by the kitchen table.

While I rested my elbows on my knees, Miki was strutting past the kitchen table wearing a derby hat. I couldn't guess where she'd found it, but the way she looked made me feel that I must have been watching a movie. No, I must have been dreaming I was watching a movie. Miki pranced back and forth across the screen in front of me, tilting the hat to different sides, experimenting to find the most jaunty way to wear the hat. She was smiling with her mouth open and looking up with sparkling eyes as if a friendly bird had just landed on her head. Then she squatted on the floor next to me and placed her left hand on my knee for balance. I pulled back my elbows and drew my knees up closer to my chest as I began to get an erection.

"My dad used to wear a hat just like this one," Miki smiled. "Not all the time, only when he was kidding around with me. We used to kid around like that all the time. He'd dress up in this hat and a funny old checked jacket, and then he'd bring out his banjo and play for me. We'd run and dance all around the house singing, 'Way down upon the Swanee River, far far away . . .'" Miki was bouncing to the tune and smiling cheerfully. " 'That's where my heart is . . .' And half the time we couldn't even finish the song, we thought it was so funny. And we'd laugh and laugh . . ."

"It sounds nice," I said softly, smiling back at her, thinking how much she looked like a little girl who was trying on her father's hat.

"My dad is terribly attached to me," she went on. "Every time I call my mom in Toronto, she tells me I really should come home to see my dad. She wants me back too, of course, but she knows how dad feels."

Suddenly, I wanted desperately to take her home with me. Not on a motorcycle, not to rumble around town with, I just wanted to show her a warm, secure, nonsterile apartment—a home.

"Have you ever been to New York, Miki?"

"I already told you."

"Well, how'd you like to come to New York with me and John?"

"You mean you'd bring Wendy and me to New York? Really?"

Wendy hadn't fit into my picture of it. But I was speeding and anything was feasible. If Wendy's presence would make Miki feel more secure about coming with us, then Wendy would also come.

"Sure, both of you can come, if you want to."

"Oh, Steve, this is wonderful!" Miki said and kissed me. Then she called across the table top to Wendy: "We're going to New York!"

Wendy skipped past the table and squatted next to Miki. She put her hand on my other knee and listened to the plan. She was as excited about going as Miki was. I was beginning to talk and *feel* like a drifting gambling man who was about to turn on the bright city lights for a couple of sweet farm girls.

"How are we going to get there? I sold my MG a long time ago," Miki said.

"Don't worry about that," I assured her. "I've done it before. All you have to do is get somebody to act as your mother and telephone the Vancouver Children's Aid Society and say you have no way of getting home to New York. They'll pay for your ticket and bill New York welfare later."

251

"If we can't do that, my mother will pay for me," Wendy said.

"Are you serious? She'll pay to ship you to New York?" I said.

"Sure, she's hip. And she's got plenty of money."

I pressed the subject further to discover that Wendy's mother sent her a regular allowance check, at one time to that girl Darlene's house and now to Ann's address.

Then I noticed Huey shaking his head again at the kitchen table.

"What's happening, Huey?" I asked.

"You can't do it. I don't know how to tell you, but you just can't. You people are so far out—Miki, Wendy, Steve, John—how can you want to leave this beautiful place to go back to the States?"

"It's another trip, Huey, just another trip," I explained.

I saw that John was observing everything, but I couldn't detect a clue in his face to reveal the way he felt about any of it. What the hell, John was tolerant; he could dig it.

It was well past midnight when the guy with the thick glasses organized the next bathroom party. The speed was free, so I wasn't going to pass it up. But I was feeling jittery so I asked Wendy if she would hit me. She sprung up off my knee. Since the bathroom was packed, we waited for a chance to take a fit and a taste of methedrine into the bedroom. I sat on the edge of the bed while Wendy did her stuff. I was impressed, as always, by the way her eyes concentrated so intently on her work. Then I noticed something else.

"Hey, are you wearing eye makeup?"

Wendy glanced up at me and then looked back down at her fit as she said, "Yeah, so what?"

"Nothing. I was only wondering. I thought it might have just been my own crazy eyes."

Wendy was uptight because she had never worn the smoky blue eye shadow nor the subtle mascara any other time I had seen her. And I guess she knew it did not fit with her image. Putting on that eye makeup made her seem about as much like Miki as putting on a motorcycle jacket would have made Huey seem like Marlon Brando.

252

Wendy pursed her lips as she poked the point into my vein. She began to pull slowly back on the flagger. And a bubble began to appear inside the syringe. A miss! Wendy's mouth was hanging wide open. She almost dropped the fit, so I took the syringe out of my arm. I felt sorry for her.

"Don't worry, I won't tell anybody."

She was still embarrassed and flustered after I hit myself, so I left her alone in the room after the rush. I went into the kitchen and sat down next to Miki and John at the table.

"Do you believe it? Ann's back out on the Island with Frank and his crew again," John said. "If nothing else, I'll give Frank credit for his energy."

"The switch from here to New York is a lot greater than the one between here and Vancouver Island," I commented.

"In some ways, I guess . . ."

"When we're in New York, will I get to fix up my own room?" Miki asked.

"Sure, Miki, any way you want it," I smiled. Just hearing her talk about it was rejuvenating my rushes. How could I ever let her down?

"How big is your apartment?"

"About like this," I said. After all, it wasn't entirely different. Our lower East Side apartment included most of the same components—a livingroom, kitchen, bedroom, bathtub, toilet—it was all just arranged differently. "Do you know what a railroad flat is, Miki?"

"Uh-uh. What is it?"

"Well, that's what they call the kind of apartment John and I have back in New York."

Railroad flat. Comfortable. "They are very comfortable apartments, Miki." A smooth way to travel. "Wonderful, I like comfort." It's a smooth way to go because the lighting bears less strain on your eyes—at least it did in our place. You notice they don't call them subway flats. Our place went well under a warm red light bulb. I remember a couple of weeks in New York City that I spent

253

hibernating inside the tiny back bedroom with thick blankets nailed over the window and a red light bulb dangling from the ceiling. John was out of town at the time. I was at home, wrapped inside a green bathrobe, seeing my world through dark shades, secure. That was a rare kind of security. I couldn't have found it in this Vancouver apartment. The light in the kitchen glared like the inside of a subway car. Of course, it was helpful in the bathroom when I had to concentrate on one point. But now in the kitchen, the light seemed to be pulsating. I was more conscious of the light itself than I was of the things it was supposed to be illuminating. When I stared at the kitchen table, everything around it blacked out so that nothing was left but that gleaming white surface with its unevenly scattered golden flecks. The light was even affecting my hearing. For a timeless period, timeless like a rush, a dull ringing sound filtered out words and left nothing but me and the surface of that table.

"Steve, are you with us?"

I looked up, guessing that it might be John's hand on my shoulder which was bringing me back into the room. But it was Huey.

"Are you with us?"

I said sure and followed him into the bathroom. We finished the last of the methedrine. The rush was what I had needed.

"Look at this cat," Huey said, making me slightly paranoid by the way his index finger was in front of my face. "He's really up there now. Look at him. Really on top of it, into his own space. Feel where his head is at, Jesse? Up there, Steve, you are really up there."

I grinned although I wasn't in a mood to have all that attention drawn to me. I was glad when Huey lowered his finger.

"Really up there. Jesse, I got it! It just hit me who you are, Steve. Brother, this is so far out. Steve, you are a pirate! Dig it, Jesse, with all that curly hair pushed back and freaking out behind his head—a pirate. Can't you just see this cat with tattoos and a saber in his fist? And a big gold hoop through his ear! That's what you need, brother, you've got to get yourself one of those gold earrings."

254

"I always thought I'd look kind of neat with an earring," I admitted. I was enjoying the pirate image. I almost turned around to look in the mirror, but I decided that taking Huey's word for it would be safer.

"Don't just think about it, brother, get one!" Huey's excitement was increasing. "Listen, one of the chicks who lives here is bound to have a sewing needle. I'll get it while you get the ice."

We went into the kitchen. I opened the freezer as Huey asked Wendy about the sewing equipment.

"What are you looking for?" Miki asked me.

"Ice. Huey's going to pierce my ear."

"And you're letting him? Don't do it, Steve, I'll hate the way you look."

I shut the freezer.

"You'll look stupid. Don't let him goad you into it," Miki said.

I sat at the kitchen table to think.

"What do you think, John? Think I should get my ear pierced?"

"Makes no difference to me, Steve."

Then Wendy burst in: "If you do it, we're not coming with you to New York."

I hated her. I hated her. She was every chick who'd ever held herself over my head as a tempting reward for when I was good. But I didn't even want Wendy. She nauseated me. I looked at her as she stood up next to Miki, and she looked pudgy and disgusting. Now I wanted more than ever to have my ear pierced.

"Are you getting the needle, Huey?"

"Can't do it, Steve. They don't have any sewing stuff."

"All right, we'll do it tomorrow." No pudgy little bitch was going to stop me from doing what I wanted to do. I went into the bedroom with Huey. Jesse and those other guys were already in there. We talked, and before long we were beginning to crash from the speed.

An hour before sunrise, I walked through the livingroom and stared with envy at the three sleeping bodies inside their sleeping bags. I rinsed my mouth out with water in the kitchen and then returned to the bedroom. Even Huey wasn't talking much.

"Know any place where I could cop another dime?" the guy with the thick glasses asked me.

I told him I knew of a place where we could cop later. Then the room rang with silence for a while. I got up again to go to the bathroom. Pissing took a long time, as it had regularly since the first time I shot MDA.

When I returned to the bedroom, the guy with the glasses looked like he was ready to start crying. He was staring at the wall. I asked him what was wrong.

"These guys are saying I'm wired out," he practically whimpered.

I looked at the gray stripes, like narrow shadows cast by syringes, shadows that trailed down his forearm halfway to his wrist. The syringes were no longer in his arm, but those shadows remained.

"Nobody's saying you're strung out," Huey assured him. "All I'm saying is that you have to draw the line someplace, know when to cool out for a while."

"And I *am* drawing a line. I just want to split one more dime with Steve. I'm not wired out. I only do it on weekends and you know it."

"What about Thursday?" Jesse reminded him.

"What about it? So I had a day off. So what? So just get off my back and leave me the fuck alone!"

Like dreams, speed parties have a way of taking sharp turns, and it all seems perfectly normal to you while you're speeding. At one point everybody is surging with a sense of the beauty of life and people, and at another point—equally real—you feel that you'd do anything just to keep the bastards from crowding you and to get them to shut up.

When you must wait, the time between sunrise and the time people wake up and climb out of their holes is one eternity.

What time does Chemical Row open for business? I could only guess, so I waited for Matthew and Jainie to come home. I tried their house early in the morning a couple of times. Nobody home.

256

Then I tried it once again before noon. Jainie answered the door.

"Where's Matthew?" I asked.

"He's at the store. What's happening?"

"Nothing, I was wondering if you knew of a particular address where I could cop some speed for a friend of mine."

Jainie was shaking her head.

"What's the matter?" I asked.

"It never does seem to dawn on you, does it? Stevie, you're one person, boy . . ."

"One person what?" I snapped. She could go to hell for all I cared. I was in no mood for pious lectures.

"You just never know when to quit, do you?"

"Look, I'll see you and Matthew later." They were two of my best friends in Vancouver, yet both of them were always coming down on me in their different ways.

I went back to Miki's place to pick up the guy with the glasses, and then the two of us went to the house on Chemical Row where Frank had copped his MDA. They sold us a dime of methedrine. We went back to Miki's and got off one last time.

Hell, I felt lousy that night. And my misery had no company because Huey and his friends were gone. By midnight, John was asleep on the livingroom floor. How I envied him. My jaw muscles were cramped. And I could barely stand without my knees buckling. I sat for another hour at the kitchen table before I decided to give sleep another chance. It was a long walk across the room. I lay down on the mattress on the livingroom floor. Then I wrapped myself in a blanket and clutched the blanket at my neck. I waited.

"We're sleeping there, Steve," Miki said just as I began to doze.

I groaned. "Oh come on, I haven't slept since Saturday."

After a pause, Miki said, "Okay, you can sleep there, but we're sleeping there with you."

My feelings were mixed. The mattress was twin-sized, meant for only one person. Naturally, I would have had no objections to having Miki alone join me. But Wendy made three. And I never liked to be crowded when I slept.

My attitude changed quickly as Miki slithered in between me and Wendy. She was wearing a soft blue nightgown. We were all lying on our backs, waiting. Miki's slinky body fit neatly into the narrow space between me and Wendy. We all lay motionless. I was thinking. What was the proper procedure? Could I exclude Wendy from this entirely? Or would I have to politely allow her to join us? No problem, I decided, I would let what happens happen.

While I was thinking, Miki began wriggling and wrestling with Wendy. They were like playful lion cubs. I felt the softness of Miki's nightgown. I felt her foot kick me as she leaned over to whisper something into Wendy's ear. And that's when I realized what was happening. Miki was interested in Wendy—not me. I couldn't remember the last time I had felt so insulted. Wendy sat up and rested her elbows on her knees. Now *she* was thinking. If she decided against it, I might still have a chance with Miki. Better to play second string than no string, I figured. But then I figured that Wendy might make it with Miki to get back at me. Who could guess what her motive would be? Who would care?

I don't know what finally persuaded Wendy. It might have been one of the things Miki whispered into her ear while she sat there thinking. I only heard the last thing Miki whispered:

"I'll give ya fifty cents!"

Ah, Miki, I would have given you at least a dollar.

28

Though I spent long periods away from New York without it bothering me, when I finally did feel a need to complete my circle by going home, the need hit me with a sense of urgency; it was as if I might fade away if I couldn't get back. That was how I felt in California in the late fall after living with Ellen and at my Uncle Mike's place. And now that's how I felt in Vancouver.

John had it easy. Through his publisher, he was scheduled to give a talk about his book at some convention of librarians in New England in October. They were paying for his plane ticket to New York.

Meanwhile, I waited an hour in the reception room of the Children's Aid Society on Broadway. When it was my turn, they took me into a small office where I told a caseworker I was a runaway from New Jersey. I told him that I was wanted by the cops back there. My caseworker was hip and friendly. He said he could arrange to have me flown home if my mother would phone him to verify my story. "But don't get your girlfriend from Winnipeg to call—it has to be your mother," he said half in jest as I stood up to leave his office. "Don't worry, I'll have my girlfriend from New York call you," I grinned.

Actually, I planned to ask my older sister, Martha, to phone Children's Aid and pretend she was my mother. Martha lived and went to college in New York, but I figured she'd be at my parents' house since school hadn't started yet. So I dialed my parents' number in New Jersey.

My mother answered the phone.

"Is Martha there?" I asked, hoping to sound like Billy Dumont, her boyfriend.

"She's not in at the moment. Who is calling?"

I paused, debating over whether or not to hang up. No, might as well talk. "It's me . . . Stevie."

"Where are you now?"

"I'm in Canada. Do you know when Martha will be around?"

"Canada? Are you making another of your phony credit card calls? I told you not to call this house with illegal credit numbers. I don't want the phone company on my back again."

I told her I wouldn't do it again. And then, figuring that getting Martha to act as my mother would involve hassles, I asked my mother to do it. I told her about the deal with the Children's Aid Society. "All you have to do is call them and say you're my mother and you want me home. Then I'll go to New York—"

"Don't ask me, Stevie. I've had enough of your shady deals. Every time I hear from you, it's another shady deal."

"But this isn't shady. Kids do it all the time to get home. All you have to say is—"

"I don't want to have to say it again. *No more shady deals.*"

I wasn't going to change her mind. So we said goodbye and I hung up.

To tell the truth, I was stunned that my mother was still bearing her grudge against me. It had been nearly a year since she and my father dropped me off at Newark Airport to send me to California. I'd only seen her once since then, when I was living in New York, and she threw me out of her house.

260

The sad thing was that I liked my family. I liked my siblings a lot, but I was a long way out of touch, practically a stranger. Christ, I had a younger brother and I barely knew him. I felt that I knew Michael from Vancouver Island better than my own brother. What kind of a brother did that make me?

I had to get back.

I set plans to fly back to New York by the end of the week. First, I asked Jainie to phone Children's Aid and act as my mother. Then I panhandled near the library. I made a dollar and a half, but I spent it right away on food. I had to do better than that. I met John at Miki's. We discussed plans. John was set to leave on Thursday, but uncertainties were still hanging like a hatchet over my head. I was pressed for time and money. Meanwhile, Miki and Wendy were giggling about something by the kitchen table. Silliness. It irritated me that they felt they could afford to be so frivolous while I was giving myself a nervous breakdown setting things up for all of us.

Much of my anxiety was relieved later that afternoon when John and I stopped in at Matthew's. Jainie was excited when we walked in.

"I did it, Stevie! Everything's cool!"

"Great, do you think they believed you?"

"I think so because I really got into it, boy. It was so funny. When I called them I asked right away to speak with your caseworker, and the lady said she'd get him, so I said okay but could you step it up because this is a long distance call, y'know. So she said yes ma'am, and went and got your caseworker. I was surprised; that guy was really nice. I told him the story you told me, y'know. I really got into it. Like I kept saying: 'I wish he'd get home as soon as possible because he's into enough trouble already and I'd hate to see him get into any more.' And the caseworker was saying: 'Yes, yes, well, we'll get him home soon.'"

"Thanks a lot, Jainie. Really, I appreciate this," I said.

Matthew was paying no attention to us. He was on the living-room floor, dividing a brick of grass into even lids.

"What are you asking for those?" John asked him.

"Fifteen, twelve," Matthew said.

"Have you weighed any of them?" John asked.

Matthew handed him a rolled-up Baggie, and John unraveled it to inspect the contents.

"Looks like an excellent dime or a very pathetic ounce," he said.

"It's a Vancouver lid," Matthew said. "If yer interested in doing some dealing fer me, I'll front ya a few of them lids and ya can pay me back ten bucks fer each."

"It's a deal," I blurted and crouched on the floor to check out the lids. They were on the skimpy side, but considering what's usually on the street, most people wouldn't complain. And if they didn't like the looks of it, well, nobody was forcing them to buy. This opportunity was a lifesaver! With the money I would earn from this, I wouldn't be landing in New York flat broke, the way I always seemed to land everyplace.

Matthew stood up while I picked out four lids. Then I looked up and all I saw were Matthew's pants like giant sticks of salt-water taffy in front of me.

"Jesus, Matthew, look at those pants! Man, I was underestimating you when I called you a fop."

The pants were skin-tight, pink, thin cotton bell-bottoms with a white tie-dye around the left knee. Yet Matthew was standing there, nonchalant, as if he were wearing any old pair of jeans. Matthew, the unflappable; he had developed a skill at ignoring people's reactions to his clothes. He enjoyed every minute of it, though.

"Yer gonna take them four? Okay, ya can pay me tomorrow."

"I'll leave them here for now," I said. "I'll start my dealing at the Travelers tomorrow."

Then I thanked Jainie again for her good work, and I went with John across the gravel driveway back to Miki's. The way everything was suddenly working out for me was invigorating, and I wanted to top that off with a long shower. John also wanted to take one. But unfortunately for both of us, Miki was occupying the bathroom. We waited with Wendy in the livingroom, and that became unpleasant because Wendy and I had developed quite a distaste for one another at this point. She was babbling about getting her hair styled and taking her turn in the bathroom before me—she reminded me of that at least three times—so I brought up the fact that she had ripped me off for twenty dollars worth of MDA when she left Vancouver Island. I didn't mention anything about the party plan, but she knew what I was talking about. Still, she managed to rationalize her way out of it, asserting that I had given her and Miki the MDA. I didn't want to bring Miki into it; I preferred to pin the whole thing on Wendy. So I dropped the subject for the time being. We waited silently for a while. Miki was taking her time. Finally, I decided to return to Matthew and Jainie's to take a bath in their tub. John waited for his turn after Miki and Wendy.

I took my knapsack across the driveway. Matthew and Jainie were in the kitchen.

"Is it cool if I take a bath here?" I asked.

"Sure," Jainie said. "But wait a minute, I have to ask you something. Did you take my potato salad from the refrigerator?"

I looked guilty. "Yeah, well, John and I were hungry and we figured it was only going to get spoiled . . ."

"Shit, man, I made that potato salad for *us,* not you. I just this minute looked in the refrigerator and I find the pot is practically empty."

"Yeah, well, I'm sorry about that. I didn't know . . ."

"You should be sorry, boy."

What more could I say? I went into the bathroom and took a bath. I tried to forget that Jainie seemed to be coming down on me again. I had better things to think about. I smoked and soaked in the tub until my toes looked like albino prunes.

Getting dressed again, I put on my purple pants. That put me into a mood for city dope-dealing. Then I went into the livingroom.

"Hey, Matthew, would it be cool if I borrowed that tie-dye tee-shirt of yours for while I'm dealing tomorrow? It'll put me more into a dealing spirit."

Matthew was hesitant.

"I'll make you more money if I'm in the right mood," I pointed out.

Matthew said all right and went into the bedroom to get it for me. He pulled it like a handkerchief out of a drawer and held it out for me. I put it on. It was a tight-fitting athletic tee-shirt that Matthew had tie-dyed pink with a big circle on the front. The circle was like a sun radiating pink all over my chest. With that shirt and my purple pants, I felt like a jet-setter.

"Hey, could you spare a smoke?" I asked.

Matthew hesitated even longer this time. That annoyed me. I couldn't believe he would ever begrudge me a smoke after all we'd been through together. Back in San Francisco, I used to shoplift whole cartons of cigarettes regularly, and I always shared them with Matthew and everybody at our apartment. We were partners back then. Had Matthew forgotten?

After finally giving me one of his Player's, Matthew said, "I set aside yer lids fer when ya want 'em."

"I guess I might as well take them now," I said. Having those lids in my possession was going to make me feel secure.

Matthew brought four lids from his bedroom. "I'll front yer some more after ya sell these."

"Man, I'll be running back here every hour tomorrow. Just watch."

That night:

Ann came home with some new friends of hers who were from a New Mexico commune. She'd met them at Wreck Bay, and now Ann was loaded on good vibes and MDA. She kissed me and told me I was beautiful at one point in the evening. Then I spoke with her one other time to ask if Frank were back in town. "Oh, Daniel?" she said. "Yeah, he drove with us, but he's going right back to the Island tomorrow to organize everything. There is a man on the beach who is going to let Daniel and Nick use some land he has in British Columbia north of here so they can start their commune." Well, I thought, that will be one commune I'll have to see.

Later, Miki told me she liked my pants and new shirt.

Then I slept with Miki and Wendy again, but tonight was different. As I was kneeling on the mattress, taking off my shirt, Miki kneeled next to me, pressing herself against me. She kissed me, deeply from the start. Then she pulled away just as I was really getting into it.

"How was that, eh?" she smiled.

Fine, Miki.

The three of us took off our clothes, Miki and Wendy under covers, and we were in bed. I wasn't even noticing Wendy.

Miki was beautiful naked. But no, she wasn't entirely naked: she still had her eye makeup on. It bothered me. I said something about it, but she only made a joke about it. She was frolicsome. In the beginning. But she grew more passionate. We were rolling around in our narrow space. I held her. She was with me all the way tonight.

Almost.

Suddenly, she was acting coy. I pulled her to me and kissed her hard, thinking this chick really knew her game.

She wouldn't let me into her.

I kissed her tenderly then, hoping she'd change her mind. I wanted to make love to you, Miki. But I couldn't wait all night.

So I took it out on Wendy.

We hitched and walked to the Travelers after the feed-in the next day. John was in exceptionally high spirits. Lucky bastard, he was set to leave for New York the next morning. I had checked with Children's Aid, and they said I would probably get a Friday or Saturday flight. Probably. I had to check back with them again because they couldn't give me the luxury of an exact departure date. And I had another worry: I still might have to help Miki make her arrangements. But maybe Wendy's mother would pay for Miki, too. I didn't know. I was still sure of little. So now I was going to use the waiting time by dealing.

Actually, like John, I was feeling pretty good. Any kind of hustle is a good way to make the time go. When I'm feeling impatient for something to happen, I can even appreciate panhandling.

A car dropped us off on Pender Street near the Little Miss Chief Restaurant. We walked along the busy street toward Gastown. At one point, we passed a pipe and tobacco shop, and I pulled John back to look at the window display.

"Check out that pipe, man," I said.

"Which one?"

"The curvy one in the middle row. Man, that's the kind of pipe I'm going to buy when we get back to New York. A soothing pipe. And I think I'll pick myself up an easy chair off the street or maybe from New Jersey. Can't you just see me? Polishing that pipe, breaking it in for myself. You know, there's a whole proper procedure to breaking in a pipe. I'll do it just right. Then I'll sit back in my easy chair, puff on my pipe with a book in my lap—it'll be a whole different life. Man, I think I might buy that pipe here if I can make enough money today and tomorrow. There's so many things I want to buy . . ."

John laughed while I was staring into that display window.

"You just want new possessions that you can cry over after you lose them," he said.

"Is that a dig?" I said, half-joking, peering at John through the corner of my eye. John laughed and then we walked on.

It was too early for many people to be hanging out at the Travelers. But dealing was easy, anyway. I casually walked by the round tables asking if anybody was interested in lids. I never came on with heavy sales raps, just let the dope sell itself. And it did. I sold two of my ounces in ten minutes. After that, John and I sat and drank beers at a table near the entrance, ready to catch new customers as they walked in the door.

Two people stood in the entranceway. With the brightness of the outdoors at their backs and the relative darkness of the inside of the Travelers, I only saw them as silhouettes. Then they stepped

266

deeper inside, and I could see that they were young kids, not more than sixteen or seventeen. They didn't look too hip. But I figured they might have money so I approached the older one with the steel-rimmed glasses and the long greasy hair behind his ears.

"Interested in some grass?"

He looked at me and grinned as if he were bursting with secrets. I started to turn around since that type of grin always bored me, but then he told me that he was dealing grass himself. So I invited him and his partner to our table to compare merchandise. I sat against the wall next to John, and the kid with the glasses glanced over his shoulders with affected paranoia before pulling out one of his lids. He pushed it across the table to me. As soon as he took his hand off it, I decided not to show him any of my lids.

"This is a lid?" I said. Without any twigs, it was at least four times as fat as the biggest of mine.

"We're selling it as an ounce for twenty because we got a good deal, but there's more than an ounce there," he said.

"You should tell me about your connection," I said.

"Yeah, it was a good one. But this is the last of his shipment."

"So he sold it to you cheap," I said, unraveling the Baggie to sniff the contents.

"Yeah. We're gonna try to sell that now, so could you give it back?"

I took my time rolling up the Baggie and then handed it across the table. I remained nonchalant, but kept studying the kid's reaction. He seemed apprehensive, but maybe he was genuinely paranoid about dealing. His stuff smelled like grass, but a lot of teas and spices smell like grass to me. I wasn't sure. John and I were silent for a few seconds as we watched those kids go to the other end of the room near the pool table.

"You think it's grass?" John asked.

"Can't be," I said. "It just can't be. Not that clean at that price."

"Y'know, if it is real grass, you'd make better profit buying ounces from them than you're making now having those lids fronted to you by Matthew," John said.

"I thought of that. That's why I don't believe that's real dope."

I ordered two more beers at the bar. Then John moved the glasses that were cluttering our table to the table next to us. As we drank, John suggested that we move on to the Gastown Inn in search of new business.

Before our glasses were empty, another guy walked briskly through the entranceway. It was Matthew. He glanced around and then walked directly to our table and sat down.

"How's it going?" he asked.

I grinned and told him I'd sold two.

"Far out. Ya got my money?"

"Yeah, sure," I said, and gave him twenty dollars from my pocket.

Matthew took a second to count it, fanning it like a poker hand. Then he stuffed the money into his pocket and went up to the bar to order a beer. By the restless way he was moving, I guessed he might be high on amphetamines. He sipped his beer before he sat down across from us again.

"A thing happened today that I ain't been able to figure," Matthew said, and he took another sip of beer. "I checked my dope stash this morning and two lids ain't there."

"So what?" I snapped, angry about what I could see coming.

"So I ain't been able to figure it out, right? Except fer a few things that fit together. Like one thing is that the dope was stashed up in the attic, and the other thing is that the last time I checked it was just before ya took yer bath yesterday."

"So what does that mean?" I said loudly, resisting an urge to punch him in his face for insulting me like that. "Man, I couldn't have gone near that stuff because I didn't even know you have an attic."

"I just thoughtcha might've saw the trap door when ya were taking yer bath and got curious."

"Matthew, I couldn't even tell you what that trap door looks

268

like. And why the hell would I rip you of all people off for dope when I see you every day?"

"I dunno. Ya might've figured that yer splitting soon anyhow. And like with that potato salad in the fridge, ya might've figured . . ."

"Potato salad! Oh, Jesus, man, you're not going to start getting on me for that now. There's a whole big difference between tasting potato salad from somebody's refrigerator and ripping them off for dope."

"I just saw Frank today. He got back from Wreck Bay, right? And he said ya ripped him off fer that MDA and a lotta stuff."

"Matthew, can't you see Frank's flipped out? It hasn't been a month since he was out on that island handing out MDA to anybody who asked for it. And just before the last time I saw him, he was giving away all kinds of things to that partner of his, Nick. So before he decided he was down on me, he was giving me stuff, too. So what's the difference? Man, Frank was practically begging me to take over management of his brain for him. And who did you say you talked to? Frank or Daniel? Huh? It was Daniel, right? If you'd ask Frank about it, you'd get a different story altogether."

"Well, it still don't figure how my lids disappeared."

I was quite heated at this point, so John took over my side of the argument. He knew I wouldn't steal dope from Matthew. I sat back drinking beer and trying to cool off while John told Matthew that he certainly never knew about Matthew's attic and that he knows Steve and knows Steve wouldn't rip off Matthew's dope. Then Matthew began to suggest that I might have done it and not told John about it, but he knew that that suggestion was far-fetched so he dropped it quickly. By that point, I suppose Matthew had decided that I was likely innocent, after all. He began to change the subject. And then I felt more insulted than ever because Matthew was taking John's word where he wouldn't take mine. He wasn't even really friends with John, yet Matthew trusted him more than he trusted his friend. In Matthew's head, what was friendship all about? I wondered. I was thinking that

269

sometimes Matthew acted as if he and I were enemies.

"How d'ya deal in this place?" Matthew asked. "I ain't never done it."

"Just go around from table to table," I said.

"Ya sold two lids that way? That ain't bad. Yer doing better than I do a lotta the time on Fourth Street."

"Yeah, well, you see those two kids down by the pool table?" I said, pointing. "That's our competition, and they're going to wipe us out of business if people believe what they're selling is real dope."

"Big lids?"

"They make ours look like nickel bags."

"I gotta check this out," Matthew said. He went to the other end of the long room, said something to those two kids, and then returned with them trailing behind him. He sat back down at our table while the two kids remained standing.

"I ain't sure yet I wanna buy," Matthew said. "But if yer deal is as good as I hear . . ."

The kid with the steel-rimmed glasses brought out the lid he'd shown me. The contents were green and fine like sawdust—or like the marijuana powder that falls to the bottom of an ounce. But I'd never seen a whole ounce of that powder.

Matthew looked inside the opened Baggie and poked around. Then he closed the top of the Baggie and looked up at the kid with the glasses.

"This stuff mixes up real good with hot water," Matthew chuckled. "I remember drinking some down in San Francisco a few times. Real nice stuff. I forget what they call it . . ."

The kid's face was turning red.

"Shall we take all their money, boys?" Matthew said to me and John in a dramatic gangster movie voice. Then there was a pause.

"We don't have any money," the kid said nervously.

"Ah, come on, leave 'em alone," John said.

"We got a good dealing scene here in Vancouver and we don't like guys coming in and dealing tea and saying it's grass," Matthew said. "Ya must've smoked this. Ya ain't gonna tell me ya got off on it, are ya?"

"Some guy just sold it to us. It's weak—we know that—so that's why we're selling at low prices."

"Weak grass, shit. I don't wantcha going around selling this."

Then the kid took his lid and went with his partner out the door. Matthew rocked back on the two back legs of his chair.

"Didja see the shit them guys are trying to pass fer dope. Same stuff I used to drink down in San Francisco. It was pretty nice tea, though."

"Ah, you could've left them alone," John said. "Nobody's going to buy from them anyway. I think you freaked them out."

"Them guys need a good freakout."

We ordered another round of beers. And after that, we walked a few blocks to the Gastown Inn, a larger beer-drinking place. My only objection to Matthew staying with us was that he meant more competition. He had a few of his own lids with him and he was working my territory. So John and I left him and went on to a third, smaller Gastown hangout.

But before we moved on, I sold another lid in the Gastown Inn. My customer followed me into the men's room to inspect the lid, and so did Matthew and John. At this point, it seemed comical when we saw the same kids from the Travelers still trying to sell their tea. Their customer was smoking a sample joint which he had rolled from their lid, and his face was practically purple from inhaling so hard. He kept saying, "I think I'm getting a buzz, but I'm not sure." Then Matthew said from the urinal where he was pissing, "After yer done with that, wanna buy some grass?" I was beginning to feel sorry for those kids myself.

Anyway, I sold my lid and then sold the other one at the next hangout. Then we went back to the Kitslano area and I bought John and me a meal of orange juice and Muenster cheese. We ate on the beach.

I was doing okay, but I was still worried about the financial situation. I discussed the fact that Miki and Wendy owed me money,

271

and John said that I ought to ask them to pay me back if I needed the money. The problem with that, of course, was that they had no money. Half in jest, John suggested that I take some of Miki's clothes as collateral, to pawn if she didn't pay me back what she owed me. But I pointed out that secondhand clothes sold for very little. "Too bad she doesn't ski, or something like that," John said.

After eating and resting on the beach for a while, I went to Matthew's to pick up more lids to sell. John stayed on the beach. Matthew and Jainie were sitting in the kitchen when I got there.

"How'd you make out at the Gastown?" I asked Matthew.

"I did okay. I got rid of three lids."

"Great. Do you have a few more lids for me to deal for you this evening?"

"I ain't gonna be fronting ya no more lids, Stevie. I decided I'm gonna deal 'em myself."

That infuriated me. I was just waiting for Matthew to blatantly accuse me of stealing lids from his attic—an attic that might not even exist for all I knew—and then I would punch him out.

"Are you still thinking I ripped you off for your dope?" I demanded.

"I ain't sure of nothing, but I'm dealing my own lids."

"Look, why the hell would I only take two lids if I wanted to rip you off?"

"I dunno. Maybe ya thought I wouldn't miss two lids. But I already told ya: I ain't sure of nothing, but I'm dealing fer myself."

He was skirting the edges of a direct accusation, because he knew I'd punch him out. Matthew knew me. He knew I didn't take that kind of insult. But the frustrating thing was that I wouldn't have punched him out. I couldn't. Even enraged, I could see that punching out my friend wouldn't accomplish anything, nor would it make me feel better. I was doomed to feeling like a lousy fucker who couldn't even be trusted by his friends.

"Are you saying you think I'll rip you off if you front me dope?" I demanded.

272

"Stevie, I don't know everything that's happening, but I wouldn't trust you," Jainie broke in. "Not these days, anyway. Every time I see you you're fucked up in one way or another. I don't think you even know what you're doing. I'm sorry to have to be the one to say it, but . . ."

So that was their attitude. I could do nothing to change it. So I left. I didn't storm out or curse anybody out; I just left.

I needed money. Dealing was out. It was too late to make what I needed by panhandling. Miki and Wendy owed me money. Miki was really the one who'd taken my MDA. That bitch thought she could casually take me off, rob me blind, while I was being dazzled like a schoolboy by her pretty face, her innocent little-girl charm. I wasn't going to let her get away with making an asshole out of me. If I had to close my eyes and think of Wendy while I did it, I was going to get back the money she'd taken from me, the same money she was supposed to have spent on the makings of a birth-day party for John. A surprise party—she liked that idea when I suggested it on the Island. Now I was going to show that bitch a surprise. . . .

I stormed across the driveway and into Miki's apartment through the sliding glass door. I would be firm at the start, but without shouting. I stood there for a second. Miki and Wendy were in the livingroom.

"Miki, you owe me twenty bucks from that MDA I lent you and I need it now."

Miki was stunned. She stood up.

"But you gave me that. And I don't have any money," she pro-tested.

"Don't give me that shit. You've got something."

Then Wendy popped up indignantly and said, "Steve, why don't you just—"

"You shut up and sit down!"

Wendy plopped back down. Then Miki went on protesting.

"How much is that watch worth?" I demanded.

"You can't take this watch," she cried and backed up.

"You'll get it back. I'll take it to a pawnshop and give you the ticket."

"No!"

Miki started to whimper. She was using all her resources. But I wasn't going to let her trick me again. I grabbed her left arm and had to pull it behind her back before I could unhook the watchband. "No! That was a present!" Miki cried. Both Miki and Wendy were screaming at me as I walked out the sliding door.

That screaming stayed with me all the way to and from the pawnshop. Miki's sobbing was getting to me whether I liked it or not. I would have given all my money at that point if it could have been Wendy's watch I'd pawned, if it could have been Wendy's arm I'd twisted. I kept picturing Miki sobbing like a frightened child. Why couldn't I have made my point with Wendy?

The watch was cheap, one with one of those wide patent-leather bands. They gave me two-fifty for it.

When I returned to Miki's with the pawn ticket, John was in the livingroom. Miki and Wendy looked up and saw me at the sliding door. Then they got up and went into the kitchen to sit at the table. They were silently staring at the surface of the table as I walked up to Miki. I held the pawn ticket in front of her. She snatched it.

"Ha! Two-fifty is all you could get? Well, you really did well, eh?"

Miki was boosting her pride back up, and I let her. I could have pointed out that I only got two-fifty because I'd taken it to a pawnshop so that Miki could buy the watch back if she liked. But I was too depressed to talk about it.

"You're not welcome to stay here anymore, Steve," Wendy said. "John can stay here, but you can't."

I was past the point of acknowledging Wendy's existence. I picked up my knapsack and sleeping bag from the livingroom floor. Nobody needed to tell me; I hadn't expected them to start serving me breakfast in bed after that afternoon. John picked up his gear, too, and we walked together out the sliding door. The sun was still hours away from setting and there was only one place to go.

"What did they say to you about it?" I asked John.

"They told me what happened, and I told Miki that she was bound to pay a price if she went around indiscriminately ripping people off."

"I wish I didn't do it. If you could have seen her face . . ."

"It's kind of funny, actually, if you think about it—all that drama over a watch that probably would have broken tomorrow."

"I don't think it's so funny," I said. "I guess it looks like we'll be pulling into New York on our own, like the way we pulled out."

"Yeah, well, that's probably best. After all your talk about easy living and the secure life we're going to have in New York, it seemed kind of crazy to me to invite Miki along, anyway."

"Yeah, but there would have been some exciting craziness."

"That's what you want?"

"Ah, I don't know."

"To tell the truth, Steve, I don't think I would have let Miki and Wendy come along with us if it had come down to that. The only reason I never said anything was that I knew all along the deal was bound to fall through."

Maybe John was right. But pulling into New York with Miki— it certainly was pretty to think about.

We went to Children's Aid and arranged to crash at Catholic Charities for that night.

We spent John's last evening in Vancouver with Tim. We made a stop at Matthew and Jainie's so that John could say goodbye, and Tim was there. He looked different from the way he had on Wreck Bay. He was clean-shaven, neatly dressed, and his hair must have been brushed in every direction with a thousand strokes. He looked more than ever like the proud Afghan.

I became better acquainted with Tim that evening, and in a way my image of him was lowered. I had been in awe of him on the Island because I didn't know him and he was John's friend. But

275

that evening, as we wandered around downtown Vancouver, I decided that Tim was a male version of Miki, a male-fatale. I realized it after we had decided to panhandle money for dinner on Granville Street. John and I went one way while Tim went the other. But when we met again in fifteen minutes, Tim was not panhandling. I asked him about it, and he told me that he never panhandled himself because he knew girls who hung out on Granville Street who would gladly do it for him. His beauty was enough to hustle those chicks.

That's one reason why he and Miki were such a match for one another. I remembered watching Miki trying to put the make on Tim a few times on Vancouver Island. She wasn't accustomed to guys who didn't climb all over her, so she must have seen Tim as a challenge. And she almost won that challenge a couple of times. I remembered seeing her and Tim playfully wrestling around on the sand. The craziest part of it was that the reason Tim's resistance to Miki was low on Vancouver Island was that there were so few mirrors around. But the few times I did see Tim near a mirror, nobody could steal his attention. People have accused me of narcissism at times, but I could never compare with Tim in that respect. He was unbelievable. I never met anybody for whom beauty was such an affliction.

I suppose some people would call this hypocrisy—that my opinion of Miki was that she was a classy chick, yet when I decided that Tim was on her level, my opinion of him diminished. That's the way it goes.

Anyway, I got along better with Tim that evening than I had in the past. He still treated me disdainfully, but it was almost in jest at this point, like a game we were playing with each other. At one point in the evening, for instance, Tim took us to a restaurant on Granville Street where he knew the cashier. The cashier had a sharply pointed, waxed mustache, and he said we could order anything we wanted. We ordered hamburgers so as not to be too extravagant. While we waited to be served, I asked Tim, "Is this the only reason you associate with this guy—to get free meals?" Tim

276

glared at me as if I were some kind of lowly creature who'd just shown its colors by insulting him. So I started to say, "Sorry, I just thought . . ." But then Tim smiled and said, "Yeah, you're right." After that meal, we went outside where John said, "Well, so long, Tim," and then John and I went to stay at Catholic Charities.

Sitting on our beds in the hostel, John and I talked about the good times that were coming in New York. Then I was amused to notice the kid with the greasy hair and the steel-rimmed glasses, the one who was dealing tea at the Travelers. Now he was trying to push one of his lids onto another kid at the end of the long room. I laughed and yelled down to his latest victim that the lid was full of tea.

After the lights went out, the same kid with the steel-rimmed glasses was sticking holes into his arm trying to hit himself up with MDA. After half a dozen misses, he whispered around the dormitory to ask if anybody else could hit him. The poor kid was desperate. So in the dark of the Catholic Charities Hostel, with the air of a couple of kids sneaking to watch television after bedtime, I hit the kid up with his fit and his MDA. And I didn't miss. In the dark. I was quite proud of that.

John left early the next morning. And when I called Children's Aid, they told me I could take a flight to New York that afternoon if I hustled.

So I hustled. First, I bought an item at the drugstore that would do more for my life in New York than would the curviest pipe and easy chair. It was a glass, self-flagging Luer-Lok syringe. It was the Rolls Royce of fits. I also bought a plastic disposable fit. Then from the drugstore I went to Matthew and Jainie's. When I told them I was leaving, they acted as if I were taking a bus to Calgary for the weekend. Well, if that's their attitude, fuck 'em. I went on to Children's Aid to pick up plane information. As I waited, I was feeling all sorts of mixed up and down feelings. So I went back to Matthew and Jainie's for one last goodbye.

They were out. The house was empty, and that emptiness made

277

me feel sad. Not only did they distrust me, but they couldn't be there for a simple farewell. Fucking Matthew. I felt like turning over the furniture. Instead, I went into Matthew's drawer and took his pink pants with the tie-dye ring around the knee. Then I located his lids and took four.

Some people might think it's funny that Matthew and Jainie didn't trust me. It's amazing where people are able to find humor. I remember a cute baby story that some of my family used to laugh over at places like the dinner table. It went like this. My sister, Lorraine, used to sit in her highchair at the age of two and point her finger at her brother and say: *"Bad . . . Bad . . ."* She'd say it over and over. And her brother at the age of three would get angry and frustrated insisting: "I am not bad!" until he was nearly crying.

Before catching my plane, I stuffed four lids of grass into my stash pockets, next to the last few caps of MDA which I'd been saving. Then I stuffed the syringes into my pants. But all this turned out to be unnecessary because they didn't even search my pack when I crossed through customs.

Between Toronto and New York, I went into the toilet cubicle and hit myself up with my plastic fit and the last of my MDA. I was flying home.

278

29

A bus deposited me in the East Side Terminal around three A.M. I wandered in a daze to the Lexington Avenue IRT subway station. A cop was patrolling the station, so I bought a token instead of hopping the turnstile. Besides, I was too weary to make the jump, almost too worn down to lift myself out of the bench when the train poured into the station. Three thirty. My eyes still smarted from the bright light of the clock when I boarded the train. Luckily, I had to share the car with only three other people. They were young. Two chicks and a guy, apparently friends, they stared at their dark reflections, familiar phantoms in the windows opposite their seats. They looked wasted. Were they crashed out on MDA, too? Or just undernourished? I was noticing the one with the teased red hair in particular. Practically no hips, or thighs for that matter, she couldn't have been more than seventeen. Her yellow teeth showed as she said something to the other chick. Then she glanced in my direction with her red hair and yellow teeth. In no shape for a staring contest, I switched my gaze to the Miss Subways placard above me. She was a black girl from the Bronx. Somehow

I took comfort in the idea that liberals still existed who would pick a black Miss Subways. The train stopped at Twenty-Third Street. The chick with the red hair stood up and whined, "How we gonna get across town now? We shoulda took the shuttle at Grand Central." Her back was to me so that I could see her black hair roots. She was not a chick, she was a guy dressed up with falsies. I squinted to study the other chick. She wasn't a chick either. The guy was a guy, though. They got off at Fourteenth Street. Before the train stopped, the red-haired one did a little dance in her red flats for nobody in particular; for me, I suppose. And she sang to the tune of *Camptown Races:* "Where do all the faggots meet? Christopher Street. Christopher Street."

I was back in New York.

And back on the lower East Side. St. Marks Place was deserted. No groups were playing that night at the Fillmore East, so no teenyboppers were hanging out late. And even the junkies were elsewhere to nod out for the night. Two cops in front of the silent, blue Electric Circus were busting one of the street's last late-night citizens. My pace automatically hastened in New York. I passed Gem's Spa, the candy store at the corner of Second Avenue. The sidewalk was wet and slimy. Rain was never enough to clean those streets, only enough to muddy the dog shit and begin turning old newspapers in the gutter into papier-mâché. I went four more long blocks, past Tompkins Square Park, and I was home.

But I still had to get keys from the landlord. It took a lot of banging to wake up his wife, and she was pissed about that, but she gave me the key. I still didn't have the key to the police lock, that heavy bar that braces the door shut. But luckily it was unlocked.

Home. Something was changed. I was too tired to pinpoint the change right away. But then I saw: the apartment had a new tenant.

Billy Dumont, my sister Martha's boyfriend, was asleep on a full-sized mattress on the livingroom floor. It was not a happy sight. Although I liked Dumont, I wasn't feeling up to seeing anybody other than John for my first week or two back in town. But Dumont had apparently moved in. John had left a set of keys with him before we hit the road. And now Dumont's KLH stereo, his most prized possession, was unpacked in the livingroom.

It wasn't enough to keep me from going to sleep right away on the lower bunk in the back room.

I woke up the next afternoon to the sound of *Music from Big Pink* on the KLH. I got up and went into the kitchen. Dumont looked up.

"Steven. Far out. I was wondering if you were going to sleep through the weekend."

I said good morning and sat down on the mattress across from Dumont.

Except that his hair was longer, he looked the same. As always, he was neatly dressed, wearing turquoise corduroy bell-bottoms and a blue tee-shirt upon which was stenciled the name and insignia of a New York boys' prep school which Dumont had attended two or three years ago, before he flipped out and went into Bellevue. His brown hair was neat, too, falling straight down to the middle of his back. He was still skinny and still barely five-seven, two facts that bothered him. And his face was handsome, though pale, and you could still tell by the way he carefully controlled his expressions that he was constantly conscious of people observing his face, whether or not they were actually doing it.

"You know, I'm really disappointed," Dumont said. "I wasn't expecting you back yet. I was expecting to have this apartment to myself for another month."

Even though Dumont laughed a bit after saying that, it annoyed me that he spoke as if I were invading *his* place.

"I wasn't expecting to see you either," I said. "I didn't think you'd take John up on his offer since you never dug this neighborhood. What happened to your place up by Columbia?"

"Oh, living with Ozzie got to be a drag so I decided to dig this place."

That meant that Ozzie had kicked him out.

"You still seeing Martha?" I asked.

"Nah, I had it with her a long time ago. Where've you been?" Dumont chuckled. "Martha and I stopped seeing each other after that time we spent down in Florida at my grandmother's. Steve, it feels far out to be free, no ties. I've lived down here alone for a month and a half, and you won't believe how many chicks I've balled since the beginning of August."

I was not in the mood to hear about it.

"I had a late flight from Vancouver, man, so I'm still kind of wrecked."

"Yeah, I heard from Sally that you and John were up there a couple of months ago. Where's John?"

"He's back, but he took an earlier flight than me. He mentioned that he might go first to visit his family in Jersey, so I guess he's there now."

"I can't say you look as well as you did when you and John first got back from Florida."

"Yeah, well, I probably lost some of that deep tan. What are you into down here, anyway? You still working at the post office?"

"Nah, I had enough of that working shit. I've just been taking life easy—you know, copping some reefer now and then. I'm very together."

"You still carry your nip bottle around?" I asked, meaning a half-pint bottle of Scotch which Dumont used to carry in his pocket for nips on the subway.

Dumont laughed for a few seconds. Then he halted the laughter and returned to his poker face. It was like switching channels back and forth.

"Is Deb still around?" I asked.

"Sure, still really strung out. I copped some skag from her a while ago, but it couldn't compare with this other stuff I had. We had a couple of junkies living across the hall last month, and they turned me on to some fine dope. I copped from Deb since then, but she's really disgusting."

I'd known Deb for a long time, and so had Dumont since all three of us were originally brought up in the same section of New Jersey. Now Deb was a junkie and she'd been hanging out on St. Marks since before John and I hit the road. I'd always dug her, even years back, back before she was a junkie, back when she was a speed freak. But Dumont put her down, as did most people who knew her.

Dumont put down a few other people as we continued our conversation, not that he hated everybody. I talked about a few of my latest road adventures, about Vancouver, and when Matthew's name came up, Dumont commented that he had never been able to understand what the big deal was about Matthew. He said that he'd met Matthew once in New York after hearing from Sally, Jainie's sister, that Matthew was one of the most amazing human beings alive. But as far as Dumont was concerned, Matthew was a dull character. Dumont was sometimes turned off when he met people about whom he'd heard praise. The time he met my friend Patrick, for instance, Dumont took an instant disliking to him. I guess that Martha had told him too much about the unusual person Patrick was.

Anyway, Dumont preferred to talk about chicks, so I told him about Miki, among others. Then Dumont talked about his sexual conquests. The topic was quickly becoming tedious. I remembered that the last winter when I was in New York, Dumont and I had often bragged like college fraternity brothers about all the chicks we balled, but we were never taking it so seriously as Dumont was now. Or were we? I didn't think we were, but I was beginning to wonder if the change in attitude was on his part or mine.

No, I'm sure we were joking when we bragged back then because we used to do it in Martha's presence and she always laughed hysterically. She used to say that Dumont and I were alike in many ways. Mainly, she said, we were both con artists. But I don't believe that he and I were all that much alike. He was more of a con artist than me because he was doing it all the time. He had more practice.

283

Billy Dumont understood the risks involved with spontaneity, and those were risks he avoided. He maintained control of his face, his gestures, and he felt most at ease when he was jiving somebody. The first time he met John, he gave John a rap about how he planned to cut his hair short and enter New Jersey politics with the aid of a few of his Mafia connections. Of course, I knew Dumont well enough to be alive to his jive. And the one time he, John and I played poker, I came out ahead. So I treated Dumont's jive lightly. I liked poking fun at Dumont because he was paranoid. He could take a joke to a point, though. He was amused, for instance, by the way John and I called him different names on different occasions. Ordinarily, we called him Dumont. But when his jive flowed in extraordinarily thick layers, we called him Bull. Martha, on the other hand, called him Billy most of the time, except when she affectionately called him Do-o-o-o-o-omont. And then there were those unusually relaxed times when John and I called him Billy, when we were very drunk, for instance.

"What are you doing for money?" I asked. "Don't tell me you're hustling all these chicks."

"Steven. What kind of charlatan do you take me for?" he said with mock indignation. I was not in a grinning mood. Then he went on: "I have enough money from the P.O. so that I won't have to find a gig for a couple of weeks. How about us observing the day of your homecoming with a taste of skag?"

Naturally, I was up for it. Dumont and I went to St. Marks Place near Gem's Spa, found a junkie acquaintance of Dumont's, and copped a couple of bags of dope.

Back at the apartment, I surprised Dumont with my new Luer-Lok syringe. He examined it as if he saw ones like it every day and was checking to see how this one compared with the others. But then something went wrong when I tried to hit myself. The self-flagging plunger didn't work. Dumont kept insisting that I must have been doing it wrong, while I kept insisting that I knew what I was doing. I later learned for sure that the fit was faulty.

"What the fuck kind of fit is that anyway?" Dumont scorned.

"An eyedropper is the only way to do it."

I put it away and used the plastic syringe. The contents of those small glassine envelopes were cut with a lot of quinine, but I got off on it.

I called John in Jersey that night, and he told me he planned to stay there for several more days. During those days, Dumont and I spent a lot of time high on junk. I ran into Deb on St. Marks often, and she looked as degenerate as ever. Seventy-five pounds of girl inside a hard shell of motorcycle jacket leather, she was a good connection.

On Thursday, toward the end of my first week back in New York, I was walking east toward Second Avenue along St. Marks Place. In my left hand I was carrying a quart bottle of Vin Rose, and in my right hand I was holding a long wooden stick which I'd picked up from the sidewalk. Bopping along with my walking stick, I was feeling pretty good.

"Grass . . . Acid . . . Mescaline . . ." I listened to the salesmen mumble names of merchandise as they passed me. "Speed, good speed . . ." Young girls were sitting on steps with their grimy toes curled over lower steps. "Change . . . Spare change . . ." It was a pleasantly sunny afternoon.

Near the East Side Book Store, a guy asked for a hit of my wine. I had seen that guy before, but I had never heard him speak except to mumble incoherently to himself. He was a young but weary black guy with tattered rags for clothing and knotted hair. Most of the time when I saw him, he was wandering around the Lower East Side with an old coat draped over his head. Somebody once told me that he had flipped out completely after eating about twelve hits of LSD in 1967.

I gave him my bottle, and he began chugging the wine down like water.

"Hit, man, hit!" I exclaimed and pulled the bottle away from him. I was thirsty, too, you understand.

He thanked me.

285

Then another black guy approached me. This guy looked healthy, though.

"Hey, Cane, how 'bout a hit offa that jug?"

I held out the bottle to him, but this time I made it clear that a hit meant a hit. This second guy only took a short sip before returning the bottle.

"Cane, is that your name, Cane?" he said, glancing down at my walking stick.

"That's right, man. So as long as your name isn't Abel, it's all cool between us."

The black guy suppressed a grin of his own as he did a mock take-back.

"You don't know my name, baby," he said. "I mean you gotta know who you're talking to, Cane. The brothers call me the clean-up man."

"That's far out because they call me the mess-up man," I said. "We might be able to get into some business together."

The black guy was amused. I quit while I was ahead and told him to take it easy.

I walked the rest of my way home along Seventh Street. Almost home, on the sidewalk next to a garbage-filled playlot between Avenues B and C, something suddenly pounded into my face. It came as total surprise, as if I'd walked into a sign or stood up quickly to bang my head on a low ceiling. For a second, I saw a huge guy, a guy I'd noticed on the streets before, standing in front of me with his fist still clenched like a hammer. "Why did you . . . ?" My words dropped with me onto the sidewalk.

Not more than a minute could have gone by before I opened my eyes again, but a crowd of people was hovering over me. They were mostly big Puerto Rican faces asking me if I could stand up. Then somebody flagged down one of the rare taxicabs that had ventured that far east. A few people helped me into the rear of the cab, and a girl paid the driver and told him where to take me.

Since they made me attend Sunday school when I was a kid, I already hated nuns. But I ended up hating them more after trying to get help in their Catholic hospital. While blood was streaming down my face, a nun was asking me questions about where I worked and about whether or not I had Blue Cross coverage. I kept asking for something to stop the bleeding, but she stalled me since she knew that she couldn't get any money out of me. "Would you please move your head back so you don't drip blood on my papers?" she said. I was trying to splash the blood onto her crisp white habit. But I couldn't do it because I was dizzy and she was out of reach. So I got up and went back to my apartment on Seventh Street.

Dumont told me that I looked a mess. I looked even worse than I had thought. Behind the blood, my nose was fractured, and only jagged pieces of my front teeth were left. The cracks in my two front teeth formed an inverted V.

"I'm gonna kill that motherfucker!"

I must have said that to Dumont a thousand times. One of the junkies on St. Marks was bound to have a pistol connection, and I envisioned myself cornering that huge fucker in an alley and taking my time to aim carefully at his head. Now *he* was going to be *my* victim. I would see him on the street again and I knew what he looked like. He was a black guy who always wore purple pants and a matching purple hat which made him look like an arrogant fool. Now I was going to show him what a fool he was. He was built like an ox, so I knew that killing him was the only way to revenge.

But I had no weapon yet, so the only immediate thing I could do for myself was to go out and cop a few bags of heroin.

Two days later, after I had abandoned the idea of murder, John came down to our apartment. While he was in New Jersey, he had celebrated his birthday so now he was loaded with presents: a few record albums including the Jethro Tull *Stand Up* album, paper and pens for writing, and two hits of LSD that a friend of his had given to him. He also brought with him a small portable television set. He had received a royalty check.

287

John unloaded his presents in our apartment, but he only stayed there himself for two nights. He gave me ten dollars for food before returning to New Jersey.

On John's first night back on Seventh Street, we hung out with Deb on St. Marks Place. Hanging out there was new to John, as it had been to me a week ago, since we looked down on the St. Marks scene during the time we lived on Seventh Street before our road trip. Now I was leaning with Deb on a parked car in front of Gem's Spa. We were on Deb's turf.

That evening was unusually pleasant with Deb; she even smiled and laughed some of the time. Saturday nights were always good nights for her because the Fillmore East was open. And that meant that hundreds of teenyboppers hung out on Second Avenue before and after rock concerts. Teenyboppers meant money. Deb claimed she could make seventy dollars on a weekend night by selling placebos to concert-goers. She would paint tiny vitamin B-12 tablets with orange Magic Marker and then approach kids with her hard sales rap about the fine sunshine acid she was dealing.

But even with the high spirits she was in on that evening, Deb spoke with a hard New York accent. And her sunken blue eyes never smiled through their gray tunnels.

In front of Gem's Spa, two guys with a videotape camera and recorder were interviewing a young girl on the sidewalk about ten feet from us.

"Wudda dem dudes askin' people about?" Deb asked me.

"Wait a second, let me listen," I said.

Behind the people who were rushing by between me and the interviewers, I could hear them asking the young girl her name and occupation. Then they asked their question: "What do you think about the death of Jimi Hendrix?" The girl had a soft voice so I couldn't hear what she was saying.

"They're asking about people's reactions to Jimi Hendrix dying," I told Deb.

Deb grinned up at John, her cheeks rippled like molded gray clay as they made that unusual expression. "Dey should ask you

288

about dat," she said. "I heard you're a writer an' all."

"I don't know how I'd answer their question," John said.

"Dey should ask me," Deb said. "I could say my name's Deb Cohen an' I'm a beat artist."

I laughed. "Right. All five-foot seventy pounds of you."

Deb was suddenly angry. "Don'tcha gimme none a dat shit, Stevie . . . I weigh seventy-five."

"Don't get paranoid," I said.

"Ah, shit, you got your hustle, I got mine," she said. Then turning to John: "I guess you gotta pretty cool hustle, too, if you can do it. . . . You got your shit together, I guess. You got your apartment, some money to eat . . . an' den you got dis tag-along here."

She meant me, and now I felt paranoid. But of course, that was her aim.

After a while, John and I went back to our apartment to sleep. Deb went back to working her beat with her brother, Robert, who was even more strung out on junk than she was.

Early the next evening, Dumont walked into our apartment and announced to John and me that he was copping dope for his sister, Betty, and anybody else who wanted a taste.

"She and Sally just came in with money from Jersey," he said. "How many bags should I pick up?"

"How ever many you want," I said.

"How about turning John onto a little taste tonight?" Dumont grinned.

John said that he was not up for it.

Then Dumont crossed the room and squatted next to the end of the mattress where John was sitting. He took John's right forearm to examine the veins. "Just check out these virgin veins, Steve," Dumont said without looking up. "They look just about nubile to me."

"They're keeping their virginity," John said.

Then Dumont turned to me. "Don't those veins look just ripe to you?"

289

"It's up to John," I said. And then turning to John: "But I must say, man, if I were you, I'd at least be curious to try it once."

"There are a lot of things to be curious about," John said.

Dumont stood up and said he'd be back in fifteen minutes with whatever he could get. Then he left.

While Dumont was out, I told John I wished that Dumont and everybody would leave so that I could find some peace for a while. John said he could appreciate my feeling, and that was why he was spending a lot of time in Jersey.

When Dumont didn't return after twenty minutes, we decided to meet him on the street. I also wanted to see Sally, who was in the city with Dumont's sister. I put on my purple pants before going out.

We met Dumont on the corner of St. Marks and Second, and he looked practically like a catatonic. His face was blank, like a rubber mask. I asked him what was wrong, and he told me he was waiting for a score to come through. Then I noticed his sister, Betty, standing next to Sally in front of Gem's Spa. My attention was diverted by Sally's beauty. Her beautiful eyes. She was tall like her sister, Jainie, but not that tall and she was very thin. She looked fragile. Her dark hair was not soft. It had grown inches since the time I'd lived with her in San Francisco, and I liked it better this way. But we were on somewhat bad terms, so I could only begin by acting superficially friendly.

"Hi, Sally, Betty, what's happening?"

Sally said hi.

"Billy just gave all my money to Robert to cop for us," Betty said.

"Robert? What the hell did he do that for? Doesn't he know Robert would rip off his best friend? If he had a best friend."

"We know it, Stevie. But Billy wasn't thinking. He's really freaked now. I wanna just forget it," Betty said.

I turned around and went to Dumont, who was still waiting at the curb.

"That Robert burned you, eh, Dumont?" I said.

"He may have been delayed for one reason or another," Dumont said, staring straight ahead.

"Oh, come on, man, don't be stupid. You know what kind of fucker he is."

Dumont said no more. His pride was destroyed.

John stood on the corner with Dumont while I went back to Betty. I asked her if she wanted me to retrieve her money for her when Robert showed up. Betty was wishy-washy about it, but she said yes, more or less. That Robert had to be shown that he couldn't get away with this. I went back to Dumont on the curb and told him I would get the money back if possible. I suppose that didn't help his pride, though.

Robert showed up in the next five minutes, and when he did, he quickly handed out a horseshit rap about how a bunch of guys had ripped him off. His tone of voice was apathetic, but the way he kept glancing from one person to another made it apparent that he was nervous that so many of Dumont's friends were around him.

Robert looked degenerate like his sister, but he looked degenerate in a way that was more disgusting than interesting. He was skinny, but unlike Deb he was tall. His posture was slumped and he was gangling, looking stupid in his black leather jacket with the STP stickers on the back; a lot of junkies look stupid. Also unlike Deb, who had had a nose job years ago, Robert had a big beak of a nose. And his head was shaved up the sides so that what hair he had sprouted out of the top of his head like a bush; apparently, he had been in jail recently.

Dumont didn't say anything to him.

"Don't give us your shit," I said. "Just give us back the money now!"

"It ain't nonna your business, Gibbons," he said. "An' I toldja I got ripped off."

"Then let me check your pockets."

"Fuck you, Gibbons. Nobody's goin' through dese pockets."

"You motherfucker, you either give me back the money now or let me go through your pockets."

"Okay, go 'head, check 'em. I don't give a shit." He raised his arms as if I were a cop. That of course meant he had stashed the money elsewhere, and now he was making an asshole out of me. So I frisked him slowly and meticulously to make him look like an asshole, letting somebody frisk him in the middle of the sidewalk.

"I toldja I got ripped off," he scorned. "So keep outa other people's business."

Then Deb walked up to us from St. Marks and asked Robert what was happening.

"Ah, dis little joik-off don't know what's his business," he told her.

And then the two of them walked away. I watched them turn left when they got to Seventh Street.

I had been counting on a taste of Betty's dope that night, so that made it my business. I went to Betty and asked her again if she wanted me to retrieve her money for her. And again she was wishy-washy. Deb was an old lover of Betty's, so Betty was slow to agree to anything that might cause an uptight scene. But again she said yes, more or less.

So I walked down Second Avenue with John next to me and Betty and Sally not far behind. I spotted Robert and Deb standing in front of a Seventh Street tenement building. John and I crossed Second Avenue, walking toward them, picking up speed.

When we were about ten yards from them, I suddenly burst forward, and running up to Robert, I slugged him in the mouth. He panicked. Right away, he was squatting like a monkey on the ground with his arms guarding his head. So I clamped my arm around his neck, putting him into a headlock. "Are you gonna give back that money now, motherfucker?" I was yelling.

But then a violent tugging at my hair and shirt distracted me, and somebody was kicking me. It was Deb. She was cursing me, and she wouldn't stop kicking my back and sides. That little girl was like a wildcat.

I looked up for help from John, but he kept standing still, frozen at ten yards distance. "Willya help me, man? Get this bitch off me!" I yelled. John was still for several more seconds, and then he unlocked himself to come and pull Deb from my back.

By that point, Robert had freed himself and run into the middle of Seventh Street. I chased after him. We started boxing, but he had no form at all. He was swinging his arms like hoses wildly through the air. I would have slaughtered him, but somehow he managed to put me into a headlock after lunging at me one time. It was a weird kind of headlock because it allowed me to put a head-lock onto him, too. So there we were, in an even match of choking one another to death. We wound up standing still, against the hood of a parked car, each of us not choking the other too much for fear that the other might choke him back equally hard.

John and Deb were standing in front of us, neither of them knowing what to do. John kept saying that it was ridiculous, that we should break it up, that nobody was accomplishing anything. To tell the truth, I would have gladly quit at that point. I was bored with the whole thing. I wanted to go home and get drunk or something. But I refused to release my hold right away when John started to try to pry our arms loose. I was waiting for Robert to loosen his hold on me first. Finally, we both agreed to release one another.

John said, "Let's get out of here," and we crossed Seventh Street.

"Well, at least I beat the money out of that motherfucker," I said, wiping a trickle of blood that was coming from my nose.

"It was a total drag," John said. "You got nothing out of it. You always seem to think you're going to get something, some kind of release. But I watch you, and you always wind up feeling shittier afterward."

"Man, he had it coming to him . . ."

Just then, I turned around to the sound of running footsteps behind me. It was Robert again, and John pulled him back by the waist before he had a chance to smash my head with the beer bottle that he was waving in his hand. Then everybody was yelling at everybody as we moved onto Second Avenue.

"Can't you cool out?" John said to Robert.

"Ah, I wasn't really gonna do it. I was pissed 'cause dis little faggot hit me when I wasn't lookin'."

"Horseshit, man," I said to Robert. "You saw me coming and you cowered because you knew you'd ripped off me and my friends."

"Stevie, you're so *stupid*," Deb yelled. "Cause I was just *talkin*' to Robert an' he *tole* me he got ripped off hisself."

"Look, just don't give me any more of your horseshit," I said and turned around to walk toward St. Marks with John.

Then Deb and Robert followed me and John up the east side of Second Avenue. They were trying to recover their pride.

"You wanna know where it's at, Stevie?" Deb shouted. "Where it's really at now is dat you're shit on da street, *boy*. You come by here all da time coppin' your attitudes . . ."

"You wanna talk about attitudes," I said.

"I *said*, you all da time comin' round here coppin' your atti-fuckin-tudes. Well, you ain't *nothin*' now, boy. You wanna cop, you just *try*, 'cause I'm tellin' Albert, Fat Georgie, *everybody* dat you're shit on dese streets."

Both Deb and I knew that she didn't carry that kind of weight on the street, so I saw no point in telling her about it.

"Makes no difference to me," I said. "I'm not strung out. I'm no fucking junkie."

"You just remembah when you come 'round dat you're shit on da street, *boy*," she repeated. "You can't even tell what's your business an' what's not."

"Look, I was up for a taste of that dope your brother ripped off. And for another thing, Betty asked me to get her money back for her, and I believe in *helping* friends. Look, here's Betty now. Ask *her* about it."

Betty and Sally were slowly crossing Second Avenue. But when Deb asked Betty if she had asked me to help her, Betty didn't answer. I glared at her.

"She ain't never asked you to do *nothin*'," Deb scorned.

"So you wanna fight me fair now, faggot? We'll go right down da block, an' dis time I ain't lettin' you hit me from behind," Robert said, tempting me to kill him.

"What are we, in junior high school?" I said. I was bored with fighting.

"You little faggot."

Finally, Deb and Robert left. I don't know what happened to Dumont, and I didn't discuss it with him later. Betty was against the wall of a bank building, avoiding my eyes.

Then Sally told me that she was amazed that I was able to do things like that. "I never could do that, just go up and hit someone like that. I'd be scared. I couldn't even stay by to watch you." Sally admired me.

295

30

"What then, you're going to let that acid sit in the freezer for the rest of the year?" I said.

"All I know is, neither of us is in any kind of shape to think about tripping," John said.

"Man, I bet it would put our heads back into shape," I insisted. I had a rut to climb out of. The week since that street fight with Robert had been filled with wine and junk.

"Hey, where'd you get those pants?" John asked suddenly. "Aren't those Matthew's pants?"

It was my first time to wear the pants in John's presence.

"Oh yeah . . . Matthew laid them on me before I left Vancouver."

"That was pretty generous of him."

We were getting off the subject. I still wanted to convince John that tripping would be good. It seemed like the only way to clear my head after that week.

That week:

The apartment was jammed, even while John was in Jersey. Deb

296

needed a place to stay, so my hassle with her brother was forgotten. And Dumont's sister, Betty, was also there every night, along with me and Dumont.

Typical of the scene at the apartment that week: We ripped off Deb's junk. About two o'clock on Friday morning, Deb was asleep, or off in some gone state which was like sleep. She was sitting up on the mattress with her eyes open. But she was totally out. I had to remove a cigarette from between her fingers so that it wouldn't start a fire on the mattress. Then Dumont and I got the idea to steal her wake-up shot. We took the glassine envelopes from the pocket of her jacket and took them into the back room to get off. Then we refilled them with pinches of flour. It was stupid; nobody burns anybody with flour. So Deb was yelling and cursing the next morning, *"Who stole my wake-up?"* She had to go out and hustle to cop some more.

We were all getting off every day that week. The only times we used any discretion were the couple of times John stopped in for brief visits before heading back to Jersey. We avoided shooting up in front of him, usually went into the unoccupied apartment across the hall.

And we squabbled stupidly. Dumont and I argued over which one of us was the better hit. Deb, on the other hand, never spoke while she was getting off. She quietly cooked her dope, drew it into her eyedropper syringe, and then she injected the skag into one of the veins in the back of her left hand. The veins in her arms were practically collapsed. When Deb rushed, she would lose hold of the fit while it was still inside her vein, and the blood would spurt onto the floor as the fit bounced on the back of her hand. That was disgusting, of course, but it was Dumont who was really getting on my nerves. We put each other down a lot that week. Once, while we were preparing to get off, I said to Dumont, "You know, next to some people I feel kind of short, but next to some other people I feel very tall." To which Dumont immediately replied: "I never feel small."

297

And now:

I wasn't left with so much as a chance to trip with John. Just in from Jersey and he went straight to sleep in the back room.

Alone in the livingroom, I screwed a red light bulb into the lamp next to the window. I sat quietly for a while. Then I got up to go outside and buy a bottle of wine. I bought a half gallon of Vin Rose at the liquor store across Seventh Street. Back inside the apartment, I started to get myself very smashed.

Deb came in after I had finished about a third of the bottle.

"Deb! Far out! Come over here and join me in a little wine," I said.

She sort of smiled. "You gettin' drunk tonight?"

"That's right. Like it should be every night! Come over here and join me."

She hung her leather over a kitchen chair and then sat next to me on the mattress. She took a good hit of wine.

"Hey, where'd you get the key to let yourself in?" I asked.

"I got Billy's key."

"Well, where *is* old Dumont? I haven't seen him practically all day."

"He right ovah dere in dat next apartment. He's gettin' hisself off like usual, an' he don' believe me dat I'm tryin' to kick, y'know?"

"You're trying to kick? That's far out. Everybody should kick."

Of course, I didn't believe that she was seriously trying to kick either. Junkies are always saying they're kicking the habit, but they rarely do it. Anyway, I was being nice to her because she was looking good to me. I watched her take another hit of wine. The bottle looked bigger around the middle than she did.

"Dis ain't a bad place at all," Deb said. "Y'know, dis apartment. I could kina get off on havin' me a place like dis."

"It's home," I said.

"Yeah, fuh you, I guess it is at dat. I guess you got things all set up fuh yourself."

"I've got what I need."

298

Deb laughed. "Yeah, I see John got all his books up dere on dem shelves. Real scholahly. Dat's *real* scholahly . . ." Then she turned to me: "Oh, but I guess I forgot. You's anothah guy who reads a lot, too, right? Anothah scholah."

I laughed.

Then she said, "Whud is dis dude John's kinda scene, anyhow? How come you kin hustle him so easy like?"

My only excuses for going along with Deb are that I was drunk and horny. Flimsy excuses. For some reason, I was convinced that Deb scorned the idea of friendship as a naive sentiment and that she would respect me more if I played the role of a hardened hustler. So I went along with her when she said that about me hustling John; I talked as if the only reason I hung around with John was to soak up his money.

"John has money and he doesn't mind sharing it," I said.

"He must at dat."

"Hey, I got an idea! What do you say we do an acid trip to-night?" I said.

"Shit, Stevie, you know how long is been since I touched any acid?"

"Come on, it'll be a gas. It'll bring your head up from junk."

I sprinted over to the refrigerator and opened it to find two hits of LSD wrapped in aluminum foil. Then I noticed on the counter a tinted jar of the vitamin B-12 which Deb sold to teenyboppers. B-12 is supposed to intensify your trip, so I opened the jar and poured the tiny tablets into my mouth like a bag of peanuts. After that, I ate one of the LSD tabs and offered the other to Deb. She took it.

Then we went back to sitting and drinking as if nothing had changed. We began getting stoned on the LSD in an hour or so. I could tell that Deb was getting off as I was because she was losing her New York accent and beginning to talk more like the way she used to when she lived in Jersey.

"There's one thing I gotta know, Stevie," she said. "I just gotta know this one thing, so please tell me, okay? Which one of you

299

guys took my wake-up last night? I just gotta know."

It seemed imperative that I keep Deb on my side this night, so I told her that Dumont took her dope.

She sprang up, enraged and cursing. "I knew it was him! I'm gonna kill that bastard!" I begged her to keep cool, to forget about it for the time being, but she ran into the kitchen before I could pull her back onto the mattress. She picked up a razor which was lying on top of the sink and ran out of the apartment. I followed her into the apartment next door where she already had Dumont backed up against the wall. She was swinging the razor and cursing. Before she could cut him, I dragged her back into my apartment. Dumont was loaded on junk, and I doubt he ever found out what she was so furious about.

Back in the livingroom, my heart was pounding. When I looked at Deb, it scared me. She looked horrible, with black shadows for eyes, like the shadowy spaces in the bone structure of a skull. Even under the red light, her face was gray, with hair like straw.

Feeling very paranoid, I drank more wine. I wouldn't look to Deb to see if she wanted any. I kept drinking. As I looked around the room, I started to feel claustrophobic. But closing my eyes would only make me feel more claustrophobic. So I put a record on the KLH. Jethro Tull. I felt LSD rushes, so different from junk rushes. Deb was saying something, but I was in a world totally apart from hers. I couldn't understand hers. It was scary, strange. I didn't want to look at her. And then I started to put the make on her, maybe automatically, maybe because I had dug her strangeness for years and now I wanted to find out about it, maybe because it was a way not to have to look at her.

She was on the mattress. She was a naked skeleton. My shirt was off. Then I was out.

A dream. I was in the livingroom. I think. But I couldn't think because they were chasing me. The old dream. The cop in my hometown, Pete Bennett, was chasing me. "I'll get you Steve Gibbons!" I am running toward a building. Can't run fast enough and my bum leg is dragging me down. The leg is okay until I start running like that. Now my shin is throbbing with pain the way my heart is pounding. I must make it to the building for cover. I have to do it. And I do. But barely in time. I am inside a hotel room. The door is locked, but the sound of Bennett outside torments me. Then I turn around and see that John is in the room. And next to him is Dean, a close friend from childhood whom I have not seen in years. They say nothing. I am still catching my breath. Then the door bursts open. Bennett is standing there, still, holding me in suspense because he know's he's got me now. I switch my glance back to John and Dean and then back to Bennett in the doorway. But now Bennett's face is obscure. He is suddenly Cohn, a psychiatrist they made me see while I was in the Children's Shelter. No, he is Bennett. And he is here to get me. I look back to John and Dean and I see a hole in the middle of the room. A pit. Looking at it, I can almost feel myself being drawn into it, falling. It has no bottom. Something strange, a new feeling comes over me. I turn around again, and Bennett is entering the room. I can't let him get me. No time to think; I just act. I push Bennett into the pit. His scream echoes. I wait for the sound to fade. Then John, Dean and I are standing in a row in front of the pit. I am still me. Yet I am shifting positions, from body to body, from mind to mind. John and Dean are thinking: he really is a psychopath, without control over himself, so maybe the best thing would be to get rid of him; but no! he is our friend! we must stick by him! The conflict is swirling through their minds. But it is all irrelevant to me at this point, because I am still wrapped up in the new feeling that has come over me. A strange feeling. The kind of feeling that makes people fall when they don't want to. Gravity. I don't know. My body steps back and pushes John and Dean into the pit. This time there is no sound. There is no sound left at all.

Something happened to the night, and it was morning. Deb was dressed again and sitting up on the mattress, in the position in which she had been sitting when we first started drinking. It was

301

strange to wake up and still be tripping, to wake up to sunlight and see a blanket crawling like a monster. I grabbed that blanket. It wasn't a monster. It was secure feeling. And monsters go with the night. A lot of things went with that night.

"You been goin' through some changes, huh, Stevie," Deb said in a spooked voice.

My jaws were crazy. I noticed a pocket comb on the floor. I picked it up to chew on it.

"Movin' all ovah like that—some real heavy changes."

The comb wasn't right. I let it drop.

"An' you spilled your wine all ovah," she went on.

"I spilled a lotta things," I mumbled, mostly to myself.

I noticed the Jethro Tull *Stand Up* album cover on the floor. I opened it up like a book. With its clever design, the opened jacket became a platform for a stand-up cutout picture of the Jethro Tull group smiling. Paper dolls. I chewed on the cutout. I chewed for about an hour.

" . . . He's trippin'. We did acid last night, an' now Stevie's goin' through some heavy changes . . ." Deb was saying.

I looked up with the album cover in my mouth and saw John. He was staring at me. He seemed to be glaring, in fact, but I couldn't read his face too well. I chewed for another half hour. When I was through, Ian Anderson was no longer smiling.

Then I needed a bath. My body felt greasy and grimy. I had to rid myself of the dirt that was crawling like bugs all over me. So I filled the tub in the kitchen and took a bath.

Everything broke down. I saw what was happening. It was Saturday. I saw what had been happening all week. All my life. John was still staring at me.

I had been using John's money to shoot dope. I had been treating everybody like piles of shit. I had stopped being a friend to anybody. And now I had stolen John's LSD to trip with Deb. I did not so much as possess the right to this trip.

John was now sitting on the kitchen chair, and I tried to say it all to him right away. But nothing came out when I opened my mouth. As in my dream, I felt horrible because I couldn't even cry out. My tub was a lifeboat in the ocean; and I was leaning over its edge, thirsty, but unable to drink the salty water.

John kicked everybody out of the apartment that day. He wasn't as nasty about it as he should have been, but he got rid of the crowd just the same.

He talked with Dumont about how the apartment was over-crowded, and then Dumont decided to go to Florida to stay with his grandmother. John helped him raise money for plane fare by pawn-ing Dumont's KLH speakers. John took the pawn ticket and then gave Dumont some extra cash as a down payment on the KLH which he would later buy. In the early afternoon, Dumont phoned a friend of his in New Jersey to get a ride to the airport. Billy must have been falling apart. And I was just watching it happen! After I had treated him as badly as I had treated everybody! He was already packed and waiting for his ride on the stoop of our tene-ment building when that hit me. I only had a few minutes in which to try to make some of it up to him. So I ran downstairs and out-side. The Jersey car had already come. Billy was ready to go. I ran up to him in the middle of Seventh Street. "Man, I can't believe you're actually splitting. I just can't believe it! I was just saying to John: 'Just try and picture New York City without Billy Du-mont. You can't do it!' And I swear, man, you really can't picture it. . . ." He was forcing a smile. Then he talked about the far-out times he was looking forward to, all the gassy times he was going to have in Florida. He was obviously falling apart. We shook hands. Then he left.

I went back upstairs and crawled under the lower bunk in the back room. There was space enough for me to sit curled up with my knees up. I hid in the corner. After a while, John crawled under there, too, so that he could talk with me. I told him I was ashamed to ask him to be the one to kick Deb out of the apartment, but that I couldn't do it. I never wanted to see her again, ever. And now, the mere fact of her presence in the apartment scared me. John assured me that he had planned to kick her out anyway.

From where I was sitting underneath the bunk, I watched John shake Deb to wake her. She had fallen asleep on the mattress on the livingroom floor. Or maybe she was faking it. Or was she dead? No, she always looked dead like that. She was faking sleep! John had to pick her up and shake her in the air to wake her. She kept her body limp like a Raggedy Ann doll. But finally she realized that John was not going to stop shaking her until she opened her eyes. So she opened them.

"You have to go now, Deb," John said.

She sat up.

"Oh . . . yeah . . . okay." Then she took her time standing up. She went into the kitchen and started brushing her hair, as if she had to pretty herself up for the street. "Like I kin unnerstan why you're tellin' me to go. Like you got your place to keep goin' an all. . . . So I'll leave. . . ." She continued brushing her hair.

"Good," John said. "I'll see you around sometime."

"Yeah. Like I been out ona streets before. Ain't nothin' new to dat to me, y'know. . . . Acourse I was tryin' to kick an' all while I was here, but I kin go back on da streets now. . . ."

She was horrible. While Deb brushed her hair with her right hand, I noticed how big her left hand was. Swollen to a size at least twice as big as the right, her left hand looked like an inflated rubber glove. The hand was dangling like a club at the end of her stringy arm.

John was thumbing through the records on the livingroom floor so that he wouldn't have to talk with Deb. She was slowly turning around while she brushed her hair, and I'm sure she spotted me under the bunk.

"Where's Stevie at?" she asked.

"He's out," John said.

"I guess he was goin' through some heavy changes dis mornin', huh?"

"I guess."

304

Finally, at a point when Deb's stalling was becoming ridiculously obvious, she put on her leather and left.

John locked the door behind her and came underneath the bunk to sit with me. We waited a while before saying anything.

"Did you see how horrible she was, man?" I said. "That whole scene, that whole junkie scene is so horrible . . . I thought she was going to fake like she was sleeping all day. It's such a relief that she's out of here, man. I hope I never see her again."

"You don't think she was faking, do you? Steve, that's crazy. She was dead asleep, believe me."

"Ah, John, can't you see through her? Nothing she does is honest. She's a fucked-up junkie, man. And I'm fucked up, too, for ever associating with her. I can't figure out what I ever saw in her, man; I'm fucked up about so many things. Hell, this last week I haven't been a friend to anybody. Nobody. Not even you, you know it? John, I just can't understand why you put up with it. You shouldn't have put up with it. That's fucked up, too."

"I know. I know. I just haven't known what I'm supposed to do, like a lot of times. It makes me feel crazy just watching all the things that have been happening. But if it makes you feel any better, I planned to kick you out this morning. I would have done it if you hadn't flipped out in the kitchen like that. I was only waiting for you to come down off the acid."

"I can't understand why you even waited. Man, I'm so fucked. I stole that acid from you. And I don't even know why I took it. But it made a lot of things dawn on me. Dawn on me, fuck, everything was hitting me right in the face. Too many things at once . . ."

I hugged my knees and went on.

"Like the way I've been treating people. The way I treat chicks. My attitude toward them. My attitude toward everybody! And Dumont. Man, when we got here, Dumont really needed a friend. He was falling to pieces, and what did I do for him? I treated him like shit, that's what."

"You two treated *each other* like shit," John said. "That's what amazed me about the way you guys acted when you were stoned on junk. I thought you'd be simply apathetic or something. But the way you two would bitch at each other!"

"He looked worse than ever today, man. Did you see him out there after we pushed him out the door? Man, he was falling apart."

"He wasn't all that bad off, Steve. I wouldn't worry about him now. He was saying he was looking forward to Florida, and I'm sure he'll be better off there, anyway."

"Man, don't you see? That was just his defense! Of course he has to keep his pride and say he's going to have a gas in Florida. I know him. Believe it, I've gotten to know him this past week, and he's falling apart. The only reason he's going to Florida instead of someplace else around here is because he thinks he has no friends left around here. And I shit on him just the way I shit on everybody else. . . . Man, you should have split on all of us."

"I know. I guess sometimes one friend follows another too far in the name of friendship."

"Really, John! And that's a good name if there is any. But you shouldn't have laid all that money on me! What kind of friendship is that? This past week, it's been no kind at all. There I was, man, running out and spending your money on junk. I swear, sometimes I wish you never got that book published. Maybe then we would have been really together all the way, with no breaks."

"Look, there were fuck-ups—it seems like there always are with money—but don't start wishing that I never got published. That wasn't what fucked us up. I just have to learn that I can't pretend money doesn't mean anything."

"Well, then I want you to start doing one thing. Start making me pay rent. I'm going to get a job so that this will really be *our* place."

"Okay."

"And fuck it to junk. The whole thing is disgusting. Junkies don't have friends. Man, I just keep thinking about all the horrible things that could have happened. Just think what might have happened if I *had* turned you on to junk. Or on to the needle so that you started digging poking holes into yourself every chance you got. What kind of a friend was I being? Look at what I could have done."

"But I would have been doing it to myself if I'd tried it. And I didn't, so that doesn't mean much to where we are now."

We sat quietly for a while. I was resting my chin and arms on my knees.

"I should have quit taking so many drugs a long time ago," I muttered.

"I guess. But it wasn't all a loss, was it?"

"I don't know. Right now it feels that way. I mean, what does acid do besides make you paranoid?"

"A lot of things. It didn't always make you paranoid."

"I know," I muttered into my knee. "I can't throw that out as a big excuse for everything. Man, it all seems so complicated. I used to try to make it simpler for myself by tripping around the country. The only decision I ever made was: do I stay or do I go? If it was good, I stayed. If it was a drag, I split. But even then, it was never so simple. I only *tried* to make it simpler by the way I did things."

"Maybe we can change things," John said.

"That's just it! I never do that! I always accept all the horseshit in myself because it seems like the most realistic way to do it. And because it's the easiest way. There are always excuses. . . . Well, maybe not always."

"Look, I've been feeling pretty damned suicidal myself lately. Every time I come into our apartment, I feel like shooting myself. But we can start changing the scene in this apartment all the way around."

I felt awfully guilty when I heard John say that about feeling suicidal. He was not a suicidal person. I didn't want to think about it. There was a long pause before I went on.

"There are so many things. Do you realize I've been in New York two weeks and I haven't even bothered to visit my own sister. That's where I've been at. Martha's right there uptown. I haven't seen her in about six months. And I can't think to spare a little time from all this bullshit."

"That's junk. But you're out of that now."

"Let's go up and visit her now, all right? Do you want to come with me?"

"Sure."

Bringing myself out from underneath the bunk took a while. By the time we were uptown, it was dusk.

Martha was not home, so we went to Riverside Park, near where she lived. John said at one point that things seemed to be back together. There were trees and it was peaceful. Maybe he was right. Things had calmed down.

31

It was dark by the time we were back on Seventh Street. We went to bed early. I was lying in the back room. But there was no way to sleep because everything was not back together. Who was John fooling? Who was I fooling?

I lay in bed in the nook formed by the bunk in the back room. I stared for hours at the wooden ceiling two feet above me that was the bottom of the upper bunk. I stared at the brown knots. I was thinking about all the things I had done that week. And I was thinking about what John had said. *He felt like shooting himself.* He felt suicidal because of a situation that I could have stopped.

It was impossible to change the scene we'd gone through that week, but it was still in my power to save John. I wasn't going to let his defensive talk about things being back together blind me from what was actually happening. I wasn't going to fuck it up.

I went into the livingroom. John was in a deep sleep; he didn't wake when I switched on the lamp over his head. I picked up the phone and slowly dialed the number of John's family in New Jersey. Ten digits. It only rang three times.

"Hello?" It was John's mother.

"Marie?"

"Yes, who is this?"

I waited. Talking with John's parents always made me paranoid.

". . . This is Stevie . . ."

"Stevie? Is anything wrong? Is John all right?"

Another pause.

"He's all right, but you should come down here to talk to him."

Another pause. Then John's mother sounded nervous as she said she'd be down as soon as possible.

I sat next to the phone for a half hour, an hour. I wasn't sure how long it would take John's mother to drive down. The light was on. John was asleep. Then I shook John's shoulder to wake him. He was difficult to wake.

"John! John!"

"What? What's happening?" He was very groggy.

"I called Marie. She's on her way down here."

"Wait. Just a minute. You called Marie? My mother, Marie?"

"I had to call her."

"Hold it. Just hold it. Did you say she's coming down here now? What for? What time is it?"

"I had to do it, man. After what you said about planning to kill yourself."

"Oh Jesus, wait a second. Oh boy. I didn't really mean . . . I mean, I meant that . . . it was figurative. . . . Hold it, do you mean my mother's on her way down here now, tonight?"

I nodded. I was confused.

"Oh boy, this is crazy . . ." John was holding his head to concentrate on waking up.

Then there was yelling in the hallway: "Stevie! Stevie!" It was John's sister.

"That's them already. Look, I'm going out to talk with them," John said, pulling on his jeans. He went out the door, and then I went into the kitchen. I sat on a chair.

John returned in a few seconds. He glanced back and forth

around the room as if he'd forgotten keys or something. Then he said, "Look, I'm going out to drive and talk. My father and sister are here. Can I leave you here alone?" His voice was shaking.

I was looking sadly at the floor. I waited. I had to give John an answer.

"I'm not going to kill myself," I said, almost too faintly to be heard.

32

Sunday. If I stayed with John at this point, it would only hurt him. John knew that now as well as I did.

I was going to do the right thing. After packing my knapsack, I told John I was going to Martha's place uptown until I figured something out. A quick goodbye. Then I walked out the door to be struck by the familiar old feeling that I did not really know where I was headed. Walking west on Seventh Street, I tried to fool myself with a strong stride. But I was weak, weak all the way across town to the A train. The ride uptown took a long time, time enough to clear my head and think about where I was going.

My body would not get up when the train stopped at the station near my sister's apartment. So I got off at the next stop, at the station underneath the George Washington Bridge bus station. Since I was not up to talking with a driver, I took a bus to my hometown in New Jersey.

For the first time in more than a year, I didn't worry about the cops in my hometown. It didn't matter. I walked home in broad cloudy daylight.

Standing in front of my parents' house, I couldn't go inside right away. I stood there crying for a while. Then I pulled myself together and went inside.

Most of them were there—my father, my mother, my brother, one of my younger sisters—all in the livingroom as if they'd been waiting for me. I stood there as they gaped at me. What could they say?

"My God, look at his hair," my mother said. What would I have said in her place?

"Jesus, I hope Pete Bennett didn't see you walking around town," my father said, referring to the main cop in town who was after me. "Does this visit mean we're going to have cops storming in here any minute?"

"Nobody saw me," I said.

I sat down in an armchair. My brother had grown since the last time I'd seen him. It jolted my parents when they saw the track marks along the veins of my left forearm. Looking at my arm, I spread it out like an injured wing—a wing that had been damaged during some high flying, I liked to think. But I was unsure of what to think.

My mother's insurance policy covered me, and I agreed to commit myself to a private hospital in New York. Between that day and the time I went into the hospital, a few days later, I began to feel better. I was getting my sense of humor back. It wasn't gone for good.

My sister Lorraine and I went back and forth between New Jersey and New York a couple of times over those days. We visited John and picked up items that I would take into the hospital.

Lorraine and I got along, as always. She was generous toward me. She gave me a pair of her pants because my jeans were shredded and I wasn't feeling up to pink or purple. Her pants fit me tightly. They were denim with rows of steel studs running like policeman's stripes down both hips all the way to the ankles. Studs for the stud. Martha teased me the way I teased her sometimes. She joked about

313

how she'd never met a guy who wasn't hung up on his masculinity. She called Billy Dumont her Exhibit A. I agreed with her, but I drew a greater generalization out of hers. As far as I was concerned, everybody was living for an ego trip. And masculinity just happened to be among the greatest ego trip sources. But some people thought I was being too cynical when I maintained that everything was motivated by ego. I developed a tendency to be quite cynical while I was waiting for an opening in the mental hospital of my choice.

I had overdone drugs, trapped myself in my own self-image. And now there was the hospital, where they would give me more drugs. Irony. Anyway, that is where I ended up.

And like being very drunk, needing to go into a mental hospital can be used as an excuse for everything you've done.

33

Janis Joplin is dead. She died on one of my first days in the nut-house, probably while I was painting.

Little Girl Blue. Thinking of her songs, I was reminded of Patrick. Who is dead, too. And for once, I was almost glad Patrick was not around. I could not bear to think of how he might have reacted to Janis dying. He was into her music—into her—and once, a long time ago, Patrick got together with Janis. It happened at the Newport Festival. Patrick was peaking on mescaline when he first saw Janis, singing her guts out. He hadn't paid for admission, so he was watching her through the fence, but he was behaving as though he were on stage with her. (Afterward he claimed that she spotted him as soon as he saw her, and that she was singing specifically for him.) He soon lost control. He scrambled over the fence. He was rabid. Guards began moving toward him to stop him, but not fast enough. On the other side of the fence, Janis' side, he was pushing and clawing through the crowd, making his own path to the stage, and screaming, "My wife! My wife! She's my wife!" Patrick was so flipped out that most of the audience he passed didn't mind the

315

pushing. In fact, they were getting into it. Janis' number stopped, and the part of the audience that was around Patrick began to chant: "Go! Go! Go! Go!" They were making way for Patrick and chanting just slowly enough so that each "Go!" was audible. Slowly, the rest of the crowd joined in. Half of them probably thought they were chanting for Janis, but it was Patrick's head that was spinning. By the time the entire crowd was throbbing with the chant, Janis saw Patrick pushing toward her with his hair flying behind him, and she dug it. So she joined the crowd, chanting into her microphone: "Go! Go! Go! Go! Go!" Then Patrick vaulted onto the stage and for a moment he wasn't sure what he should do. "You're *beautiful!*" Janis told him as she threw her arms around him and kissed him. "No, *you're* beautiful!" Patrick insisted. And then, with a Janis smile, she gave him a hit of Southern Comfort before the guards forced him off the stage.

34

Ending the story for Patrick is easier than it is to end the story for everybody else. It didn't stop in Vancouver after John and I left. Just after I entered the hospital, John got a phone call from Jainie, with Matthew in the background in a bar. They were smashed. It was midnight in Vancouver, three A.M. in New York. Jainie said she missed us and thought of us often. From the background, Matthew made a special point to say he did not forgive me for stealing his pants.

Wendy and Ann shared the apartment while Wendy went on to work her way into the Gastown hangout scene. Miki, it turned out, was a sixteen-year-old runaway, and the cops eventually caught her. Ah, Miki, are you back home listening to your father strum the banjo?

Frank never found his commune. Thinking about what happened to him is scary. Not long after we last saw him, he cut his wrists and throat. He went into the hospital for a long time. He has a scar like a snake tattoo across his neck, and they say he'll never fully recover the facility of his hands. He'll be able to pick up objects and that kind of thing, but he'll never be able to do real work with his hands, like leather work.

Jainie visited Frank in the hospital a few times and she related to John something that Frank said to her. It was not the kind of thing I could picture Frank saying. He said it was all worth it, cutting himself and everything. He said the idea that he had actually tried to kill himself was such a jolt that it caused him to stop, to take another look at the way he was running his life.

I am still indefinite about my own plans. The doctor still thinks I have a poor attitude toward therapy. That's because I refuse to kiss his ass by making a definite decision so that they can say they've cured me, made me change the way I act. I'm sure I can get on New York City welfare as a person who is emotionally incapable of holding a job, and that will give me time to think. I have ideas that I'm turning around in my head. Maybe I'll find a job and do a lot of reading for a while. I am also weighing the idea of returning to school. My father could probably help me get in as a nonmatriculated student at the college where he works. Naturally, nobody believes I'm serious when I mention that I am considering going back to school. I talked it over with John, and he says that I'll only drop out again because I obviously don't really want to go to school.

Months went by and at the time of the Christmas vacation for the kids who go to school, I went to a party in my hometown in New Jersey. I saw a number of old friends as well as some of the people I hadn't seen since high school. Ironically, many of my old friends, dropouts, talked about returning to school, while the kids who'd barely finished the first semester of their freshman year were talking about taking a year off or maybe dropping out. One kid in particular was telling me how excited he was about taking a year's leave of absence from NYU. I couldn't resist the chance to upset his enthusiasm by telling him that I was going back to school. I didn't really know what I was going to do; I said it to disturb him. He kept saying: "But you will say it was worth it, taking the time off. You did learn a lot, didn't you?" I'd never thought of it as taking time off. I said nothing more to him because that kid had always thought of me as a bum in high school and I wasn't going to give him anything now. I guess we all have to discover our own survival rules.